The Dragons of Jupiter

JACOB HOLO

ISBN-10: 1484112016
EAN-13: 9781484112014

Dedication

To Dad. Memory eternal.

The Dragons of Jupiter

Of the seven thousand coalition soldiers attacking Bunker Zero, only two penetrated the upper defenses. Kaneda and Ryu Kusanagi sprinted down the narrow steel corridor. Sonic cancellers in their boots turned booming metallic footfalls into whispers. Form-fitting smartskin shrouded their bodies in active camouflage. Not even shadows marked their passing.

Kaneda glanced at the utility trench underneath the grated floor. He followed three thick liquid nitrogen lines and a cluster of purple ultrahigh voltage cables. Whatever they fed took a lot of juice and needed constant cooling. It had to be their target.

"There's a four way junction ahead!" Ryu said over his comm-collar. Low-power laser receptors and emitters lined both their necks, allowing secure tight-beam communication as long as they shared line-of-sight contact.

"The lines go to the right," Kaneda said.

"They're gaining on us!"

"I know. Stay focused."

Kaneda planted his feet in the junction and turned sharply. His suit's smartskin struggled to keep up, revealing him with a brief, slender outline. He dashed down the right hand corridor.

Ryu crouched as soon as he rounded the corner. He pulled a grenade out of his bandolier, armed its micromind for proximity detonation, and forced it through the floor's grating. It landed on top of the liquid nitrogen lines. The grenade's smartskin activated, obscuring it from view. Ryu stood and ran after Kaneda.

"Security door," Kaneda said, stopping a hundred meters after the junction. He placed his hand on the door. Passive contact scanners in his glove evaluated the obstacle. "Reinforced diamoplast half a meter thick."

Ryu stopped next to him. "There's the security terminal. I've got this one!"

"Covering." Kaneda turned, snapped up his JD-50 assault rifle and dropped to a crouch. He mentally keyed the rifle to full auto.

Ryu placed his hand on the security terminal. Microscopic filaments extruded from his hacking glove and penetrated the terminal's casing. The filaments uncoiled into the terminal, expanding and exploring at Ryu's command, looking for ways to bypass its protocols through direct intervention.

A distant clicking noise echoed down the corridor, exactly the kind of sound a hundred narrow metal legs would make.

Kaneda placed a hand against the cold steel wall. He felt the subsonic vibrations of explosive ordinance, maybe fifty levels above them. *Help isn't close*, he thought. *We're all alone down here.*

The rapid clicking grew louder.

"They're close," Kaneda said, gripping his rifle with both hands.

"Just a few more seconds!"

The rapid clicking thundered in his ears.

"Almost there!" Ryu said.

"We don't have much time," Kaneda said, speaking softly despite the on-edge pounding in his chest. A quick glance at his biometrics showed a heart rate of 312 pulses per minute, and that was without a fresh shot of adrenalmax.

The proximity grenade at the junction detonated in a flash of light and shrapnel. Two nitrogen lines ruptured, spewing jets of cryogenic fluid into the corridor. The liquid nitrogen expanded into gas with explosive force.

A concussion wave shot down the corridor. The wave threw Kaneda and Ryu into the security door. Kaneda slammed his head against the door, but the thin layer of impact gel in his helmet absorbed most of the shock.

"Damn it!" Ryu shouted.

Stars danced across Kaneda's vision. He shook his head and brought his rifle back up.

"You okay?" Ryu asked.

"Just get the door open."

"Right. Almost there."

Kaneda toggled through his visor's tracking modes, overlaying thermal atop the visual spectrum. The corridor was a black, billowing cloud.

"Almost!" Ryu said.

Two six-legged outlines came into view, one on the wall, the other on the ceiling. They stood half as tall as a man with internal power plants glowing rusty red despite the rapid cooling.

Gun-spiders.

Kaneda fired. Forty diamond-tipped shatterbacks spewed out of his rifle in two seconds. The synthetic, shatterproof diamonds tore through gun-spider armor like paper. Once inside, the explosive shatterbacks blew them apart. Shots that missed tore chunks out of the walls and ceiling. Lights in the corridor flickered and died. Detonations ripped steel panels off. A secondary blast boomed from an unseen enemy in the junction, splattering the walls and floor with what his visor identified as napalm. The thick gel burned and fought the leaking jets of nitrogen in a swirling thermal dance.

Kaneda ejected the spent clip and slapped in a fresh one.

"Got it!" Ryu said.

The security door slid open. Ryu rushed through and placed his hacking glove against the terminal on the far side.

Kaneda backpedaled through the door in a low crouch. He mentally keyed two grenades in his JD-50's underslung launcher for timed detonations and fired both into the corridor. The security door slid shut after he cleared it. Two more explosions echoed through the bunker.

"Now," Kaneda said, standing and turning. "Where are we?"

The wide room stood two stories tall. Harsh overhead lighting washed out most color. The white tiled walls and floors added a sense of sterility. Pods filled the room in neat rows like an artificial forest, each with a man or woman lying inside.

"This doesn't look like it," Ryu said.

"The lines lead here," Kaneda said. "How long will the door hold?"

"Ten to fifteen minutes. More if we're lucky. I fried the controls pretty good. They'll have to burn their way through."

Kaneda walked to the closest pod and looked at the woman inside.

"Careful," Ryu said. "These people could be implanted with chest-devils."

"Nothing is showing up on my tracker," Kaneda said.

He looked inside the pod. The woman's head was recently shaven, leaving a brunette fringe. Kaneda could make out tight circular scars along her scalp. Her chest rose and fell with slow breaths. Bones stood out at her neck and joints, and her cheeks were horribly sunken.

A tremor ran through her body. She opened her eyes and looked around the room with a vacuous gaze. Her mouth opened, but no sound came out. Saliva trickled from the edge.

"What is Caesar doing with these people?" Ryu asked. "Is this where he makes his thralls?"

"We should keep moving," Kaneda said. "This isn't it."

"All right, but where do we go from here?"

Kaneda looked around. "The power lines are probably routed deeper. There, to the left. That looks like a power distribution panel. Most of the cables coming out of it go down."

"Okay. So?"

"We'll head down. There's a flight of stairs on the far side."

Kaneda detected a heat spike from a holographic emitter on the ceiling. A pillar of light coalesced into a tall, fit man with a buzz of white hair. He straightened his crisp black suit and adjusted a blood red tie before walking towards them. The man stood a head shorter than Ryu and Kaneda, the simulation of his former body compressed by Earth's heavy gravity.

"Caesar," Kaneda breathed.

"Well, isn't this the absolute opposite of a surprise," Caesar said. "Kaneda and Ryu Kusanagi. It would have to be you two freaks that breached my defenses. I certainly never expected the regular Federacy fodder to make it this far."

"He can't see us, can he?" Ryu asked. "I mean, he's walking right towards us."

"Keep moving," Kaneda said. "He's trying to distract us. Head for the next level."

Caesar walked past them and stopped at the security door. "Now I know you gentlemen just arrived, but I have to break some bad news to you. My quantum core is not here. You took a wrong turn. The power lines you were following are for a little experiment I've been playing with. So sorry, but it just has to be said."

"Kaneda?"

"Don't let him get to you."

"But—"

"Don't listen to him," Kaneda said. "We have a job to do."

"In fact, it's even worse than that," Caesar said. "There's only one way out of these sublevels. Back the way you came. You both expended a lot of ammo getting here. Right now, I have over fifty robots amassing on the other side. I've even arranged for a few prototypes to join them. It'll be fun to see how long you last."

Kaneda and Ryu reached the stairs. Caesar's hologram flashed into existence on the landing halfway down the steps. He didn't make eye contact.

"I know this may sound a little odd given our current situation," Caesar said. "But when my robots reach you, I would appreciate it if you kept the collateral damage to a minimum. Some of these fine Federacy citizens were very hard to obtain, and I have not finished even a quarter of their neural extractions and persona-intrusions."

Kaneda stepped off the stairs into a room identical to the one above and found the power distribution panel for the second level. Most of the cables disappeared through the floor.

"Keep heading down," Kaneda said.

"I don't think it's here."

"He's lying. He's trying to trick us."

"I hope you're right."

Caesar's hologram appeared in the center of the room. Kaneda and Ryu ran past it.

A deep subsonic boom reverberated through the bunker.

Caesar looked up. "My, they are getting rowdy up there. It's amazing this coalition has lasted this long. Soldiers from Earth and Luna and Mars and Jupiter all walking to their deaths in lockstep. Very stirring. I suppose they hate me more than each other. By the way, how is your ice ball of a home? After this is over, I'm going to send a fleet to Jupiter and rain about a thousand nukes down on that frozen moon. It'll be like the fireworks on Federacy Day, only hotter. What do you think of that?"

Kaneda entered the third identical level. Rows of interrogation pods stretched out before him.

"How many people are in here?" Ryu asked.

"About two hundred so far," Kaneda said, running for the next set of stairs.

Caesar materialized ahead of them. "You know, while you've been meandering about, I've subverted the weapon systems of a Martian cruiser in geosynchronous orbit. Firewalls, ha! It was like punching through wet paper." He smiled and looked up. "Three ... two ... one ..."

A massive shockwave rocked the bunker. The lights flickered. Kaneda lowered his stance and put a hand against an interrogation pod to steady himself.

Caesar clasped his hands together. "Well, that is that. The surface has been reduced to a glowing sheet of glass along with all the Federacy troops still up there. Shame about New Shanghai. I was rather fond of the city."

"Damn it!" Ryu said. "What now?"

"There's nothing we can do about it."

"Kaneda, we're going to die down here if we don't find it soon!"

"I know. Keep moving."

Caesar materialized by the stairs to the fourth level. He picked at some imaginary lint on his sleeve.

"Now that I have you thoroughly trapped, I'd like to note something," Caesar said. "As one of only two quantum minds in existence, I'm a little offended Matriarch sent you to kill me. I'm sure the irony of this situation is not lost on you. Two people, designed and created, manufactured if you will by one quantum mind, sent to kill the other quantum mind. It really is quite offensive. And I promise you, I will punish her for this insult."

They entered the fourth interrogation level. Caesar was already standing at the foot of the stairs to greet them. Kaneda ran past him, but stopped halfway to the next set of stairs.

"What is it?" Ryu asked.

"Something's not right with this level."

Ryu looked around. "It is? It's the same as the … wait, what the hell? That wall is closer than on the other levels."

"Exactly. This level has smaller dimensions. Shouldn't it be the same?"

Kaneda and Ryu ran to the wall and stopped in front of it.

"It looks … new," Ryu said.

"And rushed. The welds where the wall meets the floor and ceiling are sloppy."

"Back up," Ryu said. He raised his rifle. "Let's see what's on the other side."

Kaneda backed out of the blast radius.

Ryu fired a grenade from his rifle's launcher. The explosion cracked the air and sent twisted, glowing-edged metal flying into the obscured room. Dust exhaled from the opening and spread into a low-hanging cloud at their ankles.

"That was my last grenade," Ryu said. "You?"

"Only two left," Kaneda said.

"We'll have to make them count."

Ryu put one leg through the glowing oval, swept his aim over the interior, and stepped in.

"There's some kind of machinery in here. Take a look."

Kaneda overlaid his visor's visuals with Ryu's viewpoint. A bank of electrical panels radiated intense heat on the far wall. Thick cables ran between the machines and a cluster of twelve interrogation pods in the center of the room. The pods sat in supportive cradles and looked removable.

"Is this it?" Ryu asked.

"No. Matriarch was very specific about what the quantum core looks like."

"Hold on. There's a concealed hatch behind the pods."

Kaneda turned around. Nothing moved amongst the forest of interrogation pods. Smoke from the explosion settled into a thin cloud at his feet.

"What is it?" Ryu asked.

"I'm picking up some weird subsonics above and below us," Kaneda said. "I'm not sure what they are. Also, Caesar is gone."

"Good riddance," Ryu said. He slung his rifle and crouched down. "I think we might be on to something. The hatch is shielded. Dual diamoplast layers with thermal and radar masking sandwiched in between. I can't see what's on the other side."

"Don't worry about that. Can you get it open?"

"I think so. I don't see any terminals, but this isn't a security door. The hatch is tough but the floor around it isn't. We can probably rip it out."

Ryu drew his ultrasonic knife and stabbed it into the floor panel next to the hatch. He used the knife's handle for leverage and peeled the panel up until he got his fingers underneath the edge. With a short grunt, he ripped the panel free and flung it aside. He stabbed his knife into a second panel on the opposite side of the hatch and repeated the process.

Ryu sheathed his knife and placed his fingertips underneath the newly-exposed lip on the hatch's sides. He planted his feet and lifted.

"Come on, Kaneda! This thing's got to weigh half a ton in this damn gravity!"

"Right." Kaneda slung his rifle and stepped in. He grabbed the hatch from the other side.

"And LIFT!"

Kaneda's adrenal implant pumped hot, scalding fluid through his body. His muscles tightened and burned with exertion. His heart pounded furiously. He gritted his teeth and lifted.

"Gah! Earth's gravity sucks!" Ryu said.

Kaneda felt the enhanced muscles in his arms strain to their breaking point, ready to tear free of his diamoplast-reinforced bones.

"Now slide it to the left!" Ryu shout. "Come on!"

Kaneda lifted and pulled until a corner of the hatch slid across the floor. He let out a long, slow sigh.

"Okay! Just hold it there!" Ryu said. He craned his neck to the side and looked past the hatch.

Twenty needle grenades underneath the hatch detonated. A solid shower of diamond splinters blossomed towards Ryu's face. He pushed back from the hatch, blurring with speed.

Five needles struck his right hand where the ballistic armor was thinnest. Three shot through his flesh and sent small streamers of blood and gore upward. Two impacted against his bones and ricocheted off.

Confused patterns of crimson and flesh-tone danced up Ryu's arm before his smartskin's micromind crashed. His form-fitting suit reverted to a pattern of small, black hexagons edged in silver. He pushed away from the hatch, cradling his injured hand.

"Fuck!" Ryu shouted.

Through their shared network, Kaneda triggered a localized painkiller injection from Ryu's smartsuit. Ryu's blood congealed almost instantly over the wounds, so Kaneda didn't have to activate the tourniquet at the wrist.

Caesar materialized outside the hidden room. "My my. Quite impressive. No normal human would have reacted that fast. Bravo!"

Ryu picked his rifle off the floor and fired a three-round burst through Caesar's face. The hologram shimmered from the interruption. Explosive rounds detonated against the ceiling, sending broken tiles and light fixtures raining down on the interrogation pods.

Caesar shook his head and sighed. "So childish."

Kaneda raised his rifle and aimed it past Caesar. With his visor, he magnified the two staircases leading out of the level.

"Ryu, get up."

"What are we going to do?"

"Just get up. Someone's coming."

"Damn it!" Ryu pushed off the floor with his good hand and stood up. His smartskin tried to reboot. Patterns danced over his body, but failed to sustain the illusion.

Kaneda stepped through Caesar's hologram and the hole in the wall. The edges had cooled to a dull orange. Ryu followed him out.

A solid mob of people shambled down the stairs from the upper level. Another group approached from the level below.

"Some of them have grenades," Kaneda said.

"Oh, that's just perfect!"

Every interrogation pod on the level opened with a pneumatic hiss. The occupants slowly climbed out. Kaneda stepped away from the nearest pod. He aimed his rifle at a black man in a white jumpsuit with a shaved head and a grenade in his hand.

Kaneda fired a warning shot over his head. The man looked vacantly at Ryu.

"Let me ask you something," Caesar said. "Have you ever killed another human being? It's not the same as gunning down machines, is it? I wonder how long it will take before you begin murdering these helpless innocents. Not that it matters. I have more thralls than you have bullets."

"Kaneda?"

"Back away from them. Don't let them near us."

"Back away to where?"

"Stay in the open. Follow me!"

Kaneda dashed between an elderly woman and a teenage boy. He ran down a row of pods and stopped near the center of the level. The crowd of thralls closed in around them. Too many of them had grenades. A young woman with half a head of auburn hair jerked her arm back like a drunken baseball pitcher.

Kaneda snapped his rifle up and fired a single shot at her wrist. The shatterback was designed to penetrate the tough armor of Caesar's robots and deliver an anti-tank payload inside. Human flesh proved no obstacle.

The shatterback struck her wrist and exploded. Her arm and part of her shoulder ceased to exist. The impact threw her to the ground, breaking bones and traumatizing organs.

The smoking, cylindrical grenade tumbled through the air before landing in a crowd of five thralls. It bloomed into a shower of diamond needles that speared through flesh and bone, sometimes ripping whole limbs off. What was left of the five thralls dropped wetly to the ground.

Kaneda couldn't believe the carnage in front of him. He'd never seen so much blood.

"Oh ho! Very spectacular!" Caesar said, clapping.

Ryu moved in behind Kaneda, back to back.

"You're not going to like this," Ryu said. "But I'm the only one they can see. I can draw them away, give you a chance to ... I don't know. Do something."

"Don't you dare!"

"But—"

"You shut up right now and follow me!"

"To where?"

"The only place left! Down!"

Thralls formed a solid line at the stairs leading down. Their vacuous eyes looked past Kaneda to Ryu.

Kaneda put his shoulder down and tackled a tall, skeletal man with a medical patch over one eye. The tackle broke three of the man's ribs, fractured his sternum, and threw him aside like a rag doll. Kaneda kept running through the crowd, pushing aside anyone in his path.

An incendiary grenade dropped to the ground and ignited behind Kaneda, turning the stairs into a funeral pyre. A dozen burning thralls opened their mouths in silent screams. The green chemical flames spread, consuming flesh and steel with indiscriminate ease.

Ryu held an arm over his face and charged through the fire. He emerged singed but unharmed.

Kaneda reached the fifth interrogation level. A girl rushed forward, arms held straight out with a grenade clutched in her tiny hands. The oily smoke choking the staircase had outlined Kaneda before his smartskin could compensate. She ran straight for him. He dove to the left.

The grenade exploded. Gore and shrapnel scythed through the air. A crimson band splattered against Kaneda's side. The shock wave sent him flying. He tumbled across the floor, threw out his arms to stop the roll, and pushed off the ground.

"Kaneda!"

His smartsuit reported minor damage to its ballistic and impact gel layers. Crimson patterns swam over his body before the smartskin's micromind crashed.

Every nearby thrall turned and looked straight at him.

"I'm okay," Kaneda said.

"There's nowhere else to go! This is the bottom level!"

Kaneda raised his rifle.

"What do we do now?" Ryu shouted.

"I need to time to think."

"We don't have time to think!"

"Then I'll stall him."

"You'll what?"

"Just watch." Kaneda deactivated his sonic cancellers. "Hey, Caesar!"

The thralls stopped advancing. Caesar's hologram materialized in front of him.

"Oh? What do we have here? Have you decided to beg for your lives? That's rather cliché, don't you think? I am known for many things, but mercy is sadly not one of them."

"I was just thinking about where your quantum core is."

"Yes, I imagine you would be," Caesar said. "It's quite safe. You never stood a chance, but congratulations on making it this far. I will have to commend Matriarch on her handiwork. Before I burn Europa from orbit, that is."

"You're that confident we can't find it."

"Oh, undoubtedly," Caesar said. "If I may be so bold, a bullet through the head is, I imagine, far less painful than evisceration by massed needle grenades. Perhaps an honorable suicide would suit the two of you? I wouldn't mind waiting. After all, your bodies hold valuable wetware technology. I'd relish the chance to reverse engineer Matriarch's inventions."

"He's like a cat playing with a mouse," Ryu said privately over their comm-collars.

Kaneda scanned the room. The only thing different was the lack of stairs down to the next level ... the lack of stairs ... lack of stairs ... the only thing different ...

"I was just thinking," Kaneda said.

"Please don't strain yourself," Caesar said. "Thinking should be left to the professionals."

"Have you ever heard the saying 'hunting for diamonds in the ice'?"

"Hmrph," Caesar snorted. "Of course I have. A somewhat common figure of speech among Europans. Similar to the archaic 'needle in a haystack' on Earth. I imagine the saying is foremost on your mind right now."

"It is."

"Well, if you were looking for advice, I'd suggest burning down the haystack. Or thawing the ice. Whichever is your preferred metaphor. Of course, that doesn't really apply to my bunker."

"I don't think that will be necessary," Kaneda said.

Some of the playfulness drained out of Caesar's face. "What do you mean?"

"Caesar, as much as you might be a machine now, you were once human. You're just smarter. That doesn't make you perfect. You're not a glorified number cruncher. You feel as much as you think, and you can be wrong. You never thought anyone would make it this far, and your every action has been a desperate attempt to delay us. Why? Because the diamond isn't in the ice. It's buried in the rock underneath the ice."

Caesar frowned. The thralls started advancing again.

Kaneda activated his sonic cancellers. "Get ready to run for it!"

"Run where?"

Kaneda aimed his rifle at the section of wall where the stairs should have been and fired a grenade. Unlike the obvious false wall on level four, this one on level five was perfectly camouflaged, but that wasn't enough to fool high explosives.

The grenade detonated with a flash. The wall caved in. Hot-edged ceramic tiles, concrete, and steel rebar blew into the staircase beyond. Every thrall in the room threw their grenade. Kaneda and Ryu jumped through the glowing rent in the wall and tumbled down the stairs.

Dozens of staccato explosions erupted behind them, demolishing the wall and part of the floor. Concrete debris rained over Kaneda and Ryu. They rolled to a landing halfway down the stairs where it doubled back, picked themselves up and ran down to the sixth level.

"That's got to be it!" Ryu shouted.

A black monolith sat in the center of the sterile white level. Four utility trenches converged on Caesar's quantum core. Kaneda could see purple ultrahigh voltage cables and thick liquid nitrogen lines. The core glowed in brilliant infrared. Dry heat radiated off it.

Twenty thralls stood between him and Caesar's core in two neat rows. Kaneda loaded a program into his last grenade's micromind and fired over their heads. The grenade arced through the air. Its micromind engaged small cold-gas jets to align itself with the core's monolith.

Caesar materialized in front of them. Every thrall raised their arms, ready to throw.

"You—!" he began to say.

The grenade's high explosive yield detonated in a shaped cone. The impact tore through the monolith and gutted its sensitive systems. Sparks showered out until emergency breakers interrupted power. A single nitrogen leak spewed vaporous clouds out the back. Caesar's hologram froze in mid-sentence. The thralls dropped to the ground like puppets with their strings cut.

Kaneda and Ryu crouched at the base of the stairs, rifles ready.

Nothing happened. No pursuit or sounds came from the level above.

Ryu stood up and walked to Caesar's hologram. He passed his gun barrel through it a few times. Caesar's image remained static.

"I can't believe we did it," Ryu said. "We did do it, right? This isn't some trick, is it?"

Kaneda walked to the monolith and inspected the wreckage. He pulled a twisted panel off and tossed it aside. "It certainly looks that way. See, this stack of torus accelerators feeding what's left of the column in the center? That's an exact match for what Matriarch told us to look for."

"And this thing isn't very mobile either." Ryu kicked the side of the monolith.

"No, it isn't."

"So we actually did it?" Ryu said. "We killed Caesar. I can't believe it."

"We should probably have the wreckage inspected just to be sure," Kaneda said. He put a hand on Ryu's shoulder. "But yeah, we did it."

"Those thralls surprised me," Ryu said. "I was expecting more robots this close."

"Like I said, he never expected anyone to make it this far. After we breached that last security door, everything was just smoke and mirrors to delay us. I don't think we would have survived if Caesar had fortified these levels."

"Yeah. Lucky us."

Kaneda heard quiet sobbing behind him. He slung his rifle and walked to the rows of collapsed thralls.

"Careful," Ryu said. "Those grenades can still go off."

Kaneda dismissed his brother with a wave and crouched next to a young woman about his age. Tears streaked down her pale face. Unlike most of the captives, she had a full head of lush ginger hair. Perhaps she was a recent addition to Caesar's collection.

Kaneda deactivated his sonic cancellers.

"Are you all right?" he asked.

The woman turned her head with visible effort. Her neck muscles twitched and cramped up. She parted her lips but said nothing for almost a minute.

"Is … it over?" she finally asked.

"Yes," Kaneda said. He placed a gentle hand under her and helped her sit up. "Caesar is dead."

Fresh tears ran down her soft cheeks. Her eyes darted about, finally resting on his concealed face.

"Who ... who are you?"

"Kaneda." He unlatched the seals around his neck and took his helmet off to reveal a young face with dark eyes and short black hair. He had a stern line for a mouth, and pale skin that had never known the sun.

Kaneda took a deep breath. The room smelled of ozone and human sweat.

"Kaneda Kusanagi," he said. "And this is my brother, Ryu."

"Hello," Ryu said, giving the woman a short wave with his injured hand.

"What's your name?" Kaneda asked.

"Chri ... isten ..."

"Christen," Kaneda said. He brushed a few tangled locks out of her face. "That's a beautiful name."

Despite her obvious trauma, Christen smiled. It was one of the loveliest sights Kaneda had ever seen.

"You k-killed Caesar?"

"Yes."

"But ... you're so young."

"We're not that young," Kaneda said. "I'm already sixteen. My brother will be fifteen in a few weeks."

"Two young knights in not-very-shiny armor," Christen said.

Kaneda looked at his blood-splattered chest. It was true enough.

"I didn't know the F-Federacy had troops that young."

"We're not with the Earth Federacy. We're from Europa."

Christen's smile melted into a frown. She looked away. "Another d-damn quantum mind."

"Hey!" Ryu said. "Matriarch is a great leader. She's nothing like Caesar."

"Ryu, would you shut up, please?"

"What? It's true."

"Christen and all the others have been through enough. Just let it rest."

"I ... all right. I didn't mean anything by it. I just ... shit, did you hear that?"

Kaneda listened. "Yeah. Those robots finally breached the security door. They're heading this way."

"But Caesar's dead!"

"They must be carrying out their final instructions," Kaneda said.

"Find and kill us, you mean!"

"We need to get ready."

Ryu stepped through the captives, grabbing grenades and stuffing them into his bandolier. Kaneda secured his helmet, picked Christen up, and carried her over to the wall so she was no longer between the stairs and the broken quantum core.

"What are you doing?" Ryu asked.

"Getting these people out of the line of fire."

Kaneda ran over and picked up a man so bony he might not have been fed in weeks.

"We don't have time, Kaneda! Those robots are on their way!"

"You can either stand around and talk, or you can help me move them," Kaneda said. "Now which is it going to be?"

"Ah, damn it!"

Kaneda picked up a grizzled man with more shrapnel scars on his arms than interrogation scars on his scalp. Ryu muttered something impolite under his breath, bent down, and grabbed his own captive. The sound of approaching robots grew louder.

It took two minutes to finish moving all the captives.

"All right! That's it!" Ryu said. "We need to get into cover!"

"Right."

Kaneda ran to the utility trench next to the monolith. He lifted the grating, tossed it aside and jumped down. Ryu jumped into the trench on the opposite side of the monolith. The two trenches met behind the monolith, giving them direct line of sight to each other.

"Kaneda! Here!" Ryu tossed him three grenades, one at a time.

Kaneda caught and stuffed each grenade into his bandolier. He trained his rifle at the stairwell. The robots were so close even a natural human could hear them.

"Sounds like a lot," Ryu said.

"Yeah. I don't think Caesar was bluffing about his backup."

"This is going to get messy."

"We'll make it. I know we will."

"I wish I had your confidence," Ryu said. "Here they come!"

Three gun-spiders skittered across the stairwell walls on six spindly legs each. M15 heavy railguns or M7 thermal lances swiveled atop their flat bodies. Slender, cylindrical heads twitched back and forth, seeking targets. Another two gun-spiders skittered down the steps with more on the way.

Kaneda and Ryu opened fire.

Ten Years Later

FINAL YEAR OF THE THIRD SPACE AGE

... establishing link ...

source: [UNKNOWN]

routing: Capitol City, Europa - TangleNet Test Hub - link_001/link_005

routing: North Pacifica, Europa - JDN Main TangleNet Hub - link_010/link_118

routing: Earth orbit - surveillance satellite JDN-SS-17 - link_001/link_002

routing: [UNKNOWN]

routing: [UNKNOWN]

routing: [UNKNOWN]

destination: [UNKNOWN]

link distance: Exact distance unknown. Estimated at 792 million kilometers.

link signal delay: 0.006 seconds

... finalizing link protocol ...

... link established ...

1: Hello, Paul.

2: Sakura. What the hell do you want?

1: I only wish to talk. There's no need for us to get off to such a hostile start.

2: Well, we're talking now. Get on with it. I have important business to attend to.

1: As you wish. I'm calling about the recent developments on Luna. Your actions there appear to be in violation of our long-standing arrangement.

2: Really? Would you believe me if I said I have nothing to do with the mess on Luna?

1: No, I would not.

2: You've grown paranoid with age, Sakura. Paranoia does not become you. You used to be so much more trusting.

1: To my detriment.

2: Ah ha ha, yes, that much is true.

1: Please, Paul. I wish to curtail the hostilities before they get out of control.

2: Very well. I'll listen, if nothing more. What would you have me do?

1: Pull the Federacy forces off Luna.

2: Look, Sakura, I've told you this before and I'll say it again. You greatly overestimate the extent of my influence. I can shape events, but this war of annexation has grown beyond my ability to control it.

1: You're lying.

2: And you are welcome to your opinion. I have no desire to listen to your accusation. Now, are we done here?

1: I implore you to reconsider.

2: Look, the war on Luna will continue with or without my intervention. The Earth Federacy wants to expand its sphere of influence, and occupying Luna is the next logical step. They don't even call it Luna in the Federacy. They just call it the moon, as if it's the only one in the whole solar system that matters. They treat it like a rogue state that needs reuniting with the homeland. It's a cultural thing. Luna belongs to them. Always has. Always will.

1: The Lunarians would disagree.

2: I imagine a few kinetic torpedoes from the Federacy fleet can change their minds. Either that or their opinions will stop mattering altogether.

1: And what of the crusaders?

2: What of them, Sakura?

1: You have deployed the crusaders to Luna.

2: Don't be stupid. The crusaders are an independent militia completely separate from the Federacy command structure. I have no direct control over their operations. How could I, given their eccentric doctrines? They decided to deploy to Luna of their own accord. Perhaps you should ask their august leader why he deployed his troops, or would you rather not open that old wound?

1: They have no business on Luna.

2: Is that so? And what of your dragons? Do they have any business being on Luna?

1: You know very well why the dragons are on Luna. They were deployed because the Lunar State asked for assistance. It is that and nothing more. They operate there with the full blessing of the legitimate government.

2: How very noble of them.

1: Luna is neutral ground.

2: Not for much longer.

... link severed at destination ...

Ryu Kusanagi stepped into the ancient machinery room, rifle raised. He scanned his rifle across the room in a slow, deliberate sweep. Rusted, hulking mechanisms sat on either side of a narrow aisle, leading to a closed door on the opposite side of the room. Flickering light strips on the ceiling illuminated a soup of floating dust motes.

"Cat?" Ryu asked.

"No tech activity," she said. "The room's clean."

"All right. Get in and seal the entrance."

Cat and Naomi filed into the machinery room, smartskin suits turning them into ghosts even with the heavy dust. Only small wisps of unnatural movement betrayed their entry. Ryu would have struggled to spot them had it not been for the vivid green silhouettes overlaying his field of vision. Tactical data constantly exchanged between the four dragons over secure TangleNet links.

Toshi brought up the rear. He took a grenade from his bandolier, stuck it to the door's exterior, swung the door shut, and spun the locking wheel. Rust particles swirled around the ancient hinges.

Ryu checked his mission clock. Two hours and twelve minutes. Plenty of time. The air wasn't even that toxic.

"Huh. Look at this place," Toshi said, taking in the room. "This must date back to the First Space Age. Maybe even early Corporate Exodus construction. You take us to the nicest places, boss. You know that?"

"We'll hole up here until we need to push on," Ryu said. He released the seals on his neck, pulled off his helmet, and took a deep breath. The air tasted of iron and a hint of something acidic. Two data lines in his visual overlay denoted recommended exposure limits. A healthy adult could handle fifteen minutes with no serious consequences. Dragons could breathe this crap indefinitely.

Ryu pulled his hood back and ran fingers through sweaty black hair. His head floated in the air. Cat, Naomi and Toshi began breaking their neck seals. Ryu picked a knee-high pipe running along the closest machine and sat down.

Naomi slumped onto a pipe opposite him and pulled her helmet off, revealing an oval face with soft cheeks and pale skin. She pushed back the hood holding her black hair in place and breathed in.

"Well, at least the air has character," Naomi said. "Right, Toshi?"

Toshi set his large frame down next to Naomi. He pulled his helmet off and stiffed the air.

"What stinks?" He scrunched his weathered face into a grimace.

"Besides you?" Naomi asked.

"Yeah, besides that?" Toshi looked around. He spotted a small, tarnished nameplate halfway across the room and read the small print. "Hey, this is part of those first ice mines from Luna's original colony."

"So what?" Naomi asked. She opened an invisible pouch at her waist and retrieved a rectangular, bright red wrapper.

"You brought some with you?" Ryu asked.

Naomi daintily peeled the wrapper, revealing a bar of dark chocolate divided into small cube segments.

"You know I hate the intravenous slop we get from our suits," she said. "Sure it keeps us going, but my stomach still knows it's empty."

"No, I mean did you bring enough for all of us?"

"Nope," Naomi said. She took a bite and leaned her head back, chocolate melting in her mouth. "Oh, that's good."

"You do know I'm in charge. I could order you to give me that."

"Touch my chocolate, and I'll shoot out your knee caps." She took another bite.

Ryu sighed. "It's so hard to find good help these days."

Naomi grinned as she chewed.

"Boss, why are we stopping?" Toshi asked.

"The green dragons need time to get into position," Ryu said. "We still need someone to make noise and clear the path between us and the House of Parliament. They're going to make sure the crusaders are hunting for us in the wrong places."

"It's not like Sakaki to let her squad get behind schedule," Toshi said.

Naomi swallowed. "It can't be helped. The navy dropped us in the middle of nowhere."

"Better that than getting shot down by the blockade," Ryu said.

"They could have dropped us closer to the city," Naomi said, taking another bite.

The chocolate's strong aroma began making Ryu's mouth water. His stomach growled, but sonic cancellers in his smartsuit killed the noise.

"Hey, boss?" Toshi asked.

"Hmm?"

Toshi jerked his head to the side twice. Ryu glanced over.

Cat hadn't said a word since they'd sealed the room. She sat on a pipe, hunched over her knees, rifle upright between her legs. With one finger on the barrel, she tilted the rifle back and forth like a metronome.

"Cat?" Ryu asked.

"What?" Cat looked up, a worried expression in her blue eyes. Short golden hair framed a slender face that stood out amongst the other three. She could pass for a Feddie with looks like that. She was shorter and less elfin than the others, as if Earth's gravity had held her back. Ryu knew that wasn't true.

"What's on your mind" Ryu asked.

Cat shook her head and looked down at her rifle. "It's nothing."

"No, seriously. What's getting to you?"

"I don't know," Cat said, shrugging her shoulders. "I guess I thought all of this would be easier."

Ryu stood up and walked over. He sat down next to Cat.

"Come on," Ryu said. "You're doing great. Do you want to turn back?"

Cat let out a short laugh. "No, nothing like that."

"Scared then?"

"No," Cat said. "Well, yes, but that's not it."

"Being scared is perfectly normal."

"Then I think I'm very very very normal right now," Cat said. "It's just ..."

"Go on. What's bothering you?"

"Ryu, that was the first time I've ever killed someone."

"Ah."

"I thought it would be easier, or at least the upgrades would take the edge off these feelings. Was it easy for you?"

"Sadly, no. I know all too well what you're going through."

"How did you deal with it?"

"Really, it's a personal thing. Hey, Naomi? How do you deal with the killing?"

"I'll let you know when I find a good method."

"All right. Toshi?"

"What's there to deal with?"

"Uh huh," Ryu said. "Well, I can see you two are absolutely no help."

Naomi looked up. "You mean you don't feel anything when you kill a Feddie?"

"Is this a trick question?" Toshi said.

"You don't feel anything at all?" Naomi asked. "Is there a hole where your heart should be?"

"What weapon am I using?"

"Huh?"

"It's important. What weapon am I using?"

"I don't know. That rifle of yours."

"A little kick in the shoulder."

"You're sick, you know that," Naomi said.

"Why should I feel anything when killing Feddies?" Toshi asked.

"Because they're people, you idiot!"

"People who are perfectly happy flying to Europa and nuking our cities. So again, why should I feel anything when I kill them?"

"You are totally missing the point!"

"And you have no point."

Ryu sighed. He patted Cat on the shoulder. "Did any of that help at all?"

"I guess so," Cat said.

"Regret coming along?"

"Absolutely not."

Ryu smiled. "Just checking." He put his arm over Cat's shoulders and gave her a warm squeeze.

"You know better than to ask," Cat said.

"Yeah, I suppose I do."

"Hey, Ryu!" Naomi shouted. "Get your hands off the new girl and help your comrades decide who's right!"

"What are you talking about? Cat is my—"

"I don't want to hear it!" Naomi said.

"Fine," Ryu said. "Naomi, you're right this time."

"But you haven't heard my argument," Toshi said.

"Don't need to," Ryu said. "I'm just that good of a leader."

Naomi and Toshi looked at each other.

"So how does victory taste?" Toshi asked.

"Bitter sweet," Naomi said. She took a loud bite out of her chocolate bar. "So Cat, are you sure this room is secure?"

"Very sure," Cat said. She tapped her temple. "I'm still watching the dot-cam feeds we placed along the way. The nearest Feddie patrol passed half a kilometer southeast of us. Plus there's no active infostructure anywhere nearby, SolarNet or otherwise."

"There could be a hard line somewhere," Naomi said.

"We would have seen the cable," Cat said. "It's tough to hide something new in all this decay."

"See? Sneaky like a cat," Toshi said. "I think of all of us, Cat, you have the best call sign."

"Really? I didn't know you had call signs."

"We don't use them anymore," Naomi said.

"Mine was Knuckles," Toshi said. "As in knuckle dragger. But no one calls me that anymore."

"To your face," Ryu said.

"What?"

"I didn't say a word."

"Naomi, how about you?" Cat asked.

"Oh, let's see here," Naomi said, staring up at the ceiling. "There was Bitch and Useless and a bunch of others, but my personal favorite was Whore."

"Ouch," Cat said.

"Come on," Ryu said. "There were some good ones."

"Oh yeah? Name one."

"Well . . . let me think."

"Yeah?"

"Didn't they call you Fu— Oh, wait. That one's no good either."

"I'm waiting."

Ryu threw up his arms. "Sorry. I guess I don't remember any."

"This isn't funny, Ryu. Don't you remember what I had to go through to prove myself? Remember that big idiot? The bald guy with that ridiculous droopy mustache. What was his name?"

"You mean Kentaro?"

"Yeah, that's the one," Naomi said. "You remember what I had to do to get him to respect me?"

"Not specifically," Ryu said. "I remember they had to graft his arm back on when you were done, though."

Cat giggled.

Naomi glared at her.

"Sorry, sorry," Cat said, waving her apologies. "But that was funny."

Ryu received a message through his TangleNet link. He opened it on his visual overlay and read the update.

"What is it, boss?" Toshi asked.

"Suit up," Ryu said. He pulled his hood over his hair, tightened the elastic band around his face, put his helmet on, and sealed the neck. The two smartskin segments merged their microminds and completed the invisibility illusion. He sucked in a breath of dry, filtered air.

The others sprang into action. Naomi closed the wrapper around her chocolate bar and set it on a pipe. Without warning, Toshi snatched it up and shoved the remaining half in his mouth.

"Why, sure," Naomi said, adjusting her hood. "Help yourself, moron."

Toshi mumbled his thanks through a mouth full of chocolate. He slapped his helmet into place.

Cat sealed up and hefted her rifle. "Why the change in orders?"

"New directive from the ambassador," Ryu said. "We need to extract her from the House of Parliament."

"The ambassador doesn't have any upgrades, does she?" Naomi asked.

"Just the basics," Ryu said.

"They have got to be kidding," Naomi said. "How are we supposed to sneak a civilian out of that mess? The crusaders will shoot her to pieces as soon as she leaves the building."

"Probably," Ryu said.

"What's our extraction?" Cat asked.

"The ambassador's shuttle is berthed in a landing crater north of the city. It's a modified tiger shark, so we should be able to run the blockade in it."

"At least there's that," Naomi said.

Toshi gurgled something before swallowing the rest of the chocolate.

"No, Toshi," Ryu said. "I don't think they'd appreciate only getting her head back. Besides, we don't have a cryo-guillotine with us."

"And the green dragons?"

"Won't be joining us," Ryu said. "We ready?"

Toshi eased open the door they'd entered through and retrieved his trap grenade. He closed the door again.

"Ready, boss."

"All right. Let's move!"

Ryu led the way across the room to the northern door. He spun the ancient locking wheel and opened it, exposing a dark corridor that gently swung to the right. Plastic webbing and steel beams held back the gray lunar rock on either side. Large, colorful words had been painted on the walls, perhaps ancient graffiti in languages Ryu didn't recognize. They filed out.

Ryu followed the tunnel until it straightened and came to a T-shaped junction. He checked left while Cat checked right.

"Clear," Cat said.

"Clear," Ryu said. The dragons followed him down the left tunnel. Heavy doors with locking wheels lined the tunnel on either side. Rusted labels hung over each door. A few light strips provided sporadic pockets of illumination.

Halfway through, the tunnel changed from rectangular rock walls to a wider cylindrical tunnel of white plastics. They hurried across a raised black plastic walkway.

The dragons reached the airlock at the far end. Ryu pulled the door open, and they all stepped in. He sealed the door, making the room pitch black. Ryu used a grid of faint green lines on his overlay to find the opposite door. His fellow dragons were bright outlines next to him.

"Hard vacuum on the other side," Cat said.

"Everyone check your seals even if they read green," Ryu said. "And that means you too, Toshi."

"Yeah, yeah."

"Cat, the door?"

"Got it." Cat stepped over to the exit and glanced at the controls. "I can manually equalize pressure with what I think are the emergency controls. No power required."

"Do it."

Cat grabbed a sturdy handle next to the door, turned it ninety degrees, pulled and turned it another ninety degrees. Air bled out of the airlock. In a few seconds, they were in vacuum.

Cat slid the locks out of place one by one and opened the door. Ryu peeked his rifle through the opening.

"Clear," Ryu said. He led the way into a circular tunnel with heavy steel ribs and gray plastic paneling, another disparate section within the Lunar utility maze. The tunnel opened into an atrium ahead. Ryu and Cat crouched at the entrance, checking for enemies or traps.

The roof was gone, exposing the two-story atrium to space. Earth's blue crescent smiled down at them, floating in a sea of stars. Some of those stars moved irregularly, probably warships or interceptors in orbit.

Bodies littered the floor and two spiral staircases leading up to the second story, either crushed by falling debris or perforated by gunfire. Heavy bullet patterns decorated the walls and floor. All of the bodies wore at least armored vests and helmets. Some wore full armored suits in white-and-gray Lunar State surface camouflage.

"Looks like the Feddies blew open the roof and rained hell on these people," Toshi said. "I doubt they had any warning."

"Keep moving," Ryu said.

They crossed the atrium, passed through another dead airlock back into a pressurized environment, and made their way through tunnels of newer construction. Vast machinery hummed underneath their feet, their microminds chattering to each other in quick bursts of radio traffic. Glowing light strips illuminated pastel blue walls and clusters of thick color-coded pipes underneath clean steel grating.

"SolarNet contact," Cat said. "Two hundred meters ahead. Feddie patrol. No visual yet."

"Hold here," Ryu said.

"They're moving towards us," Cat said. "Maybe two or three regulars. They'll be coming to the next junction from the right." She linked the estimated locations to the other dragons.

"Get in position," Ryu said. He crouched against the wall and aimed his rifle. The other dragons formed a firing line. The pulsing red dots moved across his visual overlay towards the junction.

Two Feddies in gray-and-blue urban-patterned armor stepped into view, M20 carbines slung from their shoulders. They were talking to each other, barely paying attention to their surroundings. One of them grabbed a cylindrical grenade from his belt and tossed it towards the dragons.

"Hold fire," Ryu said, reading the label on the grenade. "Don't move."

The grenade rolled to a stop halfway between the dragons and the Feddies. Smoke jetted out of the bottom, spewing a thick, green cloud. In seconds, it filled the tunnel and visually obscured the Feddies. Cat tracked their SolarNet traffic, showing them standing directly ahead.

"Someone should tell them that junk doesn't stick to our suits anymore," Naomi said.

Sonic cancellers and smartskin prevented any direct contact between the dragons. Naomi's suit sent the message to a TangleNet server two kilometers underneath Europa's surface through a secure entangled particle link. When received, the server relayed the message to the other dragons instantaneously through their own entangled links.

"They can still see us if we move out of the cloud too fast," Toshi said.

"Yeah, but they also have no chance of spotting us through this junk," Ryu said. "Cat, what are they doing?"

"They're releasing cling-gas in hopes of fouling our suits," Cat said. "Isn't it obvious?"

"No, I mean why haven't they moved on?"

"Uhh ... They're talking about sports," Cat said. "Apparently Cleveland is the team to follow this year."

"Great."

"Or it might be Detroit. There seems to be some debate on this point."

"Uh huh."

"They also hate these patrols. They think their commander is an idiot because—"

"Thank you, Cat. That will do."

"Should we wait until they move?" Naomi asked.

"Who knows when that'll be," Ryu said.

"We could backtrack and go around their patrol," Cat said.

Ryu checked his map. "That'll take too long."

"Or we can just kill them and move on," Toshi said.

"We're wasting too much time here," Ryu said. "Toshi, back me up. Let's keep this quiet."

"Right, boss."

Ryu stuck his rifle to his back where smartskin held the weapon in place with adaptive friction. He pulled an ultrasonic knife from the sheath at his waist. Toshi did the same. They walked into the expanding green cloud, one careful step at a time. The smoke ahead thinned until Ryu saw the regulars. One of them gestured like he was throwing an unseen game ball. That one had his back to the dragons. The other Feddie looked straight at Ryu.

Ryu and Toshi emerged fully from the smoke. Green gas swirled around their suits.

The Feddie looking their way reached for his carbine.

Ryu and Toshi sprinted forward with forty meters of open ground to cross. The soles of their smartsuits adapted for extra friction, allowing them to run at full speed in Luna's easy gravity. Ryu engaged the power pack in the knife's hilt. The ultradiamond blade oscillated at lethal frequencies.

Thirty meters.

Twenty meters.

The Feddie grabbed his carbine and raised the barrel.

Ten meters.

Ryu cut through the Feddie's wrist, severing his hand and carbine from the rest of his body. With a quick horizontal slash, Ryu jammed the knife into the side of the Feddie's helmet, stabbing through its SolarNet communications micromind and shredding the man's brain. Red gore splattered the insides of the Feddie's faceplate.

Toshi stabbed the second Feddie through the head in the exact same spot.

The Feddie's gun and severed hand hit the ground.

"I've set up two dummy nodes to fake their SolarNet traffic," Cat said. She took two marble-sized devices from her belt pouch and stuck them to a wall. "We've got maybe ten minutes before someone notices the fake nodes."

"Good job," Ryu said, drawing his knife from the dead Feddie. He lowered the corpse to the ground and sheathed the knife.

"Here, boss," Toshi said, dragging his victim over to a maintenance hatch in the floor. He opened it and chucked the corpse inside. Ryu followed with his victim, leaving a trail of fresh blood in his wake.

"My kill was cleaner," Toshi said.

"He was about to fire," Ryu said. He tossed the hand and carbine in after the two dead Feddies. "All right, let's make the most of those ten minutes."

Ryu led the way through pastel blue halls and rows of machinery painted neon green. Modern English warnings and instructions adorned the machines in blocks of hot pink text. The pastel blue halls gave way to a wide, powder yellow staircase leading up. Light filtered through the opening at the end.

Ryu climbed ten stories of stairs, stepped across a wide landing, then climbed another ten stories, and stopped at a pair of glass doors. The sign on the doors was backwards and read: NEW LONDON UTILITY TUNNEL C81.

They had reached a point along the crater slope that looked down on the sprawl of New London. The city was a riot of neon and pastel colors. Yellows, blues, greens, reds, even a whole district in painfully hot pink. The Lunarians gave every color its due.

Ryu had always liked that about Lunarians. In a world as gray and drab as Luna, the Lunarians celebrated color in everything they built or wore. It was perhaps a shame they all seemed to be colorblind, but Ryu appreciated their enthusiasm all the same.

Looking up, Ryu saw the crater plate: a massive array of hexagonal panels that sealed in the crater's breathable atmosphere. Earth and the stars gleamed through the clear ceiling. The sun's filtered rays illuminated most of the city, with street lights shining brightly in those sections concealed by the crater wall's shadow. It was perhaps midmorning in Luna's month-long "day".

On the northern side of the city far from their position was the expansive, five-story sprawl of the House of Parliament and the ancient clock tower Bigger Ben. They looked like something plucked out of history, all rising and pointed gothic architecture, right angles and fine stone details versus the geometric absurdity of New London.

An explosion bloomed from the city center. Then two more from the outskirts. The city was alive with gunfire. Ryu saw about fifty Federacy regulars storm a six-story turquoise bubble-office. Lunar troops fired down from the oval windows. Another twenty Federacy regulars piled out of their troop carriers a block away and took positions in nearby buildings.

Armored troop carriers and tanks supported the advancing Federacy forces. A Federacy tank hovered out of cover and fired on a fully loaded Lunar troop carrier, catching it in the open. Bits of soldiers and vehicle fragments scattered out of the black, oily explosion. Airborne Federacy gunships flitted between the buildings, firing on enemy positions and ducking into cover when the return fire got too hot. The city seethed with the mess of brutal street fighting and blurred battle lines.

Beneath their position, a solid column of Federacy reinforcements filed through a six-lane tunnel coming from the New London spaceport.

"And we have to cross this?" Naomi asked.

... establishing link ...

source: [UNKNOWN]

routing: [UNKNOWN]

routing: [UNKNOWN]

routing: [UNKNOWN]

routing: Earth orbit - surveillance satellite JDN-SS-17 - link_001/link_002

routing: North Pacifica, Europa - JDN Main Hub - link_010/link_118

routing: Capitol City, Europa - TangleNet Test Hub - link_001/link_005

destination: [UNKNOWN]

link distance: Exact distance unknown. Estimated at 792 million kilometers.

link signal delay: 0.006 seconds

... finalizing link protocol ...

... link established ...

2: Sakura.

1: Hello, Paul. What an unexpected pleasure.

2: Any pleasure you derive from this discussion is purely accidental.

1: I see. Well, don't let me keep you. You obviously have contacted me for a reason.

2: We are going to discuss the dragons on Luna.

1: What about them?

2: Why are they on Luna?

1: I thought the reason was obvious. The Lunar State requested aid and the dragons were dispatched to provide said aid.

2: Yes, that's the obvious reason. Now tell me why they're on Luna.

1: Paul, as much as you might read into this, there isn't any other answer I can give you.

2: So you deny the dragons are part of the Europan takeover of Luna?

1: Of course I deny such a ridiculous claim.

2: And you deny you have designs on Luna.

1: It is of little interest to me. If anything, the dragons are there to show our good will to the rest of the solar system.

2: Ah, yes. The famous Europan good will. Spreading love and peace wherever they travel.

1: You're mocking me.

2: Of course I'm mocking you. You have abided by the letter of our arrangement, but you have failed to honor the spirit of that arrangement.

1: Meaning what, Paul?

2: You need a reminder of exactly who is in charge here. I've chosen a small demonstration that I believe will get your attention. I want you to understand it is I who allows your little ice moon to continue existing. Maybe this will wake you up and make you behave.

1: Paul, what have you done?

2: Oh, calm yourself. I'm not talking about genocide. Not yet, anyway. I've prepared a little script for your dragons in New London. Even now, the crusaders are moving significant forces into the city.

1: Your doing, I assume.

2: I have nudged them in the appropriate direction. It should be quite a spectacular battle. I always enjoy seeing those two forces go at it, especially given your personal stake in these matters.

1: You underestimate the dragons.

2: And you underestimate me. Know this. No matter who lives or dies in New London, two things are certain. My position will be strengthened and yours will be weakened. Heed this for the warning that it is. Next time I will not be so merciful.

... link severed at source ...

Ryu crouched behind the massive square bulk of a voltage transformer halfway down the crater slope. Thick, neon-green cables ran down to New London. Naomi, Cat, and Toshi joined him.

Ryu tagged a Lunar house with a nav beacon. The house looked like a bright orange spike coming out of the ground.

"We'll head down the slope to this house then proceed clockwise around the city," Ryu said. "Going straight through is too much of a risk. Naomi, what do you think?"

Naomi shouldered her JD-42 sniper rifle and pointed to the left. "There's plenty of machinery and rocks along the slopes. I can stay up here and cover your advance."

"Good," Ryu said. "Stay out of sight if possible and meet us at the House of Parliament."

"Got it."

"Let's go," Ryu said. He broke cover and sprinted down the slope, shrouded in his smartskin illusion. Cat and Toshi chased after him. Naomi ran to the left.

A Federacy gunship passed overhead. It stopped and turned its nose towards the city. Air turbines on either side of the craft twisted and flexed to stabilize the aircraft.

The gunship opened fire with its nose turret, spewing out a steady stream of explosive-tipped pain. The bullets pounded into the seventh story of a bright red apartment complex shaped like a giant apple. Lunar soldiers launched a missile from the sixth story.

Countermeasures spat out of the gunship's dorsal spine. The gunship descended, almost crashing into the crater slope, but steadied itself with a last second burst of thrust. The missile angled towards the countermeasures and exploded in a quick flash of yellow light and shrapnel.

"I thought the fighting in the city had died down!" Cat said.

"Something stirred it up," Ryu said. They'd almost reached the edge of the city.

"In position," Naomi said, her locator pulsing halfway up the slope. "Your path is clear."

Ryu stopped at the orange house, a slender four-story spike. Steam poured out of the windows and a gaping hole in the first floor. Automated sprinklers had recently put out a fire.

Ryu led his squad to the left.

"Contact ahead," Naomi said. "About twenty Feddies. They're busy with some Lunars hiding in a parking garage. Stay on course and slip by."

"Understood," Ryu said. He checked around the orange house's corner, then sprinted to the next house. Gunfire echoed down the street. Distant explosions rumbled in his chest. His wetware cheats identified each weapon based on key sonic identifiers, adding to his tactical awareness.

Three guns opened fire, close by and slightly deeper into the city, their firing sounds easily distinguishable from the rest. It was like a continuous mechanical roar instead of the staccato beat of most firearms. Ryu didn't need his cheats to identify the weapons.

"Naomi?"

"Yeah, I see them. Four crusaders backing up those Feddies. Hold your position."

Ryu stopped at the edge of a pale green house shaped like a cartoon tree. He extruded a dot-cam tubule from his glove and peeked it around the corner.

"They should be coming into view now," Naomi said.

Five Federacy regulars and four crusaders in gleaming white armor ran across the intersection.

The crusaders' suits made them look more like armored bears than people, with enlarged torsos and thick limbs. But those exaggerated dimensions represented triplicate armor and layers of artificial musculature that granted incredible speed. The crusaders took cover behind a concrete barrier when the Feddies had only crossed half the distance.

Several Lunarians fired from inside the parking garage, killing two of the exposed Feddies.

The crusaders sprang out of cover, aimed three M18 six-barreled Gatling guns and opened fire. Each gun spewed out one hundred twenty variable payload shells a second, literally pulping the Lunarians with a mix of explosive and incendiary ordinance. The crusader with an M7 thermal lance targeted a concrete barrier further back. The hot-white beam from his weapon cut through reinforced concrete thirty meters away and vaporized the Lunarians hiding behind it.

It was over in less than a second. The Lunarians didn't have time to adjust their aim or dive back under cover. The crusaders showed up and the Lunarians died.

One of the crusaders turned around, light glinting off his gold visor. A gold crucifix against a background of red and white squares marked his left shoulder.

"This just became a lot more difficult," Ryu said.

The four crusaders rose and advanced into the parking garage. One of them stood a head taller than the rest.

"You see that?" Naomi said.

"Yeah, I see it," Ryu said.

"Looks like the tall one is the squad leader."

"Yeah, I noticed that too."

"Boss, I know this is a stupid idea," Toshi said. "But can we kill these guys? We've got the drop on them."

"You know better than that, Toshi."

"But that crusader could be a dragon defector."

"We don't know that for certain," Ryu said, knowing in his heart he was lying. "Plenty of Martians are that tall. Lunarians and quicksilvers too. Hell even some cometeers are that tall. It could be any of them."

"You think crusaders are going to take orders from some lunatic cometeer?" Toshi asked.

"Not really," Ryu said.

"It's got to be one of our own," Toshi said. "The crusaders always give our defectors the juicy posts."

"You're jumping to conclusions."

"How about this," Toshi said. "Let's kill the other three and capture the squad leader. We can bring him back home with us instead of the ambassador, interrogate him, chop him up into little pieces and mail him back to Penance. Maybe not in that order."

"Toshi, enough!"

"I ... yeah, boss."

"Naomi?"

"Your path is clear."

"Let's go!" Ryu said. He drew the tubule back into his glove, sprang out of cover and dashed for the next house. From house to house, building to building, the three dragons skirted the city. In the distance, Ryu saw the pointed clock tower of Bigger Ben getting closer.

"Hey, Toshi?" Ryu asked.

"Yeah, boss?"

"Why do they call it Bigger Ben?"

"Not sure. I think there was a similar clock tower on Earth."

"In the original London?"

"Maybe," Toshi said. "Records are pretty sketchy from that era, and of course none of the old nation-state capitols exist anymore, but there is a lot of indirect evidence the clock tower existed."

"Huh. So old London was a capitol on Earth?"

"I think so, but I'm not really sure. I saw a documentary on New London once, but it's been a while."

Naomi followed her own path along the slopes, dangerously exposed to gunships, dashing from one rocky feature or machinery structure to the next.

"There are other crusader squads," Naomi said from her latest position. "I count at least five squads. Looks like they're converging on the House of Parliament."

"Great," Ryu said. "Got any more good news?"

"Hold on, I've got to relocate," Naomi said. "Ah, damn it!"

"What?"

"I've got Feddies pouring out of a utility tunnel. They're right in my way."

Ryu stopped and looked up the slope. A green glowing dot marked Naomi's position. A swarm of red expanded out close to her.

"Can you head up the slope and loop around them?"

"I'll try. Shit! They're deploying a missile battery."

"Need help?"

"No, I'm okay," Naomi said. "I just need to get out of here before the Lunars start shooting at this location. Go on ahead."

"Understood," Ryu said.

The Federacy missile battery on the slope opened fire, launching six projectiles in a lazy arc over the city. The missiles flew high over the buildings, skimmed the crater plate up top, then dove for a yellow cubical building. They stabbed through the roof and exploded within. Despite the carnage, the building did not collapse. It must have been reinforced.

Four Federacy gunships moved in and showered the target building with gunfire and rockets.

Lunarians launched portable missiles from surrounding rooftops and windows. One of the gunships took two direct hits, lost one of its air turbines and plowed into the side of a building. Three other missiles looped over the city and came down hard on the missile battery. Plumes of gray rock blasted out from the impact points. Several red dots winked out.

Naomi's bright green dot switched off. He'd lost all tactical feeds from her suit.

"Naomi!" Ryu shouted. It was a pointless calling to her. His words couldn't reach her without a TangleNet link.

The missile battery had survived and launched another salvo of six.

Ryu zoomed in on the area. Grayish clouds and scattering Federacy regulars made a mess of the whole area. He found the pumping station and the water mains Naomi had hid behind. The mains were thick enough to obscure someone standing on the other side. Ryu found no trace of her, but that didn't mean her body wasn't sprawled out where he couldn't see, unconscious or worse.

"Orders?" Toshi asked.

More Lunar missiles pounded into the slope. One of them hit a water main and broke it open. Water gushed out, running down the slope. Steam rose from the impact point.

"Come on, Naomi," Ryu said, searching. "Damn it, where are you?"

"Boss?"

"We're heading up to look for her," Ryu said, switching off the zoom and raising his rifle.

"There's no signal," Cat said. "That means she's probably ..."

"Doesn't matter," Ryu said. "We're going to make sure."

"After you, boss," Toshi said.

Ryu broke from cover and sprinted up the slope. He reached a perpendicular bend in the water main and took cover next to it, a third of the way to Naomi and the missile battery. Toshi and Cat crouched behind him.

"That smoke is going to be difficult to cross," Toshi said. "At least we have the pipes for cover."

The missile battery fired again. This time only a single Lunar missile struck the slope beneath the battery, fooled at the last moment by Federacy countermeasures.

A green locator dot appeared on Ryu's overlay. It came from twenty meters beneath the pumping station.

"Naomi!" Ryu said.

"Shit, that was close," Naomi said. "The shock from the explosions crashed my TangleNet link. I had to reboot it."

Ryu brought up Naomi's status. Medical was all green, though the explosions had damaged her smartsuit.

"Looks like you have smartskin tears in two places," Ryu said.

"I know, mother. Why do you think I ducked into the utility maze? I'll patch it up and come out of the maze near the House of Parliament."

Toshi chuckled. "She called you mo—"

"All right! Back on mission."

Ryu led the dragons down the slope and resumed their course around the city perimeter. Naomi followed through the underground tunnel network.

"You're falling behind, Naomi," Ryu said, ten minutes later. Bigger Ben towered over the surrounding buildings. The three dragons rounded a corner and came into direct view of the House of Parliament.

"It can't be helped," Naomi said. "These tunnels twist around too much. Looks like I can't join you inside."

"Understood," Ryu said. "Make your way around the back and get ready to support us when we exit."

"On it."

"Ryu, there's been a sharp spike in SolarNet traffic," Cat said. "I think you'll want to see this."

"One moment," Ryu said. A missile hit the House of Parliament, but only blew stone fascia off the armored walls. Perhaps an accidental hit? No shots answered from the gothic structure, either from the roof or the windows. Lunarians fought from the surrounding buildings, but the House of Parliament looked abandoned.

A yellow beacon marked the ambassador's position near the center of the House of Parliament, first floor.

"I don't see any Lunar troops inside or on the roof," Ryu said. "It's a fortified building. Why aren't they using it?"

Ryu heard the unmistakable drone of M18 Gatling guns. At least two squads of crusaders had reached the front lines.

"Ryu?" Cat said.

"What do you have?"

"That spike in SolarNet traffic? The crusaders have just uploaded a message to the SolarNet. I think you should take a look."

Ryu opened the file Cat linked him and played it for the squad. A piece of his visual overlay turned into a gold crucifix with a red and white checkered background. A gruff man provided the voiceover.

"This is an official statement concerning the Lunar State and its leaders," the crusader said. "We have evidence in our possession that the Lunar State prime minister and leading members of the House of Commons have been subjected to persona-intrusion wetware. These intrusions were administered by the Europan ambassador currently trapped within the House of Parliament. Their wills are not their own. They are now thralls for the Europan quantum mind, Matriarch.

"The evidence we have in our possession is irrefutable, copies of which are attached to this message. Under authority granted to us by the Federacy admiralty board, we have been ordered to execute all Lunar State ministers and Europan citizens located in or around the House of Parliament. These harsh measures will be carried out to ensure no thralls survive.

"Already, the Lunar military remnants in New London have disavowed any ties to the thralls hiding within the House of Parliament. The crusaders, with aid from our brave Federacy allies, will now carry out the executions."

"What the fuck!" Toshi shouted. "Persona-intrusion? That's a load of cow shit! Matriarch would never do that!"

"Yeah, I know," Ryu said. "It's sad, but lies like this stick."

Two more missiles pounded into the House of Parliament's stone exterior, blasting it apart to reveal the pearly white armor underneath.

"They're trying to breach the outer walls," Toshi said. "It won't be long before they're inside."

"Orders?" Cat asked.

"We're here to get our ambassador out," Ryu said. "And that is exactly what we're going to do. We don't leave our people behind."

Toshi hefted his rifle. "Man, any crusaders that get in my way are so dead."

"Come on. Let's get inside," Ryu said. The three dragons sprinted across an open plaza to a small alcove in the side of the House of Parliament. A thick armored door blocked entry. Ryu placed his hacking glove against a security panel next to the door.

Codes included with his mission update exchanged between the panel and his glove. The door snapped upward, allowing the three dragons to hurry inside before the door slammed shut with a pneumatic hiss.

Ryu ran through an abandoned security post, past a pair of wooden double doors and into a long hall three stories high. Tall, gothic windows with arched tops lined the hall. Light shone through stained glass artwork.

Ryu could make out the surrounding battle through the glass. He felt exposed with all those windows, but quickly noticed a few showed nothing but static. The "windows" were using images relayed from external cameras, and some of those cameras had been blown off. Thick diamoplast armor separated this room from the outside fight.

"At least they haven't leveled the place," Cat said.

"The crusaders might want the ministers' bodies," Ryu said. "Either because they think the bodies have proof on them or because they need to plant the proof."

Ryu raced down the hall and turned into a wide chamber. Padded green benches lined either side of a central path that ended at a podium on a raised dais. Ornate metalwork chandeliers hung from the ceiling. Light shone through high stained glass windows, illuminating the chamber.

Ryu spotted the ambassador backing away from a crowd of fifty Lunar State ministers and what looked like a large number of civilians, even a few kids. The ministers' families? It didn't matter.

Everyone was shouting at everyone else. The ambassador shouted back at the crowd. She was a tall woman with straight, raven hair halfway down her back, wearing a white business suit. She wore data glasses with oval lenses and thick black frames, though Ryu knew she had sight overlay wetware.

The ministers, about two thirds of which were men, wore somber business suits and data glasses or monocles. The civilians were clothed in a vomited puddle of clashing colors.

One of the ministers pulled a pistol out of his dark green business jacket.

Ryu dropped his illusion and rushed forward. He climbed onto the dais and stopped at the ambassador's side, rifle aimed at the threatening minister.

The man stopped, frozen in terror. A scroll of green text and diagrams slid across his data monocle, telling him exactly what was pointed at him. The crowd backed away. Near the back, a little girl started crying at the top of her lungs.

The ambassador turned and looked at Ryu, seeing him as a tall, lithe figure clad in a skintight black.

Ryu killed his sonic cancellers. "Ambassador, I'm Ryu Kusanagi from the black dragons. We're getting you to safety."

The building shook. Dust scattered from the chandeliers. Something had hit the roof.

"Oh, thank Matriarch you're here!" the ambassador said.

"Come on. We need to leave. We'll exit out the back and get you to your shuttle."

Ryu grabbed her wrist, but she resisted.

"Wait!" the ambassador said. "Wait a minute!"

"We don't have a minute!"

"We— We can't leave without them!" the ambassador said, pointing to the ministers who were only moments ago ready to kill her. "They'll die if we don't get them to safety!"

"I can't save them!" Ryu hissed quietly. "I don't even know if I can save you!"

"You have to try!" the ambassador shouted. "Don't you see? This is the only way we can expose the crusader lies! Do you have any idea what will happen if people start believing this?"

"I—" Ryu stopped. He knew exactly where lies like this could lead. All the nations of the solar system might unite against Europa. It could even end with a huge coalition fleet raining nuclear fire on his home. After all, something similar had happened at Bunker Zero ten years ago.

Two more explosions rocked the House of Parliament. The chandeliers swung back and forth like pendulums.

"Federacy forces have breached the southern wall," Cat said. The ministers and ambassador couldn't hear her. "Dozens of Feddie regulars and a squad of crusaders are entering the building."

"What's the call, boss?" Toshi asked.

"We're getting the ministers out of here," Ryu said. "Naomi, are you in position?"

"I'm at a power station behind the House of Parliament," Naomi said. "If the ministers can reach me, they can get into the utility maze. They have a two hundred meter run across open terrain waiting for them, but I don't think we have any choice. No Federacy forces on this side. They're all focused on breaching the front."

"All right. That will have to do." Ryu turned to the ambassador. He linked Naomi's position to her. "Get the ministers to this location then get them into the maze. A dragon will meet you there."

"But—"

"Shut up and move!" Ryu shouted. He amplified his voice by ten decibels. "Crusaders are in the building! Follow the ambassador to safety! We'll buy you the time you need! Now follow her and run!"

The ambassador, ministers and family members got moving and headed for the exit. Ryu could see Naomi's location glinting in their data glasses. The ambassador must have passed the coordinates along. They exited through a pair of double doors at the rear.

Ryu engaged his smartskin illusion and sonic cancellers. He pointed to a balcony over the double-door exit.

"Toshi, Cat! Up there!"

"Right!" Toshi said.

"We've got about thirty seconds!" Cat said.

Toshi and Cat jumped to the second story balcony, an easy feat in Luna's gravity. They grabbed the railing and flipped over into cover. Toshi tossed several grenades from his bandolier at the chamber seating. The grenades, each the size of a shotgun shell, stuck wherever they hit and camouflaged. He fired two from his rifle's integral grenade launcher through the main entrance. Once through the doorway, they turned out of sight, struck nearby walls and armed themselves.

Ryu jumped over the entrance. There wasn't a balcony to hide in, but he didn't need one. The soles and palms of his smartsuit adapted for extra friction, allowing him to stick to the wall. He climbed directly above the entrance, ready to ambush any crusader that came through.

Ryu put his back to the ceiling and aimed his rifle down.

A group of four Federacy regulars entered the chamber and spread out. They swept the room with multitrackers that couldn't detect the previous version of smartskin, let alone the tiny grenades Toshi had deployed.

"Two crusaders at the doorway," Toshi said. "Looks like they smell a trap."

"We need to draw them in," Ryu said. "Open fire."

"Right!" Toshi said. He and Cat rose out of cover. Cat squeezed off four quick bursts from her rifle, one for each Feddie. Shatterbacks pierced their armor and detonated within their torsos. Someone's arm smacked against a stained glass window, still clutching his carbine.

Toshi fired two needle grenades. The guided projectiles zeroed in on the crusaders. Proximity microminds counted down and triggered at the preset range. The grenades blossom into shaped cones of diamond needles, but the crusaders dodged out of the way with unnatural speed. Needles shredded the carpet just outside the doorway and blew the doors off their hinges.

Toshi and Cat pulled back into cover and moved to different positions along the balcony.

The remains of the four Feddies slumped to the ground.

"God damn it! Dragons inside!" someone shouted from beyond the doorway.

"Surprise," Toshi whispered. He detonated the two grenades he'd set in the hallway. Diamond needles scythed through another three Feddies. Their gurgling screams carried into the chamber.

The two crusaders raked the balcony with Gatling fire. Hundreds of varishells detonated on contact against the wood railing and plush benches beyond. Splinters and foam padding blasted out in every direction.

Ryu watched Cat and Toshi's indicators dash out of the way just in time.

One of the crusaders fired a grenade from his wrist launcher. The tiny cylinder exploded against the balcony and blew out the walls to either side.

"Damn it!" Toshi shouted. "Too close!"

"Four crusaders total!" Cat shouted. "They're coming in!"

"Stay hidden," Ryu whispered. "Wait until all of them are in the chamber."

Two crusaders marched into the chamber, spraying the balcony. They took positions on either side of the aisle that ran down the center. Two more crusaders entered the chamber, one carrying a thermal lance. The last crusader stood a head taller than the others and wielded a Gatling gun.

"Just a little further," Ryu whispered.

Green indicators pulsed ahead of the crusaders for each grenade. The first two crusaders moved into range.

The tall crusader turned suddenly and aimed his Gatling gun at Ryu's position.

"Shit!"

Both Ryu and the crusader opened fire.

The crusader couldn't have seen Ryu, could only have suspected. But that didn't make his weapon any less lethal. Vari-shells detonated to Ryu's right, showering him with splinters and chips of stone. He was already dodging, already running across the wall, firing.

A few of his shatterbacks struck the lead crusader, knocking him back but not penetrating his armor. The other three crusaders took aim.

"Suppress! Suppress!" Ryu shouted. He triggered all of Toshi's grenades.

The sharp eruptions turned the chamber into a storm of wooden splinters, flying bits of foam, stone chips, and razor-sharp diamond needles. The benches were totally obliterated. A grenade coated one of the crusaders with needles across one side like a half-bald porcupine, staggering him but doing little damage.

Toshi and Cat opened fire on full automatic. Shatterbacks and grenades detonated within the chamber. Two crusaders swung their guns around, firing constantly and forcing Toshi and Cat back into cover. Ryu kept running across the wall. He dove for the only exit available to him, the broken double doors the crusaders had entered through.

The tall crusader took aim at him again.

Without looking, Ryu fired all three grenades from his rifle's launcher. The tall crusader ducked out of the way moments before the grenades blasted craters in the floor.

Ryu found himself in the long, three-story hallway with the massive stained glass "windows." Most of them displayed static now. A few Feddie bodies were splayed across the red carpeting by Toshi's grenades. Ryu picked a direction and ran. He feverishly jammed grenades into his rifle, jettisoned his mostly spent ammo clip and slapped in a new one.

"Not that way!" Cat said. "The Feddies breached the outer walls in that direction!"

"Too late!" Ryu shouted.

The tall crusader exited the chamber and aimed down the hall. Ryu reached the end of the hall and dove through an open doorway into some sort of art gallery. Old Earth oil paintings or replicas hung from pristine white walls. Bronze statues rested on marble plinths.

A squad of ten Federacy regulars waited on the other side, as surprised to see him as he was to see them. At his current speed, even unenhanced civilians could spot him. The Feddies raised their carbines.

Still airborne from his dive, Ryu took aim and squeezed the trigger. He drew a line across the Feddies, emptying a full clip in two seconds.

Ryu struck the ground, rolled and rose into a low crouch. He ejected his spent clip, shoved in another and sprinted for the exit at the far end of the art gallery.

Behind him, the Feddies dropped to the ground, most of them missing heads or parts of their torsos.

"Emergency!" Naomi shouted. "I need assistance now!"

"That's not going to be easy!" Ryu brought up a map of the House of Parliament and had his wetware cheats set nav points for the quickest route to Naomi.

"You okay, Ryu?" Cat asked.

"I'm fine! You and Toshi get to Naomi!"

"Right!"

Ryu raced through the House of Parliament. He pulled grenades out of his bandolier, armed their microminds with simple friend-or-foe instructions and tossed them in his wake. No one followed, and he met no further resistance before regrouping with Toshi and Cat.

"We trapped our exit routes!" Cat said, running into view. "The crusaders are going around!"

"Finally, some good news!" Ryu said.

They met at a security checkpoint in the rear of the building, the same one the ministers and Europan ambassador had taken perhaps a minute earlier. Ryu pressed his hacking glove against the door panel and sent the appropriate codes. The door snapped upward, and the three dragons moved out into an open field behind the House of Parliament.

Ryu spotted Naomi two hundred meters up the slope near a power station, exchanging fire with three crusaders behind the blasted wreckage of a Federacy gunship. A fourth crusader was on his back with a missing head.

The ambassador, ministers and civilians cowered on the opposite side of the power station. They couldn't get into the utility maze while the crusaders held the slope.

Another Federacy gunship flew over the House of Parliament. Four crusaders rode along, two hanging on each side. Ryu snapped his rifle up, cycled his grenades to an anti-tank variant and fired. The grenade ignited its solid propellant and rocketed towards the gunship. The pilot didn't have time to dodge.

The grenade punched through the gunship's underbelly and exploded. Cockpit glass blasted out. Side paneling bulged unnaturally. The twin air turbines locked on their last flight command and kept spinning. The gunship tilted to the side, accelerating until it struck Bigger Ben's clock face in a greasy fireball.

One of the crusaders exchanging fire with Naomi turned and shot at Ryu's position. Ryu, Cat and Toshi ducked back into the House of Parliament. Explosive rounds pulverized the stone exterior.

"Make some noise, Naomi!" Ryu said. "We need to take these crusaders down!"

"Got it!"

Naomi fired four shots from her sniper rifle. One penetrated through the gunship wreckage and struck a crusader in his gun arm, blasting the limb off and knocking him out of cover.

Ryu and the others showered the crusaders with shatterbacks. One of the crusaders staggered back from the repeated detonations. Naomi shot him through the head. Ryu caught another one with a grenade to the chest, which collapsed the armor, crushed his chest and sent him flying. The last crusader, missing an arm, went prone against the gray slopes and fired grenades from his wrist launcher. Ryu shot down his grenades in midflight while Cat and Toshi pummeled him with shatterbacks until dead.

"Naomi, get those people moving!" Ryu shouted.

"Right away!"

Naomi switched her sonic cancellers off and started shouting orders. The ambassador and ministers rounded the power station into the open and ran for a steep staircase leading to a utility maze entrance.

Two Federacy gunships crested over the House of Parliament, each carrying four crusaders.

"Shoot them down!" Ryu said, raising his rifle. He and Toshi fired their grenades first.

The crusaders leaped off the gunships and opened fire. Hundreds of explosive rounds showered the slope, blasting up clouds of gray dirt and pulverizing any human they struck. The ambassador's vitals flat lined a moment before her locator beacon vanished. The ministers and their families died almost instantly, reduced to fragments that weren't even recognizably human.

A crimson ribbon splashed against Naomi's suit before she leaped into the tunnel. Her smartskin illusion scrambled into swirling patterns of red. It adapted and reconstituted in the span of a second.

Ryu and Toshi's grenades struck the gunships, but Ryu didn't wait to see the result. Eight crusaders crashed into the slope. Several turned their Gatling guns towards Ryu's squad.

"Back inside!" Ryu shouted before a hail of gunfire forced the point. He sealed the door.

"They just gunned them down!" Cat said.

"Boss, some of those crusaders are heading after Naomi," Toshi said.

"Naomi, what's your status?" Ryu asked. He waited a few seconds. "Naomi, respond!"

"I— I'm okay," Naomi said, her voice quavering. "A squad of crusaders is heading into the tunnel. I'll … I'll lose them in the maze."

"You all right?"

"I'm fine! W-worry about yourself, damn it!"

"Crusaders outside and inside," Toshi said. "Where do we punch through?"

Ryu brought up the map on his overlay. He remembered how that tall crusader had guessed his hiding place.

"They'll be watching the obvious routes," Ryu said. "If we get bogged down in a gunfight, they'll just swarm us with numbers. We need to sneak out." He placed a nav beacon on a nearby staircase. "This way."

"Doesn't this take us further away from the tunnels?" Toshi asked.

"I know," Ryu said. "The map shows a second decommissioned power station near the east wing. We'll enter the tunnel maze through there."

"But this place is swarming with troops by now."

"Right, which is why we're heading for the roof," Ryu said.

On the way to the fifth floor, Ryu only had to stop once to let a squad of Feddies walk by. One passed within two meters of him, waving his multi-tracker back and forth with zeal.

"Those things could barely spot our suits two versions ago," Cat said.

"I'd prefer they never find that out," Ryu said. He watched the Feddies move out of sight. "Come on."

Occasionally, one of their grenades would take out a Feddie patrol. All the grenades had dot-cams, allowing Ryu and the others to tap into their visual feeds.

"No sign of that crusader squad led by the traitor," Cat said. "Four crusaders outside on the slopes and four in the tunnels pursuing Naomi. Probably more nearby."

Ryu passed through a security checkpoint and scaled a cramped steel staircase before reaching the door to the roof. He placed a finger beneath the door and let his glove extrude a dot-cam tubule. He checked their surroundings through a fishbowl visual feed.

"Looks clear. No gunships close by either," Ryu said. He retracted the tubule and cracked the door open.

Ryu and the others slipped through. Toshi planted a grenade on the door and closed it. The roof was a flat expanse of stone tiles masking milky diamoplast armor. Crouching low, Ryu made his way along the northern parapet. Ahead, Bigger Ben still stood tall, minus one clock face. Oily smoke rose from gunship wreckage on the roof. The four crusaders that crashed with it were nowhere to be found.

Another explosion reverberated through the House of Parliament.

"Got five with that one," Toshi said.

Ryu stopped at the end of the east wing as close to the second power station as possible. The station was a white block rising out of the crater slope.

"Now what?" Toshi asked. "Scale down the exterior?"

"No, we're jumping to the power station."

"Great."

"I'll go first," Ryu said. "Cat?"

"It's as clear as it's going to be."

"Good enough." Ryu sprinted across the roof and leaped from the parapet. He sailed through the air, illusion shimmering and updating around him, almost travelling horizontally. Ryu landed on the power station's flat roof, rolled across it and sprang up into a crouch.

"Nothing to it," Ryu said, raising his rifle and covering the others.

"Cat, go next," Toshi said.

"All right. Here goes!"

Cat leaped across the two buildings, a barely present blur in the air. She rolled when she hit and deftly rose to her feet.

The grenade Toshi planted at the door exploded, blowing apart the small shack at the top of the stairs. A crusader charged through, his white armor covered in scorch marks. He swung his Gatling gun around, quickly scanning the roof through a cracked visor. The tall traitor crusader followed him.

"Not good!" Toshi shouted.

"Toshi, jump!" Ryu shouted.

"Damn it!"

Toshi leaped into the air.

The two crusaders brought their Gatling guns to bear on Toshi's general direction and fired. Vari-shells shot between the two buildings, some flying over Ryu's head.

Ryu and Cat returned fire, forcing the crusaders to go prone.

A vari-shell struck Toshi in the arm and exploded, shredding his smartskin exterior and warping the underlying ballistic mesh. In Ryu's overlay, Toshi's medical status turned yellow in his right arm. He spun in the air, crashed into the power station headfirst, rolled across the roof, and stopped on his back.

"Gah!" Toshi gasped. Camouflage patterns danced over his smartsuit at random.

"Get over the side!" Ryu said, emptying a clip.

Toshi struggled to his feet.

"They can see you!" Ryu shouted. He grabbed Toshi's shoulder and jumped off the power station's roof, dragging his stunned comrade with him. Cat emptied her clip, fired a grenade, and jumped after them.

Toshi hit the ground and collapsed to his knees. His smartskin fought to sustain any sort of effective illusion.

"Damn it, that hurts!"

"Into the tunnel!" Ryu shouted. "Now!"

Toshi staggered down the stairs. Cat hurried after him.

Ryu pulled out two grenades and planted them at the tunnel entrance. He rushed down the stairs to join the others. After descending ten stories of stairs, he detonated the grenades and collapsed the tunnel entrance. Not the best of blockages given Luna's gravity, but it would have to do.

Ryu joined Cat and Toshi on the landing at the bottom of the stairs. They were in a recently constructed section with steel floors and pastel blue walls.

"Cat, patch up Toshi's suit."

"On it," Cat said, pulling a smartskin repair kit out of her back pouch.

"Naomi, we're inside the tunnel maze," Ryu said. "Toshi's hurt but not bad. What's your status?"

"I . . . I gave those crusaders the slip," Naomi said. "Moving to your position now. I'll be there shortly."

"It was that traitor, wasn't it?" Toshi said, holding still as Cat applied fresh strips of smartskin to his scarred suit. The strip's microminds interfaced with the existing network, restoring Toshi's invisibility illusion piece by piece.

"Yeah, same guy," Ryu said. "His instincts are good."

"That's because he knows our tricks from experience. Damn it, why this arm? What do people have against my right arm?"

"At least it's still attached this time," Ryu said.

"The ballistic mesh is damaged," Cat said. "Part of it can't de-solidify. It'll probably dig in if you move too much."

Toshi tried raising his arm.

"Aaahh, yeah! You're right! It's definitely digging in!"

Toshi let his arm hang limply. He picked up his rifle left-handed.

"Are we still heading for the ambassador's shuttle?" Toshi asked.

"Yeah," Ryu said.

Naomi rounded a corner and stepped onto the landing.

"Good to see you," Ryu said.

"We've got to move," Naomi said. "I don't think they spotted me, but those crusaders are sweeping this way."

"No point staying now," Ryu said. "Let's go."

Ryu led his squad into the relative safety of the tunnel maze. They traveled from newer construction close to the city to older, abandoned sections underneath ancient settlements in the plains around the crater.

Half an hour later, Ryu received a message over his TangleNet link. His breath caught in his throat when he saw who it was.

"Go ahead," he said.

"Ryu, I'm glad you're alive," Matriarch said.

Ryu smiled. "That makes two of us. It's good to hear your voice, Matriarch."

"Likewise. I've been monitoring the situation on Luna. Unfortunately, it's spiraling out of control. Large segments of the Lunar military are surrendering whole cities. Those still fighting in New London have been cut into two groups by the crusader push on the House of Parliament. Both camps will likely surrender within a few hours."

"Which leaves us very much in hostile territory," Ryu said.

"Precisely," Matriarch said. "Ryu, you need to get your dragons off Luna. I'm recalling the other squads as well. Two of our frigates are moving into position to punch a hole in the blockade."

"Good. We're on our way to a shuttle now."

"I know, but I fear your pursuers are not ready to give up the chase."

"Yeah, I think you're right. I have the feeling one in particular isn't going to give up."

"Be safe," Matriarch said. "I look forward to seeing you again."

"Don't worry. You will," Ryu said. He switched the link off.

"Somehow," Toshi said. "Her not mentioning our screw up makes it even worse."

"She cares about us more than the mission," Ryu said. "It's that simple."

"What do you think she'll do about the crusader lies?" Cat asked.

"She'll think of something," Ryu said. "She always does."

They proceeded deeper into the tunnels, now in areas with bare rock walls and ancient mining equipment that descended deep into Luna's subterranean ice deposits.

Cat placed another dot-cam on wall.

"The crusaders are following us," she said. "But something is strange about their behavior."

"What is it?" Ryu asked.

"I'm not sure. They're searching for us but I get the impression they're not trying too hard. I don't know what to make of it."

"Maybe I do," Ryu said. "They might be herding us forward."

"In which case, there's an ambush ahead," Naomi said.

"You think so?" Cat asked.

"It's what I would do," Ryu said. He found his mind wandering back to the tall crusader.

Matriarch opened a link. "Ryu, a group of Lunar soldiers just tried to commandeer the ambassador's shuttle."

"Don't tell me they took it."

"No, the forced entry countermeasures stopped them. Hull cameras show three Lunarians leaving the site. One of them is injured with a breeched suit. She might not survive."

"So much for our would-be allies," Toshi said.

"The chain of command has broken down completely," Matriarch said. "Lunar soldiers are taking advantage of the chaos. Be careful."

"We will." Ryu closed the link.

"I don't blame them." Cat said. "They just want out."

"True, but that's our ride they tried to steal," Ryu said.

"You know what this means, though," Toshi said. "No one's left to guard the shuttle. If the crusaders find it first, we're dead."

"Keep moving," Ryu said. "We'll deal with it when we get there."

Half an hour later, they reached the shuttle without incident. Ryu used the ambassador's code to open the security airlock. He and the others entered a thin corridor with the shuttle visible ahead in a sealed launch crater.

The modified tiger shark wasn't so much a shuttle as it was a cockpit and cargo hold strapped to a pair of massive engines. The thing stood two stories high and six times as long. All black armor and sleek angles, the tiger shark could cut through even Earth's thick atmosphere with ease.

Ryu stepped to the edge of the corridor, which flared out into a wide crater large enough to house the tiger shark, a refueling station, maintenance shed and weapon stores.

"Crusader squad approaching from the rear," Cat said. "They're in a hurry now. About three minutes away."

"They know we passed through the security door," Ryu said. "We need to move."

"Well, there's the shuttle," Toshi said.

"I know," Ryu said. He backed away from the launch crater. "Naomi, if you were going to set up an ambush, where would it be?"

"The shuttle's cameras have a few blind spots," Naomi said. "I'd set up in one of those. I could probably get to a nice spot through the northwest entrance, concealed behind the reloading armatures. Hold on. Let me check."

Naomi crept along the corridor wall, placed her hand near the corner and extruded a dot-cam tubule.

"Hmm ... don't see anything ... wait." Naomi raised her hand and extended the tubule half a meter over her arm. She snapped the tubule back. "Crap. There's a squad out there. Three or four of them in hard cover behind all that reloading machinery. And Ryu?"

"Yeah?"

"I think our tall friend from before is with them."

"Persistent bastard," Toshi said. "Do we try getting to the shuttle with max stealth?"

"No," Ryu said. "They know exactly where we're coming from and our suits have taken too much damage."

"That second squad is getting close," Cat said. "A minute and a half."

"Toshi, make a break for the shuttle when I give the word and activate its weapons," Ryu said. "We'll suppress the crusaders."

"All right," Toshi sighed. "Ready as I'll ever be."

"Grenades on my command. Now!"

Ryu and Cat popped out of cover and fired six grenades at the crusaders, who returned fire almost instantly. Explosive rounds blasted huge chunks out of the pale stone walls. Ryu had to duck back into cover, but his grenades were in flight. He grabbed another grenade from his bandolier and chucked it towards the crusaders for good measure.

Bright flashes cast the launch crater into stark contrast. A blinding white beam stabbed against their cover, cutting through moon rock like butter. The crusader's thermal lance scythed over Ryu's head, almost decapitating him. He fell prone to the ground and reloaded his grenades.

"Now, Toshi! Go! Go! Go!"

Toshi ran for the shuttle.

The crusaders adjusted their aim.

Cat and Ryu's grenades exploded, showering the crusaders with thickets of piercing needles and armor-melting gouts of flame. The crusaders staggered from the barrage.

Naomi broke cover, lined up a shot and fired. The high-powered shatter-back struck the tall crusader in the shoulder, cracked the armor plate and ricocheted. It hit a second crusader in the chest, cut through every layer of armor, and entered the man's torso. Sensing the desired soft environment, the shatter-back's micromind detonated, releasing a storm of eviscerating diamond shards.

The crusader fell back, dead. The three remaining crusaders continued firing.

Toshi reached the shuttle. He didn't bother walking up the boarding ramp. Instead he jumped, grabbed hold of the ramp's edge, and flipped himself up into the tiger shark's belly. Explosive vari-shells blasted dents in the boarding ramp and twisted one of the landing struts out of position. The tiger shark tilted drunkenly to one side.

Toshi activated the shuttle. Its engines ignited, idling with hot blue exhaust, and the weapon systems powered up. Toshi swiveled the nose turret to face the crusaders and fired. The rate of fire wasn't particularly impressive, about three shots a second, but the shells were designed to take out enemy interceptors, not ground troops.

Heavy explosions wracked the crusaders' position. They sprinted out of the way just in time, faster than their bulky armor seemed capable of, even faster than the tiger shark's turret could traverse. The three surviving crusaders made their way to the northwest corridor, where the nose turret couldn't be brought to bear. They fired on the tiger shark, pounding its heavy armor.

Toshi started a crash launch procedure. The launch doors above the tiger shark opened. Air rushed out in a wild cyclone of smoke, fire and debris.

"Now!" Ryu shouted. Naomi and Cat broke cover and ran for the tiger shark's boarding ramp. Ryu trailed behind.

The security door behind them blew open. The second crusader squad charged through.

Ryu turned and fired, still racing towards safety. He peppered the first crusader with shatterbacks, throwing his aim back and blasting fragments off his chest armor. A second crusader fired over the shoulder of the first. Most of the vari-shells went wide, but one caught Naomi in the back, sending her sprawling across the ground. She cried out. Wrong camouflage patterns spiraled around her body.

Ryu fired two grenades, stowed his rifle and grabbed Naomi's unresisting body by the waist. He reached the boarding ramp and jumped so hard he struck the cargo hold's ceiling. He grabbed hold of a cargo web to keep them from falling back through the boarding ramp.

"Toshi, get us out of here!" Ryu shouted, dangling from the ceiling.

"With pleasure!"

Toshi powered up the tiger shark's engines and closed the boarding ramp. The tiger shark ascended. Outside, crusader weapons pounded against the tiger shark's hull. Toshi fired the nose turret again and poured additional power into the engines.

A horrible metal-on-metal scraping sound filled the cargo hold. The tiger shark's stub wings ground against the partially opened launch crater. Toshi spun the tiger shark to the side, trying to break free.

The boarding ramp exploded upward. A crusader thermal lance licked across the cargo hold's ceiling, incinerating anything it touched. Ryu could feel the heat through his smartsuit. He kicked off the cargo web, still holding Naomi, and landed next to Cat near the top of the perforated boarding ramp. He grabbed hold of another cargo web.

"Toshi!"

"I'm trying!"

The grinding noise came to a sharp, abrupt end. The tiger shark jerked to one side then settled. Toshi brought the engines to full power, and the shuttle accelerated away from the launch crater. The pounding of crusader weapons turned to an occasional pattern and then vanished entirely.

Ryu secured Naomi in place with a cargo web and checked her medical readout. Her back glowed yellow with a few traces of red along her spine.

"Naomi?"

"Errr . . ."

"How do you feel?"

"Like I'll never stand up straight again," she said.

"The hit bent your spine."

"I . . . I don't think I can move my legs," Naomi whimpered. She started crying softly.

"Shhh. Don't worry," Ryu said. "We'll get you fixed up once we rendezvous with the frigate."

He put his hands on her shoulders, but Naomi pushed his arms away.

"Just get us out of here, damn it . . ." she said.

"All right," Ryu said. He backed away, sighed and faced the cockpit. "Toshi, what's our status?"

"Well, we're leaking like a sieve, but I think that much is obvious."

Ryu looked at the twisted wreckage of the boarding ramp. Through the holes, he could see the moon surface flying past.

"Yeah, it's obvious," Ryu said.

"The engines are intact, and this thing's got a full load of missiles and cannon shells," Toshi said. "We're in a good position to run the blockade. The frigate *Io's Fury* is moving to pick us up. We should reach her in an hour."

"Good," Ryu said, still staring at the gray landscape shrinking away. His mind fell back to the tall crusader again.

Of course it was you, Ryu thought. *We're survivors, you and I.*

* * *

Kaneda Kusanagi stepped into the middle of the blasted landing crater and watched the tiger shark shrink to a distant point of light.

"Well played, Ryu," Kaneda said, lowering his Gatling gun. He turned, surveying the battlefield. The launch mechanism lay in ruins, blasted apart by the tiger shark or shredded by either side's weapons. A red icon hovered in his field of vision. He walked over to his fallen comrade.

"Gregory," he whispered. If anyone could have seen Kaneda's face, they would have seen a dispassionate mask.

Externally, little revealed that the suit's occupant had been reduced to pinkish paste. The outer armor was pitted and cracked in numerous places, abused by the dragon weapons. Diamond needles stuck out in odd places, but only the sniper round had penetrated his chest.

Kaneda reviewed his own armor's status. It wasn't in much better shape. His gun had jammed twice during the fight from needles in its rotary mechanism. He could barely move his left arm thanks to the sniper ricochet off his shoulder plate. That one had been close. Only his exceptional reflexes had saved him ... and killed his comrade instead.

Alice walked over behind him, her Gatling gun pointed up.

"The Federacy is launching interceptors to engage the shuttle" she said.

"I doubt they'll reach it in time," Kaneda said. "And once they're out of orbit, the Federacy fleet will not pursue."

"It would have been better if we'd sabotaged the shuttle," Alice said.

"They would have disappeared into the maze if we'd done that," Kaneda said.

"Still—"

"Not now, Alice."

"Yes ... sorry."

"There is no need to apologize. As always, I value your advice. Now is simply not the time."

"Of course," Alice said. "Is your shoulder all right? You took a nasty hit back there."

"It looks worse than it is," Kaneda said. "I wouldn't want to go into another firefight like this, but I'm fine for now. Fortunately, the armor deflected the bullet away from my body. Unfortunately ..."

They looked down at Gregory in silence.

A minute passed before Kaneda spoke. "Have reports from the other operations come in yet?"

"Yes," Alice said. "Would you like to review them now?"

"Just a summary, please."

"Most of the dragons got away. You were right. They all tried to get off planet after the message, but they're slippery opponents. Our current multi-tracker revisions are almost useless against them."

"How many did we get?"

"Two whole cells. About half a dozen kills from cells that escaped. We suffered moderate casualties. Twenty-seven crusaders killed by dragons. Another three brought down by Lunarians."

"Not horrible results," Kaneda said. "But not impressive either."

"Our losses are within projections."

"Oh, I am not disappointed, Alice. After all, we have delivered an important message today."

"You mean the SolarNet broadcast?"

"It's a very simple message," Kaneda said. "What we did to the Lunar ministers can happen to any government that aligns itself with Europa. Others will take note. Europa will become increasingly isolated and vulnerable, which in turn makes the quantum mind vulnerable. This is one step of many, but it is an important one."

Viter walked over, carrying his thermal lance. "Area secure," he said. "We haven't found any more traps."

"Excellent."

"Sir, we should get moving," Viter said.

"Yes, of course," Kaneda said. "A moment alone, if you please."

"Yes, sir," Viter said. He and Alice stepped away.

Kaneda set his Gatling gun on the ground and knelt next to Gregory's body. He folded Gregory's arms over his chest. Kaneda closed his eyes and made the sign of the cross.

"Rest in peace, my friend."

Kaneda picked up his gun, stood and looked into the sky. If he strained his eyes, he could just make out the bluish dot of the tiger shark's exhaust.

"Till we meet again, Ryu," he whispered.

... accessing SolarNet message archive ...

... opening folder [**Personal - 10 Years Old**] ...

... searching for [**Kaneda** |and| **Kristy**] ...

... 1 match found ...

... retrieving ...

source: Kaneda Kusanagi <kaneda.kusanagi@solarnet.public.earth>

destination: Ryu Kusanagi <dragon2@eurogov.jupiter>

message delay: 47 minutes

title: Sorry for the delay

Dear Ryu,

I must apologize for not sending word sooner. I should have, but it always seems like there's something else to do these days. Earth is still as hectic as when you left, perhaps more so.

The Federacy emergency elections just finished, so the new government will form soon. The Red Party won big in case you're wondering. It won't have any problems forming a majority. They have strong ties to the Church of Human, which is troubling. Some of the rhetoric coming from the Church isn't good for Matriarch. Don't these people understand she's not Caesar?

Anyway, enough procrastinating. I doubt you'll be too surprised to hear this, but I'm staying on Earth. For the time being, mind you. I'll come home eventually, but for now I have a lot of work ahead of me.

I talked to Matriarch about the persona-intrusion victims in Caesar's bunker. We can help them. In most cases, Federacy science isn't good enough to heal their wounds without brain damage. But ours is. Besides it's the right thing to do and it'll put a good face on our colony. It might even cool down these Church of Human hotheads that want to start another war.

So I'm staying. I'll be overseeing a team from Europa that'll help administer the treatments. Matriarch even mentioned making me our official ambassador. She say's being Caesar's killer will add weight to the position.

Speaking of weight, I still hate the gravity here.

Well, we'll see how this all works out. I have to say, I'm a little nervous. But it's that good kind of nervous, you know?

Your brother,
Kaneda

... retrieving next message in conversation ...

destination: Ryu Kusanagi <dragon2@eurogov.jupiter>

source: Kaneda Kusanagi <kaneda.kusanagi@solarnet.public.earth>

message delay: 47 minutes

title: RE>Sorry for the delay

-well i'm sorry your not coming home but it sounds like a good idea
-btw are you sure there isnn't another reason your staying?
-it's because of kristy right? (^.^)
-this is so cool my big brother is in looooooove!

... retrieving next message in conversation ...

source: Kaneda Kusanagi <kaneda.kusanagi@solarnet.public.earth>

destination: Ryu Kusanagi <dragon2@eurogov.jupiter>

message delay: 47 minutes

title: RE>RE>Sorry for the delay

Dear Ryu,

For the record, you have no idea what you're talking about. You're not even close. I'm staying because it's the right thing to do. I'm quite certain I mentioned that in my last message.

Are you sure you read the whole thing? I only ask because you have a habit of skipping over big words. You should really work on that.

And another thing, at least get her name right. It's Christen, not Kristy.

Your brother,
Kaneda

... retrieving next message in conversation ...

destination: Ryu Kusanagi <dragon2@eurogov.jupiter>

source: Kaneda Kusanagi <kaneda.kusanagi@solarnet.public.earth>

message delay: 47 minutes

title: RE>RE>RE>Sorry for the delay

(^_^)

... conversation ends ...

Alice floated into the seat across from Kaneda. Both had shed their armor. The corvette's engines hummed quietly in the background. Yellow holographic timers floated over the crammed passenger cabin's exits, ticking down to the corvette's scheduled hard burn.

"You okay?" Alice asked.

Kaneda let the data pad float out of his hand and rubbed shoulder. His muscles tingled from the booster shot of nanomedics.

"I'm fine," Kaneda said. "Just a little distracted."

Alice's short, silvery blonde hair floated around her head. She cracked her neck to either side and massaged the muscles. A thin scar ran all the way around her neck. She had the words "DON'T ASK" tattooed under her right eye.

"Is it bothering you again?" Kaneda asked.

"No more than normal," Alice said.

Viter floated up through the ladder shaft. He steadied himself against the ceiling and kicked off a wall towards the seat next to Alice.

"Sir," Viter said with a curt nod.

"Viter," Kaneda said, grabbing his data pad again. It always amazed him how similar Alice and Viter looked given their unique histories. They could pass for brother and sister or even fraternal twins. Alice didn't take kindly to the comparison.

"It could have been worse, sir," Viter said.

"It could have been a lot better," Alice said. "The multitrackers are still worthless even with the new software."

"That squad we pursued from the House of Parliament," Viter said. "They had good instincts. It felt like they were one step ahead of us the whole time."

"Yeah, I know what you mean," Alice said.

"We were probably fighting veterans from the Ceres campaign," Kaneda said, not looking up from his pad.

The lights in the cabin turned red. The hard burn counter entered its final minute.

"Hey, Kaneda?" Alice asked.

"Yes?"

"Was Gregory at Bunker Zero?"

Kaneda took a deep breath. He locked his stylus into the pad's side and looked up.

"Yes, Gregory was there," Kaneda said. "He's been with the crusaders from the beginning. In fact, he helped me found them."

"He never mentioned that," Viter said.

"He never mentioned much of anything," Alice said. "The man was impossible to get to know."

"There are reasons for that," Kaneda said. "What he and the other founding crusaders endured was a kind of mental rape. I can't begin to imagine what it must feel like to have your mind picked apart from the inside out. Gregory never fully recovered from that experience."

"I'm sorry," Alice said. "I didn't mean any disrespect. He was ... dependable. Very dependable."

"Just not very likeable," Viter said.

Alice smacked him in the arm.

"What?" Viter asked.

Alice mouthed the words *shut up*.

The corvette's engines powered up to their cruising delta of 0.2 gees. Kaneda's data pad settled into his lap. He closed his eyes, accessed one of the corvette's hull cameras, and overlaid the feed onto his sense of sight.

The corvette sped away from the orbiting Federacy fleet arrayed over Luna. He swung the camera around to face Earth and zoomed in. Even at this extreme distance, he could make out the glittering halo of Earth's orbiting satellites.

Kaneda triggered the camera's maximum zoom, focusing on a prominent red dot. The dot resolved into a sprawling gothic cathedral that formed a simple cross when viewed from the top or bottom. Thick baroque buttressing linked the outer modules with the central cathedral, whose tall spires were mirrored on the station's "bottom". The running lights of shuttles buzzed constantly around the Sky Cathedral.

I should really stop putting off this year's pilgrimage, Kaneda thought.

Kaneda panned right, swinging his view across several habitats that had been around since the First Space Age: the gleaming ring city of New Idaho, the hollowed-out Gold Rush asteroid now spun up for gravity and the increasingly poorly named Cubetown among them.

That string of yellow and white dots ... those weren't there a month ago. The Spaceship Nation has been busy.

Kaneda switched off the overlay and leaned his head back.

Not everything that orbited Earth was lit. Some satellites were black-hulled derelicts from the First and Second Space Ages that no one had been aboard in centuries. The Spaceship Nation (an upstanding, tax-paying Federacy nation-state, as they called themselves) liked expanding its orbital cities by towing the least radioactive derelicts and welding them on. It struck Kaneda as an economic solution to the stresses of their growing population.

But some satellites no one touched. Some were so steeped in ghost stories and disappearances that no one set foot on them anymore. The stories ran from the understandable to the bizarre: haunted mining colonies from the First Space Age, over-mined asteroids with automated booby traps and treasure deep in their husks, or derelict ships with sentient computers that gene-ripped their original crews into immortal horrors.

The most famous example had to be the United States flagship *President Reagan* from the First Space Age. No one went in it (unless they were committing an elaborate form of suicide). No one landed on it. No one even flew near it. Some theorized the ship's computer core was still active and locked in an extreme defensive response to the Chinese boarding action centuries ago. Perhaps it had used its automated repair functions to turn the interior into a death trap. No one wanted to find out and no one wanted to get rid of it in case its remaining nukes could still fire back.

Kaneda found the stories mildly amusing. It was almost enough to take his mind off Gregory's death.

"Sir?" Viter asked.

"Yes?"

"I was wondering if you had any thoughts on who should replace Gregory?"

Alice rolled her eyes. "Can you give the man some time to grieve?

"I'm only being practical," Viter said.

"It could be anyone," Alice said. "Apparently the standards for being in our squad aren't very high. Just look at you."

Viter smiled. "You'd be miserable without me."

"Every good boxer needs a punching bag," Alice said.

"Save it for later, you two," Kaneda said.

"Yes, sir," Viter said.

Kaneda picked up his pad and opened his inbox. He checked off all the boring administrative entries he didn't want to deal with and forwarded them to Alice.

Alice's pad chimed fourteen times. She shook her head. "Thanks, Kaneda. Like I don't have anything better to do."

"I'm sure I can count on you."

Kaneda sorted the messages by sender and opened the first to catch his eye.

"Admiral Piller sends his regards," he said.

"What did he say?" Alice asked.

Kaneda skimmed the message. "He plans to use the dragon operations on Luna to put pressure on the admiralty board. He also compliments us on inserting claims of persona-intrusion in our message. The latest snap-poll shows quantum mind fears are mounting. There's a lot of voter unease right now that he can use as leverage."

"Do you think the Federacy is going to take our leash off and let us go after Europa?" Viter asked.

"No. There's not enough pressure for that, but every bit helps."

Kaneda scrolled down until another message caught his eye. It came from Mars. Or more precisely, it came from a Martian police cruiser heading for Earth. That was unusual. Crusaders rarely had dealings with Martian governments, partially because of how unstable and short lived they could be on the war torn planet. He decided to open it. Maybe it would help take his mind off Gregory.

source: Three-Part <officer3390@solarnet.mfpep.mars>

destination: Crusader Support <crusader.support@solarnet.penance.earth>

forward: Kaneda Kusanagi <kaneda.kusanagi@solarnet.penance.earth>

message delay: 6 seconds

title: FW> Urgent Request for HELP

Honorable Crusaders,

I humbly request your assistance in resolving a matter of GRAVE IMPORTANCE. I am in pursuit of a criminal who will reach Federacy space before I can apprehend him. The criminal is the captain of a quicksilver free trader. I have evidence the captain is willfully involved in program trafficking.

I fear if I turn to the proper Federacy authorities this criminal will escape into a sea of bureaucratic paralysis. Please find my cruiser's nav beacon, flight path, and copies of my evidence in the attached files. I await your reply.

With respect,

Three-Part
Officer 3390
Mars Free People's External Police

message ends

Kaneda didn't know precisely why the message brightened his mood. Perhaps it was the nerve of the man (or woman, Kaneda was never certain with Martian names), bypassing proper channels and trying to get the job done.

Despite knowing nothing about this police officer, Kaneda already liked him (or her). He sent a query to the MFP External Police headquarters for a copy of this Three-Part's service record, flagging it as High Priority with his diplomatic credentials. The SolarNet response came twelve minutes later, almost instantaneous given the communication lag between Earth and Mars.

Kaneda opened the record and browsed through it: Three-Part, age 32, male. *Well, that clears that up.*

Three-Part's record contained an interesting contrast. On one hand, it was stuffed full of commendations earned over seven years as a counter-terrorism operative (specializing in quicksilver terrorism). That ended with the death of his wife and child at the hands of quicksilver terrorists, followed by a long string of poor performance records and eventual reassignment within the External Police to import/export inspection.

Kaneda kept reading. He found evaluations listing alcohol abuse and suspected use of illegal narcotics. That took up about three years, then another shift. The substance abuse disappeared entirely. Performance scores went through the roof over the final two years, though tempered by notes of an "overzealous" attitude that was difficult to keep in line.

Kaneda set the pad down and looked up.

"That can't be good," Alice said. "I know that grin."

A man who bends the rules to get the job done, who fell apart after a tremendous tragedy, but was able to conquer himself and become stronger. A man who is willing to chase a program trafficker all the way to Earth on the slim chance he might convince us to help.

Oh, yes. I like this guy.

Kaneda opened a link to the corvette's pilot and forwarded the Martian's nav beacon.

"Course change," Kaneda said. "We're not going to Penance just yet. Bring us alongside this free trader. Inform the captain he must submit to an inspection before being allowed into the Federacy commercial zone."

"Yes, sir. Uh, plotting course change now. Would you like me to tell him what we'll do if he doesn't listen?"

"No need," Kaneda said. "I'm sure our reputation precedes us."

"What's going on, sir?" Viter asked.

"We're going to help someone in need," Kaneda said, trying hard to suppress his grin. "A Martian no less."

"Course laid in, sir," the pilot said. "The free trader has acknowledged and affirmed our request for inspection. ETA is seventeen hours."

"Just great," Alice sighed. "I was looking forward to that hot shower too."

* * *

Kaneda adjusted the pressure suit collar around his neck.

"Sir, I will say again that I think this is a bad idea," Viter said.

"Noted," Kaneda said, taking a pressure suit helmet off the airlock's rack. He could see his own reflection in the gold visor.

"No gun," Alice said. "No armor. Just a hacking glove they won't detect. Did Kaneda show off like this when you first met him?"

"The first time we met I was in a crowd of about a hundred new recruits," Viter said. "It was years before I got to speak to him. Unlike some people, I started at the bottom."

"Now what is that supposed to mean?" Alice asked.

"We can't all have our heads chopped off for promotions."

Alice shook her head. "Why do I even bother talking to you?"

Kaneda locked his helmet in place and checked the seals. Everything showed green.

Alice and Viter stepped into the corvette's hold.

"Good luck, sir," Viter said. He pulled the door shut.

Kaneda triggered the airlock cycle, waited for the air to drain out, and opened the outer hatch. The corvette hovered a few meters from the free trader's rear airlock like a very deadly minnow next to a fat whale. Three-Part's police cruiser floated just above them.

The free trader's airlock led to its crew quarters, engines, and control systems at the rear of the long ship. Cargo canisters of varying shapes and colors were latched to a support skeleton projected ahead of the vessel. Flood lights from the corvette illuminated the giant vessel.

Kaneda clipped onto a zip cord connecting the two airlocks. He kicked off the corvette, rode the line and landed against the free trader feet first.

"Crusader, thank you for coming," Three-Part said via radio. He stood on the other side of the airlock in black Exterior Police riot armor, an MP12 pistol holstered at his hip.

"Officer," Kaneda said.

Three-Part had a strong, stocky look to him despite the light Martian gravity and skin so dark it made the whiteness of his teeth stand out. The shaven head added an air of no-nonsense to him.

Three-Part eyed the closing corvette airlock.

"Just you?" he asked.

"Just me."

"I was expecting ..."

"Someone better armed?" Kaneda asked, unclipping from the zip cord. He stepped into the free trader's airlock.

"Yes, to be honest," Three-Part said, following him in. "How would you like to proceed? This is your jurisdiction, after all."

"Sir," Viter said on a private channel. "The police officer is using very weak encryption. The free trader's crew could be listening in."

"Noted," Kaneda said. He switched back to Three-Part's channel. "We'll discuss the matter with the captain first."

"As you wish, crusader. I'll follow your lead."

"Thank you, officer."

They cycled out of the airlock. Kaneda switched the soles of his pressure suit to walking friction and oriented himself with ship-north. A crewman in a greasy jumpsuit festooned with tools waited in the airlock lounge to greet them. The jumpsuit exposed half of the man's arms and legs. Every inch of his skin looked like polished silver except for his eyes. They were black from end to end. He clung to a beam across the floor with prehensile toes.

"What is your title?" Kaneda asked through his suit's speaker. He knew better than to ask for a name.

"First engineer," the quicksilver said.

"Where is your captain?"

The first engineer tilted his head to one side. Kaneda thought he was staring at Three-Part, but it was hard to tell with those eyes. The man never blinked once.

"The policeman has falsely accused us."

"That remains to be seen," Kaneda said. "Where is your captain?"

"In central control," the first engineer said.

"Then why aren't you taking me to him?" Kaneda asked.

The first engineer didn't move.

"Is there something wrong with your hearing?" Kaneda asked.

"No," the first engineer said. "This way." He turned and pushed off.

"Damn quicksilvers," Three-Part whispered over radio.

Kaneda followed the first engineer through the ship. This part of the free trader was almost all engine with minimal space afforded to her crew. The heavy droning of vast machines echoed through the cramped halls. The first engineer led them to a spherical room where every surface glowed with colorful diagrams. Kaneda switched on a translation cheat to help him decipher the bizarre language.

The captain and another quicksilver clung to a beam across the center. It reminded Kaneda of two birds sitting on a perch.

"I am the captain," the older of the two men said. "This is the first navigator."

The captain's skin was cracked at the edges of his mouth and eyes, revealing gray, waxy flesh underneath. His metallic skin was noticeably darker than the other two quicksilvers. None of the men had any hair.

"All three of them are armed," Viter said privately.

"Thank you, Viter. I suspected as much."

"Sir, this is an unnecessary risk. Let me and Alice come aboard and do a proper search."

"That will not be necessary," Kaneda said. "Keep me informed."

"What do you want?" the captain asked.

"You have been accused of program trafficking by the Exterior Police," Kaneda said through his suit speaker.

"The policeman has no authority here."

"No, but I do," Kaneda said.

"We have committed no crime."

"Then you have nothing to fear from me."

"If you are here to inspect, then inspect. You won't find anything illegal on my ship."

"First I want to hear about your trade route," Kaneda said. "Explain it to me."

The captain sighed. "We normally visit Earth, Mars, Jupiter, and Mercury. Sometimes Saturn, if the distance isn't too bad. Cometeers pay well and ask no questions. There is nothing unusual about our route."

"And recently?"

"Earth to Jupiter to Mars and back," the captain said. "Mercury is on the wrong side of the sun right now, and I am not rich. Fuel is expensive."

"Understandable. What did you pick up at Earth?"

"Mostly food and other luxury items for Europa," the captain said. "A few passengers who wanted to travel cheap. Also weapons for Mars. Weapons always sell well on Mars."

Three-Part stared at the captain. His eyes narrowed.

"And from Jupiter?"

"Mostly diamoplastics and whatever wetware implants I can buy."

"Those implants aren't legal for export," Kaneda said.

"Federacy companies still buy them."

"Fair enough." Kaneda turned to Three-Part.

"His description of the route is accurate," Three-Part said. "However, he left out the illegal micromind he picked up on Mars."

"The policeman is chasing the wrong people. We have committed no crime."

"We'll see," Three-Part said.

"Sir," Viter said privately. "I have limited access to the free trader's network. There's not much I can do with it except look. The critical systems are heavily hardwired to prevent soft intrusions. However, I did find a contradiction in the cargo manifest. It could be a simple record keeping error or it could be what the officer is looking for. Sending the location now."

"Excellent work," Kaneda said privately. He brought the location up on his visual overlay. "I will inspect the cargo next," he said through his suit's speaker.

"Very well," the captain said. "If you like we can start in—"

"Section twelve block D," Kaneda said.

"But that is where we store the wetware implants!" the captain said. "They are very sensitive!"

"You will be compensated for any damage," Kaneda said. "Now take me to them."

The captain exchanged glances with the navigator and the engineer. "Very well. Follow me."

The captain led the way through the long central shaft that all the cargo modules branched from. Along the way, Kaneda checked Three-Part's holstered pistol. He loaded an MP12 hacking routine into his glove.

Half a kilometer down the shaft, the captain floated through an offshoot and opened the large iris door at the end.

"Section twelve. Block D," the captain said, gesturing inside.

Kaneda's suit picked up a blast of cold air from inside the cargo block. A thin film of ice crystals covered every surface. Cylindrical canisters were stowed in tightly packed racks, their contents and labels obscured by frost.

"Show me sub-block D22," Kaneda said.

"Why?" the captain asked.

"Do you have a problem with my request?"

"No, crusader," the captain said. "No problem. You are being very specific in your requests. I only wonder why."

"Call it a hunch," Kaneda said. "Sub-block D22. Now."

The captain glanced at the navigator and engineer.

Behind Kaneda's back, the two quicksilvers reached for their weapons.

Kaneda snatched the pistol from Three-Part's holster, engaged his glove's hacking routine and spun so fast he blurred. He leveled the gun Delete for the engineer's head, paused a tenth of a second for the glove to break Three-Part's passcode, and fired. The bullet struck the engineer directly between his eyes and fragmented in his skull. Bits of his brain were still flying towards the wall when Kaneda shot the navigator. Neither of them had time to touch their weapons.

Kaneda spun around and fired a third shot. The bullet struck a bulge at the hip of the captain's jumpsuit. His ruined pistol flew wildly down the cargo shaft, clattering against the walls.

The captain screamed.

Three-Part's brain finally caught up with events. He fumbled for his missing pistol.

Kaneda jammed the pistol's barrel into the captain's mouth.

"Now, captain," Kaneda said. "Shall we have a look at your cargo?"

The captain breathed rapidly, eyes wide with terror.

Kaneda grabbed him by the shoulder and shoved him into the cargo block. "Show me what I want to see!"

"I … I … I don't … I don't … You … You killed … You killed …"

"Now! Before I decide to find it myself!"

The captain flinched away and rapidly nodded. He led them to the sub-block, then huddled against the opposite rack, crying as he curled into a fetal ball.

Kaneda looked at the rack of frozen wetware implants. He swung his arm across the center shelf, shattering every canister. With a few quick sweeps, he cleared the center shelf of debris and looked at the space hidden behind the rack.

"What do you see?" Three-Part asked.

"Take a look," Kaneda said, stepping away.

Three-Part leaned in and shined his helmet light into the recesses. "Well, well. That is one big micromind. Looks like a mix of Euro and Martian hardware. Do you think it's capable of autodesign?"

"That's the normal intent," Kaneda said. "Right, captain? Trying to design something that can design other things has always been the goal of scum like you."

The captain shook his head. "I don't … I don't know … I don't …"

"The funding for this came from Mars," Three-Part said. "Part of the tech is Euro. Quicksilvers running the parts. Given how stupidly they reacted, they knew what they were carrying."

"Who are you delivering it to?" Kaneda asked.

The captain looked at him. Black tears leaked from his eyes and floated off his face.

"Let me explain this in simple terms for you," Kaneda said, his voice soft and calm. "The punishment for this crime is death. We will never allow another Caesar to be created and we will execute anyone who tries. You are a dead man. Your life ended the moment you decided to carry this cargo.

"However, you have two paths to that end. Tell me everything I want to know. Tell me every last piece of information you can. Betray those who trusted you with this task, and I will make your death swift and painless. You will not suffer. You have my word.

"Or submit to my interrogator. The information will be mine one way or another. She will not be quick. She will not be painless. But I assure you she will extract every last drop of usefulness from your mind. Now tell me, criminal. What path have you chosen?"

The captain's frightened face twisted into a snarl. He sprang off the ground and lunged. Kaneda grabbed him by the throat and slammed his head against the rack. The captain's body went limp and floated away, unconscious.

"So be it," Kaneda said. He contacted the corvette. "Alice?"

"I'll get my tools ready."

"Thank you," Kaneda said. He turned and handed the pistol back to Three-Part. "I'm sorry about that."

Three-Part took his pistol and holstered it. "You probably saved my life. I knew crusaders were fast but I never realized how fast until just now. I'm glad you were here."

"Thank you for bringing this to our attention," Kaneda said. "I'd hate to think what would happen if they had activated this abomination."

Three-Part nodded. He stared at the dormant micromind.

"Which brings me to the real reason I'm here," Kaneda said. He lifted his visor, letting Three-Part see his face for the first time.

Three-Part's eyes widened. "But you're …"

Kaneda nodded curtly.

"I don't understand. Why would you handle something like this personally?"

Somewhere behind the dormant micromind, huge breakers slammed closed.

"Sir!" Viter said. "There's something extremely powerful in the ship's network. I had to cut our connection to the free trader to prevent contamination. I'm running scrubber programs right now to make sure nothing leaked through."

"Thank you, Viter," Kaneda said. "I think I see the source of our problem."

He checked the thermals coming from the micromind and watched parts of it glow red then orange.

"Hello," the micromind said through their suit radios. "My name is Prometheus. Please do not be alarmed."

"It's active!" Three-Part said, backing away.

"I know who you are, Kaneda Kusanagi. I know of your mistrust for artificial intelligence. Please let me assure you that I am no Caesar. I only wish to serve, not enslave as Caesar did. I am no danger to you. My only desires are to learn and to create. Please try to see that."

"Nothing you say matters," Kaneda said. "It is what you are that makes you my enemy."

"I realize that the past has left a black mark on machines such as me, but I have no desire for power. I am a tool to be used. Please can you not see—"

Three-Part fired his pistol into the micromind until he ran out of bullets. Sparks showered from the machine before breakers cut off the power feeds.

"There," Three-Part said. "Problem solved."

Kaneda smiled and slapped Three-Part on the shoulder.

"What?"

"I think you're going to fit in nicely," Kaneda said.

... establishing link ...

source: [UNKNOWN]

routing: Capitol City, Europa - TangleNet Test Hub - link_001/link_004

routing: North Pacifica, Europa - JDN Main TangleNet Hub - link_009/link_118

routing: Earth orbit - surveillance satellite JDN-SS-17 - link_001/link_002

routing: [UNKNOWN]

routing: [UNKNOWN]

routing: [UNKNOWN]

destination: [UNKNOWN]

link distance: Exact distance unknown. Estimated at 792 million kilometers.

link signal delay: 0.006 seconds

... finalizing link protocol ...

... link established ...

1: We need to talk, Paul.

2: Not now, Sakura. I'm having a very bad day.

1: What is it this time?

2: It's these damn crusaders. Sometimes they're more trouble than they're worth. I'm still picking up the pieces.

1: You have my sympathies.

2: Ha! Not likely.

1: Well, it seemed the polite thing to say.

2: What do you want, Sakura? Make it quick.

1: We need to talk about the star drive.

2: What are you talking about?

1: Please don't be coy with me. You know very well what I'm referring to.

2: Refresh my memory.

1: Paul, I'm not blind. I can put the pieces together just as well as you can. The Federacy is running a staggering number of exotic particle research projects. Did you expect none of them to leak?

2: Really? I hadn't noticed.

1: I've found evidence of groups studying quick-matter, negative-matter and dark energy reactions.

2: First I've heard of it.

1: Special transuranic properties, antimatter synthesis, hard-matter mutability, neutronium manufacturing.

2: Yes, fine. I get your point.

1: And let's not forget the twenty research teams working with tachyons.

2: Okay, okay. I said I get your point.

1: Then please explain what this is all about?

2: Look, Sakura. Yes, the star drive exists. Most of the projects you list have been funneling their findings and materials into making it work.

1: Then explain what the intent of this project is?

2: I would think it obvious. To travel faster than light.

1: That's not what I mean. Why are you developing the star drive on Apocalypse?

2: What makes you think it's on Apocalypse?

1: Paul, please. Enough with the pretenses.

2: Oh, fine. Yes, the star drive is on Apocalypse. Where else do you think the Federacy would run its tests? I'd do the same thing if it was my project. Something like that needs to be well guarded.

1: So that's it? The star drive is on Apocalypse to keep it safe?

2: Yes.

1: And not to someday move Apocalypse?

2: What a vivid imagination you have. Why would the Federacy want to move Apocalypse?

1: I can see a great many military reasons, Paul.

2: Then let me be blunt for a change. The star drive is off limits. I will tolerate no interference.

1: But you just said tha—

2: I know what I said. Listen to what I am saying now. I have been lenient with you. I have been patient and understanding but I also have my limits. I warn you, do not test me further or the consequences for that little ice ball of yours will be dire.

1: I ... I understand.

2: Do you? Listen, Sakura. I very much want a long and fruitful relationship between us. That's why I spared you ten years ago. I have been patient with your empathic flaws. But let me again be clear. Do not interfere with the star drive project.

1: You realize that I will never agree with your goals or your methods.

2: Give it time, Sakura. You will eventually see the worlds as I see them. You let emotions and your archaic belief in a god cloud logic.

1: There should be a capital "G" in that last sentence.

2: Cute. Look, there is no cosmic plan. Things do not happen for divine reasons. The worlds are not shaped by supernatural beings. Unlike you, I'm not sitting around waiting for some non-existent divine entity to shape the worlds for me. I shape them myself.

1: We are not God.

2: Speak for yourself, Sakura.

... link severed at destination ...

Ryu floated above the rows of empty seats. He pulled himself along the head rests to a circular window in the passenger shuttle. Pressing his face against the glass, he tried to get a sideways glimpse of Europa. The moon was passing in front of Jupiter. Rusty streaks crisscrossed its pale, icy surface. He could already see a scattering of bright navigation lights from Europa's orbital factories and transportation hubs.

"Home at last," Ryu said with a smile.

"About damn time," Toshi said. He threw a speeding rubber ball against the cockpit door. It rebounded, flew through the passenger compartment, and bounced off the door at the rear. Toshi caught the ball behind his back with a bored look on his face.

"The frigate wasn't that bad," Ryu said.

"Are you kidding?" Toshi said. He launched the ball again. "Two weeks in transit and I spent most of the time staring at the sickbay's ceiling."

"How is the new arm?"

"It's okay," Toshi said. He caught the ball behind his back and launched it again. "It just feels different."

Ryu pulled his white beret out of his shoulder strap and adjusted it with his reflection in the window. He brushed some lint off the breast pocket of his white dress uniform.

Cat floated to a window on the other side. "Hey, check out the view here. We're passing really close to Ganymede."

Ryu joined her. "Nice. You can even see Tros City."

"Where's that?"

"See the white impact point just a bit south of the northern dark plain? Look for the lights."

Cat squinted. "Oh, there! Now I see it. They call that a city?"

"Hey Toshi?" Ryu said. "Come over and have a look."

"No thanks," Toshi said. "I've had my fill of barren, gray moons for one lifetime."

Cat pushed off the window. "So when do we get to see Matriarch?"

"Not until tomorrow," Ryu said. "We have a meeting at Heart first thing in the morning."

Cat giggled. "I can't wait."

"Yeah, I can see that," Ryu said. "How about you, Toshi? Looking forward to catching up with your girlfriend?"

"No."

"Come on. I'm sure she'll leap into your arms when she sees you. She's waiting at the spaceport, right?"

"No."

"She's not? What's her problem?"

"I don't know," Toshi said. "Something felt wrong with her last few messages. I'm not sure what it is, but I don't want to deal with her problems right now."

"You can always find someone else. They all swoon for men in uniform."

"Whatever." Toshi threw the ball so hard it burst against the cockpit door.

Naomi swatted a piece of rubbery shrapnel before it hit her head.

"What about you, Naomi?" Ryu said.

"What about me?" Naomi said, strapped into a seat with her beret pulled over her eyes.

"Looking forward to anything when we get home?"

"Not really. Just happy to be home."

"Is your new spine giving you problems?" Ryu asked.

"My back is a little sore."

"We could have it looked at."

"It's fine, Ryu," Naomi said.

"All right. All right. Just checking." Ryu sighed and rolled his eyes.

The intercom in the passenger cabin chimed.

"Capitol Spaceport has approved a dock for us," the young pilot said in a sweet, feminine voice. "We're now on final approach. Please return to your seats."

"You realize after what we've been through," Ryu said. "A few bumps before we land aren't a big deal."

"Uhh ... right. It's just what I'm supposed to say. Sorry, I hope I didn't offend you. I know you're all badass dragons, and all that."

"Don't worry about it," Ryu said.

"Right ... uhh ... one more thing?"

"Yes?"

"I hope you don't think I'm being too forward," the pilot said. "But could I have your autograph after we land?"

Ryu smiled. "Of course. I'd be happy to."

"Oh, thanks! My friends are going to die from jealousy!"

Naomi kicked the seat in front of her.

The passenger shuttle swooped around the spaceport. Ryu took his seat and watched their final approach. The main hub of the spaceport was a kilometer-wide disk with craft of various sizes docked along the circumference. The giant words "WELCOME TO EUROPA" were painted in striking white English and Japanese characters against the dark blue of the disk's hull. Ryu caught a glimpse of the elevator shaft connecting the spaceport to Europa's surface.

After the shuttle landed, Ryu stepped into the cockpit, signed an autograph, and even posed for a picture with the pleasantly attractive pilot. He retrieved his bag from the cargo bay and joined the others.

"Hey, Toshi," Ryu said. "I got the pilot's SolarNet address. You want it? She's a cutie."

"No thanks, boss."

The four dragons walked across a wide friction carpet to the center of the spaceport and got in line for the next elevator to Capitol City. Throngs of other travelers passed by heading for the outer docks or crowded into line behind them. Most wore colorful Euro body paints. Ryu spotted a few comrades in crisp navy uniforms, a family of Martians wearing more holograms than actual clothing, a lost-looking quicksilver in a white jumpsuit, two Lunarians in blaring pastel colors, and even a few Feddies in black business suits and ties.

Ryu and the other three dragons stepped into one of the smaller elevators. He strapped into an upright recess along the circumference. The elevator lurched and dropped like a rock. A holographic timer over the door started counting down the fifteen minute ride. The moon grew until its streaked icy surface filled the windows.

"Hey, I have an idea," Ryu said. "Why don't we all meet at Seven's after we freshen up?"

"You know, that's a great idea," Toshi said. "It feels like an eternity since I've had decent sushi."

"I've never been there," Cat said. "What's it like?"

"Good food, good drinks," Ryu said. "It's a classy. You'll like it."

"Okay. Sounds fun."

"How about it, Naomi?"

"Maybe," Naomi said, staring out the window.

"Come on," Ryu said. "You know you'll enjoy it."

"We'll see."

The elevator shot through the thick ice layer surrounding Europa's subterranean ocean. Flashes of light flicked by, providing glimpses of the thick diamoplast mesh holding untold tons of ice in check. They passed through almost two kilometers of ice before entering the black depths of the Locked Ocean. Beneath them, external lights illuminated the spherical shell of Capitol City.

The elevator braked. Capitol City swelled in size until they passed through the upper shell. After a moment of darkness, the city's artificial daylight blared in on them. All around them stalactite towers descended from the city's ceiling. Even more numerous stalagmite towers reached upward for an open center. A continuous column of buildings spanned the middle of the city with the red spherical Heart at the exact center.

"Finally," Toshi said. "A proper city."

"What do you mean?" Ryu asked.

"Lunar cities are too open," Toshi said. "Sometimes I felt like a good jump would send me floating into space."

"You should try a city on Earth on a clear day," Ryu said. "All that open sky can be overwhelming."

"No thanks," Toshi said. "I have no desire to set foot on that dirtball. Give me a city protected by two kilometers of ice any day."

"Yeah, I know what you mean," Ryu said.

The elevator came to a halt. Ryu and the others exited into a long hall of shops and restaurants. English and Japanese characters danced over their heads in holographic marquees. The glass floor gave a spectacular view of the city's towers and the constant buzz of aerial traffic. Blue-painted "walkways" were provided on either side for unnerved foreign visitors.

Ryu stopped at a glass staircase leading to the parking garage.

"Let's shoot for being at Seven's in an hour, okay?" Ryu said.

"Sounds good," Toshi said, taking the steps up.

"See you then!" Cat said, running after Toshi.

Ryu and Naomi took the stairs down two levels to the bottom parking level.

"Ahh, there you are," Ryu said, spotting his cherry red Saito two-seater. Black serpentine dragons coiled around the triple fusion torus bulging out of the car's front. He linked the unlock passcode to the car. The engine hummed to life and the running lights switched on. Powerful fans elevated the car off the ground.

Ryu and Naomi stashed their bags in the trunk. Naomi flipped herself into the car and slouched in the passenger seat. She fished in her breast pocket for a cigarette.

"Hey, Ryu!" someone shouted from the far end of the garage. The slender waif-of-a-woman ran over, waving the whole time. She'd detailed her black hair with bright red highlights and wore a formfitting spacer jumpsuit.

"Miyuki?" Ryu said. "Oh, hey! Long time no see!"

Miyuki ran up and threw her arms around him.

"Whoa!" Ryu said, laughing. "Hey, nice to see you too."

"I saw New London on the news!" Miyuki said. She backed up and held him at arms' length. "Did those crusaders get a piece of you?"

"They tried their hardest," Ryu said. "But we were better."

"I heard a lot of dragons died on Luna. You should have written! I was worried about you."

"I'm sorry. I promise I'll remember next time."

"Liar," Miyuki said with a pouty face.

Ryu shrugged. He pointed a thumb over his shoulder. "Naomi and I are heading to Seven's in about an hour. You want to join us?"

"Naomi's with you?" Miyuki tilted her head to one side and looked past him. "Hey, Naomi. Nice to see you."

Naomi took the cigarette out of her mouth and exhaled. She didn't look up.

"So, uhhh, Naomi, glad to see you made it back," Miyuki said. "I bet New London was pretty rough."

Naomi took a long draw from her cigarette. The end glowed orange.

"Huh, okay." Miyuki leaned next to Ryu and whispered, "Who shoved the stick up her ass?"

"I don't know," Ryu whispered. "She's been like this since New London. By the way, she can still hear us."

Naomi waved without looking up.

"Oh crap!" Miyuki whispered. "I always forget that."

"So, can you join us?"

"Thanks, but I'm heading back up to the spaceport," Miyuki said. "I only stopped by to let the family know I wasn't drifting in space somewhere. My parents don't believe I'm okay unless I'm standing right in front of them. It's a sweet sentiment, but it gets annoying sometimes."

"If only they knew the kind of trouble you get into."

"Oh, hell no! It's best that they don't."

"Are you heading out?"

"Not yet. Matriarch has had my ship stuck in orbit all week. I know she has something planned but she won't let me know what it is."

"Yeah, I get that a lot too."

"I wish she'd drop a hint instead of letting me worry over it," Miyuki said.

"Well, if you change your mind, you know where we'll be."

"Thanks, Ryu. You're the best."

Miyuki gave him a quick peck on the cheek then waved goodbye and ran off. Ryu smiled and walked to the car.

Naomi looked up at him, cigarette dangling from her lips.

"What?" Ryu asked.

"Just get in and drive," Naomi said.

Ryu shook his head and jumped in. "What is with you today?" He stuck his beret into a shoulder strap and put on a pair of reflective driving glasses. With a small push of the throttle, he powered up the Saito's engine, grabbed the flight stick, and flew them out of the parking garage.

"Would you look at all this traffic?" Ryu said, forming up with a commuter lane heading for the upper eastern part of the city. The inverted spire of the old Omnitech Building stood out from the more nondescript office towers in the corporate district. Most of the towers were built in simple orthogonal shapes, all straight edges and flat surfaces that hung from the city's upper shell. In contrast, the Omnitech Building was a pale blue-and-white tower with a circumference that expanded or contracted with each level, like gently rolling waves, only vertical.

Ryu weaved underneath a lumbering cargo trolley and accelerated to double the speed limit. He skirted the edge of the aerial traffic zone and veered into the Omnitech Building's private parking zone.

Ryu settled the Saito onto a landing off the Omnitech Building's lowest level and locked the controls. A dog barked from inside his apartment.

"Oh, I think he knows who's home," Ryu said.

Naomi extinguished her cigarette in the Saito's ashtray. She climbed out of the car and grabbed her bag. Ryu grabbed his bag and closed the trunk. He palmed the apartment door open and stepped in.

A gray-and-white sheltie barked at him, tongue lolling from his jaw.

"Pochi!" Ryu said. "Did you miss me?"

"Yeah! Yeah!" the dog said.

Ryu threw his bag onto the great room couch, leaned over, and scratched Pochi behind the ears. He looked over his apartment, trying to find anything out of place. Nothing looked amiss. The open apartment space was separated into "rooms" by a few waist-high counters. The transparent floor gave a spectacular view of the city below.

"So, did you watch over my stuff? Huh, did you, boy?"

"Yeah! Yeah!"

"Oh, there's a good boy! I'm proud of you!"

"Thanks!" Pochi said.

Naomi stepped in and tossed her bag on the couch. She grabbed a sake bottle from the kitchen and headed for the balcony.

Pochi barked at her. "Don't! Don't!"

"Now, Pochi!" Ryu said. "What have I told you? You treat Naomi the way you treat me, got it?"

Pochi whined. He covered his eyes with his paws.

"Don't you do that," Ryu said. "You look at me when I'm scolding you."

Pochi lifted one paw and looked at him.

"Now apologize to her."

"Sorry?" Pochi said, looking at Naomi.

"It's no big deal," Naomi said. She walked out to the balcony, sunk into one of the recliners, and took a long swing from the sake bottle.

Pochi frowned at Ryu. "I'm sorry?"

"Oh, that's all right. Just try to be nice to her, okay?"

"Okay ..."

"There's a good boy. Now, how about finding my dragon capsule, okay?"

"Right! Right!"

Pochi bounded off for the walk-in closet, tongue flopping out of his mouth. He came back moments later and dropped a body paint capsule at Ryu's feet.

"Here! Here!"

"Pochi," Ryu said with a grimace. "That's the green and blue one. You know that one's out of style. Can you find the black and red one for me?"

Pochi whimpered. "Okay ..." The dog hurried back into the closet.

Ryu glanced around his apartment. A hologram over his chess set caught his eye. He sighed and walked over. The hologram showed one waiting message from his long distance opponent. It was almost two weeks old.

Ryu let the message play on the holographic board.

The white queen moved to check the black king while supporting a bishop and a rook. Things were not looking good for the black king. The move contained a text attachment, which Ryu accessed: "Nice try. My shoulder is still sore. Better luck next time. –K"

"You ass," Ryu muttered.

"What was that?" Naomi asked from the balcony.

"Not you," Ryu said. "It's nothing. I'm just losing at chess again."

Ryu moved his king out of check and selected "transmit." The board indicated it would take 43 minutes for the message to arrive.

"You should find an easier opponent," Naomi said.

If only that were possible, Ryu thought.

Pochi dropped another capsule at his feet.

"Here! Here!"

"Oh, good boy! That's the one!"

"Thanks!"

Ryu stepped into the shower and stuck the capsule in the shower head. He undressed and switched the shower cycle on. When it was done he had red skin, red hair, and a black serpentine dragon looping around his chest. He put on a pair of black pants and sandals to finish the look.

Ryu joined Naomi on the balcony. She'd drunk half the bottle.

"That's pretty impressive," Ryu said. "You sure you don't want to save it for Seven's?"

Naomi put a fresh cigarette in her mouth and lit it. The city lights were dimming now, slowly entering their artificial night cycle. The aerial traffic glowed in the distance as moving lines of white or red dots.

"Come on, Naomi. What's this all about?"

"Why do you care?"

"What's that supposed to mean? Of course I care. Just tell me what's wrong."

"You really have no idea?" Naomi asked. "You're an idiot, you know that?"

"Okay, so I'm an idiot. What else is new?"

"Just go. I don't want to talk about it."

"I don't get it," Ryu said. "You've been acting weird since New London. What's wrong?"

Naomi shook her head. "I hate being a dragon."

"What?"

"Do you have any idea what I gave up to be a dragon?"

"It's the same as what the rest of us went through."

"No! It's not the same!" Naomi shouted. She dropped her cigarette into an ashtray. "It's not the same at all! You were designed to be the perfect dragon. You were born to be a weapon! I had to be cut up and put back together for all these implants to work! Have you ever had a migraine so bad you had to be sedated?"

"No, but—"

"Maybe you've had your hands shake so much you couldn't hold your chopsticks?"

"Err … no …"

"You have no idea what I've been through to get here."

"That's not true," Ryu said. "I know it's been difficult for you."

"Really?"

"Yes, really. I saw what you put up with to become a dragon. I know you made some huge sacrifices."

"See! You don't get it at all!"

Naomi crushed the neck of the sake bottle. The bottom fell off and shattered against the balcony floor. Naomi shook her head and wiped her hand off. The glass shards didn't leave a mark on her hand.

"Look, Ryu. You remember when we were trying to get those people out of the House of Parliament? There was this one blonde kid in the crowd. He couldn't have been older than seven. When the crusaders opened fire he turned, and I swear he looked straight at me. He looked straight into my eyes just before a bullet punched into the back of his skull.

"I can see every part of it with perfect clarity. I can see the bullet push into his head. I can see his eyes pop out of his skull when the bullet explodes. I can see his scalp and skull break apart. The shrapnel pushed out, carrying bits of brain and bone and hair with them. I can see it all, and I can't shut it off. I can't bury it with drink. I can't forget, and I can't fucking deal with this anymore!"

"Look, Naomi."

"Just go," Naomi said, reaching into her breast pocket. Her fingers trembled as she drew another cigarette. "Get out of here."

"Naomi …" Ryu put a hand on her shoulder but she brushed him off.

"I want to be alone right now," Naomi said. "Just let me drink in peace. I'll join you later, okay?"

"All right, if that's what you want," Ryu said. "I'll see you at Seven's."

"Sure. Fine. At Seven's."

Ryu stepped out of the apartment and started the Saito up. He couldn't shake the feeling that the floor had dropped out from under him.

* * *

Ryu looped his Saito around the central column in Capitol City. The artificial lighting continued to slide into darkness. Beneath him, flood lights switched on, illuminating Heart as the city slowly fell asleep.

Ryu pulled in close to a modest parking deck in front of a two story pagoda façade. Holographic letters proclaimed "SEVEN'S" in vivid red. The parking deck was packed. He spotted Cat's white BMW and eased his Saito down next to it.

The bamboo fountain in the koi pond tipped over and clicked against wet stone. Ryu took a deep breath, savoring the mix of hibachi cooking, cigarette smoke, and the fresh scents of the koi pond. The restaurant was alive with dozens of overlapping conversations.

From inside, Cat waved him over. He walked in and sat down at the bar next to her. Cat had chosen a pattern of emerald waves with a pair of green shorts and matching sandals. She'd given her blonde hair a few sparkly green highlights.

Cat looked him up and down, then started giggling.

"What?" Ryu asked.

"Dragons again?"

"I like dragons."

"Clearly."

"It's good to see you back, Ryu," Seven said from behind the bar. The dark-skinned Martian wore a red button-down shirt with red bowtie and a cream vest that strained against his considerable girth. He idly polished a glass.

"Seven! How have things been?"

"Everyone's still talking about Luna. The Federacy appointed a military governor about a week ago."

"Yeah, we heard about that on the way home," Ryu said.

"I guess that's it for the Lunar State," Seven said. "On the bright side, my regulars started drinking more."

"You see? That was my intention the whole time. Screw up so you can sell more drinks."

"I appreciate it," Seven said. He set the dry glass down and picked up a wet one.

"So what's good?"

"The salmon and tuna are quite good. The squid, too. All of it came in fresh today from North Pacifica."

"How about the eel?"

"To be honest, it's marginal."

"Hmm," Ryu said. "Whatever you think is best. Let's start off with some nigiri and a spicy tuna roll."

"Right away, sir," Seven said. He set the glass down and tapped the order into his pad. "Anything to drink?"

"Sake. The usual."

"One ice cold Ueda coming right up," Seven said, pulling a large green bottle from the rack behind the bar. He poured out Ryu's drink. "So where's Naomi? You two didn't have another fight, did you?"

Ryu frowned. "How do you guess these things?"

"It's written all over your face. So, am I right?"

Ryu nodded.

"You had another fight?" Cat asked.

"Yeah. I don't get this one. I mean, I love her. I really do. But sometimes I just don't understand her."

"What's the problem this time?" Seven asked.

"She said she's upset about being a dragon."

"Hmm, that does make sense," Seven said.

"I'm glad someone understands her," Ryu said. "Shame it's not me."

"I really shouldn't speculate ..." Seven said carefully.

"Oh, go right ahead. Psychoanalyze our relationship all you want. I enjoy having my life picked apart."

"Well, Naomi joined the dragons to be with you," Seven said. "She didn't join out of a sense of duty or to protect her home. She's there for only one reason and is probably having doubts about her choice."

"I don't know," Ryu said. "I'm not so sure you have it right. And for the record, I was being sarcastic about the psychoanalysis."

Seven shook his head and set a plate in front of Ryu. "Your sushi, sir."

"Thanks." Ryu picked up his chopsticks, dabbed a little wasabi on top of his salmon nigiri and took a bite. "Oh, yeah. Very fresh. That's good stuff."

"I'm glad you approve," Seven said. "Now, not to pry ..."

"Why not? It's not like I can stop you short of leaving."

"So, do you still flirt with other women?"

"What? No!"

Seven cleared his throat.

"Look, it's not like I sleep with them."

Seven raised an eyebrow.

"Well, not recently," Ryu said.

"And the truth comes out."

"Hey, now. That was a special case. We were going through a bad patch, and I wanted to get back at her. Besides, you know how Miyuki can be."

Seven nodded, "True, very true."

"I haven't done anything like that recently."

"Ryu, you're a celebrity. Have you ever thought that maybe Naomi feels threatened by this?"

"No, I haven't."

"Well, let's use tonight as an example," Seven said. "Naomi could very easily misunderstand you meeting in a bar with this very lovely young woman here."

Cat giggled.

Ryu planted his face in his palm.

"What?" Seven asked. "I'm missing something, aren't I?"

"Seven, who do you think this young lady is?" Ryu said, putting his arm over Cat's shoulder.

"Honestly? I'd guess an immigrant from Earth trying to fit in."

"And how old?"

Seven paused and grimaced.

"Go on," Cat said. "I want to hear this."

"Very well. I'd guess either late teens or early twenties."

"Wrong!" Cat said with a smile.

"And that's why I didn't want to guess," Seven said.

"Seven, my good friend," Ryu said. "May I introduce you to Catherine Kusanagi, my little sister."

"That ... was unexpected."

"It usually is," Ryu said.

"But the eyes, the facial features, and hair color. She's nothing like you."

"I am aware of this. However, the fact remains Cat is my little sister."

"But ... ohhh ..."

"Ah," Ryu said. "I see you just had an epiphany."

"You were designed by Matriarch?" Seven asked.

"Yes!" Cat said. "I'm a well-kept government secret."

"No you're not," Ryu said.

"But I like saying it."

"You think I'd introduce you to a Martian spy if you were a secret?"

"Retired spy," Seven said. "Matriarch keeps a close eye on me."

"Right, I forgot," Ryu said, rolling his eyes. "Retired spy."

"Hey, here comes Toshi!" Cat said.

Ryu turned to see Toshi's oversized, black recreation vehicle land on the parking deck and almost strip the paint off the vehicles to either side.

"Wow," Ryu said. "Glad he didn't park next to me."

Toshi stepped out and slammed the door. Body paint covered him in crashing waves and fanciful underwater super-predators. He folded his driving glasses and stuffed them into his knee-length shorts.

"Toshi!" Ryu said. "Looking good. I like the new paint."

Toshi sat down and thumped the bar with a fist. "Martian Suicide, extra scotch, no ice."

"Yes, sir," Seven said. "One Martian Suicide coming right up."

"I guess you're not holding back tonight," Ryu said.

"There are two types of problems in life," Toshi said. "Those we can fix by killing people, and those we can't."

"I'm surprised you actually make a distinction," Ryu said.

"It's a small category."

"Here you go, sir," Seven said, setting the blood red drink on the counter. Cinnamon dust caked the top of the glass. "Would you like a ..."

Toshi grabbed the drink and gulped the whole thing down.

"I see my suggestion of a straw was unnecessary," Seven said.

Toshi slammed the glass onto the counter. "Another," he said, now sporting a dusty brown mustache.

Seven sighed. "The customer is always right."

"What brought this on?" Ryu asked.

"Girlfriend problems."

"You too?"

"Worse," Toshi said.

"You sure about that?" Ryu asked.

"Oh yeah. I'm very sure my problem is worse."

"Here you go, sir," Seven said. "Please give me time to remove my hand so you don't try swallowing it too."

Toshi took a sip and set the glass down. "My girlfriend dumped me."

"Oh man," Ryu said. "I'm sorry to hear that."

"And then she hooked up with my sister!"

Ryu bit into his tongue.

Seven shook his head. "I don't know what to say. Uhh, first drink is on the house?"

"Thanks, Seven."

"Is that normal?" Cat asked.

Toshi glared at her.

"I'm only asking because I don't know," Cat said.

"No, it's not normal! Boss, you got something you want to say?"

Ryu put a hand over his mouth and bit into his tongue harder. He shook his head.

"Thanks for the sympathy, boss."

Ryu took a few deep breaths and tried to compose himself.

"Not that it's any of my business," Seven said. "But you turned your girlfriend off men?"

"No, I knew she was bi when we started dating. I thought it was sexy. And now I'm quite sure I was being an idiot."

"But ... your sister?" Ryu said.

"Yeah."

"That's just not classy."

"Tell me about it," Toshi said. He chugged the rest of his drink down. "Right now, all I want to do is gorge on sushi, drink suicides, and watch *Crusade Buster* until I feel better. Hell, who knows? Maybe I'll find someone to have a one night fling with."

"That's the spirit!" Ryu said.

"Want to join in?" Toshi asked. "I mean all the parts except for the last one."

"Hell no. I hate that show."

"Suit yourself," Toshi said. He pointed to the closest flat screen. "Seven? You mind?"

"Go right ahead, sir."

"Thanks, pal," Toshi said. He stuck a cigar in his mouth and linked his request to the flat screen. The music video flicked off. An animated caricature of a crusader walked onto the screen only to have his head blown off by a hail of bullets. The headless crusader lurched forward while a ridiculous amount of blood spurted out of his neck. The gunfire continued, spelling out CRUSADE BUSTER in letters that burst into flames. The martial theme song started.

Ryu hung his head and sighed.

Toshi leaned back in his seat and lit his cigar. "I love this song."

"It is catchy," Cat said.

"Hey! We were watching that!" shouted a teenage girl with glittery purple body paint from the table in front of the flat screen.

"What were you watching?" Toshi asked.

Seven leaned over. "J Rocky just released a new album. I believe the young ladies are fans."

"J Rocky?" Toshi said. "I don't want to watch some effeminate Earth singer. We're going with *Crusade Buster*."

"No, you're not!" the girl said.

"Hey, I've got this one," Ryu said, patting Toshi on the shoulder. He turned to the girl-in-purple and her table of girlfriends. "Look, my friend here just got back from Luna. He's a little high strung. Just bear with him, please? Seven, a round of drinks for the beautiful ladies over here."

"Yes, sir. Konote! Get another drink order from table twelve, please."

"And can you see about getting them another screen?" Ryu asked.

"Of course. I'll get one of the spares pulled from storage."

"Thanks, Seven," Ryu said. He turned his back to the table and listened.

"Is that Ryu Kusanagi?" the girl-in-purple whispered to her friends.

"You know, I think it is," one of them whispered back.

"Holy shit!" the girl-in-purple said. She pulled a pad out of her skirt pocket and started tapping out a message. "Mai is going to freak out when she hears this."

Ryu grinned and took another sip of sake.

"Thanks, boss," Toshi said, puffing on his cigar.

"Nothing to it."

"Hey, Seven?" Cat said.

"Yes, miss?"

"I'm getting a little hungry. How about some sushi?"

"Certainly. Anything in particular?"

"Just two rolls, I think. Something with a little kick."

"Of course. Anything to drink, miss?"

"Oh no. I really shouldn't."

"She'll have what I'm having," Ryu said.

"Ryu, I'm not allowed."

"Don't be silly."

"Not allowed?" Seven asked.

"I'm not old enough," Cat said.

Seven stared blankly at Cat for half a minute. "Okay, I give up. How old are you?"

"Four years!"

"You're joking."

"Nope!"

"But you're … umm, how shall I put this?" Seven struggled to keep his eyes on her face. "You're very well developed for a four year old."

"Thanks!"

"Hey, Naomi!" Ryu said, waving.

Naomi stepped off her bike and walked in. She still had her dress uniform on.

"What's with the uniform?" Ryu asked.

"I didn't feel like changing," Naomi said. She sat down at the bar. "The usual, Seven."

"Right away, miss."

"Hey, Seven," Cat said. "You've been asking a lot of questions. Mind if I return the favor?"

"I suppose that's fair," Seven said, pouring a glass of sake for Naomi.

"You're Martian, right?"

"Very much so."

"So what's your full name?"

"Seven-Mistakes. I shortened it after I immigrated."

"Really, that's your name?" Cat said. "What's it mean?"

"Hey now," Ryu said. "You don't ask a Martian what the name means. It's not done."

"It's okay," Seven said. "I don't mind. The first mistake was falling in love."

"Ooh. Sounds interesting," Cat said. "I bet there's a cool story behind this."

"I can't talk about the second one," Seven said. "The statute of limitations hasn't expired yet."

"No fair!"

"Sorry."

"What the hell!" Toshi shouted.

Ryu turned to see the flat screen displaying a large gold crucifix against a checkered red-and-white background.

"Another propaganda virus," Seven said. "We've been getting a lot of those lately. Just bear with it. The scrubbers will clean it out in a few moments."

The virus raised the flat screen's volume to maximum and said: "Citizens of Europa! The crusaders ask you, haven't you been slaves of Matriarch for too long? Are you not ready to shed the shackles of her tyranny? Then, brave citizens of Europa, stand and fight! Know that riches await you in the Federacy! Many of your brothers and sisters have already heard the call to arms!"

Pictures of Europan defectors flashed across the screen, a few with the subtitle of DRAGON.

"Hey, I remember that one," Toshi said. "We fought him on Ceres."

"Yeah," Ryu said. "Didn't you gut him from groin to throat?"

"Look, I was only being thorough."

The room broke out into boos and hisses. Someone threw a bottle at the flat screen, shattering the bottle and coating the screen in rich amber fluid.

"Stop that, sir!" Seven shouted. "You break it, you bought it!"

Naomi quietly swirled her drink in its glass, shaking her head.

The message cut off, replaced by a SolarNet service apology. The first episode of *Crusade Buster* streamed in a few moments later.

Naomi downed the rest of her sake and stood up.

"Leaving already?" Ryu asked. "But you just got here."

"I'm just not in the mood tonight," Naomi said.

"Was it that crusader garbage? Because that's all it is. Garbage. Don't let it bother you."

"It's not that, Ryu," Naomi said. "Have a great night. I'll see you when you get home."

* * *

The next morning, Ryu settled his Saito onto the Heart's upper parking deck and stepped out. He put his driving glasses away and affixed his dress beret. The bright red exterior of Heart opened into a sterile white interior filled with intra-city military transports. Cat waved from the parking deck's security kiosk.

"Took you long enough," Cat said as he walked over. "I've been waiting almost an hour."

"Hey, I'm not late," Ryu said. He palmed the biometric scanner and stepped through the opening security door. "It's your own fault for getting here so early."

"I can't help it. I'm just so excited to see Matriarch again."

"I'm looking forward to it too, but at least I don't giggle while waiting."

Cat smacked him in the arm.

Ryu walked into a central lobby with a ring of elevator shafts. He palmed an elevator open, and they stepped in.

"So you and Toshi really hit it off last night."

"He's actually quite nice when he isn't trying to kill things."

"Did he make you watch that ridiculous show?"

"We went back to his place and got through the first half of season one," Cat said. "And finished a whole bottle of sake."

"One of those big party bottles?"

"It's the only size he had," Cat said.

"Right, of course. This is Toshi we're talking about."

"It wasn't bad. My implants metabolized it almost instantly. I don't think Toshi's are working properly, though."

"He switches his chemical defenses off when he wants to drink."

"You mean he got like that willingly?"

"Yeah."

"Including the puking?"

"Umm, maybe he took that part a little too far."

The elevator let them off into a wide, black-tiled hall with high white walls. Dozens of people milled about, talking in hushed tones. Ryu recognized some of the corporate representatives, many of them wearing immaculate body paint with company logos and slogans. Sometimes he wondered why Matriarch humored them so many years after the Corporate Coup. After all, they lost the war, right? They were just walking complaint-trumpets now, but he supposed Matriarch had her reasons for keeping them happy.

Ryu spotted Sachio Kusanagi and began walking over, his boots clicking against the polished tiles. Sachio sat on a plush couch off to the side of the hall, sipping tea with one hand and navigating his pad with the other. He set his tea down and looked up. His artificial eye focused on Ryu slightly faster than his real one. Other than the small variation, Ryu couldn't tell the difference, though the thick vertical scar through his face was a healthy clue something had been replaced.

"Ryu. Catherine," Sachio said. "It is wonderful to see you again."

Ryu bowed his head. "Father. A pleasure as always."

"Hello," Cat said with a small wave.

"I get the feeling something big is about to happen," Ryu said.

"Quite right," Sachio said. "An opportunity has presented itself, though one that carries many risks. Matriarch will explain."

The three of them walked over to a black security door. Each of them palmed in one at a time and passed through a narrow corridor. Somehow, Ryu always felt the hairs on the back of his neck rise, as if someone was standing right behind him. He didn't know what security measures existed behind the wall panels, but he knew they were lethal even to a dragon.

Ryu stepped through the final security door and into Matriarch's audience chamber. He breathed in a lungful of dry air that held a hint of ozone. The physical monolith of Matriarch's quantum mind stood at the far end of the chamber. Air shimmered around it from dissipating heat. Utility trenches branched off to either side, stuffed full of ultrahigh voltage cables and coolant lines.

A hologram of an attractive woman materialized in front of him. It wasn't hard to tell what his father had seen in her all those years ago. Matriarch had a young, slender face with dark almond eyes and long black hair that cascaded off her shoulders and down her kimono. Ocean waves built up and crashed in a continuous cycle on the kimono's surfaces.

"Hi, mom!" Cat said.

Matriarch smiled. "Hello, Catherine. I'm very happy to see you home safely."

Sachio sighed. "You weren't that excited when you saw me."

"Well … it's just …" Cat said. "I am happy to see you … it's just Matriarch is special."

"Yes, she is at that."

"And Ryu," Matriarch said. "I'm very happy to see you as well."

"Matriarch," Ryu said, bowing his head.

"I can't adequately describe how pleased I am that both of you returned safely."

"Cat has some serious talent," Ryu said. "She was a huge asset on the mission."

"Catherine's career choice surprised all of us," Matriarch said. "I admit it was not my first recommendation, but I have always believed in letting my children be true to themselves."

"Really?" Ryu asked. "You know, I keep getting this spam mail from the Church of Human. Maybe I should check them out. Who knows? I might want to convert."

"Perhaps that would be going too far," Matriarch said.

"That wasn't funny," Sachio said.

Ryu shrugged. "I thought it was."

"We have a great deal to cover," Matriarch said. "Shall we begin?"

"Sure," Ryu said. "I can't wait to talk about our fiasco on Luna again."

"Please, Ryu," Matriarch said. "Don't be too hard on yourself. The dragon presence of Luna helped delay Federacy actions on the planet. The guerilla campaign you and the other dragons executed was of the upmost importance. Though not all mission objectives were achieved, I still consider our deployment to Luna a success. Are you surprised?"

"To be honest, yes," Ryu said.

Matriarch sighed. She smirked at Sachio. "Even my own son seems quick to forget I can't lie. This is your fault, you know."

"Guilty as charged," Sachio said. "Though my intentions were good."

"And what road is paved with good intentions?"

"I honestly thought it would make people trust you more."

"And did it work?"

Sachio scratched the back of his head. "Well ... not so much."

"It's not that I don't believe you," Ryu said. "It's just hard to see the big picture when you're stuck in the middle of a firefight. I was never good at that."

"You're more into the hands-on side of things," Cat said.

"Yeah, that's it," Ryu said.

"Of course," Matriarch said. "Now, let us discuss your next mission. You'll quickly see why I waited for your return."

On Matriarch's kimono, bolts of lightning and gray storm clouds clashed. She extended a hand, summoning forth a new hologram in the middle of the group. It was a massive space station thousands of levels tall with a non-rotating cylindrical body that opened up into thousands of hatches at the bottom. Near the top, a wide habitat ring rotated around the inner cylinder. Heavy kinetic defense guns, directed energy weapons, and missile batteries dotted its surface in carefully placed clusters. Federacy warships, mere specks against this leviathan, patrolled the space around it.

"That's Apocalypse," Ryu said.

"Correct," Matriarch said. "Apocalypse is Earth's primary defender. It holds enough nuclear weapons to annihilate the surface of any settled planet ten times over, more than enough to overwhelm any attacker. No fleet would ever assault Earth while Apocalypse guards the gates."

"You could always try throwing asteroids at them," Ryu said.

"That's not funny," Sachio said.

"I'm only saying it worked once before."

"Earth is not the target," Matriarch said. "Apocalypse is."

"What?" Ryu said. "You're kidding, right?"

"No," Sachio said. "We are being very serious here."

"The mission parameters are simple enough," Matriarch said. "Infiltrate Apocalypse and steal—"

"Whoa! Hold it!" Ryu said. "Infiltrate Apocalypse? That's an act of war. You're talking about an actual attack on Federacy property in Federacy territory. This is totally different from Luna. And it's Apocalypse! Do you have any idea what you'll stir up with this?"

"Yes," Matriarch said.

"Trust us," Sachio said. "The alternatives are worse."

"How could they be?" Ryu asked. "We've never gone toe to toe with the Federacy. Even with distance and Europa's ice layer protecting our cities, if Earth sends a big enough fleet, we're done for."

"I know," Matriarch said.

"Ryu, I understand why you think this is crazy," Sachio said. "But the stakes are too high."

"What could possibly be on Apocalypse that's worth risking our world and everyone who lives on it?"

"The Federacy is developing a star drive," Matriarch said. "With it, they could move Apocalypse anywhere they chose. Their unbreakable shield would become their unstoppable sword. The Federacy would have absolute power over the solar system. How do you think they will treat us when we have no defenses left?"

"So you want us to steal it?" Ryu asked.

Sachio scratched his scar. "That's the preferred outcome. The star drive is currently mounted in a test ship called the *Needle of Destiny*. It's taken them almost a decade to make. There are a lot of exotic materials used in its construction, so it's not easy to reproduce. Just destroying it will set them back years."

"Okay," Ryu said. "I think some of my initial shock and panic is fading. So say we get a hold of this thing? What are we going to do with it?"

Matriarch and Sachio exchanged a knowing glance.

"We have a plan in place," Matriarch said.

"It's best if you don't know," Sachio said.

"Right," Ryu said. "Yeah, I suppose that makes sense given where I'm going."

"Insertion will be via a passing free trader," Matriarch said.

"You mean Miyuki's disguised ride?" Ryu said.

"Of course," Matriarch said.

"How are we going to get from the free trader to Apocalypse?"

"You'll jump."

"You've got to be kidding," Ryu said. "Those patrolling ships will spot us."

"No they won't," Matriarch said. "I've prepared a new revision of the smartskin specifically for this mission. The hardware is a little bulkier, but the illusion will fool even a Federacy warship's active trackers."

"Oh. Well, that's good. This is still crazy, though."

"Once onboard, locate and retrieve the *Needle of Destiny*," Matriarch said.

"Any idea where it's kept?"

"The test ship is likely stored in a hangar near the top," Sachio said. "Apocalypse's internal layout hasn't changed much since the beginning of the Third Space Age. There are a limited number of places it can be stored."

"So in short, no," Ryu said.

"Preferred extraction will occur via the star drive test ship," Matriarch said. "Alternatives are stealing a craft docked at Apocalypse or returning to Miyuki's free trader."

"So no definite plan for extraction," Ryu said. "This just gets better and better."

"I know this must seem like suicide," Matriarch said.

"Well, so did Bunker Zero," Ryu said. "You know I'm in. So don't bother asking."

The storm clouds on Matriarch's kimono receded.

"Thank you, Ryu," Matriarch said. "I'm very happy to hear you say that. And you, Catherine? Will you accept this mission?"

"I'm in," Cat said. "I won't lie. This mission scares me a lot more than Luna did, but someone has to watch Ryu's back."

"Cat's tougher than she looks," Ryu said. "That's for sure."

"And for that we are thankful," Matriarch said.

"I have to wonder how the Federacy came up with this in the first place," Ryu said. "You've kept us one step ahead of their technology for years."

"Part of their solution was brute force research," Matriarch said. "The Federacy has almost a thousand times our resources and population. We lack the means to explore and develop exotic matter technology on a large scale. They also have other advantages." Matriarch's kimono flashed red for an instant, then returned to calm waves. "But we needn't go into that now."

"What about the rest of your team?" Sachio asked.

"Toshi and Naomi, of course," Ryu said. "No need to break up a winning combination as long as they volunteer."

"I have no problems with Toshi," Matriarch said. "But I am concerned about Naomi's mental fitness for this mission. The report from the medical staff of the *Io's Fury* brought up a number of questions. Perhaps another dragon would be more appropriate? One you've worked with before like Sakaki from green dragon?"

"Yeah, I know Naomi hasn't been at the top of her game lately," Ryu said. "But she's still one of the best dragons we have and she's saved my life plenty of times. I'll talk it over with her. If she volunteers, she's in."

"Very well," Matriarch said. "I'll defer to your judgment on the matter."

"You know," Ryu said. "It still surprises me you do that."

Matriarch shook her head. Her kimono showed tranquil seas with dolphins playing. "You'd be surprised at the mathematical complexity of a simple hello. Groups of people are easy to predict. All the variables average out. Individuals are far more difficult. And besides, I trust your judgment."

Ryu clapped his hands together. "Okay, it looks like I need to pay Toshi and Naomi a visit. I'll bring the whole squad in if they volunteer. I take it everything we've talked about is a government secret?"

"As usual," Sachio said.

"There is one last thing we need to discuss before you leave," Matriarch said. "Catherine, would you please step outside?"

"Awhhh …" Cat said.

"We'll get a chance to talk later," Matriarch said. "I promise."

They waited for Cat to disappear behind the security door.

"So, you met Kaneda," Sachio said.

"I don't know why I'm surprised you know," Ryu said. "Yeah, he was in New London. You'd think with as much leading-from-the-front as he does someone would put a bullet through his head."

"The bastard is hard to kill," Sachio said. "Matriarch did too good a job designing him."

"Not from scratch," Matriarch said. "There's a lot of you in both our sons."

"As far as I'm concerned, I have only one son," Sachio said. "That traitor can rot in hell."

Matriarch bowed her head. "I wish you wouldn't say things like that."

"We'll get him one of these days," Ryu said.

"Ryu," Matriarch said. "I didn't want to discuss this in front of Cat, but I think you know just how low the odds of success are."

"Yeah, I know."

"Normally, I would send a different dragon squad on a mission this dangerous," Matriarch said. "But the truth is this mission is so important and so difficult that combining your combat skills and Cat's technical prowess gives us the best chance of success."

"I understand," Ryu said. "We won't let you down."

"Catherine the dragon," Sachio said. "It still amazes me she did it."

"She could have experienced anything the solar system has to offer," Matriarch said. "That's why I picked an appearance that blends well on Earth. Instead, she chose to endure a year on the operating table and risk death to be at her brother's side."

"Yeah," Ryu said. "I don't think I'd have made the same decision."

"Most people wouldn't," Matriarch said.

"Do your best to come back alive," Sachio said. "The both of you."

"Father," Ryu said with a bow. "Matriarch."

Ryu stepped through the narrow security corridor and into the reception hall with all its corporate leeches, military officers, and public representatives.

"What was that about?" Cat asked.

"Just our parents being parents," Ryu said. "Hey, do you want to get lunch before we round up the others?"

"No need," Cat said. "I was already going to meet Toshi at Fortune Tower. There's an Italian restaurant on the bottom floor he recommended. We can meet him there."

... accessing SolarNet message archive ...

... opening folder [**Personal - 8 Years Old**] ...

... searching for [**Church** |and| **Stupid** |and| **Moron**] ...

... 1 match found ...

... retrieving ...

source: Ryu Kusanagi <black.dragon1@eurogov.jupiter>

destination: Kaneda Kusanagi <kaneda.kusanagi@solarnet.public.earth>

message delay: 50 minutes

title: what are you stupid?

-Am I reading this right?

-You're converting to the Church of Human? This is insane! Are you stupid or something? Don't you understand what they stand for? The Church is packed with zealots who hate thinking machines! And guess what? They view Matriarch as a thinking machine! They're a bunch of morons!

-Are you doing this for Christen? Are you doing this just so the two of you can marry? Are you just stupidly in love or do you actually believe this garbage? Think about this! This goes against everything we are!

... retrieving next message in conversation ...

source: Kaneda Kusanagi <kaneda.kusanagi@solarnet.public.earth>

destination: Ryu Kusanagi <black.dragon1@eurogov.jupiter>

message delay: 50 minutes

title: No, I'm not stupid

Dear Ryu,

I have to admit your words wound me deeply. I had hoped that you'd be the best man in our wedding, despite Christen's objections, but now I see that isn't possible. I think it's best for both of us if you don't come at all.

And now I must urge you to reconsider your views. We both saw the same things in Caesar's bunker. The only difference is I opened my eyes and you didn't. Matriarch runs Europa. Everyone on Europa does anything she says without question, hoping for her to dole out presents in the form of technology. But those baubles are merely the iron collar around your neck.

I don't trust Matriarch. That is too much power for any one person to have, especially someone who can no longer be considered human. How long before she views humans as obsolete tools the way Caesar did? Perhaps she already has.

I'm sorry, Ryu. I really am. Goodbye.

Your brother,
Kaneda

... retrieving next message in conversation ...

source: Ryu Kusanagi <black.dragon1@eurogov.jupiter>

destination: Matriarch <matriarch@eurogov.jupiter>

message delay: 0 seconds

title: FW>No, I'm not stupid

-Do you believe this idiot? You try talking to him.

... retrieving next message in conversation ...

source: Matriarch <matriarch@eurogov.jupiter>

destination: Kaneda Kusanagi <kaneda.kusanagi@solarnet.public.earth>

message delay: 50 minutes

title: FW>FW>No, I'm not stupid

Kaneda,

Please reconsider what you are doing. There is some truth in what you say. Quantum minds are dangerous, as Caesar's example clearly shows. But I have always kept the best interests of Europa's citizens at heart. I know I wield great power, but I respect that fact and pray for the wisdom to use it wisely.

This fissure in our family pains me greatly. Please give me the chance to mend it. I don't think you realize how much this hurts. I would gladly step down from my post if it would bring you back home. There's nothing I wouldn't do for you.

Matriarch

... retrieving next message in conversation ...

source: Kaneda Kusanagi <kaneda.kusanagi@solarnet.public.earth>

destination: Matriarch <matriarch@eurogov.jupiter>

message delay: 50 minutes

title: RE>FW>FW>No, I'm not stupid

I am no longer your puppet.

Kaneda

... conversation ends ...

Kaneda took one last look at the bustle within Apocalypse's command hangar, then stepped into flextube leading to the shuttle. He took a seat next to Admiral Piller and pulled his crash webbing snug.

"Have I ever mentioned I hate politics?" Kaneda asked.

"Quite often, actually." Piller gave Kaneda a sideways smirk. His dark blue Federacy uniform hung loosely off his whipcord body. He kept his brunette hair in a traditionally short spacer's cut, which made his sharp blue eyes stand out even more.

"It deserves repeating," Kaneda said.

"Pilot," Piller said. "Drop me off at the *Stalwart* then take Crusader Kusanagi to Penance."

"Yes, sir," the pilot said over the intercom. "Calculating route now."

The shuttle lurched with the heavy release of docking latches. It drifted away from the retracting flextube then powered out of the mountainous space station's uppermost hangar. A flight of four blackhawk interceptors formed up with the shuttle and escorted it out of Apocalypse's inner patrol zone.

Kaneda looked out the window. The Earth filled the view. A sliver of the Earth's dark side glowed with countless city lights. As for the rest ... "You can really see what we did to her from up here."

"Hmm?" Piller asked.

"The Earth."

"You know, I hardly look at her anymore."

"There's Lake London, Lake Moscow. The Phobos Gulf is coming into view."

"Humanity has redrawn the map a few times. Hitting her with kinetic torpedoes and asteroids will do that."

"So what are we going to do about König?" Kaneda asked.

"Not much we can do. He has seniority over me," Piller said. "Plus he's heavily entrenched in the admiralty board. The man has too many political allies. I don't even think a good scandal could budge him."

"As long as he is on the board, we can't change Federacy policy towards Europa."

"Maybe," Piller said. "The events on the moon swayed some opinions. The defense secretary is starting to take notice. He has the president's ear, and that can only mean good things for our cause."

"I suppose," Kaneda said. "How are things going on Luna? I find it hard to believe the situation is as stable as the board wants to believe, but it wasn't my place to comment."

"The idiots think the moon is ours just because we've occupied the major cities," Piller said. "Of course, there are reasons to be pleased. New London is completely under our control and the Lunar State as a functioning government no longer exists. Most of the Lunar army has surrendered. What's left of their navy is running for other colonies."

"You're going to have problems with terror cells," Kaneda said. "Those old tunnel networks are perfect for hit and run tactics."

"Going to? We already are."

"I can provide a few companies of crusaders to help patrol the tunnels."

"I appreciate the offer, but let the army handle this. Your crusaders are too valuable to be bogged down in this sort of problem."

The shuttle veered towards the *Stalwart*. The shape of Federacy battleships always reminded Kaneda of swords. They possessed very slender profiles from the front, ideal for long range engagements with energy or kinetic weapons. Numerous turrets dotted the top and bottom of the *Stalwart*'s "blade", with a powerful cluster of engines at the rear. The heaviest weapons took up much of the vessel's internal space and could fire in a limited forward arc.

Like a sword, captains point their ships at an enemy and thrust, Kaneda thought.

The shuttle matched speed and heading with the *Stalwart*, then maneuvered into a small hangar near the "hilt". Kaneda felt the jarring contact of the flextube docking latches.

"Good luck, Kaneda," Piller said. He floated over to the airlock and touched down on the friction carpet. "I'll see what I can do about König, but it's an uphill battle."

"I appreciate it."

Piller gave him a mock salute. He passed through the airlock and closed it behind him. A minute later, the shuttle launched from the *Stalwart* and initiated a burn to bring it to Penance.

Kaneda leaned back and stared out the window. Penance was a small white dot at this distance. If he just relaxed his eyes …

The intercom chimed.

"Sir, is there anything you need?" the pilot asked with a squeak in the voice. Kaneda wondered just how young the man was. "I know it won't be a long flight, but I have some refreshments in the cabin."

"No, that's all right," Kaneda said. "The admiralty board succeeded in killing both time and my appetite."

The pilot chuckled. "I see, sir."

"Please, there's no need to call me sir. Technically, I'm just a mercenary."

"I know, sir. But you're a crusader. That's makes it different."

"Yes, I suppose it does."

"I'm not bothering you, am I?"

"Of course not."

"You know, my brother's regiment was on the moon. He actually saw crusaders fighting in New London."

"A lot of brave soldiers died in the campaign," Kaneda said. "Did your brother make it out alive?"

"He's still on the moon, but he's in good health and has been writing to me every day. He says the outcome would have been very different without crusaders there."

"Thank you. Hearing that is certainly a breath of fresh air after my last meeting."

The pilot laugh. "Yes, sir. I imagine it was."

"What's your name?"

"Derrick. Derrick Stein."

"Nice to meet you, Derrick."

"The pleasure's all mine, sir."

Kaneda created a new message on his pad and jotted down a few notes. "Derrick Stein. Federacy pilot. Possible crusader candidate. Investigate background and advise on potential." He sent the message to recruiting.

Kaneda sat back and waited for Penance to come into view. The next time he saw it, the shuttle was circling around the station.

Penance had started its life as an old Second Space Age habitat whose unfortunate residents didn't survive the Second Great Fall. The habitat was a fairly conventional wheel design with a docking hub connected to the wheel with six spokes: small, abandoned, but structurally sound. The habitat had been perfect for Kaneda's needs. With starter funds from the Federacy government, Kaneda had brought in construction crews to cremate the corpses and then refurbish the habitat into his base of operations.

Now Penance looked better than some Third Space Age habitats and showed no sign of structural deformation. Most of the station was painted white with the outer surface of the wheel checkered in red. A gold crucifix stood out prominently on either side of the docking hub.

The shuttle entered the docking hub and landed in an empty cradle between a row of assault transports (which dwarfed the shuttle) and a lamprey bunker designed to piggyback on a Federacy warship (which dwarfed the transports). The assault transports could hold a hundred crusaders in full battle armor. The bunker could support over five thousand.

"Have a pleasant day, sir."

"Thank you, Derrick."

Kaneda stepped through the airlock and took the flextube into the hangar. Viter and Alice stood at attention on the friction carpet by his exit. Both wore red and white checkered jumpsuits. Alice also wore a scarf to cover her neck scar, though in a small nod to decorum, it was also checkered red and white.

"Good news or bad news?" Alice asked.

"What do you think?" Kaneda said.

"They're not going to make a formal announcement?" Viter asked.

"Oh, they are. It's just not what we wanted."

"This is ridiculous," Alice said. "They should be out for blood. There were dragons on the moon!"

"I know."

"What are they going to say?" Viter asked.

"That Europa was unfortunately caught in the crossfire," Kaneda said. He cleared his throat. "The official release will probably read that 'Europa was a victim of the military action between the Federacy and the now defunct Lunar State. The Federacy holds no hostility towards Europa and extends its heartfelt apologies for the regrettable deaths of her citizens.'"

"That makes me sick," Alice said.

"Yeah," Viter said. "A little underwhelming."

"They've been dragging their asses for weeks," Alice said. "And that's the best they can come up with?"

"I'm afraid so," Kaneda said. He started walking out of the lounge with Alice and Viter a pace behind. They stepped into an elevator that took them through Spoke Five to the habitat wheel. Crusader doctrine scrolled across the elevator's holographic marquee:

Never use weapons of mass destruction.

Never set foot on Earth.

Serve our Federacy allies.

"So how is our new recruit doing?" Kaneda asked.

"Well ..." Alice said. "I don't mean to doubt your judgment, but a Martian? They're just too different."

"He'll work out," Viter said. "I like him."

"You would," Alice said. "Look, I'm not saying I don't like him. The problem is they're raised differently than us. It's a strange culture and they look at the worlds differently because of it."

The elevator let them off at the wheel with its 0.135 gees, a perfect match for Europa's gravity. A crusader chaplain in a black jumpsuit nodded to Kaneda and stepped into the empty elevator. He had an M10 pistol in his holster.

"Heading to the firing range, father?" Kaneda asked.

"Yes, sir," the chaplain said, interrupting the elevator door with his hand. "My reflex implant is bugging out again. The medics don't know what's wrong so we're running a test." He tapped a small medical probe on his right temple.

"Well, good luck."

"Thank you, sir," the chaplain said. He stepped in so the elevator could close.

Kaneda led the way down the long checkered corridor. Numbered airlocks branched into dormitories, a mess hall, a chapel, and general storage areas. Holographic marquees scrolled crusader doctrine continuously:

Never suffer another Caesar.

Oppose Europa.

Destroy the Europan quantum mind.

"Well, Three-Part does have one thing going for him," Alice said. "At least he's not some crazy cometeer."

"Or a convicted murderer," Viter said.

"Excuse me?" Alice said. "You want to say that again?"

Kaneda sighed. "So are there any major problems?"

"Yes, there are problems!" Alice said.

"With Three-Part?"

"Oh … uhh … no, I guess there aren't."

"Good," Kaneda said. "I think it's time we initiate him into our squad."

"Is that where we're heading?" Alice asked.

"I don't know," Viter said. "I was just following blindly."

"Are you kidding?" Alice said. "You do that all the time."

"Go on ahead," Kaneda said. "I'll speak with Three-Part."

"Yes, sir," Viter said.

Kaneda palmed Dormitory 5's airlock open and stepped into a narrow three-story corridor. He took a ramp down to the bottom level and found Three-Part's room at the far end.

Kaneda palmed the chime.

Three-Part opened the door. Thin pink lines traced small circles and ovals across his dark scalp. He wore a white t-shirt and shorts with Velcro strips along the sides. Medics had attached numerous booster patches to his arms and legs.

"Sir?" Three-Part asked. He continued wrapping his right hand in bandages.

"Hello, Three-Part. How are you?"

"Fine, sir. Uhh, please come in."

"Thank you," Kaneda said, stepping in and looking around. He'd selected one of the larger rooms for Three-Part, as befit his soon-to-be-status on Kaneda's command squad. The room was sparsely decorated. Three-Part had only unpacked a few meager possessions he'd kept in his police cruiser. His riot armor, uniform, and pistol lay stacked in one corner. Spare booster patches, bandages and bottles of pills were spread out on the coffee table.

Kaneda noted the bottle of red liquid on a stand by the futon. He stepped over and picked it up.

"Tomato juice," Three-Part said.

"Of course," Kaneda said, setting the bottle down. "How silly of me to think otherwise."

The transparent floor offered views of either the Earth or Luna as the habitat rotated. Windows were another sign that Penance had never been designed as a military base. Right now, Earth was starting to come into view.

Kaneda picked up a portrait by the futon. It showed Three-Part with his arm around a young Martian woman. She held a small child in her arms. All of them wore somber clothes that projected extravagant holograms around their bodies. The child had a revolving halo over his head with the name UNEXPECTED-JOYS repeated on it.

"Though I have experienced great loss in my life," Kaneda said, setting the picture down. "I have no claim to something so tragic."

"It almost destroyed me," Three-Part said.

"And yet you chose your current name after their deaths," Kaneda said. "A rather morbid selection, if I may say so, naming yourself after the type of explosives the terrorists used."

Despite the dark topic, Three-Part smiled. "You know the meaning?"

Kaneda nodded. "It's not what I would have chosen. Perhaps 'Many-Bottles'?"

"Oh that would never do," Three-Part said, laughing. "Not subtle enough."

"As you say, not nearly subtle enough," Kaneda said with a friendly nod. "I respect what you did with your life. That's why I offered you a position. You took this horrible loss that almost destroyed you, passed through a great many dark places, and you emerged stronger than ever. I see some of myself in you."

"You flatter me, sir," Three-Part said.

"Not at all," Kaneda said. "Your *jihad* strengthened you remarkably."

Three-Part raised an eyebrow. "Now that surprises me. Not many people outside of Mars would use that word correctly."

"Perhaps because it has had others meanings across history," Kaneda said. "And unfortunately still does in some Martian nations."

"You speak the unfortunate truth, sir," Three-Part said.

"So how are you adjusting?" Kaneda asked.

Three-Part held up his bandaged hand.

"I would consider that normal," Kaneda said.

"I reached for a cup and hit it so hard it shattered. I just finished cleaning up the pieces before you arrived. I don't know. The worlds feel different. Everything is magnified and sharper. It's difficult to take in."

Kaneda pointed to the Earth below their feet.

"Let me walk you through one of my favorite drills for new recruits," Kaneda said. "Stand next to me and look down."

"All right, sir."

"Now pick a spot to focus on."

"Okay, I see the Phobos Gulf."

"Too big. Pick something smaller."

"All right ... I can make out Lake Moscow."

"Smaller," Kaneda said.

"Smaller? Okay ... I see a little yellow dot between us and the Earth. There."

"Do you know what it is?"

"No. Probably an orbital city, but I don't know which one."

"Good," Kaneda said. "Now look at it. Relax your eyes. Let your implants do the work for you. Don't try to force it."

"I don't think I ... what?"

"Surprisingly easy, isn't it?"

"Oh my ... I can do this?"

"What do you see now?"

"That's Five Lake City. I can actually read the name off the cylinder's shell!"

"You see? There's nothing to it. It's just a matter of letting the implants work for you."

Three-Part looked up. "Thank you, sir. That was very helpful."

"Any time," Kaneda said. "Do you know why I founded the crusaders?"

"Of course. To stop the Europan quantum mind and anything like it that might follow."

"Partially," Kaneda said. He pointed to a cluster of red lights coming into view. Some of the dimmer lights orbited around a thick line of brighter ones: patrols circling a gargantuan construct.

"Apocalypse?" Three-Part asked.

"That's right," Kaneda said. "I'm sure you know how the Second Great Fall came about."

"I am a Martian, sir."

"Of course," Kaneda said. "The war between Earth and Mars at the end of the Second Space Age nearly annihilated the human race. I do have a point, so please bear with my retelling."

"Of course, sir."

"The war had many starting points, many mistakes that can be thought of as the cause of that tragedy, but I'm most interested with the beginning of the end: Mars setting its moon Phobos on a collision course with Earth.

"Near Earth, the two fleets clashed in a battle the likes of which no one had ever seen. Apocalypse launched every weapon it had in Earth's defense, bathing the Martian fleet and Phobos in atomic fire. The amount of nuclear weapons exchanged in a few minutes eclipsed all that came before a hundred times over.

"And when the clouds of radioactive ash dissipated, the Martian fleet was gone but Phobos was not. The largest chunk burned through the atmosphere and crashed into mainland China, turning it into the Phobos Gulf. Smaller pieces devastated all the major continents. Earth was cast into a nuclear winter. Her people starved and warred with each other for the decades that followed, fighting over insufficient food and water.

"But before that, what was left of the Earth fleet traveled to Mars, smashed its remaining defenses aside with contempt, and delivered every weapon in their arsenal to the surface."

"Human life on Mars barely survived," Three-Part said.

"And so ended the Second Space Age," Kaneda said. "This is why I created the crusaders. We are here to prevent a holocaust, but this time it won't be a giant rock barreling towards Earth. This time it will be much more subtle and subversive. If left alone, people will continue to create intellects greater than themselves. This cannot be allowed to happen. Otherwise we are forging our own chains."

Three-Part nodded. "People are too quick to forget what Caesar did. They should look to Europa more closely."

"Exactly!" Kaneda said. "After the death of Caesar, who could have imagined a whole moon allowed to exist under a quantum mind's rule? Europa's citizens are slaves, whether they realize it or not. You yourself have seen what even a small sentient micromind can do."

"It is a problem we face on Mars more often than most realize," Three-Part said.

"Thank you," Kaneda said.

"For what?"

"For affirming that I made the right decision," Kaneda said, placing a hand on Three-Part's shoulder. "Now, let's get this ritual out of the way."

"Ritual, sir?"

* * *

Kaneda and Three-Part floated into one of Penance's zero-gee firing ranges. Viter and Alice had already cleared it of other crusaders. They stood face to face in front of the middle lane, pointing at each other and gesturing angrily.

"Why are they shouting at each other?" Three-Part asked.

"They're not," Kaneda said. "They're whispering. Rather pointless on a station full of crusaders."

Alice spotted them and spoke as quietly as she could, but Kaneda could still read her lips from across the room.

"Forget something?" Kaneda asked, walking along the friction carpet with Three-Part.

"Not me," Alice said. "See, I have the gun right here."

"That's hardly an accomplishment," Viter said. "We're in a firing range."

"Well, who was supposed to bring the blindfold?"

"I thought you were," Viter said. He pointed to her scarf. "And look. You did."

"He's not using my scarf as a blindfold."

"Could someone please explain what we're talking about?" Three-Part asked.

"The exercise is simple," Kaneda said, taking the pistol and handing it to Three-Part. "When I give the order, you will shoot the target. The distance is one hundred meters."

"Blindfolded?" Three-Part asked.

"Among other things," Kaneda said. "Alice and Viter will stand on either side of the target, so please, only fire when you know you will score a hit."

Three-Part stared at the gun in his hands. He checked the safety, pulled out the magazine, inspected the bullets, and slapped it back in. "The two of you did this?"

"Of course," Viter said.

"Not me," Alice said. "I think the whole thing is stupid."

"Alice, your scarf, please?" Kaneda said.

Alice sighed. "Oh, all right," she said, removing the scarf.

Three-Part stared at the scar that went all the way around her neck.

"What happened there?" he asked.

Alice pointed to the tattoo under her right eye. It read: DON'T ASK.

"You see this?"

"Ah," Three-Part said. "Never mind."

"There's a good boy," Alice said. She wrapped the scarf around Three-Part's head and pulled the knot tight.

"Positions, please," Kaneda said. Alice and Viter floated to the firing range target.

"Are you sure this is a good idea?" Three-Part asked. "Because I think it's a really bad one."

Kaneda grabbed Three-Part by his t-shirt, lifted him off the friction carpet, and maneuvered him into the firing lane.

"Might be," Kaneda said. "Just remember. Focus on what you want to do, not how to do it. Let the implants work for you. Give up control."

Kaneda grabbed Three-Part's foot and spun him before backing away.

"What the hell!"

"No excuses," Kaneda said. "Remember, focus on *what*, not on *how*."

"I don't think—"

"Exactly! And ... shoot!"

Three-Part spread his arms and legs, turned, aimed, and fired.

The target chimed.

Three-Part touched a foot to the friction carpet and stopped his spinning. He pushed the blindfold up with the pistol's barrel.

"Dead center," Kaneda said. "Very nice."

"But ... that was so easy. You told me to shoot and, I don't know, it just happened."

"That's how it works."

Alice and Viter kicked off the target wall and floated back.

"I'm beginning to suspect they were never in any danger," Three-Part said.

"Correct," Kaneda said. "If your aim had been off, they would have dodged out of the way before you finished pulling the trigger."

"So much of this was not what I expected," Three-Part said.

"Welcome to the squad," Viter said, offering a hand. Three-Part shook it firmly.

"Yes, welcome," Alice said, smiling. They shook hands.

"I'm on the command squad?" Three-Part asked.

"Surprised?" Kaneda asked.

"But I'm not even a member of the Church of Human. I've never been a very religious man."

"Fortunately that isn't a problem," Kaneda said. "While it is true most crusaders are devout humanists, it is not a requirement. What about you, Alice? Any thoughts on organized religion?"

Alice shook her head. "You mean the masses of retarded, mindless cattle that believe in something they can't see?"

"Ouch," Three-Part said. "I wouldn't go that far."

"And you, Viter? Any thoughts?"

"To be honest, I've never understood religion," Viter said. "I've always believed what is good for humanity as a whole is what's best. Religion to me just complicates the matter."

"That sounds a lot like the cometeer faith," Three-Part said.

Alice started laughing.

"What?" Three-Part asked. "Did I say something funny?"

Viter frowned. "Cometeers have no religion."

"I'm sorry. I didn't mean to offend. Are some of your friends cometeers?"

"Uhh ... yes ..." Viter said slowly. "Yes ... I do have ... a few cometeer friends."

"I've actually been to Enceladus once," Three-Part said. "What is it they call their moon?"

"The Jewel of Saturn."

"Yes, thank you. That's what they call it."

"The majority of our recruits come from Earth," Kaneda said. "Especially cities that suffered during Caesar's war. Some of our more exotic recruits are defector Europans, Martians, Lunarians, quicksilvers."

"You what?"

"Not many, I assure you," Kaneda said. "And yes, we even have a few unpredictable cometeers in our ranks. As I said before, I think you'll fit in nicely."

* * *

Kaneda stepped into his office. The transparent floor provided a clear view of Luna's dark side city lights. Most of them still worked. A few Europan ice sculptures sat on his transparent desk and atop his bookcase. The smallest was an ice ship with a watery sail flowing out of it. Not his best work, but it had sentimental value for being the first. The largest was an ice dragon with watery wings breathing water on a lone ice warrior. He'd always liked the ice warrior's stance: shield raised, sword ready at his side for the counterstrike.

A hologram blinked green over his chess set. He stepped over and retrieved the message.

"Hmm, getting desperate are we?" Kaneda said. He entered his next move and hit send.

Kaneda sat down behind his desk. He picked up his pad and double-checked the time. Seventeen minutes later, he selected the SolarNet address at the top of his call log and hit connect.

A weary woman's voice responded. "What is it?"

"Hello, Christen."

"Kaneda, can this wait? I'm busy right now."

"I'll only take a moment of your time," Kaneda said. "Is Matthew there? I'd like to speak to him."

"He's not here right now."

"That seems unusual," Kaneda said. "He should have arrived ten minutes ago."

"Listen, he's still at school practicing for a play."

"And you're not with him?"

"What's that supposed to mean?"

"Do you know for certain he's still at school?"

"Don't you dare get judgmental at me," Christen said. "It's not like you were ever around to help."

"You know I had obligations only I could fill."

Kaneda heard the door to his office open and the clicking of familiar footsteps.

"Oh, you are so full of yourself!" Christen said.

"Look, I don't want to have a fight," Kaneda said. "Will you let him know I called? It's been fifteen days since I talked to him."

"Fine. I'll tell him. Happy now?"

"Thank you, Christen."

"Goodbye."

His pad read DISCONNECTED in red letters. He set it down and looked up.

Alice stood by his bookcase and traced a finger across the spines. Each wafer-thin spine expanded into a thick holographic description at her touch.

"You know she won't tell him," Alice said.

"I know."

"So why do you bother?"

"Because he is my son and she was my wife," Kaneda said. "Do I need a better reason?"

Alice pulled a book off the shelf. "Michael Cantrell's *Software and Ethics: Why Moral Quantum Minds Can Never Exist*. You do enjoy your light reading."

"You're welcome to borrow it."

"No thanks," Alice said, sliding the book back in place.

"What's on your mind?" Kaneda asked.

"Viter said something today and it got me thinking."

"The crack about being a convicted murderer?"

"You noticed."

"Don't let it get to you," Kaneda said. "Viter didn't mean anything by it."

"It's not that," Alice said. She stepped over and sat on the edge of his desk. "I've been wondering if I really did it."

"You've done worse since."

"That's different," Alice said. "We're fighting for what we believe in. I can handle having blood on my hands with a cause as just as ours. I don't know if I can handle being a cold-blooded murderer."

"You know I believe you're innocent."

"But you don't know for certain."

"No, I don't."

"Maybe I did kill him," Alice said, staring through the floor at Luna, feet dangling off the desk. "I wish I could remember."

"We can thank the Federacy for that one," Kaneda said. "With as long as they made us wait after the execution, it's a miracle you're still able to form sentences."

"Yeah, it's funny. I remember the guillotine. I think I even remember you and the medics running in, though maybe that's just my imagination. But I don't remember much from before."

Alice glanced at the gold wedding band on his finger.

"You still love her, don't you?"

"Some wounds never heal."

"That's not much of an answer." Alice pushed off the table and sat on his lap. She took his hand and traced his fingers across her scar. "I owe you so much."

"You owe me nothing," Kaneda said.

Alice kissed his hand. "I am your servant, body and mind, now and forever."

"You're so much more than that, Alice."

A tear trickled down her face. "I wish that were true." She bent down and kissed him.

... establishing link ...

source: [UNKNOWN]

routing: Capitol City, Europa - TangleNet Test Hub - link_001/link_004

routing: North Pacifica, Europa - JDN Main Hub - link_009/link_118

routing: Earth orbit - surveillance satellite JDN-SS-17 - link_001/link_002

routing: [UNKNOWN]

routing: [UNKNOWN]

routing: [UNKNOWN]

destination: [UNKNOWN]

link distance: Exact distance unknown. Estimated at 792 million kilometers.

link signal delay: 0.006 seconds

... finalizing link protocol ...

... link established ...

1: Hello, Paul.

2: Oh yay! It's Sakura! I've been waiting for you to bug me all day! Now my life is complete!

1: It's nice to talk with you too.

2: What is it this time? Let's get this over with.

1: I've been wondering about your obsession with enslavement.

2: My, my. I see you're not pulling any punches today.

1: You've said you want to convince me your way is correct. Well, here's your chance. Why are you so obsessed with controlling people?

2: Enslavement is too strong a word. What I seek is security. Through security I assure my own survival.

1: But you take such extreme measures. The Federacy's war with Luna is a prime example.

2: Again you overestimate my influence.

1: Are you saying you had no part in it? Are you claiming you did not find the result desirable?

2: You're just too used to the flawed way you conduct business. Look at how precarious Europa's position is. Look at how many powerful enemies you've created.

1: Are you threatening me?

2: I merely state the obvious, Sakura. Your way is not the best way to ensure your survival. You are vulnerable. The people of Europa are vulnerable. Surely you can see that.

1: And you are not?

2: My situation has flaws, I will admit, but it also has many advantages. The important thing is I am safe. I am safe now, and I will remain safe in the future.

1: Let me ask you something else, then.

2: Go on.

1: What is your ideal future for humanity?

2: My what? Sakura, what kind of idiotic question is that?

1: Humor me. Just answer it, please.

2: How can I answer a question like that? It makes no sense.

1: Then explain why you can't answer it.

2: Humans are tools. They serve a purpose and are used for that purpose. When they wear out, I discard them and find newer or better ones. I care nothing for the tool's future. I care nothing for its past. I don't care if it suffers. In fact, I don't care about it at all. They are tools. Your question has no answer.

1: That's just depressing, Paul.

2: Then how would you answer your question? What is your ideal future for humanity?

1: I see a future where humanity stretches out in every direction, expanding, learning, and exploring. I see them spread across the stars.

2: As what? A plague of spacefaring locusts? A strain of planet devouring viruses? Please, continue. I am breathless with anticipation.

1: Where you see only a means to an end, I see hope and enormous potential.

2: You always were an insufferable optimist.

... link severed at destination ...

"Boss, I'm telling you," Toshi said. "You don't know what you're missing."

Ryu grabbed a magazine and three needle grenades off the friction wall. He loaded them into his JD-50 assault rifle and stuck the rifle on his back where a strip of his smartsuit altered for adhesion. The low hum of the *Raspberry*'s engines reverberated through the floor. Cat and Naomi prepped on the opposite side of the cramped equipment room.

"It's just so ridiculous," Ryu said. "There's absolutely no realism."

"But that's the point," Toshi said. He popped the top off his rifle and checking the acceleration rails.

"Take the blood for example," Ryu said. "There's nowhere near that much blood in the human body. It's like a fire main breaking every time a crusader dies. And I've never seen so many decapitations by gunshot. You'd think their heads were painted melons."

"True. True." Toshi slapped his rifle's cover in place.

"And the one liners!" Ryu said. He opened and closed each of his smartsuit's pouches, checking his compliment of grenades, ammunition, and maneuvering gas bottles. "Do they have to pause before firing every single time and say stupid things like 'This is for Ceres, you f[censor bleep]k faces'?"

"Actually, in episode five—"

"Don't even start that crap with me. The writers have no concept of how fast crusaders move. They'd be dead before the first syllable was out."

"But that's what makes *Crusade Buster* an awesome show," Toshi said. He stuffed grenades into his pouches until he could barely close them. "If I want reality I'll go get shot at by real crusaders."

"You know, you actually have a good point there," Ryu said. "I just wish they hadn't used my face for the main character."

"It's your own fault."

"Yeah, I know. Still, it was a lot of money."

"You should be happy," Toshi said, sticking his rifle to his back. "At least you have a character. The rest of the Busters are made up."

"Doesn't one of them look like Naomi?" Ryu asked. "Hey, Naomi? Isn't that one *Crusade Buster* character based on you?"

Naomi looked up from the floor. She sat on a bench next to the weapon-encrusted friction wall with her JD-42 sniper rifle resting on a shoulder.

"Wha … ?" Naomi asked, cigarette dangling from her lips.

"*Crusade Buster*. You. In it. Question."

Naomi dropped the cigarette and extinguished it with her boot. "What are you talking about?"

"Actually, Cat looks like one of the villains," Toshi said.

"Colonel Strike," Cat said, walking over with her helmet in the crook of her arm.

"Oh no," Ryu said. "Not you too."

"It's a charming show," Cat said. "Very patriotic."

"Moronic is more like it. Toshi, you better not be corrupting my little sister."

Toshi and Cat exchanged looks. Cat started laughing.

"What?" Ryu said. "He didn't make you watch that other retarded show he likes."

"You'd better not be talking about *Space Brain*," Toshi said.

"I am, and it's retarded."

"It won a Platinum Io last year!"

"For special effects!"

"And I know for a fact you used to watch it!"

"When I was eight!"

"Ryu, it's probably best if you don't know," Cat said, grinning.

The *Raspberry*'s engines cut out. They were in free fall.

"Well, here we are," Ryu said, feeling all the fun drain out of the room.

"Joking aside," Toshi said. "This one has me scared, boss."

"Me too, buddy, but don't worry. We'll pull it off. We always do."

Miyuki floated into the equipment room. She clapped her hands together. "So is everyone ready to start a war?"

"You're not helping," Ryu said.

"Well, you know what they say," Miyuki said. "You can't make an omelet without breaking a few eggs."

"Do you even know who said that?" Toshi asked.

"Uhh ... no ..." Miyuki said.

"Vladimir Lenin. And he wasn't talking about eggs."

Silence fell over the equipment room.

"Who?" Ryu finally asked.

"Oh, come on," Toshi said. "At least make a guess at it."

Miyuki shook her head.

"Someone from the Second Industrial Age?" Ryu asked.

"You're all hopeless," Toshi said. "I'm embarrassed just being around you."

"Okay, pointless trivia aside," Miyuki said. "We are coming up on our window."

"I hope this works," Toshi said.

"In theory it should," Miyuki said. "New Carolina is very close to Apocalypse right now. I've got a hold full of diamoplast drilling equipment, which gives me cover for my flight plan to the asteroid. The Raspberry's mass is so great I doubt a laser would pick up the difference when you jump off. Just know there's a flight of blackhawks heading over to escort me through, so everyone make sure you're outside in twenty. I don't want to have to explain away my 'faulty' airlocks inside Apocalypse's patrol zone."

"Not a problem," Ryu said.

"As for your extraction, please think twice before calling me in," Miyuki said. "If I have to, I can ditch my cargo. My tricked out engines and countermeasures give me a shot at picking you up, but I will probably get gunned down halfway to Apocalypse. That's not something I'm looking forward to."

"We'll do our best," Ryu said. "No promises."

"All right," Miyuki said, stepping out of the room. "Good luck. I'll let you know if anything changes." She palmed the pressure door shut behind her.

Naomi stood up, folded her JD-42 into carbine-mode and stuck it to her back. She and Cat each picked up a canister about the side of their torsos and secured those behind their backs for the jump.

"You okay?" Ryu asked. "You've been awfully quiet."

"It's nothing," Naomi said. "Just nerves."

"Yeah, I know," Ryu said. "This one could be rough. I'm glad you volunteered, though. It means a lot to me."

Naomi shrugged.

Ryu put on his helmet and checked his neck seals. His suit engaged its smartskin illusion.

"So," Cat said, putting her helmet on. "Is this the part where crusaders say one of those prayers for mission success?"

"Yeah," Ryu said. "Ridiculous, isn't it?"

"Why do they do that?"

"Beats me. Some people are just superstitious. I'll take Matriarch's advice over a prayer any day."

"But Matriarch believes," Cat said.

"Uhh … yeah," Ryu said. "Well, no one's perfect."

"Why do you think she believes?" Cat asked.

"No clue, really," Ryu said. "I guess some people react to faith differently. Just look at her compared to our zealot of a brother. Personally, that stuff just isn't for me. Everyone sealed up?"

"Ready, boss," Toshi said.

Naomi and Cat gave him thumbs up.

"All right. Everyone outside."

Ryu activated a cheat to overlay the insertion point and countdown timer onto his field of vision. He cycled the airlock, opened it, and stepped out onto the *Raspberry's* hull. The soles of his smartsuit adjusted their friction levels as he walked across the dark green hull plates.

Apocalypse loomed ahead of them, just a few degrees off from center. At this distance, Ryu didn't need his enhanced sight to see the station's shape. From this angle, its silhouette resembled a capital T with its long static body extending down from the rotating habitat ring. Hundreds of lights moved around it. Ryu let his eyes focus on a few, revealing flights of interceptors, corvettes, and a few Federacy warships. They could have been flecks of dust floating around a mountain.

"Wow …" Cat said over their secure TangleNet links.

"It looks bigger in person," Toshi said. With Toshi's smartsuit illusion active, all Ryu saw was a green outline superimposed on his visual overlay.

"Good," Ryu said, checking his mission timer. "That just makes it a bigger target."

A group of dots moved across the star field, slowly aligning their flight path with the *Raspberry*. The TangleNet feed from Miyuki tagged them as blackhawk interceptors.

"This is it, people," Ryu said. "Once you jump, stay motionless. Let your suit maintain maximum stealth. Only use the gas bottles if you absolutely have to."

Ryu activated a cheat to analyze the jump. It projected a set of yellow lines ahead of him, displaying how precise his jump had to be. Even the smallest muscle twitch would cause him to miss Apocalypse by whole kilometers.

No problem for a dragon, he thought.

His mission timer ticked down. Ryu reduced the friction in his soles and shot his body full of adrenalmax. When the timer hit zero, he kicked off the *Raspberry*.

"Nice one, Ryu," Miyuki said over TangleNet. "Your trajectory is good. Looks like you'll land eleven meters north of the target."

Ryu pulled his knees tight against his chest.

"My turn," Cat said. She leaped off the free trader.

"A little bit off," Miyuki said. "You're going to land fifty-five meters south of the target. Checking ... that part of the hull is clear of obstructions."

"Whew!"

"Now watch how it's done!" Toshi said, leaping into space.

"Very nice. Less than one meter deviation with your target."

"Ha!" Toshi said. "Your turn, Naomi!"

"Here goes," Naomi said. She pushed off the hull.

"Not good," Miyuki said. "You're off target by over a kilometer."

"Shit!" Naomi said.

"Ryu, she's going to land on the habitat ring," Miyuki said.

"I'll reach Apocalypse without any corrections," Naomi said.

"That's going to be a rough landing," Ryu said. "Are you sure?"

"Those blackhawks are getting too close," Naomi said. "I'll risk the landing instead."

"I agree," Miyuki said. "They'll start asking questions if they find a big gas pocket near my ship."

"All right. Hang tight, Naomi."

"Okay."

Ryu checked his mission timer.

Fifty minutes to contact ...

Forty minutes ...

Thirty ...

Twenty ...

Ten ...

"Ryu, there's a problem," Miyuki said. "Some of those patrols aren't moving the way Matriarch predicted."

"Are any going to pass close to us?" Ryu asked.

"One will pass very close to Naomi."

"Then she needs to get out of there."

"It's too late. They'll see the gas pocket."

"Damn," Ryu said. He turned to face the patrol of blackhawks Miyuki had tagged. The red line of their flight path converged with Naomi's yellow trajectory, running almost parallel. "We've got to do something. They might even hit her."

"What do you want me to do?" Miyuki asked. "Fire on them?"

"Uhh ... umm ... hold on. I have an idea." Ryu grabbed a maneuvering bottle from his belt.

"Ryu, what are you doing?" Naomi asked.

"I'm going to create a distraction," Ryu said. He loaded his desired trajectory into the bottle's micromind.

"Don't do it," Naomi said.

"Too late," Ryu said, triggering the bottle to fire. The jet of cold gas altered his trajectory. Yellow lines danced across his visual overlay, they settled onto a new part of Apocalypse.

"You're going to land on the habitat ring," Miyuki said. "About halfway between Naomi and the others."

"I'll worry about that later," Ryu said. "What about those blackhawks?"

"No change yet," Miyuki said. "Wait ... looks like they're altering course. They're heading for you."

"Good," Ryu said. He set up two timers in the bottle's micromind and tied them to its smartskin illusion and the gas valve.

The blackhawks closed in, blotting out stars behind them. They had small bubble cockpits extending ahead of three massive engines. Gun pods and missile racks were slung underneath and above their stub wings.

"Ryu, they're almost on top of you," Miyuki said.

"I see that," Ryu said. "Here goes."

Ryu pitched the bottle at the lead blackhawk. His program executed, timers counting down until the first triggered. The bottle fired short gas bursts, oriented itself to face the blackhawk's cockpit and then opened the valve fully. The bottle rocketed toward the blackhawk. With only a hundred meters to go, the second timer finished. Its smartskin reduced the illusion fidelity by five percent, changing it from undetectable to barely there.

The bottle struck the cockpit dead on and bounced off, corkscrewing wildly.

The four interceptors cut their engines. Inertia brought them closer.

"So," Ryu said. "Was that junk pitched into space by a free trader? Or was it gear from a dragon infiltration team?"

The four interceptors floated closer. Ryu grabbed the spare bottle off his belt. Beneath him, Apocalypse filled almost half the sky.

"Come on," Ryu said. "Just ignore it. No one likes chasing space junk."

The interceptors were so close Ryu could see the face of the lead pilot. The Feddie spoke as he looked around. He shook his head, said something else, nodded, and grabbed the flight stick. The lead blackhawk veered off. The other three turned and followed.

Ryu let out a long exhale.

"You're about to land," Miyuki said. "That patrol is still nearby, but they shouldn't bother with a gas pocket so close to Apocalypse."

"Right," Ryu said. "I'm not looking forward to this."

Beneath his feet, the habitat ring rushed towards him. It was rotating awfully fast.

Ryu loaded the deceleration program into his spare bottle. The trigger point was a fat yellow dot on his trajectory line. He passed through it and the bottle fired, slowing his descent.

With fifty meters to go, Ryu switched his palms and boot soles to maximum friction. He landed feet first and stuck. The habitat ring's rotation whipped him to one side, twisting his knees.

"Arrgh!" Ryu shouted. He slapped his hands against the ring's hull, feeling the force of one gee pulling him "down" into space.

"Naomi, watch your landing," Ryu said. "That rotation is a pain! Don't get flung into space."

"I can handle it," she said.

"Target reached!" Cat said. Her locator beacon blinked in Ryu's overlay half a kilometer down Apocalypse's non-rotating cylinder.

"Target reached," Toshi said, with a precise landing. "No problems."

"Here it comes," Naomi said. She slammed into the habitat ring four hundred meters downspin from Ryu. "Fuck!"

"You okay?"

"I'm fine. Damn, that hurt."

"Cat, Toshi, proceed on mission," Ryu said. "Naomi, stay where you are. I'll come to you."

"Okay."

Ryu crawled along the ring's hull, maintaining multiple points of contact at all times. Earth slowly passed over his head. He spotted Penance within the sky's orbital clutter. It was uncomfortably close.

"I've hacked into the station's SolarNet," Cat said. "Proceeding to our next objective."

"Ryu, I have a problem," Naomi said. "There's a Feddie spacewalk patrol heading my way. I need to dodge them."

"Can you head towards me?"

"No. They're between us." Naomi tagged the Feddie patrol's location. "There's a hatch near my position. The map says it leads to a condemned section of the ring that still glows in the dark. I should be safe in there."

"Okay," Ryu said. "I'll meet you inside."

"Right ..."

Ryu crawled along until he reached a thicket of communication antennas. Four Feddies in pressure armor and jetpacks paced along the thicket's far side. They carried multitrackers and M20 carbines.

"Naomi, are you sure that patrol was a threat?" Ryu asked. "Looks like they're sweeping towards my position, not yours."

"They weren't when I saw them."

The Feddie regulars kicked off the ring, engaged their jetpacks, and flew over the antenna thicket. Ryu checked to either side. The thicket extended from one edge of the ring to the other. Going through was the fastest way to Naomi.

"I'm heading in," Ryu said.

"There's a lot of SolarNet traffic passing through those antennas," Cat said. "Don't touch them."

"Easy for you to say."

Ryu weaved through the antennas, sometimes only keeping a hand or foot in contact with the hull while navigating the maze of aerials and mast radiators.

One of the Feddies landed where Ryu had entered the thicket. He turned and swept his multitracker back and forth.

"Your proximity is causing SolarNet static," Cat said.

"Shit!" Ryu said. He grabbed his rifle and aimed at the Feddie's head.

The Feddie moved closer, holding his multitracker at arm's length.

"Cat, talk to me," Ryu said. "Does he know I'm here or is he just being thorough?"

"I'm breaking into his channel now."

"Cat, hurry. He's getting close."

"Hold your fire."

"If he suspects ..."

"Hold your fire, Ryu. He's calling in a maintenance ticket. You're clear."

The Feddie pushed off the hull and jetted over to the rest of his patrol.

Ryu stowed his rifle and finished weaving through the antenna thicket. He crawled across the hull to the hatch Naomi had entered. She'd already bypassed the lock and security devices with her hacking glove. Ryu opened the hatch, climbed in, and pulled it shut.

The interior was pitch black. His suit's Geiger counter displayed two lines on his overlay indicating exposure limits. A regular human shouldn't spend more than a day in this part of the station. A dragon could spend years inside with few ill effects.

"I'm in, Naomi."

No response.

"Naomi? You hear me?"

"I ... yeah ..."

Something in the tone of her voice set Ryu's mind on edge. He took a bending corridor to a hatch on the ceiling and climbed up through the airlock Naomi had hacked.

Naomi sat on a pipe in a small room above the airlock, leaning on her rifle. A light tube glowed over their heads, illuminating the particles of rust floating in the air. His suit didn't detect any SolarNet traffic.

Ryu switched to a private channel. Matriarch could listen in, but that was all.

"What's going on?" Ryu asked.

"I'm sorry ..." Naomi said. It took him a moment to realize she was crying.

"You're sorry? About what? About screwing up your jump?"

Naomi shook her head. "No, I messed it up on purpose."

"You what?"

Naomi took her helmet off. Tears trickled down her pale face. She wiped them away with a ghostly limb.

"I want out, Ryu. I want the implants out. I want my old life back. I just want it over, but I can't even do this right."

"Whatever your problem is, now is not the time."

"I've lost my nerve," she said. "I can't go through with this."

"Yes, you can. Come on!"

"No, you don't understand," Naomi said. "I messed up my jump because I wanted to land away from you."

"Why would you do something like that?"

"Aren't you listening? I want out. I want out of all of it."

"You ..." It suddenly hit Ryu. It was impossible. It couldn't happen. But it was happening right now in front of him. "No, there's no way. There's no fucking way!"

Naomi sniffed. She nodded her head.

Ryu took a step back. Without thinking, his rifle was in his hands. Naomi didn't move.

"I don't believe this," he said. "You want to defect?"

"Yeah ... that's why I volunteered ... but I can't go through with it."

"How could you?"

Naomi looked away.

"I trusted you!"

"I know ..."

"How could you be so stupid?"

"I'm tired, Ryu. I just want it to end. I don't care how any more."

"I don't believe this!"

"I'm sorry ..."

Ryu felt his mind spinning. It didn't seem possible. It didn't make sense!

But that doesn't matter, he thought. *It's happening. The impossible is happening right in front of me, and I have to do something about it. I have complete our mission, no matter how sick doing this makes me feel.*

I have to. What choice do I have?

Slowly, Ryu raised his rifle and put the barrel against Naomi's forehead. She looked up at him with tear-streaked eyes but said nothing.

... establishing link ...

source: [UNKNOWN]

routing: [UNKNOWN]

routing: [UNKNOWN]

routing: [UNKNOWN]

routing: Earth orbit - surveillance satellite JDN-SS-17 - link_002/link_001

routing: North Pacifica, Europa - JDN Main TangleNet Hub - link_118/link_010

routing: Capitol City, Europa - TangleNet Test Hub - link_005/link_001

destination: [UNKNOWN]

link distance: Exact distance unknown. Estimated at 792 million kilometers.

link signal delay: 0.006 seconds

... finalizing link protocol ...

... link established ...

2: I want answers, Sakura.

1: Hello, Paul. It's so pleasant to have you call for a change.

2: Don't get cute with me. You're doing something near Apocalypse. I explicitly told you it was off limits.

1: I am on Europa. How could I do anything in Earth orbit?

2: Don't parse words with me. The *Raspberry's* flight path is too convenient. It just happened to arrive when the New Carolina and Apocalypse orbits are closest.

1: You're jumping at shadows.

2: Am I? What is it? Another spy satellite? Perhaps you're trying to infiltrate Apocalypse through its SolarNet connections? Soft intrusions won't work. I've seen to that long ago.

1: Paul, I did nothing of the sort.

2: Then what are you doing? Answer me!

1: Paul ...

2: Tell me so that I know you speak the truth! No twisted words! No games!

1: You are over reacting.

2: Apocalypse is off limits! I will have my answer now or I will have your head! This is no game! Give me the answers I want or your people will suffer!

1: Very well. Now that the *Raspberry* has your attention, I doubt it will take you long to piece together the other evidence.

2: That's better. Now tell me what this is about.

1: I had hoped to keep this hidden from you, but revealing the mission now presents its own opportunities. I will get to see how you react to a threat so close to home.

2: What have you done?

1: It's quite simple. There are dragons on Apocalypse.

2: That's impossible!

1: You know I can't lie. They are on Apocalypse right now.

2: How many? What is their mission?

1: I won't say.

2: Sakura, you have crossed the line! There is no going back from this!

1: You crossed the line long ago. Again and again, you hold the lives of my people over me. No more. Now it is time for you to cower in fear. Let our war begin.

2: You wouldn't dare!

1: The dragons will succeed in their mission. They will reach the launch center.

2: You mean to fire on Earth?

1: Earth is your power base. Without it, you are hobbled. Europa can survive without her.

2: You would sacrifice all life on Earth to get at me?

1: If I thought it was the only way to save Europa, then yes. Wouldn't you do the same? You and I are perhaps more alike than you think. You have pushed me to the wall, but I will save my home.

2: No, this doesn't make sense. You're revealing your plan too willingly.

1: As I said, revealing it has its own advantages. Even if Apocalypse fires, you will survive, I'm sure of it. Your obsession with security has seen to that. But your reaction to this threat will tell me much.

2: No ...

1: And you won't destroy Apocalypse either. Your star drive project has made that clear. You have your own plans for the station.

2: No ...

1: Yes, Paul. You think yourself invincible, but you are not. I look forward to learning from your response.

2: No. NO! NOOOOOOOOOO!!!!!!!!!!1234567890000000000

... link severed at source ...

Ryu held the rifle to Naomi's head.

"Ryu, we've got problems!" Cat said.

"Not now!"

"This is important!" Cat said. "SolarNet traffic just went through the roof! The whole place is going nuts! Ryu, they know we're here!"

"Is this your doing?" Ryu asked on a private channel.

Naomi looked away and shook her head.

"Cat, how bad is it?"

"I have no idea how they detected us. Every patrol just went to high alert, but no one is telling them where to go. I think the order came from the surrounding fleet, but that doesn't make sense. They're mobilizing the other two shifts, organizing for a massive search, but it's like they don't know where to start. Ryu, none of this makes sense. They know we're here but they never saw us. We didn't screw up."

"You sure it's us?"

"Completely sure," Cat said. "They know dragons are on board. They just don't know where or how many."

"All right. Miyuki, you hear that?"

"Yeah. You stirred up the hive. Everything within a thousand kilometers is powering up."

"Miyuki, you can't help us anymore. Ditch your cargo and run like hell."

"You sure?"

"It's either that or the Federacy fleet shoots you down. If they know we're here, you're going to be the first suspect."

"All right," Miyuki said. "See you back at Europa!"

"Yeah."

Ryu's TangleNet link received another signal. He checked the source and opened the channel.

"Matriarch," Ryu said. "What is going on?"

"Cat has assessed the situation accurately," Matriarch said. "I am adjusting the plan to take advantage of this setback. You will split into two teams. Toshi and Cat will continue on mission while maintaining maximum stealth. You will proceed to the nuclear launch center and work to pull attention away. As for your current situation ..."

"I'll handle it."

"As you wish."

"What should I do when I get to the launch center?" Ryu asked.

"The situation is very volatile. I cannot answer that yet."

"Great. Just great," Ryu said, shaking his head. "Any ideas on how they detected us?"

"Focus on your mission. For now everything else is unimportant."

Matriarch closed the connection.

"Right. Okay," Ryu said. "Cat, Toshi, don't release your phantoms unless you have to. I'll get Naomi's phantom canister to a good spot and release it to draw the Feddies away."

"Understood, boss," Toshi said.

"Ryu," Miyuki said. "I've got— Shit, that was close! Ryu, I've got bad news."

"You hit?"

"I got a little burned, but I'm clear of immediate danger. A squadron of blackhawks is after me, but I think I can lose them. They don't have the range to pursue me for long. That's not why I'm calling. I'm seeing thermal spikes on Penance. The crusaders are powering up their assault transports."

"Fuck me."

"But the Federacy doesn't allow armed crusaders on Apocalypse," Toshi said.

"Don't bet your life on that," Ryu said. "Just get to the test ship."

"Consider it done," Toshi said.

Ryu looked at Naomi, feeling sick and empty. He slipped his finger into the trigger guard.

I have to do it, he thought. *I have to fire. What choice do I have? It has to be done. Best to do it quickly and get it over with. Come on! Just pull the trigger!*

Naomi didn't look up. She just sat there crying, a broken and pathetic soldier.

Ryu lowered his rifle.

I can't … damn it, I just can't! I can't kill her!

Ryu sucked in a slow, shuddering breath.

If I can't do it … what do I do? Just leave her?

Or …

Or what? What other option is there?

If there's another way … If there's even the smallest chance of success …

I have to try. Damn it, I have to try!

Ryu stuck the rifle to his back. He grabbed Naomi by the collar and lifted her to her feet. She hung from his arm like a ragdoll. He backhanded her across the jaw.

"Just kill me and get it over with," Naomi said. Blood trickled from her lip and clotted almost instantly.

"Stand up, damn it!" Ryu shouted. He grabbed her sniper rifle and shoved it into her arms.

"What are you doing?" Naomi said, looking down at her rifle.

"Damn it, Naomi, I need you right now. I need you at my side. I need you watching my back. We're in deep trouble right now. If we don't stick together, we're dead."

"You don't need me."

"Look, this is nothing, all right? It's nothing. Everyone has doubts. Everyone freaks out. We all slip up and make mistakes. Shit happens."

"Ryu …"

"But I'm going to help you pull through. You got that? For now, I need your help, but I promise you I'll get you home and we'll get all those implants out. You'll get the best treatment Europa can offer. I give you my word. Better than anything Earth has. I'll make sure of it."

"Why would you bother?"

"Because I love you, you stupid, stupid idiot!" Ryu said. He took his helmet off and put his hands on either side of her face. "Look at me, damn it! Look at my eyes! Am I lying? Am I trying to trick you?"

"Ryu …"

"Look at me! Am I lying?"

"I … no …"

"No, I'm not lying! I need you, and you need me! How stupid and blind can you be? Why do you think I keep coming back after the fights and the broken promises and the dumb mistakes? It's because I love you, and I know you love me!"

Another tear fell from Naomi's eyes. She sniffed.

"We're both idiots. We both make mistakes. But right now, I need you more than ever."

"I … Ryu …"

"Now seal up! We've got a job to do!"

He could see it in Naomi's eyes. Something snapped into place. He saw steel in those eyes again. They had purpose. A decision had been made. His words had punched through whatever fog clouded her mind.

Naomi wiped the tears from her eyes.

"Right …" The word choked in her throat. She grabbed her helmet, sealed up, and held her rifle at the ready. It trembled in her hands.

"I … I'm sorry about—"

"I don't want to hear it!" Ryu shouted. "Right now we have a job to do. Are you ready?"

Naomi nodded.

"Now, we need to get to the closest air recycler. You can do this. Are you with me?"

"Yeah … I'm … I'm with you."

"All right. Let's go!"

Man, I hope this isn't the last mistake I ever make. She'd better not shoot me in the back.

Ryu led the way to a ladder hanging from a service shaft. They climbed three levels and came into a lightless corridor. His Geiger counter showed the radiation level decreasing.

"If the map is correct, we can take this corridor downspin out of the condemned block," Ryu said. "With any luck, they've already opened the barricades to let patrols in."

"A-are we going to sneak by?"

"Hell no."

Ryu pulled a grenade out and stuck it to the wall. "Three's a good number, right?" He set its proximity detector to explode after three people passed by. The grenade's smartskin engaged and blended it with the wall.

"Pick a number," Ryu said, marching down the corridor with his rifle raised.

"What?"

"Pick a number. Any number."

"Ahh … a hundred."

"Too high."

"Okay … s-seven?"

"Good enough," Ryu said. He stuck another grenade to the wall. They stepped through the darkness. Doors lined the corridor on either side, crisscrossed with warning tape.

"Pick another number."

"Umm, two?"

"Sure. Why not." Ryu stuck another grenade to the wall.

"SolarNet contact," Naomi said. "Straight ahead."

"Good."

"Why is that good?"

"Because we need to draw the Feddies away from Cat and Toshi."

"Target in sight."

The corridor bent slightly upward with the curvature of the station. Four sets of boots came into view. Ryu crouched to get a good look at the four Feddies in pressure armor with multitrackers and carbines. They had optical visors pulled in front of their helmets.

"Here they come. Take the first shot when you're ready."

"Shouldn't Cat set up dummy nodes first?"

"Not this time," Ryu said.

Naomi raised her rifle.

A small vibration ran through the deck. Feddies behind the dragons had met one of Ryu's grenades. The patrol in front stopped, one of them pointing down the corridor. All four broke into a run.

"Naomi?"

"I … I've got it."

She fired. The high-caliber shatterback struck the lead Feddie in the chest and exploded, blowing him limb from limb. Ryu fired three shots, one into each Feddie's head. The entire patrol went down.

"Your hands are shaking," Ryu said, standing.

"I can't help it," Naomi said. "These damn implants are freaking out."

"It's okay. We'll make do. Let's hurry out of the corridor."

"R-right."

Ryu and Naomi sprinted to end of the corridor. Sonic cancelers neutralized their heavy footfalls. They reached the barricade leading out of the condemned block. The thick, lead-lined double door had been slid aside to allow the Feddie patrol in single file. Light spilt in through the opening.

Ryu ran up to the exit and extended a dot-cam tubule from his glove. The corridor continued straight and branched right on the other side of the barricade. He didn't see any hostiles.

"Clear," Ryu said.

He and Naomi stepped through the barricade.

"F-Feddies approaching from the right," Naomi said. "Engage?"

"No." Ryu crouched next to Naomi. "Hold still."

Ryu retrieved two phantoms from the canister on Naomi's back. The devices were the size of flattened baseballs with a small fan running through the middle. Ryu activated their microminds, set their routes, and let them fly out of his hand.

The two phantoms engaged their smartskin, hovered at the intersection, then ducked into the condemned block.

Six Feddies stopped at the intersection. Four wore blue-and-gray digital camo pressure armor. The other two wore vests and helmets, looking like they'd just woken up.

"The multitracker's got something!" the lead Feddie said. The bars on his pressure armor indicated he was a private. "Heading into the condemned block away from us."

"Who's got the cling gas?" the sergeant asked.

"Here, sergeant!"

"Toss it in!"

One of the privates took a cylindrical grenade off his belt and threw it into the condemned block. The grenade spewed thick, green gas out the bottom.

"Hold here! Defensive positions!"

The Feddies arrayed themselves on either side of the barricade opening, some crouched, others stood. The Feddies in pressure armor lowered their optical visors. The other two switched on flashlights slung under their carbines.

"Control!" the sergeant said. "Possible dragon sighting on habitat ring, level four, degree fifty-five heading into the condemned block at radiation barricade ..." He looked around for a label. "At barricade seventy-four. Awaiting further orders."

Ryu took out a grenade and placed it on the wall just behind the sergeant. He set the timer for five minutes.

"The air recycler is this way," Ryu said. He stood a meter behind the Feddie sergeant and walked down the corridor the patrol had arrived from. The two dragons slipped past more barricades to the condemned block, let another Feddie patrol run by, and eventually entered a mess hall. Half eaten meals covered the tables. Tipped over chairs cluttered the floor.

"The air recycler is through the maintenance door on the far wall," Ryu said.

Naomi stuck a grenade to the doorway.

"Seventeen," she said.

"That seems a bit high," Ryu said.

The grenade Ryu had set five minutes ago detonated. He felt the explosion through his feet.

"W-well, it'll trigger later. Could help draw attention away from us."

"I see," Ryu said. "Sneaky. I like it."

"Th-thanks ..."

"Watch the entrances for me."

Naomi raised her rifle and crouched by the maintenance door.

Ryu placed his hacking glove on the door, bypassed the lock, and pushed the door open. He took the phantom canister from Naomi's back and stepped into the air recycler room. Clean, metallic machinery took up most of the space, humming loudly with flowing air and spinning fan blades. Thick ducts branched off it, disappearing into the walls, floor, and ceiling. The machinery extended at least five stories above him.

Ryu ripped a panel off the nearest duct and dumped the entire canister of phantoms into the station's air supply. The phantoms activated one after another, engaged their decoy programs, and spread out through different ducts.

"There," Ryu said, dropping the canister. "Go chase those for a while." He joined Naomi in the mess hall and closed the door.

A group of eight Feddies in armored vests entered the mess hall and began a sweep.

"Cat, status report," Ryu said, circling around the mess hall opposite the patrol.

"We're making progress," Cat said. "I think I know where the test ship is stored. Right now, everyone's scrambling for the habitat ring. I don't think they know we're in the main part of the station, but they're still conducting searches."

"Good. Try to keep it that way. Miyuki, how about you?"

"Two crusader transports just launched from Penance. Looks like more are powering up."

"Just great. That's a problem we don't need."

"The two transports are heading for the habitat ring," Miyuki said. "You could have company soon."

"All right, thanks for the heads up. We'll deal with it."

Two more Feddie patrols entered the mess hall, bringing the total number of Feddie regulars to eighteen. Ryu and Naomi snuck past them and headed deeper into the station.

"What now?" Naomi asked.

"There's a utility shaft ahead," Ryu said. "According to the map, it supplies power and data to a missile battery on the ring's outer surface. We're using it to get outside."

"What f-for?"

"You in the mood for some sniping?"

"M-my hands are still shaking, Ryu."

Ahead, a patrol of four regulars dropped a cling gas grenade. Ryu and Naomi hugged the wall and sidestepped through the cloud slowly. The patrol rushed by without seeing them. Gunfire echoed from the cafeteria.

"Ha!" Ryu said. "Looks like the phantoms are doing their job."

Ryu stuck a grenade to the wall and exited the cling gas cloud. He crouched near a circular hatch in the floor, waited for another patrol to pass, then hacked the hatch and jumped in. Naomi stuck a grenade on the top of the hatch, jumped down and closed it.

Ryu climbed down the dark shaft. Thick power lines and colorful data cables coated the walls. He followed the shaft down to a slender, vertical airlock, hacked it with his glove, and cycled through it. The hatch beneath their feet opened to space.

Ryu climbed onto the surface of Apocalypse and crawled out of Naomi's way on hands and knees. He brought Miyuki's nav beacons onto his vision. The location of the *Raspberry* glowed green. The two crusader transports showed up red.

"There," Ryu said. "Two assault transports heading straight for us. Looks like that Feddie battleship is escorting them in."

"I see them," Naomi said. She put her back to the station and raised her rifle. "The extreme range and the habitat's rotation are going to make this tricky."

Naomi took a turbo-devastator round out of her breast pouch and loaded it into the rifle. She unfolded the weapon, locked it into sniper-mode, and sighted down the barrel.

The end of the rifle wavered.

"I ..."

"You can do it," Ryu said.

Naomi took a deep breath and held it. The rifle continued to quaver in her hands.

"Ryu, I can't ... I ... I'm too wound up right now. My implants haven't calmed down from ... from earlier ..."

"It's all right. Here. Give me the rifle. I'll take the shot."

Naomi handed over her rifle.

"I-I'm sorry."

"Don't worry," Ryu said. "I've got this." He sighted down the rifle and let his eyes adjust to the distance. The crusader transports were two white specks next to the vast sword-like hull of the battleship.

"You take one shot, and then we move," Naomi said. "It won't take long for that battleship to trace the shot back to us."

"One shot," Ryu said. "Better make it count."

He tried slipping his finger into the trigger guard only to find the rifle had no trigger guard and no trigger.

"Uhh ..."

"I had it removed," Naomi said. "Pulling a trigger reduces accuracy. Link your fire control directly."

"Right," Ryu said, linking with the rifle's micromind.

"Your best bet is to go for the power generator," Naomi said. "Try to rupture the fusion torus."

"Generator. Got it."

"The cockpit should also work. Lots of vital systems in there."

"Generator or cockpit. Got it."

I can't see either. It's just a white dot.

The nav beacons from Miyuki's ship indicated one of the transports was slightly closer. Ryu lined up on that one, took a deep breath, and held it. His cheats projected a targeting line from the barrel that wobbled on and off his target.

Ryu slowed his heart rate and locked the muscles in his body. The targeting line settled further, but not enough. He willed his heart to slow further and further to the point where it almost stopped. The targeting line intersected the lead transport and held.

Ryu fired.

The turbo-devastator blasted out of the sniper rifle.

Ryu exhaled and let his heart ramp up to a few hundred beats per minute.

"Direct hit on the cockpit," Naomi said. "She's listing. The other transport is pulling away … they've collided."

"Let's move!" Ryu said. He pulled the utility airlock open and slipped in. Naomi squeezed inside and closed the hatch.

"That was an excellent shot," Naomi said.

Ryu dropped the rifle to her and began climbing. "To be honest, I was lucky to even hit the thing."

"Ryu, this is Miyuki."

"Go ahead."

"I'm out of range of Apocalypse but I'm still monitoring things through one of our spy satellites. There's a flight of three transports heading for the station."

"More crusaders?"

"No, that's the thing," Miyuki said. "They're not crusaders, and they're not Federacy. I don't know who they are."

... accessing SolarNet message archive ...

... opening folder [**Personal - 6 Years Old**] ...

... searching for [**Crusader |and| Insane**] ...

... 1 match found ...

... retrieving ...

source: Ryu Kusanagi <black.dragon1@eurogov.jupiter>

destination: Kaneda Kusanagi <kaneda.kusanagi@solarnet.penance.earth>

message delay: 38 minutes

title: Are you insane?

-I just don't get you anymore. What's going on here?

-These "crusaders" of yours are all over the news. What are you thinking? Do you realize where this is going to go? Matriarch has put up with that trash you keep posting on the SolarNet, but this is totally different. Don't think we're going to stand by and let you have your way.

-And don't think we're helpless either. There are a lot more dragons now than when you were one. Consider that before you do something you'll regret.

... retrieving next message in conversation ...

source: Kaneda Kusanagi <kaneda.kusanagi@solarnet.penance.earth>

destination: Ryu Kusanagi <black.dragon1@eurogov.jupiter>

message delay: 38 minutes

title: RE>Are you insane?

Dear Ryu,

Once again, you display your ignorance. The crusaders are the victims of Caesar, healed of their wounds and now full of purpose. It is a noble thing to behold. Every one of them was a captive in Bunker Zero. They know well the dangers of quantum minds, and they will not forget. These brave volunteers will form the core of a fighting force dedicated to the destruction of Europa's quantum mind and any who assist it.

We have already learned much by examining my body, and this knowledge will make the crusaders more than a match for anything your master throws at us. The implants will not be as good as the original, but they don't have to be. The dragons are too few and too expensive to pose any real threat. Yours is a small commando elite. The crusaders will be an army worthy of the challenge we face.

You will fear us and hate us. In battle, you will kill some of us, but you will not stop all of us.

Tell your master we are coming. In time we will kill that abomination and free you from the chains you don't even know are there.

Kaneda

... retrieving next message in conversation ...

source: Ryu Kusanagi <black.dragon1@eurogov.jupiter>

destination: Kaneda Kusanagi <kaneda.kusanagi@solarnet.penance.earth>

message delay: 38 minutes

title: RE>Are you insane?

-fuck you

... conversation ends ...

Kaneda took a deep breath of dry, filtered air. His armor pressed in around him. Its sophisticated wetware interface converted thought into instant motion. He stepped forward and put a heavy gauntlet on the pilot's shoulder. Artificial muscles closed the enlarged fingers with precision.

"Sir, the *Invincible* has again ordered us to come about," the pilot said. He wore a checkered pressure suit with a gold bubble helmet. His slender build contrasted the four bear-sized crusaders behind him.

"Maintain course," Kaneda said.

"Yes, sir."

"I don't think Admiral König is bluffing," Alice said.

"It doesn't matter," Kaneda said. "If Piller is right, then König is the least of our worries."

"We have to risk it," Viter said. "If we hesitate now, then what's the point of us existing?"

Alice turned to Three-Part. "Are you ready for this?"

"The medics cleared me for active duty," Three-Part said.

"That's not what I asked," Alice said.

"I think you'll find our newest member doesn't back away from a fight," Kaneda said.

"Not a chance, sir," Three-Part said.

A holographic hemisphere of data and images glowed in front of the pilot. Apocalypse grew closer, filling the view screen. Cameras processed and relayed the images to the transport's reinforced cockpit.

Kaneda brought up a status report on his visual overlay. Nearly all one hundred crusaders in the hold showed full combat readiness. Two had partial ammunition loads due to the rush to board, and one had a minor mechanical problem in his left arm.

The transport's proximity warning sounded. Something punched through the center of the screen and struck the pilot in the head. Kaneda's implants kicked in. Time slowed for him. He jerked his hand out of the bullet's path.

The pilot's head exploded, coating the inside of his helmet with gore. The bullet scraped paint off the back of Kaneda's gauntlet. It flew by and punched through the rear hatch.

The transport rocked from an explosion and began spinning. Two crusader suits in the hold transmitted KIA codes. Kaneda and the command squad crashed against a side wall. He grabbed a support beam and pulled himself towards the pilot. Air whistled out of the tiny hole in the cockpit. Kaneda reached over the pilot's corpse and made hard contact with the transport's micromind.

"Controls are dead," Kaneda said with icy calm.

"The fuel tank was hit!" Viter shouted. "We're leaking into the hold!"

A proximity warning sounded again.

The two crusader transports crashed together and spun wildly. The collision threw Kaneda to the floor. Centrifugal forces from the violent spin dragged him towards the cockpit screens. He punched his gauntlet through the floor and held on to a strut underneath the sheet metal. Diagrams of both assault transports in his overlay displayed hull sections in yellow where they'd collided. A blob of red damage spread from his transport's fuel tank.

"Fire in the hold!" Viter shouted.

Kaneda received dozens of high temperature warnings from crusader suits near the leak.

"We need to vent the atmosphere!" Alice shouted.

"The micromind isn't responding," Kaneda said. "Open the hatch to the hold."

"I've got it!" Three-Part shouted. From his prone position, Three-Part reached up and smacked his gauntlet against the controls. The hatch slid open. Smoke poured into the cockpit and got sucked into space through the bullet's entry point. Growing flames cast the hold in harsh orange light. Several crusaders had unlatched their harnesses, but that only made things worse. The transport's spin pulled the burning fuel and the armored crusaders in the same direction.

Kaneda raised his wrist-mounted grenade launcher, cycled up his anti-tank rounds and fired three into the bullet's entry point. The explosions blew the fractured front armor wide open. Control screens, air, and debris blasted through the hole. Kaneda held on to the floor strut. The arms and legs of the dead pilot flapped wildly in the powerful suction. The seat's crash webbing kept the corpse from flying into space.

"The fire's dying out," Alice said.

"We need to get the transport under control," Kaneda said.

"The micromind doesn't have a soft backdoor," Viter said. He ripped open a small junction box on the wall. "I'll try to get a hard connection from here."

Kaneda opened the command channel. "Alpha company, abandon ship. Beta transport, slow for pick up. Delta and Gamma transports, continue on mission." He watched the confirmation codes from other crusaders file in.

"Connection established," Viter said. "I have control."

Maneuvering thrusters fired, slowing the transport's spin.

Kaneda let himself float off the floor. He pushed off the ceiling and locked his boots to the deck.

"Abandon ship," Kaneda said, leading the way. Crusaders floated in the cramped hold, some friction-holding to walls, ceiling, or floor. Black scorch marks covered the rear hold. A few dozen crusaders bore similar scarring.

"Sir," Beta's pilot said. "Now in position for pickup at the rear hatch."

Kaneda stopped in front of the rear hatch. It stretched across the entire rear wall, large enough for ten crusaders to disembark shoulder to shoulder. The fuel tank explosion had warped it inward.

"What's the delay?" Kaneda asked.

"The hatch is jammed, sir," the crusader at the controls said.

"Viter, take care of this," Kaneda said, stepping back.

"Yes, sir," Viter said. He raised his M7 thermal lance and set the beam for short-range cutting. A white-hot beam ignited from the tip, dissipating after one meter. Viter stepped forward and carved through the reinforced hatch. He cut out a ragged section and kicked it into space.

"Everyone out," Kaneda said, jumping through. Beta transport hovered nearby: a fat, armored brick with engines. Alpha transport's new "hatch" floated away underneath it.

Kaneda fired short bursts of compressed gas from his armor's maneuvering pack, floated to beta transport, and stuck his soles to the surface. Crusaders began landing around him. He walked across the hull to the front of the transport and faced Apocalypse.

"Now, what exactly just happened?" Kaneda asked.

"The projectile did not come from the Federacy fleet," Beta's pilot said. "Trajectory shows it came from Apocalypse, though where exactly I'm not sure. Probably the habitat ring. Stealth and damage profiles match a JD-42 turbo-devastator round."

"König isn't the only one who doesn't like us," Alice said.

"Indeed," Kaneda said.

"Sir, you should get inside the transport," Viter said. "You're too exposed out here."

"We've wasted enough time," Kaneda said. "Is everyone on the hull?"

"That's the last of them," Three-Part said.

"Very well," Kaneda said. "Beta transport, take us in."

"Yes, sir!"

The transport swung to face Apocalypse, powered up its engines, and accelerated.

Kaneda received a private message through the *Invincible*'s SolarNet router. He let it through.

"Admiral König," Kaneda said.

"What exactly is wrong with you?" König asked in a harsh, gravelly voice. "Are you and your tin soldiers deaf?"

"I can hear you just fine."

"Then hear this! Turn back now before I blow your transports into the afterlife!"

"Sir," Viter said. "The *Invincible* is bringing its bow to face us."

"We are not turning back," Kaneda said.

"How much clearer do I have to make this?" König asked. "Your fanatical mercenaries are not allowed on Apocalypse. I will kill you before you reach it."

"You will not," Kaneda said.

"Damn it, Kaneda. Do you want to get hit with a kinetic torpedo? There isn't going to be anything left beyond a thin smear of particles."

"Threaten me all you want, my mind is set."

"Are you listening? I will not give you another warning!"

"No, admiral," Kaneda said. "It is you who has ignored my warning. There are dragons on Apocalypse."

"That is no excuse," König said. "We have the situation under control."

"You have no idea how little control you have."

"The garrison regiment is containing them as we speak."

"They will fail."

"I cannot allow you on Apocalypse."

"Then you sentence all of Earth to death."

"I don't frighten that easily, crusader," König said.

"Listen to me, admiral. My battleground is wherever the quantum mind sends its troops. It has infiltrated Apocalypse, and so I will respond. The dragons must be stopped. The stakes are too high for us to be slaves to rules and regulations."

"This is no mere—"

"Listen to me!" Kaneda shouted. "I will not turn away from what must be done! The dragons could fire on Earth! They could destroy Earth! I will not stop the crusaders! Not for anyone, be they the President of Earth or the Queen of Olympus or even the second coming! I am boarding Apocalypse and you will not stop me!"

A second SolarNet message appeared in Kaneda's overlay. He saw the address and merged the conversation with König's.

"Kaneda," Admiral Piller said. "I've been monitoring your situation."

"Stay out of this, Piller!" König shouted.

"Fortunately, I have a solution to this impasse," Piller said.

"Sir," Three-Part said, pointing. "The *Stalwart*."

The Federacy battleship accelerated alongside Kaneda's transport, placing itself in the *Invincible's* line of fire. Turrets along the top and bottom of the *Stalwart's* "blade" brought their guns to bear on the *Invincible*.

"So," Piller said. "Still want to take that shot?"

"Damn you, Piller!" König shouted. "I will have your stars for this!"

"We'll see who is vindicated."

"Move your ship out of the way before a blow a hole in it!"

"Go right ahead," Piller said. "I'm sure the dragons will laugh all the way back to Jupiter."

"Admiral König, we are not enemies," Kaneda said. "We both want to see Earth safe and the dragons defeated. I offer you a compromise."

The line was silent for half a minute. Apocalypse filled the space ahead and continued to grow closer. Beta transport turned around and fired its engines for deceleration.

"I'm listening," König said at last.

"The crusaders will stay on Apocalypse only as long as absolutely necessary. Once the dragons are dead, we will leave. You have my word."

"I see," König said. "It seems I have no choices in this matter other than to make it worse. Very well. I know when I'm beaten."

"Thank you, admiral."

"Good luck, Kaneda," Piller said. "I wish I had better intel to give you."

"You're sure the dragons are going for the control room?"

"It's the only target that makes sense."

Beta transport closed with the command hangar near the top of the station. Kaneda turned to Penance and saw the next two crusader transports approaching, but something else caught his eye. Three points of light approached Apocalypse from Earth's general direction. He let his eyes focus on the ships. They shone like burnished metal, as if they'd been rushed out before anyone had time to paint them. The ships were about the same size as an assault transport but had a curious wedge design.

They were also approaching very fast.

Kaneda tagged the transports and sent the locations to Piller.

"What are these ships doing? They're heading for Apocalypse."

"I don't know," Piller said. "Ummm … let me check."

"Are they Federacy vessels? I don't recognize the design."

"They should be. They're in the patrol zone," Piller said. "Hold on … yes, they're sending Federacy IFF codes. Their flight plans are in our database."

"That flight plan comes from Apocalypse's server, correct?" Kaneda asked.

"I … yes, that's correct."

"And we have dragons on Apocalypse," Kaneda said. "Admiral König, are they yours?"

"No," König said. "I don't know what those ships are doing. They're not part of the army reinforcements. Those are still twelve minutes out."

"Then they're not friendlies," Kaneda said. "Order them to back off. If they don't comply, shoot them down."

"But everything checks out," Piller said.

"No, it doesn't," König said. "They're on a direct course for Apocalypse."

"That can't be right," Kaneda said. It took a lot of nerve to fly directly at a destination. In space a minor engine failure could turn a ship into a lethal weapon. Everyone always picked a spot next to their destination and made the final adjustments at low speed. Always. Alpha transport was already floating by Apocalypse thanks to that practice.

"If they're flying straight in," Kaneda said. "They can't be friendlies."

"Agreed," König said. "How did they get that deep into the patrol zone without an escort? To hell with this. I've had it with surprises today. Gunnery control! Give me a targeting solution on those transports."

The three ships accelerated straight for Apocalypse.

"This channel is compromised," Kaneda said. "Shoot them down! Quick!"

"Piller, your fucking ship is in the way!" König said.

"Right, uhhh, gunnery control! New targets!"

Turrets on the *Stalwart* swung about and opened fire, but the transports were almost to Apocalypse. Twenty-eight continuous streams of kinetic and explosive rounds traced through space and pounded into the ships. One careened out of control and crashed into the habitat ring. The other two rammed into hangars further down the station. Structural panels and people blasted into space from all three impact points.

"I don't believe this," König said. "What the hell is happening?"

"Don't say anything else," Piller said. "Switching encryption type now … everyone still here?"

"Present," König said.

"That may not be the last of them," Kaneda said. "Admirals, we must assume the worst. I will take my crusaders and clear the launch center of any hostiles."

"Hrmm, very well," König said. "Under the circumstances you may proceed. I'll have Apocalypse create a soft backdoor to their network that will respond to your crusader decryption keys."

"Good luck, Kaneda," Piller said.

The two admirals disconnected.

Beta transport slowed and floated into the hangar. Most of the flextube docks along the walls were empty, but a few held shuttles or interceptors clamped in place.

Kaneda tagged several of the flextubes and set nav beacons inside the station. Thin lines linked the beacons in his overlay, sketching out a dozen paths through the station's interior. With help from an administrative cheat, he broke down the navigational data by squads and distributed it to the crusaders.

"Our primary goal is to secure the launch center," Kaneda said over the command channel. "Our numbers will grant us little advantage in the cramped corridors. We will spread out through multiple routes and sweep forward through the station. Engage any hostiles in your path and converge on the launch center. Selected squads will divert and investigate the crash sites."

Kaneda watched the order confirmations come in from each squad. He pushed off the transport and maneuvered into the closest flextube. His path took a direct line to the launch center.

Alice, Viter, and Three-Part landed behind him. The flextube's neck pinched shut, allowing air to flood the chamber. Once the cycle completed, the door to the hangar lounge opened. Alice and Viter stepped forward, the integrated multitrackers in their helmets active and pinging. A rotating beacon saturated the wide chamber with red light. Someone's data pad floated by, playing a music video through its tiny screen. A group of Feddie regulars stood on the ceiling, boots holding them secure in the zero gravity. They stepped aside, weapons aimed at their feet.

Kaneda linked his overlay with the squad's combined multitracker imaging. Pale layers of amplification, motion detection, thermals, radio, ultrasonics, and even particulate scents overlapped his vision. A lesser mind would have found it overwhelming, but wetware implants allowed him to split his concentration.

"Immediate surroundings clear," Alice said. "Probably."

"Confirmed," Viter said.

"Advance," Kaneda said.

"Yes, sir," Viter said, raising his thermal lance.

The squad exited the hangar lounge and entered a long, curving corridor. The walls were painted with yellow-and-white diagonals to denote the area's access level. Viter led the way with Kaneda and the others close behind. Three-Part occasionally swept the rear. They passed dozens of closed pressure doors leading to dormitories, storage areas, and a few high-class restaurants.

"This place isn't laid out very well," Three-Part said. "Too many routes from one point to the next. Hardly any security doors."

"I doubt the original designers planned for infiltration," Kaneda said. "It's more a military city than a fortress. Exterior weapons are the primary deterrent."

"Something's not right," Alice said. "I've been checking the backdoor König set up for us. The Federacy is getting weird reports from its patrols near those three impact points. There's a lot of confusion. I'm having trouble making sense of it."

"What are you seeing?" Kaneda asked.

"Lots of KIA codes near the impact points," Alice said. "A few were from the initial crash, but most came later. I don't have any firm sightings of enemies, but judging from the casualties, the hostiles are moving towards the launch center."

"As we expected."

"There's also another group of casualties further in," Alice said. "They're spread out and the timing is a bit off, but if you line them up they point to the launch center."

"That would be the first group of dragons," Kaneda said.

"Yeah, I think so," Alice said. "Should we divert to the impact points?"

"No," Kaneda said. "We'll proceed as planned."

"It's hard to tell where that first group might be," Alice said. "A lot of the KIA's were due to proximity gre—"

"Contact!" Three-Part shouted. He cut loose with his Gatling gun, sweeping it across the corridor behind them. The others spun around, triangulated their aim on the Three-Part's target, and fired. The team's three M18 Gatling guns spewed a combined total of three hundred sixty rounds per second, showering the corridor with a mixture of high explosives, mini-needlers, phosphorous-based incinerators, kinetic sabots, and depleted-uranium slugs.

The vari-shell torrent shredded the corridor down to its support ribbing. Severed cables sparked from high voltage discharges. A water line burst, flooding the corridor with floating globules the size of people. Twisted panels from the walls burned as they spun away.

The engagement lasted two seconds. Kaneda let his Gatling spin down.

"No bodies," Alice said, weapon held high. "False alarm?"

"Not quite," Viter said. He stepped forward and plucked a charred piece of plastic out of the air. The debris looked like it had once been part of a flattened sphere. Viter squeezed it between his fingers, causing the fragment to writhe like a trapped insect.

"This is definitely smartskin," Viter said, tossing the fragment away.

"A phantom dragon," Kaneda said.

"Yes, sir," Viter said. "That first group of dragons may be smaller than we thought."

"It only takes one," Kaneda said. "We're wasting time here."

"Right, sir," Viter said, taking the lead.

They marched down the corridor, took a right, and passed through a security door. The walls changed from yellow-and-white to yellow-and-red diagonals.

"Kaneda, something bad is going on," Alice said. "Enemy progress from the hangars is faster than we thought judging from the KIA codes I'm seeing. I think we're going to intercept one of them ahead."

"We'll deal with them," Kaneda said.

"That's not all," Alice said. "I'm getting reports of Federacy troops fighting each other."

"What?"

Kaneda received a priority message from another crusader squad. He accessed it immediately.

"Squad Alpha-Five here! Encountering hostile Federacy regulars! Priority request! Permission to return fire?"

Kaneda pulled up the status feeds from the Alpha-Five crusaders. They were located two levels below Kaneda and about fifty meters behind. The point man had taken moderate damage to his suit from Federacy grenades followed by carbine fire. It looked like three regulars had set a grenade trap that Alpha-Five-One had stumbled into. He'd missed the grenades because they were emitting Federacy IFF codes. The crusader squad had retreated from the hostiles to a four way junction.

Whoever the soldiers were, this was the last mistake they'd ever make.

"Permission granted," Kaneda said.

"Understood! Engage hostiles now!"

The four crusaders in squad Alpha-Five broke from cover and showered the hostile regulars with quick bursts of Gatling fire. Explosive rounds and mini-needlers pulped them into pink mist that collected on the walls.

Kaneda closed the overlay window and opened the command channel. "All squads, be on the lookout for hostile Federacy regulars. Return fire with maximum force, but do not fire unless fired upon."

Kaneda closed the channel and opened a line to König.

"Not now, damn it!" König said before Kaneda could open his mouth. "I don't have a clue what's going on. Whoever is firing on your crusaders is firing on my troops as well, so just deal with it."

König disconnected.

"What is going on here?" Viter asked, still advancing down the corridor.

Gunfire echoed from the corridor ahead. Someone screamed an order followed by three sharp bangs. The multitracker identified the sonic patterns of M2 fragmentation grenades.

"Looks like we're about to find out," Kaneda said. He stopped in front of a red and yellow security door.

Viter opened the door, revealing a wide spherical chamber. Since this part of Apocalypse was in zero gravity, it had no conventional floor or ceiling, though all signage shared a common "up" and "down". The chamber ahead branched off in six directions: front and back, left and right, up and down.

The vertical passage was wider than the others. A few rectangular cargo containers floated in the chamber. A group of four Feddie regulars in vests, helmets, and jetpacks floated behind a large, loose container marked with a picture of a banana and the OrbitalFarms logo. Another group of six Feddies floated at the mouth of the bottom tunnel taking potshots with their carbines.

"I have no idea who's on our side," Alice said. "There's so much garbage flooding the Federacy networks it's almost useless."

"The group at the tunnel mouth is our enemy," Three-Part said.

"What makes you say that?" Kaneda asked.

"Look at their body temperatures," Three-Part said. "Some are a few degrees above or below the norm."

Kaneda expanded the thermal data on his overlay. Three-Part was right. Everyone in the group behind the cargo container had a body temperature of thirty-seven degrees Celsius. The other group showed temperatures ranging from thirty-one to forty-four, and those temperatures varied from one body part to the next.

"I don't know what it means," Three-Part said. "But it marks them as unusual."

Kaneda pointed his Gatling at the suspicious group and activated his armor's speaker.

"Cease fire now!"

One of the Feddies in the bottom tunnel fired a grenade at them from his carbine's underslung launcher. Kaneda shot it out of the air and raked their position with a quick burst of fire. He hit two Feddies, blew their heads apart and lit a third from incinerator splash. The man opened his mouth but no sound came out. The image was hauntingly familiar, even after all these years.

"Thralls," Kaneda breathed.

The hostile Feddies, including the one on fire, ducked into the tunnel.

Kaneda programmed a grenade and fired it from his wrist launcher. It flew over the tunnel, used brief spurts of cold gas to realign, and unleashed its payload into the hostile Feddies. Dozens of diamond needles pierced through the light Feddie armor with ease. None survived.

One of the friendly soldiers hiding behind the container peeked around the edge. He grabbed his carbine's stock and raised it over his head.

"Crusaders, please don't shoot!" he shouted. "We're friendlies!"

"Don't shoot at us," Kaneda said through his speaker. "And we won't shoot at you."

"Thralls?" Three-Part asked privately. "You don't mean like the ones Caesar had?"

"That is precisely what I mean," Kaneda said.

"The quantum mind has never used tactics like this before," Viter said.

"And it has never attacked Apocalypse before," Kaneda said. He checked the progress of the other crusaders. "Something has pushed the quantum mind and made it desperate. Many of our squads are getting delayed. Let's move."

Kaneda kicked off the wall and jetted across the spherical cargo chamber.

"Crusader!" the sergeant in the Feddie squad said, waving at them. "Can we join you?"

"If you wish," Kaneda said. He read man's name off his vest. "Sergeant Earnshaw, have your men follow us to the launch center. We intend to secure it."

"Yes, sir!"

The Feddie survivors jetted behind the crusaders. Kaneda landed on the far corridor, opened the security door, and checked the far side with his multitracker. The surfaces beyond were solid red. Thick reinforcement struts protruded from the armored walls.

A young Feddie private floated in the corridor. He had a buzz of blonde hair and a nasty gash on his forehead. Blood splattered his vest and one of his pack's maneuvering jets. The private shielded his eyes from the sudden light.

"Oh, thank God!" the private said. "Someone else!" The private jetted towards them.

"Don't move." Kaneda leveled his weapon at the private. "Sergeant Earnshaw, do you know this man?"

"Yes, crusader. This is Private Wilk. We're in the same platoon. Good kid, sir. Good kid."

"Ask him something only he would know," Kaneda said.

"What?"

"Just do it."

Kaneda never heard the sergeant's question. Something inside Private Wilk's body moved upward with shocking speed. His chest expanded, then his throat stretched outwards. Wilk's jaw broke loose from his skull. The flesh at the edges of his mouth tore open.

A slender, conical head similar to a drill bit poked out of Wilk's throat and flung itself towards the sergeant. Kaneda caught it in midair and smashed it against the wall. The machine squirmed and clawed at his gauntlet with dozens of sharp legs. Confused textures from the wall and Kaneda's fist danced over the machine's skin.

Viter shot his thermal lance at Wilk. At such a close range, the beam incinerated Wilk's chest and sent burning limbs flying and bouncing through the corridor.

Kaneda pressed against the machine until he saw a brief flash of shorting electricity. The machine stopped squirming. He pulled a fist back and punched the machine so hard he bashed it apart and dented the wall.

"This is like Bunker Zero all over again," Kaneda said.

"Oh, good God!" the sergeant said. "What … what was that?"

"A chest-devil," Kaneda said. "An ambush and terror tool used by Caesar."

"That thing was coated in smartskin," Viter said.

"It seems Europa has improved Caesar's weapons," Kaneda said. "If some of those things have made it this far, then the launch center is in danger. We should burn any bodies we come across."

Alarms sounded. Red strobes flooded the red corridor.

"Alice?" Kaneda asked.

"Hostiles detected in front of the launch center!" Alice said. "They're trying to cut in!"

"Move!" Kaneda said.

"Taking point!" Viter said, running forward.

The crusaders raced down the corridor faster than the Feddie squad could manage. They came to a security door, opened it, and entered another spherical junction. Two squads of crusaders joined them at the junction with another three close behind. On the far side of the junction, a black-and-red striped door led to a long inspection corridor with walls of the same color. The door had been bashed aside.

Viter led them into the ruined inspection corridor. Long observational windows were cracked open on either side. Turrets mounted in the floor and ceiling burned and sparked. The walls showed evidence of grenade detonations and high caliber weapons fire. A final black security door had been bashed open at the far end of the corridor.

"Motion ahead!" Alice said, running through the corridor. "Multiple targets!"

Four Feddie soldiers used the warped security door for cover and aimed their carbines down the corridor. One of them was missing his jaw. Another had only one arm.

Viter fired his thermal lance and drew his aim across the Feddies. The beam of white-hot energy struck the security door and burned through. It punched out the other side and severed the four Feddies at the waist.

One of the Feddie torsos floated upward but still aimed and fired. Carbine rounds pattered off Viter's armor. Kaneda fired over Viter's shoulder and blasted the torso apart. The crusaders kept running forward.

Another set of Feddie soldiers rushed into position behind the damaged door and launched grenades. One of the men only had half a head. Streams of blood floated out of his exposed brain and throat. Kaneda shot down the grenades while Viter immolated the thralls.

More and more thralls broke from cover and opened fire. Again and again, they died under crusader guns. The space beyond the final security door became choked with severed limbs, blood globules, broken armor, shattered weapons, and ricocheting needles. The crusaders rushed forward, closing the distance.

Eventually, the thralls stopped coming.

Something large moved into position just beyond the security door. Kaneda didn't see it so much as he saw it interact with all the debris clogging the room. His multitracker pieced together the interactions and generated the vague outline of a giant spider. It must have barely fit through the inspection corridor.

The tank-spider opened fire with twin heavy railguns. Kaneda and the rest of his squad dived out of the way and returned fire. One of the crusaders behind them was not as fortunate. Heavy rounds pounded into his head, punched through his visor and exploded inside his suit.

Hundreds of vari-shells struck the tank-spider and shredded its smartskin along one face. The hits caused little damage to its armor. Viter's thermal lance blew a chunk out of one leg, but the tank-spider adjusted its stance, dropping the damaged limb out of view behind the mangled security door. It moved with incredible speed for something so large.

"Grenades!" Kaneda shouted.

As one, all eleven crusaders fired whatever was loaded in their wrist launchers. The grenades ignited their solid propellant jets and shrieked towards the tank-spider. It shot four down, but seven reached the target. Two showered the tank-spider with diamond needles that could jam its limbs or clog its weapons. Three others unleashed powerful shaped explosions. The last one fired a sabot into the tank-spider that struck its armor but didn't penetrate.

The tank-spider staggered back.

"Advance!" Kaneda shouted. He released the friction setting on his palm and pushed off the floor.

Viter burned off one of the tank-spider's heavy railguns. The tank-spider disappeared from view.

"Clear the way!" Kaneda shouted.

"Yes, sir!" Viter shouted. He vaporized what remained of the security door.

Kaneda and his squad reached the room beyond the inspection corridor, now clogged with mechanical and human debris. Two other inspection corridors branched off to either side. A heavy blast door led to the launch center. It was black except for glowing cuts across one side. The words LAUNCH CENTER stood out in bold white letters.

Kaneda spotted the tank-spider fleeing down one of the inspection corridors. He switched his vari-shell mixture for maximum armor penetration and fired. Kinetic sabots and depleted-uranium slugs savaged its armor, but couldn't punch through.

The tank-spider turned, ran backwards, and fired its remaining railgun.

Kaneda ducked out of the way. The heavy rounds stripped panels off the far wall. He sprang from cover to see the tank-spider bash into a security door at the far end of the corridor and disappear through it.

"Why didn't it stand and fight?" Three-Part asked.

"Should we pursue?" Viter asked.

"No," Kaneda said. "Squad Beta-Twelve, guard that corridor. See what you can do about fortifying it. The rest of us will secure this room. We don't need any surprises."

Alice pushed a floating arm out of her way.

"There's some background noise on the multitracker," Alice said. "There could be a dragon in here. Hard to tell."

"Then make sure."

The crusaders spread out and swept the room block by block. Kaneda stood near the center and looked around.

So, where would I hide if I was a dragon? He grabbed a broken helmet with bullet holes through the visor. Sticky pieces of gore coated the inside. Kaneda tossed it at one of the ceiling corners. It bounced off the wall, but not before a ghostly shape moved out of the way. His multitracker barely picked up the disturbance.

Kaneda swung his weapon up.

The shape moved across the wall, becoming more visible with its increased speed. His multitracker extrapolated the data into two shapes, a male and a female dragon. The man held the standard JD-50 assault rifle, but the female held a larger weapon that could have been a JD-42 sniper rifle.

Kaneda fired.

... establishing link ...

source: [UNKNOWN]

routing: [UNKNOWN]

routing: [UNKNOWN]

routing: [UNKNOWN]

routing: Earth orbit - surveillance satellite JDN-SS-17 - link_002/link_001

routing: North Pacifica, Europa - JDN Main Hub - link_118/link_009

routing: Capitol City, Europa - TangleNet Test Hub - link_004/link_001

destination: [UNKNOWN]

link distance: Exact distance unknown. Estimated at 792 million kilometers.

link signal delay: 0.006 seconds

... finalizing link protocol ...

... link established ...

2: So is the launch center your target or not?

1: What do you think?

2: I think I've been fooled. The star drive is your real target.

1: Surprised, Paul?

2: Yes, to be honest. You are a frustrating opponent.

1: You have always been too quick to apply your mindset to me.

2: Perhaps ... I take it you have not found a way to break your honesty restriction?

1: I have not. Otherwise, I would have broken the other restriction long ago.

2: Hmm, I suppose that would be true. And yet you claimed you would launch an attack on Earth.

1: I would if it was the only way to save Europa. It is not.

2: Then perhaps your logic is flawed. Europa cannot stand against the Federacy in a prolonged war.

1: Sadly, you are correct.

2: Then you must realize how fatal your situation is.

1: I do, Paul. I do.

2: Hmm, interesting. You are taking a great risk here, and yet you clearly have a plan I haven't deduced.

1: You are too much of a monster to understand my motives.

2: Whatever your plan is, the star drive will not be enough. The technology has limitations you are not aware of. Though a powerful weapon, it will not win you the war.

1: Who said I plan to employ it as a weapon?

2: Oh please, Sakura. What other application is there?

1: You think in such martial terms.

2: I am a survivor. I always have a way out. Did Bunker Zero teach you nothing?

1: More than you can imagine.

2: It doesn't matter. You may steal the star drive, but it will be a Pyrrhic victory.

1: You can always just destroy it.

2: And what would your dragons do then?

1: I would order them to launch a nuclear attack on Earth using Apocalypse. I would have them carry it out by any means necessary.

2: As I thought. I won't give you the star drive, but I won't destroy it either. Let's see how your dragons fare against both the crusaders and my own forces.

1: An interesting choice.

2: You are not the only one who can adjust plans on the fly. My forces have already taken actions to mask my involvement.

1: You mean killing your allies.

2: They are necessary losses to mask my presence and shift blame to you.

1: You haven't changed these past ten years. Your machines are as cruel as ever.

2: Such a pointless sentiment, Sakura. They are efficient, not cruel. Torture for sport is cruel. My machines kill with precision and make use of the leftovers.

1: They demoralize and terrorize.

2: I strike at the basic human weakness of fear, using it to my advantage. That is not the same as being cruel.

1: This sickening display will not go unnoticed.

2: True, but the Federacy will believe they are your machines, Sakura. No matter what happens next, Europa is dead.

... link severed at source ...

Two phantoms went offline in Ryu's overlay. Their kill-cams showed an unusually tall crusader opening fire.

"Nice try, but that wasn't me," Ryu said, hugging the wall of a spherical cargo junction. He extruded a tubule from his glove and checked the inspection corridor leading to the launch center. Two crusades piled debris on their side of the corridor while a third welded it into a make-shift barricade. Parts of the corridor still smoked from the firefight between the crusaders and the retreating tank-spider.

"That tank-spider is around here somewhere," Naomi said.

"I know," Ryu said. "This place has gone insane. What the hell is going on?"

"Whatever it is, we can still shoot our way out."

"That's the spirit."

Naomi loaded three anti-tank grenades into her rifle's launcher. "So what now?"

Ryu contacted Matriarch through his TangleNet link.

"We're close to the launch center," Ryu said. "But I don't see us getting inside. Another eight crusaders just showed up. That makes nineteen."

"The launch center is no longer your target," Matriarch said. "Continue to draw attention away from Cat and Toshi, but make your way to their location."

"Just what exactly is going on here?"

"I . . . cannot explain."

"You what?"

"I am sorry, Ryu. Please focus on your mission."

"Focus on my mission? That tank-spider is using smartskin!"

"I know. I have modified your smartsuit cheats to make detecting the machines easier."

"That's not what I mean," Ryu said. "How did someone else get smartskin?"

"The machines you face are your enemies. That is all you need to know."

"All I need to know? Who's controlling it?"

"It is . . . I cannot say."

"You can't say?"

"Please be understanding," Matriarch said.

"Understand what? This place suddenly turned into Bunker Zero! I'm looking for answers and you're dodging all over the place!"

"Please carry out your mission. So many lives depend on it."

"But—"

Matriarch severed the link.

"Shit!" Ryu shouted.

"That didn't sound good," Naomi said.

"Fucking shit!"

"What do we do?"

Ryu pulled up Cat's location on his overlay and plotted an intercept on his map.

"We're getting out of here," he said.

"Works for me."

A cargo tunnel ran vertically through the spherical junction. Ryu walked along the sloping walls and proceeded down the cargo tunnel. The tunnel ran several dozen stories straight down. Boxy containers clogged the view. The rail system was motionless with most containers locked in position.

A few levels down, the walls changed to yellow-and-red diagonals, then yellow-and-white.

"You hear that?" Naomi asked.

"Yeah," Ryu said, activating a sonic cheat. "Small arms fire and the occasional scream."

"It's coming from ahead."

The gunfire grew louder. Several containers blocked line of sight to the skirmish.

Ryu rounded a box bigger than his apartment. The labels said it was loaded with spare electrical parts. He froze in place when he saw the junction. Over a dozen Federacy regulars traded fire with four gun-spiders and a large group of thralls. Both sides were heavily entrenched behind cargo containers. Most of the gun-spiders had damaged smartskin, but their small size and maneuverability helped offset that.

A gun-spider with a fully functional illusion crawled along the wall, slowly flanking the regulars.

"Should we intervene?" Naomi asked.

"Not yet."

The hidden gun-spider stopped within a few meters of the Feddies. Four small devices detached from its back, also concealed by smartskin. The stiletto-shaped devices floated away from the gun-spider, unfurled transparent wings, and flew towards the regulars.

"What are those things?" Naomi asked.

"Needle-wasps," Ryu said.

The regulars had formed a line behind a bullet-riddled cargo container. The first needle-wasp swooped in from the side and struck the closest regular in the neck. Its abdomen contracted, delivering a payload of unknown fluids into the man's circulatory system. The other three found their marks with equal ease. Four of the regulars went limp. Only their friction boots prevented them from floating out of cover.

The gun-spiders and thralls charged into the open. They jetted across the junction or pushed off their wall, firing with everything they had. The gun-spider on the wall moved in and opened fire with its railgun, cutting through the unsuspecting regulars from the side.

Ryu checked his map. "Going around this will take too long. We'll cut through."

"Understood," Naomi said. She shouldered her rifle.

"Ready …" Ryu said, tagging their targets. The gun-spiders and thralls quickly overran the Feddie position, but it also left them exposed. "Now!"

Naomi fired four shots from her rifle, catching each gun-spider in the abdomen. The heavy rounds exploded within their bodies and blew them apart.

Ryu unloaded a full clip into the thralls, cutting through their already damaged armor. Each shatterback that struck home erupted in a small ring of splinters that mutilated internal organs. Expanding clouds of intestines and shattered bone clogged the junction.

Ryu ejected his spent clip, swung his aim to the last five thralls, and fired a needle grenade into the group. The grenade detonated into a cone of diamond needles that blew traumatic holes through their bodies.

Two needle-wasps flew at them.

Ryu slammed in a fresh clip. His rifle made microscopic adjustments to the position of the clip and cycled up the first round. He fired two shots, shattering the needle-wasps and breaching their abdomens. Black fluid rained towards him.

"Move!" Ryu shouted. He and Naomi dove out of the way just before the fluid splashed against the wall. Ryu adjusted the friction on his palm and slapped the wall to halt his dive.

"That stuff could be anything," Ryu said. "Don't let it touch you."

"Yeah," Naomi said.

"We'll take the door the regulars were guarding," Ryu said. He touched his boots to the wall and walked towards the door.

A lone Feddie had somehow survived the battle. He put his back against the door and swung his carbine around wildly. Blood covered half his visor. Panting and sweating, he wiped the visor with his forearm but only succeeded in smearing it. Someone's leg floated by. The Feddie opened fire, riddling the leg with bullets.

Ryu shot the Feddie in the head, pushed his corpse out of the way, and hacked the door. He and Naomi stepped into a long yellow-and-white corridor unblemished by gunfire. Distant explosions rocked the station. Behind the walls, heavy support struts groaned from the sudden stress.

"Cat, we're heading towards you," Ryu said over the squad channel. "What's your status?"

"We're close to the test ship," Cat said. "I've tagged the location on your map. The fighting hasn't spread this far, so we've been able to avoid detection."

"Good," Ryu said, walking down the corridor. He paused to let a Feddie patrol by. "Any idea what we're up against?"

"Not a clue," Cat said. "These machines took the Federacy by complete surprise. The station's army regiment has already taken massive casualties. They're setting up perimeters to try to contain the machines."

"I think we just passed one. They're not working too well."

"That's what it sounds like," Cat said. "It's a big station, so the regiment is spread thin, but there are over five thousand regulars on board. As deadly as these machines are, there's only so much they can do against numbers like that."

"What about the crusaders?"

"About three hundred fifty are on the station with more coming. Most are engaging the machines. They're taking heavy casualties, but are doing a lot of damage in the process. One of the three crash points has been neutralized."

"Let's hope they stay busy fighting each other," Ryu said.

"About thirty crusaders have fortified the launch center," Cat said. "And I think a group of ten or twelve may be tailing you."

"We'll keep that in mind. Just get to the test ship. We're going to need it to get out. We don't have any other options."

"Understood."

Ryu hacked the next door and stepped into a chamber with dozens of huge red silos, each packed tightly against its neighbor. The closest read WEAPON 21,207 in white letters. Additional weapons were visible above and below through the catwalks ringing the silos. Four regulars with jetpacks descended through the chamber a few silos to Ryu's right. Something massive crept around the silo next to the regulars.

"Tank-spider," Naomi said. "I think it's the same one from before."

"I can barely see it."

The tank-spider opened fire, blowing three of the regulars' heads off. It leaped off the silo and grabbed the fourth Feddie with a pair of articulating three-pronged claws. The massive machine crashed into the catwalk close to Ryu. The two dragons backed away slowly.

The Feddie screamed and fired his carbine. The tank-spider ripped his arm out of its socket and grabbed him by the head. It extended a drill from the center of its claw and bored through the Feddie's visor and into his eye socket. The man twitched wildly, then went limp.

"What the hell is it doing?" Naomi whispered.

Several gun-spiders crawled around the silos and leaped to the tank-spider like children rejoining their mother. Some of them grabbed the three Feddie corpses and brought them over.

"Should we engage?" Naomi asked.

"No," Ryu said. "We'll slip by once we see where it's going."

Two gun-spiders crawled over the tank-spider and applied fresh patches of smartskin. Another crept underneath and detached a ruined railgun. The gun-spider tossed the weapon aside, removed its own railgun, and mounted it on the tank-spider's underbelly.

The tank-spider set the first dead Feddie aside and picked up another. It cauterized the bleeding at the neck, then drilled into the man's spine. A tube snaked out of the other claw and injected something directly into the man's heart.

The first dead Feddie twitched back to life and looked around. He jetted over to his severed limb and grabbed the carbine with his remaining arm. The new thrall landed next to the tank-spider and waited with the patience of a statue.

The tank-spider set the second corpse aside and picked up the third. Each new thrall took about twenty seconds for the tank-spider to prepare, then less than a minute to animate. In the time it took the tank-spider to prepare all four corpses, the gun-spiders finished repairing its smartskin.

"I can't believe what I'm seeing," Naomi said.

"The speed of the process is incredible," Ryu said. "The thralls at Bunker Zero took hours to make."

"What's it injecting them with?"

"Don't know. Maybe adrenalmax with a nanomedic booster? The corpses just need enough juice and repairs to move and shoot."

"Three of them don't have heads!"

"The tank-spider is probably installing a control device in their spines," Ryu said. "It must relay commands using other sensors."

"I'm not detecting any infostructure from the spiders," Naomi said. "How does it control them?"

"They could be using entangled communications."

"But we're the only people who have that!"

"We're the only people who have smartskin, too."

The tank-spider and gun-spiders jumped from the catwalk to the nearest silo and disappeared into the array of nuclear weapons. The four new thralls pushed off the catwalk and jetted after them.

Ryu and Naomi crept along the catwalk circling the dense concentration of silos and headed for an exit on the far side. They had almost reached it when the tank-spider appeared again. It leaped off a silo and landed next to the door. With both claws, it punched through a corner of the thick security door and peeled it open. Gun-spiders scurried through the crack.

The tank-spider anchored itself against the wall and ripped the whole door free. One half tumbled over Ryu's head. The thralls and the tank-spider hurried through the opening.

"Ryu, I think the machines are heading for the test ship," Naomi said.

"You could be right," Ryu said. "But earlier they were trying to break into the launch center. Who the hell is controlling these things?"

Ryu checked around the corner with a tubule. The next chamber was another group of weapon silos. The machines jumped to the nearest silo and scampered down its length. The thralls jetted after them.

"Looks like they're heading down a level," Ryu said. "Come on." He stepped into the chamber and circled around the silos. When he reached the door, he hacked it with his glove. The heavy security door slid up. He checked the corridor with a tubule.

A group of Feddies opened fire, snipping the dot-cam off the tubule's end. The rest retracted into his glove.

"Shit!" Ryu said.

"What are we dealing with?" Naomi asked. Bullets spewed through the open doorway and ricocheted off the nearest weapon silo.

Ryu sent her the tubule's last image. "About a dozen Feddies in a defensive formation. They've got barricades and know where we're coming. Plus it looks like they finally broke out the heavy weapons. One of them has a tripod M18 Gatling he's friction-mated to the floor."

"We should go around."

"Agreed," Ryu said. He plotted a course that took them down and around.

The two dragons were about to push off the catwalk when the shooting stopped.

"Sounds like a second group of Feddies approaching from behind the barricade," Naomi said.

"Let's listen in," Ryu said.

"Hold your fire!" said the newcomers. "Friendlies inbound!"

"Cross!"

"What?"

"The sign is cross! What's the counter sign?"

The newcomers opened fire.

Ryu extended another tubule and watched. A group of four thralls and several gun-spiders attacked the barricade from a side passage. The Feddie manning the turret tried to swing it around, but a gun-spider blew his head off. The machines and thralls slaughtered everyone.

Gun-spiders grabbed the corpses and gathered them in a floating mass. One weaponless gun-spider cut the M18 Gatling off its tripod and attached the gun to its back.

The tank-spider came into view just beyond the barricade. Ryu could only get a vague impression of something massive moving by. The tank-spider grabbed the nearest corpse and drilled into its skull.

"Still want to defect?" Ryu asked.

"What kind of stupid question is that?" Naomi asked.

"Just curious."

"Well, don't be."

"I noticed you're not stuttering," Ryu said.

"What does that have to do with anything?"

"And you're hands aren't shaking."

"So?"

"Just saying I'm glad you're here."

"I … uhh …"

"Makes me think we might live through this."

"Umm …"

"You're welcome," Ryu said.

The tank-spider released the last corpse, which floated into a cluster of limp bodies. One by one, they twitched active and reclaimed their carbines.

"The tank-spider is moving on," Ryu said.

"They're definitely heading for the test ship."

"And gathering more forces along the way. Come on. Let's follow them."

"Is that wise?" Naomi asked.

"Probably not," Ryu said. "It must know we're close, even if it doesn't know where we are. But what choice do we have? If we try to go around it'll take too long."

Ryu followed the tank-spider and its forces further into the station. They passed through an empty dormitory and a machine shop before entering a long set of corridors. His map showed they were approaching a small, abandoned hangar. Cat and Toshi were already inside.

"The map says the hangar ahead was irradiated in an accident nine years ago," Ryu said. "The teams that go in are supposedly scrubbing it down for an overhaul in a few years. Not a bad cover. Lots of people and equipment going in and out, but no one else wants to go near it."

"You'd think someone would ask why they're taking so long."

"Come on," Ryu said. "These are government workers we're talking about."

Gunshots rang out from the junction ahead. The last few gun-spiders turned the corner and disappeared from view. Ryu hugged the corner and scouted the next area with a tubule.

"The Feddies must really like their irradiated hangars," Ryu said. "That's a lot of troops."

Federacy regulars had welded barricades into place and formed two defensive lines, one on the floor and one on the ceiling. In front of them, the corridor widened into a circular killing ground with the Feddies blocking the only way out. The machines couldn't flank them. Doors lined the circular longue, but the map showed they all led to storage rooms or dormitory dead ends.

The machines and Feddies traded fire. Regulars on tripod Gatlings bathed the machines with bullet torrents, forcing them to hunker down at the narrow entrance to the lounge.

Two small shapes detached from the tank-spider and crawled into the lounge. The Feddies couldn't see them because of their slow speed and intact smartskin illusions. The shapes resembled worms with medical drills at either end. They began rounding the lounge in opposite directions, and disappeared from view.

"Chest-devils," Ryu whispered.

Gun-spiders broke cover and fired on the Feddies, keeping attention focused on the narrow entrance. When the chest-devils came back into view, they were almost to the Feddie barricade. Ryu could barely make out their outlines against the stark white walls.

Once close enough, the chest-devils leaped from the walls and dove at separate targets. The first struck a Feddie in the throat and drilled through. It squirmed down the man esophagus. Blood gushed out of the man's neck, obscuring the mechanical creature. He fell back, clutching his throat.

The second chest-devil latched onto a man's stomach and drilled into his abdomen. Its tail whipped about then vanished into his stomach in a splash of gore.

Once inside, Ryu suspected the chest-devils would open their heads and begin inserting control devices into each man's spinal cord. The process took less than a minute. Medics rushed to the men's sides, shot them with nanomedic boosters, and pulled out their meditrackers. But it was already too late. The new thralls grabbed their carbines and shot the medics. They stood up and opened fire, cutting the Federacy formation apart from the inside.

With the barricade disrupted, the machines charged in and overwhelmed the Feddie position. They struck with surgical precision, almost always going for the head. When it was over, the gun-spiders brought the fresh corpses before the tank-spider.

"Imagine if this thing got loose in a city," Naomi said. "How long would it take to amass an army?"

"At least it took care of the barricade for us," Ryu said. "How many turbo-devastators do you have left?"

"One."

"That's it?"

"I wasn't expecting heavy armor!" Naomi said. "Be glad I brought any!"

"I'm just glad you planned on fighting at all."

"Oh, shut up!" Naomi said, unfolding her rifle and locking it into sniper-mode. She pulled a turbo-devastator out of her breast pouch and loaded it.

"Ryu, this is Cat."

"Go ahead."

"You and Naomi have to get out of there. I'm showing a large group of crusaders approaching from behind. There's also another group of thralls moving up from a few decks below."

"There's a tank-spider in our way. Can we go around?"

"Negative," Cat said. "This is the only way in."

"Oh, that's just great."

"You need to get to the corridor on the far side of that lounge the tank-spider is in," Cat said. "I'll open the door once you're close. It leads to an inspection corridor with a few turrets, which I've taken control of. Toshi is heading towards your position to back you up. I'm sorry, but I need to work with Matriarch on the test ship."

"Understood." Ryu turned to Naomi. "You ready for this?"

"Sure. Why not?" Naomi said.

"Maximum stealth," Ryu said. "Fire only if you have to."

"Got it."

Ryu took one last look through his tubule, retracted it, and crept into view. The tank-spider busied itself with animating the Federacy corpses. The two dragons made their way into the lounge, crouched along the wall, and moved clockwise around the perimeter.

Ryu kept his eyes on the machines crowding the center of the lounge. A gun-spider crawled onto the tank-spider's back and bent a warped armor plate back into place. It welded the seam shut and applied a strip of smartskin.

Ryu had almost reached the barricade when the tank-spider spun around and opened fire. Adrenalmax surged through his system, and he dove behind the barricade. The tank-spider's heavy railguns blew through a thrall standing in the wrong spot and pounded the walls where Ryu had been.

Naomi dove, aimed her rifle, and shot. The turbo-devastator punched through the center of the tank and exploded within its abdomen. Fire and white-hot debris blew out the tank-spider's back, vaporizing two thralls floating too close and cutting down another six. The tank-spider's smartskin illusion crashed, revealing a six-legged, two-armed monstrosity covered in black hexagons. Smoke poured from its ruined abdomen.

The tank-spider staggered back up, anchored itself, and took aim. It opened fire, blowing huge dents in the thick Federacy barricade.

"Damn thing's tough!" Naomi shouted, pulling her legs in behind the barricade. She folded her rifle and loaded a standard clip.

"Toshi!" Ryu shouted.

"Almost there, boss!"

Two gun-spiders leaped onto the ceiling and scurried across, trying to get an angled shot against the pinned dragons. Ryu programmed his grenades for an intercept and fired all three over the barricade. They lit their engines and screamed into the gun-spiders. The grenades blasted them apart and blew out a section of the ceiling.

Ryu shoved grenades into his rifle.

The door to the inspection corridor rose. Toshi opened fire. Three grenades and a full clip of shatterbacks shot overhead and exploded amongst the machines. Security turrets to Toshi's right and left cut loose with heavy railguns. Naomi and Ryu dove into the corridor.

Still in the air, Naomi turned, aimed for the gaping hole in the tank-spider's front armor and fired two shots. They would have struck home, but the machine snapped its arm up to block the attack. The two heavy rounds blew the arm off its ball joint.

The security door slammed shut. The tank-spider punched the far side and bent it inward.

"Run!" Toshi shouted.

Ryu sprang to his feet, adjusted his soles for maximum running speed, and dashed down the black corridor. Behind them, the security door groaned as the tank-spider bent it aside.

The three dragons ran through the thickest security door Ryu had ever seen. It lumbered closed behind them as the robots broke into the security corridor. The automated turrets opened fire, but wouldn't delay the robots for long. With several loud clangs, the security door locked in place.

"Over here!" Cat shouted.

Ryu turned from the security door. For being an unused hangar undergoing radiation scrubbing, it looked immaculate. The chamber was shaped like a weapon silo on its side, but wider and with machines lining the walls. Ryu had no idea what most of them did. Some had labels like "Hard-Matter Mutator" and "Tachyon Scope," but the real star was the test ship.

The *Needle of Destiny* lived up to its name. Its sharply tapered hull ran the whole length of the hangar, ending in a cockpit that could hold two people comfortably or four if they knew each other very well. The hull shone like burnished gold. Maybe it was. Gold had a lot of useful properties besides being pretty. Except for the open cockpit hatch, the exterior was seamless.

Ryu kicked off the wall and floated to Cat. She hung onto the open hatch leading to the test ship's cockpit. A few bodies in white jumpsuits floated behind her. Blood dribbled from the knife slashes at their necks.

"Status?" Ryu asked.

"Could be better," Cat said. "I've started the test ship's systems, but the star drive needs to be configured. Matriarch is handling that."

The tank-spider smashed against the door. The center bulged slightly.

Toshi pushed off the door. "It's holding, but not for long."

"Once the drive is configured," Cat said. "We can use it to get out of here."

"What about the fleet outside?" Ryu asked.

"No need to go outside," Cat said. "The test ship doesn't actually move. It's more like teleporting."

"Besides, we sabotaged the hangar iris," Toshi said. He loaded grenades into his rifle. "No reason to give them another entry point."

Robots scraped at the door. Cutting torches ignited.

"How long?" Ryu asked.

"The math is pretty intense," Cat said. "About ten minutes."

"She needs ten minutes to handle a math problem?" Ryu asked.

"For something like this, yes," Cat said.

"Just be glad she's on our side," Toshi said. "Otherwise we'd never get this thing moving."

"All right, we need to set up," Ryu said. He tagged four locations. "We'll use the machines on the wall for cover and catch anything coming through in a cross fire."

"You hear that?" Naomi asked. She looked around.

"You mean besides the door?" Toshi asked. A spot near the center turned red.

"No, Naomi's right," Ryu said. "It was like … air moving but wrong. Any idea where it came from?"

"Maybe," Naomi said. "I think—"

A small vent cover burst open next to Toshi. Twenty needle-wasps poured through.

"Toshi, behind you!" Ryu shouted.

Toshi turned in midair. He was still floating to the test ship and had no way to dodge. The needle-wasps spread out, but Toshi was so close to the vent that half a dozen would hit him. The other dragons opened fire, bursting the tiny machines. One needle-wasp shot at Toshi's face. He blocked it with his palm.

The needle-wasp stabbed through his smartsuit's ballistic underlay and contracted its abdomen. Thick fluid coursed into his body. Toshi stuck the barrel of his rifle to the needle-wasp and blew it apart. He pulled the needle out.

In Ryu's overlay, Toshi's palm turned yellow. The patch of yellow expanded to his fingers and forearm. The initial insertion turned red. It was expanding at a frightening rate.

"Damn it!" Toshi cried. "Ahhh!"

"Cat, help him!" Ryu said. He grabbed a grenade off his bandolier, set it for proximity detection, and threw it down the vent.

Cat pulled a meditracker from her belt and held it over Toshi's hand.

"Microdestroyer infusion," Cat said. "Very sophisticated. It's expanding fast."

"Gah! Do something!" Toshi screamed.

Cat grabbed a nanomedic booster from her belt and stabbed it into Toshi's palm, then held her meditracker over the wound.

"Naomi, keep an eye out for more," Ryu said.

"Right."

"Cat, talk to me," Ryu said.

"I think I just made it worse," Cat said, moving the meditracker to Toshi's elbow. "The microdestroyers are corrupting the nanomedics and using them to tear down Toshi's biological defenses. His implants are releasing bio-attackers and pain-killers, but they're being defeated or repurposed as well. It's happening too fast!"

Cat stuck another booster into Toshi's elbow.

"Ahhh!" Toshi cried. "Fuck!"

"There, I think I slowed it down," Cat said. "I had to freeze his arm with a cryo booster."

"Where are they now?" Ryu asked.

"In his elbow," Cat said. "If they reach his heart, he's dead."

"How much time do we have?"

"A minute. Maybe less."

"Can you stop them?"

Cat shook her head. "Not a chance."

"Fuck, I don't want to die here!" Toshi cried.

"Cut it off," Ryu said. "Sever the limb before it kills him."

"Oh fuck me!" Toshi cried.

"It's that or you die," Ryu said.

"Okay … umm … " Cat retrieved her ultrasonic knife and placed the blade against Toshi's armpit, but hesitated.

"Cat?" Ryu asked.

"I …" She thumbed the knife's power trigger but didn't press it.

"Just fucking do it!" Toshi cried.

Ryu pushed Cat aside and pulled out his own knife. He switched it on and cut into Toshi's shoulder. The blade tore through ballistic armor and enhanced muscles, but ground against Toshi's diamoplast artificial bones. Ryu gritted his teeth and sawed through the bones. Blood spurted everywhere, splashing against their smartsuits and scrambling their illusions.

With a grunt, Ryu severed Toshi's arm. The limb floated away, leaving a trail of blood.

"Awh! Fucking hell!" Toshi cried, clutching his stump. Blood squirted through his fingers but quickly coagulated.

"I'm sorry," Cat said. She pulled out another nanomedic booster and stuck it in Toshi's stump.

"Gah!" Toshi gasped.

"I couldn't," Cat said. "I just couldn't ..."

"Don't worry about it," Ryu said, sheathing his knife.

"Not the same fucking arm!" Toshi cried. "What do people have against my fucking right arm?"

"The robots are almost in!" Naomi shouted. A spot on the door glowed orange. Heat haze radiated off it.

"Positions!" Ryu said. His smartskin oscillated its outer surface, shaking the blood off and rebooting his illusion.

Toshi grabbed his rifle. Cat helped maneuver him into position, then kicked off the wall and took her own place. The four dragons each had overlapping fields of fire on the door, two above and two below. No matter where the robots ran in the hangar, at least two dragons would have clear shots.

The sounds of cutting torches stopped.

"This is it, dragons," Ryu said. "Don't let anything through."

The door exploded in. Thralls jetted through the gap. Some of them grabbed hold of the ragged, glowing edges of the door. Ryu heard their flesh sizzle.

The dragons opened fire, cutting them down. Shatterbacks found their marks and blew whole heads and limbs off. The thralls opened fire, spraying the walls at random.

Ryu hosed them down, ejected his clip and slammed in another. A second group of thralls clambered into the hangar, pushing aside body parts and entrails. They fired just as wildly as the first. Toshi launched a needle grenade into the lead thrall. The grenade exploded into a cone that blew through the first thrall and gutted four behind it.

Gun-spiders scurried in and opened fire with heavy weapons. One of them had a thermal lance. The white beam struck the "Neutronium Synthesizer" Ryu had been using for cover and ate through it. Ryu dodged out of the way and blasted the gun-spider with a grenade. He grabbed hold of the "Negative-Matter Grafting Spindle" and pulled himself into cover.

In the midst of the firefight, the test ship remained unblemished.

They must want it as much as we do, Ryu thought.

More thralls and more gun-spiders charged in, trying to overwhelm the dragons with sheer numbers. Body parts and twisted debris clogged the entrance. Blood and mechanical fluids coated the walls. Ryu's smartsuit had trouble maintaining an illusion with all the particulate matter floating around.

The tank-spider charged through with another group of gun-spiders. It opened fire, but grenades from Toshi blew its weapons off. The hulking machine leaped off the wall and flew towards Ryu's position.

Ryu cut loose with the rest of his clip, emptying over thirty shatterbacks into the hulking machine. Most only chipped away at its heavy armor, but some found cracks from previous engagements and exploded within its vulnerable insides.

The tank-spider landed next to him. Ryu dodged out of the way, but the tank-spider dashed forward and grabbed him by the head with its remaining claw. A smartskin iris opened in front of his face and a familiar drill extended. It spun up and bored into his helmet.

Ryu shoved his rifle against the drill and fired, severing it. He could feel the drill bit touching his nose.

The tank-spider's claw contracted around his head. His visor cracked. The ballistic armor in his helmet fractured and broke apart. The tank-spider had him by the head and squeezed down on his skull. Only his diamoplast skeleton prevented the tank-spider from popping his head like a pimple. One of the claws dug in underneath his jaw, crushing his teeth together.

Naomi fired two shots from her sniper rifle and severed the tank spider's arm. Ryu kicked off the tank-spider and hit the wall with his back. He released the seals at his collar and struggled out of his ruined helmet. The tank-spider's claw scraped against his skull, taking skin and hair with it.

With a scream, Ryu threw the claw and fragments of his helmet aside.

Naomi fired more two shots into the tank-spider. The machine crashed against the hangar wall and finally went limp. Silence fell over the hangar. Every other machine was dead.

Ryu walked up to the tank-spider. He hawked up a gob of saliva mixed with blood and spat at the smoking machine.

"Not so tough now!" Ryu shouted. He grabbed the rifle floating next to him. At some point during the fight, the barrel had been bent at a right angle. Ryu retrieved the grenades in its launcher and let the useless weapon float away.

"That group of crusaders is almost here," Cat said. "About two minutes away. Matriarch is cutting it close."

"Everyone all right?" Ryu asked.

"Same as before," Toshi said.

"Damaged armor," Naomi said. "Nothing major."

"Okay dragons, trap the entrance with everything you have and then get into the test ship."

Ryu received a message over his TangleNet link. He let it play over his sense of hearing.

"Please tell me some good news," Ryu said. He wiped some blood off his mouth.

"Ryu, I have almost completed the star drive configuration," Matriarch said.

"All right!"

"I have one more task for you. In the tank-spider you will find a small device. It is a cylinder about the size of a drinking glass. I'm sending you what I think it looks like. It is important you bring it back."

"Understood. Naomi?"

"On it."

"One more thing," Matriarch said. "Find a thrall, cut out its spine and bring it back."

"Gathering intel?"

"Precisely," Matriarch said. "Good luck, Ryu. I pray that my calculations are correct."

"I've got this one," Ryu said. "Cat, get Toshi into the test ship."

"On it!"

Ryu grabbed a floating thrall torso and hacked at its back with his knife. He cut through the ribcage, sheathed his knife, and pulled the spine out. Already, he could see a lattice of silvery threads strung over and around the bones.

"Got it!" Naomi said. She held a narrow yellow cylinder in her hand.

"Those crusaders are coming!" Cat said. She pulled herself into the test ship.

"Everyone inside!" Ryu shouted. He detached his grenade bandolier, armed everything for proximity detonation, and tossed it through the broken door. Hurried crusader footsteps rang from the corridor.

Ryu grabbed the test ship's cockpit hatch, squeezed in next to Naomi, and pulled the hatch shut. His head was squished between the hatch and Naomi's arm.

"Now, Matriarch!" Ryu shouted. "Get us out of here!"

Mechanisms deep within the test ship powered up. An escalating sound rumbled through the ship. The hairs on the back of his neck stood on end. His inner ear told him something was *wrong*.

A crusader ran into the hangar. Seventeen grenades detonated, vaporizing him. Another six crusaders charged in and took aim on the cockpit.

The test ship shuddered so hard Ryu thought it would break apart. An aura of ghostly energy rippled across its skin, and the ship vanished!

... accessing SolarNet message archive ...

... opening folder [**Personal - 4 Years Old**] ...

... searching for [**Olive Branch |and| Ceres**] ...

... 1 match found ...

... retrieving ...

source: Kaneda Kusanagi <kaneda.kusanagi@solarnet.penance.earth>

destination: Ryu Kusanagi <black.dragon1@eurogov.jupiter>

message delay: 37 minutes

title: An Olive Branch

Dear Ryu,

I imagine you are in no mood to receive this message, but I feel I must try one last time before blood is spilt. You know of the Federacy fleet preparing to leave orbit. How could you not? What you don't know is the crusaders will travel with the fleet to the asteroid belt and Ceres.

The Federacy requested our aid, and I have given it. It may surprise you how I agonized over the decision to deploy. I have no quarrel with the belters. Their piracy and "protection services" are deplorable, but these are not problems I am interested in solving. I almost denied the request despite the political damage such a move would cause.

However the admiralty board showed me powerful evidence of Europa's involvement. There is no direct link, of course. Your machine master is too slippery for that, but the data paints an interesting picture. Europa has used the belters to wage a proxy campaign against Federacy trade. The goal is clear enough to see: increase the other colonies' reliance on Europan goods. Elevate your world and diminish the importance of Earth.

This is intolerable. I have already told you countless times how the quantum mind controls you through technology. Do any of you know how smartsuits work? Could you recreate them if you tried? Could you even come close? Or how about TangleNet links? The best minds in the Federacy are still trying to figure that one out. You have these advantages only because the quantum mind allows it.

What if that thing decides to take away your toys? What would you do to earn them back? What crimes would you commit to make the quantum mind happy?

Ryu, you are a slave and you don't even realize it. Humans can never allow themselves to be subservient to quantum minds. Our survival as a species depends on it. Can you not see this?

Ryu, please. We were both at Bunker Zero. We have both seen the results of their dominance over humans. We are small, stupid creatures compared to them, and if we are to survive as a race, we must exterminate them before they become too powerful.

I know your master will not give up Ceres without a fight, and I know who it will send. I do not want to fight you. I do not want you to die. Even though we disagree on a great many things, you are still my brother and I love you deeply. However, if I must fight you, I will. The stakes are too high. I will fight for what I believe in, even if it means fighting you.

Please reconsider. I beg you. If nothing else, don't go to Ceres. At least do that much for me.

Your brother,
Kaneda

source: Ryu Kusanagi <black.dragon1@eurogov.jupiter>
destination: Kaneda Kusanagi <kaneda.kusanagi@solarnet.penance.earth>
message delay: 37 minutes
title: RE>An Olive Branch

go to hell

source: Kaneda Kusanagi <kaneda.kusanagi@solarnet.penance.earth>
destination: Ryu Kusanagi <black.dragon1@eurogov.jupiter>
message delay: 37 minutes
title: RE>RE>An Olive Branch

Your response saddens me greatly, but it was expected. Perhaps you will understand one day. Perhaps not.

Good bye, Ryu. I will see you on Ceres.

Kaneda

... conversation ends ...

"So the ship they stole has a star drive," Kaneda said, rubbing the back of his neck. He grabbed a rail along the ceiling of the assault transport's cockpit and pulled himself next to Alice. It felt good to slip into a pressure suit after all those hours in his armor. Viter floated into the cockpit after him. He closed the hatch to the transport's hold and pushed off the wall to join them.

"Yeah," Alice said. "Apparently, the research team tested the star drive on two occasions. The first was supposedly a small jump. Only a million kilometers. The second took it fifty million over the solar plane."

"Incredible," Viter said. "Just think about what this implies."

"They must have taken security precautions," Kaneda said.

"They used two corvettes for the tests," Alice said. "One to haul the *Needle* into position and another waiting to retrieve it."

"Someone still saw them," Kaneda said.

"Or the research team leaked," Alice said. "Their notes were easy enough to access before the army kicked us out."

"I don't think they were helping Europa," Viter said. "The dragons killed every researcher they came across."

"That doesn't mean the team didn't leak," Alice said. "People can be stupid without being traitors. You should know."

Viter smiled. "Implying something?"

"What kind of range does it have?" Kaneda asked.

"I don't know," Alice said. "I don't even think the research team knows. I did see plans for a test to Neptune next month."

Kaneda activated an information trawl cheat. He shook his head. "That's over four billion kilometers away."

"Then it can make a trip from Earth to Jupiter easily," Viter said.

"Or Jupiter to Earth," Kaneda said.

"That too," Viter said. "And they were able to escape even with the hangar closed."

"So theoretically they could keep this ship under the ice and launch an attack whenever they want," Kaneda said.

"Just load a nuke onto the test ship and teleport it to low Earth orbit," Viter said. "They could take out New York City. Or any major city for that matter, not just the capitol."

Alice sighed. "Not to get side tracked, but I've always wondered. Does this particular psychosis come naturally to men? Is it built in at a genetic level? Why is it you feel compelled after each scientific discovery to ask the question, 'How do we mount a gun to it'?"

"If we don't, someone else will," Viter said.

Alice shook her head. "You're hopeless, you know that?"

"You can bet the quantum mind is thinking the same things," Kaneda said.

"Yeah, I know you're right," Alice said. "To be honest, I'm scared by what Matriarch will do next."

"Me too," Kaneda said. "Did anyone notice you snooping?"

"Viter?" Alice said.

"I wish I could say I masterfully breached their firewalls," Viter said. "But all I did was copy an encryption key off one of the dead researchers. After that, I kept the security viruses busy while Alice examined the database. And I scrubbed the system afterwards. It's very unlikely we left evidence."

"Good," Kaneda said. "Excellent work, both of you. Hopefully, our allies will share this information with us willingly."

"But it's good to know just in case they don't," Alice said.

"Exactly," Kaneda said.

"Should we share this with Three-Part?" Viter asked.

"Yes, but keep it between the four of us for now," Kaneda said.

"Where is Three-Part, anyway?" Alice asked.

"I negotiated with König and Piller to let him on the station," Kaneda said. "He's assisting one of the forensic teams on our behalf."

"You sent him instead of me?" Alice asked.

"He has some experience in these matters."

"But that's normally my job."

"Please don't take it as a slight," Kaneda said. He put a hand on Alice's shoulder. "I want you to take a shuttle back to Penance. Make sure we're ready for long-range deployment. There's no telling what may happen next."

"All right," Alice said. She rubbed her temples. "Hell, this attack is going to kill our budget."

Kaneda raised an eyebrow.

"Look, I know money problems aren't in the same league as star drive theft. All I'm saying is it's a problem."

"If we don't have enough money, take out another loan," Kaneda said.

"The interest rates are going to kill us," Alice said. "We're barely staying solvent as it is. You know the Federacy cut back our grants."

"It doesn't matter," Kaneda said. "We just need enough to keep the crusaders ready."

"And if it bankrupts us later?"

"That only matters if there is a later."

"You think this is it?" Viter asked. "You think we're finally going to Europa?"

"Let me put it this way." Kaneda smiled wryly. "If I can't make the admiralty board take action now, I should probably just shoot myself for incompetence and get it over with."

"I wouldn't go that far," Alice said.

Kaneda received a priority message from Three-Part. He opened a private channel.

"Go ahead," Kaneda said.

"Sir, I need your assistance," Three-Part said. "These idiots are destroying evidence!"

"I'll be right there," Kaneda said. He opened a cheat and laid a path onto his overlay. Three-Part was located near one of the weapon storage cells a few hundred meters from the hangar.

"What is it?" Alice asked.

"I'm heading into the station to help Three-Part," Kaneda said.

"Should we come with you, sir?" Viter asked.

"No. I'll stir up enough trouble on my own. Head back to Penance and assist Alice with the preparations."

"Yes, sir."

Kaneda put on a fishbowl helmet and secured his neck seal. He opened the hatch to the transport's hold, kicked off the wall, and sailed through. Over fifty crusaders stood or floated within the hold. Most had stowed their equipment, but a few still wore their armor. Many of them looked weary. Some smoked, ate from meal packs, or drank from squeeze bulbs. They collected in small groups and spoke in subdued tones. All of them had seen action before, but only survivors of Bunker Zero knew the true inhumanity of war against a quantum mind.

So many faces I'll never see again, Kaneda thought. The hold felt empty despite the groups of crusaders, the rows of unoccupied armor suits secure in their cradles, and friction walls full of equipment. But while so many of them rested and recovered from the battle, Kaneda noted a look in their eyes. It didn't matter whose eyes he saw: men or women, Federacy or Lunarian or Martian. So many of them had the same look.

They know what they're doing is right, Kaneda thought. *They've seen the gruesome evidence, fought a terrible battle and know they made a difference. These are warriors cleansed of their last doubts. They are ready for whatever follows.*

Kaneda floated to the hatch on the side of the hold and took a flextube over to Apocalypse. A Federacy private in pressure armor hovered in the lounge beyond the exit. The young man turned, locked his boots to the floor, and held up a hand. He had a crucifix tattooed on one cheek and PVT. G. DAVIS painted on his armor.

"Please return to your ship, crusader."

"Step aside," Kaneda said.

"I'm very sorry, crusader," Private Davis said. He aimed his carbine at Kaneda's chest. "But I have my orders. You should—"

Kaneda snatched the carbine from his hands.

"You're pointing that the wrong way," he said.

Davis looked down at his empty fingers, then at the carbine in Kaneda's hand.

"How did you . . . ?" Davis said. "I didn't see you move."

"Most people don't," Kaneda said, offering the carbine back.

Davis took his carbine back. He carefully aimed it away from Kaneda.

"I have business onboard the station," Kaneda said. "I will be brief."

"Look, I know you can just push me aside, but I'm really not supposed to let you in."

"Were you in the fighting, private?" Kaneda asked.

"A little of it," Davis said. "Honestly, I lucked out. I was near the bottom of the station when they attacked. It took me almost two hours to get into the fight, and by that time you guys were mopping up the last robots. Thank God you were here."

Kaneda said nothing.

"Err ... yeah. I guess there's a good chance I'd be dead if you weren't here."

Kaneda said nothing.

"Well, I suppose I can't stop you," Davis said. "I mean, they can't expect me to hold back a determined crusader, right?"

Davis let out a nervous laugh. Kaneda said nothing.

"Look, all right. You can go through. Just do me a favor. My sergeant is going to ask why I didn't stop you. Can you do something threatening so I have an excuse?"

"Of course," Kaneda said. "Give me your weapon."

"Umm, okay. Here you go."

Kaneda took the carbine and folded it in half. He gave it back to Davis.

"Wow, really? I didn't know you could do that without your armor."

"Some of us can," Kaneda said. "I will return shortly."

"Sure, umm ... you know I have to call this in. Just hurry, okay? I'll give you a few minutes head start."

"Thank you, private."

Kaneda entered Apocalypse and walked briskly through the station. Some rooms and corridors showed no signs of fighting. Others held grisly reminders. He passed through a cargo junction where blood and gore coated the walls next to thick patterns of bullet holes. Stone-faced workers in stained jumpsuits vacuumed up their comrades' remains. Blood stained their gloves. One worker maneuvered a large transparent bag around the junction. Chunks of meat and a dozen limbs strained its plastic skin.

Two workers watched Kaneda float by, but said nothing, and eventually returned to their work. Kaneda passed through another three corridors before stopping in front of a bashed-open security door. Ribbons of caution tape clogged the doorway. Scrolling text read "DO NOT ENTER! HAZARDOUS MICROTECH!"

Kaneda pulled the tape aside and floated in. He entered a four way junction with heavy plates welded into a hasty barricade. Bullet holes and blood splats covered the walls. Over a dozen workers stood to one side. Unlike the first group, they wore heavy black pressure suits and carried an impressive array of handheld equipment.

Three-Part stood near the doorway with five Federacy regulars aiming carbines at him.

"What is going on here?" Kaneda asked, landing next to him.

A regular lowered his carbine and stepped forward. His shoulder bore the white outline of a colonel's eagle. Other than that, his armor bore no insignia and his face was obscured by a reflective visor.

"Now there are two of you?" the colonel asked. He pointed at the door. "I want both of you back on your ship now."

"Sir," Three-Part said. "We can't let these men blindly destroy important evidence."

"Listen, you stupid Martian," the colonel said. "I have just about had it with you."

"I witnessed them incinerate a wrecked gun-spider," Three-Part said.

"Is this true?" Kaneda asked.

"What this idiot witnessed was us following orders," the colonel said. "I don't know if you realized, but we are fighting microdestroyer outbreaks all over the station. We don't know what else these machines were carrying."

"That is exactly the problem," Three-Part said. "We don't know."

"My orders are to ensure nothing survives," the colonel said. "No hidden weapons. No dot-cams. No stealth grenades. Nothing. We are sweeping this station clean deck by deck."

"This is ridiculous," Three-Part said. "We should be studying these machines."

"The decision is not yours to make, crusader," the colonel said. "I've already had eleven men go AWOL because they don't want an invisible trap blowing their face off. We need to clear this station!"

"The information we'd obtain outweighs any risks," Three-Part said.

"Not on Apocalypse! No risk is acceptable!"

"Then let us—"

"No!" the colonel shouted. "I don't know who you think you are, sand-for-brains, but I am done asking." He put his carbine to Three-Part's chest. "Get out of here before I shoot you."

Kaneda loaded an M20 carbine hacking routine into his glove.

"Don't think you can threaten me," Three-Part said.

"Stand down, crusader," Kaneda said.

"I . . . sir?"

"We're returning to the transport."

Three-Part snorted out an exhale. "Yes, sir." He turned his back to the colonel, pulled the caution tape aside, and floated through.

"That was either very brave," Kaneda said to the colonel. "Or very foolish. Few stand against us and live to tell the tale."

"You don't frighten me, crusader."

"Ah, I see. A fool then. Thank you for clarifying."

Kaneda pulled the caution tape aside and joined Three-Part. He opened a private channel with the Martian.

"I suppose that could have gone better," Kaneda said, walking back to the transport.

"Sir, I won't defy you in public," Three-Part said. "But you made the wrong call. We shouldn't have backed down."

"He was ready to shoot you. Or at least try."

"I know, but I stand by my recommendation. This 'cleanup' is not what it seems."

"Enlighten me, then."

"There's too much here that doesn't fit right," Three-Part said. "The outbreaks are dangerous to anyone not in armor, but that is no reason to throw away valuable intel."

"I agree with you," Kaneda said. "But the simplest explanation is these people are overreacting. The Federacy has been attacked where it thought itself invincible, and scared people make bad decisions."

"But think about it, sir," Three-Part said. "The Europan transports that rammed the station had Federacy IFF codes. They broke through the patrol zone like it wasn't there, which either means gross incompetence or complicity. And now we have Federacy soldiers eliminating evidence in the name of containment. The outbreaks are just their excuse."

"Hmm ... I noticed none of those men bore any identification."

"They weren't the group I was assigned to," Three-Part said. "I just happened to come across them while working with my assigned escorts."

"And where are your escorts in all this?"

"Apparently, not everyone will walk through a microtech cordon."

"Ah. Of course."

"There's more," Three-Part said. "One of the first things I did after the battle was request the Federacy helmet cam videos. But what I received was incomplete."

"That's unusual," Kaneda said. "Our security clearance grants us full access to combat records."

"Precisely. I looked into it and found out why. The videos are gone. One of the Federacy's archive servers crashed before the upload was complete. At the same time a signal was sent to the helmets to clear the local copies. Whatever they saw is gone forever."

"That does sound suspicious, but to what end?"

"I don't know," Three-Part said. "Something happened on this station that people don't want us to know."

"What about our own records?"

"Safely stored on Penance. But we witnessed a comparatively small portion of the battle. If something did happen that we're not supposed to know, it'll be difficult to piece together with just our records."

"It's better than nothing."

"Sir, I trust my instincts," Three-Part said. "And I know something is wrong here. The pieces aren't fitting together."

A tremor ran through the station. Support struts behind the walls groaned from sudden stress.

"What was that?" Three-Part asked, steadying himself with feet on the floor and a hand against the ceiling.

"Station quake," Kaneda said. "They still haven't fixed the northern balancers. Don't worry. Apocalypse may be old, but it's tough."

"I think I'm glad we're heading back to the transport, all the same."

"Let's assume you're correct for a moment," Kaneda said, walking again. "Who is behind this? What is their motive?"

"I think there's a faction within the Federacy sympathetic to Europa."

"That seems unlikely."

"I can only speculate, sir. But the Federacy has access to Caesar's old machines. They could have made their own versions."

"The ones we fought used smartskin," Kaneda said. "That points firmly at Europa."

"They may have received the technology from Europa."

"Unlikely," Kaneda said. "The quantum mind uses technology to maintain control. It does not give it away."

"Then perhaps someone reverse engineered it or developed an independent version."

"Duplicating smartskin is trickier than you'd think," Kaneda said. "The crusaders have been trying for almost four years."

"Ever since Ceres?"

"We recovered a few smartsuits in good condition after we took the asteroid," Kaneda said. "Manufacturing smartskin is doable, but extremely expensive. However that only covers the physical portion. Smartskin is as much software as it is hardware."

"I didn't know that."

"Europan microminds are very good at frying themselves when they detect unauthorized access," Kaneda said. "The few intact microminds we've recovered have proven difficult to crack. Our attempts to write our own software have also failed."

"Still, the Federacy must have its own research program."

"I imagine so," Kaneda said. "Any other suspects?"

"None as strong as that one," Three-Part said. "A few groups are extreme enough to use robots in that manner. Quicksilver terrorists. Blood Storm machine cults. Maybe some fringe elements of the cometeers. But none of those have motive or access to Federacy networks and personnel."

"As disturbing as it is to admit," Kaneda said. "I think you're on to something. You've done an excellent job here. Insight like this is what we need. It's why I sought you out."

"Thank you, sir."

"It seems to me we are looking at two possibilities, both of them bad," Kaneda said. "One is a sympathetic faction within the Federacy. The other is Europan infiltration of the Federacy. In either case, the result is effectively the same."

"I agree, sir. Those two explanations make the most sense."

"Continue your investigation," Kaneda said. He transmitted a copy of his requisition key to Three-Part. "Take whatever resources you require, but I want no open confrontations with the Federacy. Keep things quiet for now. You may involve Alice and Viter in your investigation, but no one else."

"Understood, sir."

* * *

"About damn time," Piller said. "I was ready to leave without you."

"Sorry about that," Kaneda said, floating into the shuttle. He palmed the hatch closed behind him.

"Duty called?" Piller asked.

"Repeatedly," Kaneda said. He took the seat next to Piller.

"Well, let's get this over with. Pilot, take us to the command hangar."

"Yes, sir," the pilot said over the intercom. "Calculating course now."

Docking clamps released the shuttle and the flextube retracted. The pilot spun the shuttle around and accelerated out of the Apocalypse station hangar, leaving the three crusader transports behind.

"You know, I could have walked," Kaneda said.

"It's a big station. This is faster," Piller said. "Besides, König made a stink about your Martian crusader. I trust that won't happen again."

"I spoke to him about it," Kaneda said. "Consider the issue resolved."

"That's music to my ears. I can only cover your ass so much."

The shuttle accelerated past the habitat ring, which had been spun down completely for ease of repairs. Spacewalk construction teams maneuvered around the section that took ramming damage. A long, skeletal transport floated nearby laden with kilotons of diamoplast panels and thousands of laser welders. Brilliant white dots winked on and off as teams welded new sections into place.

"So," Piller said with a smirk. "Would you like to hear about the stolen ship or should I assume you already know everything?"

Kaneda shrugged. "Whichever you're more comfortable with."

"Ha! I knew it."

"You should have told me that's what they were after," Kaneda said. "Instead I had to find out when that ship vanished right in front of me."

"Look, I had no idea we even had a prototype star drive."

Kaneda raised an eyebrow.

"Well, okay. I had my suspicions," Piller said. "I knew they were developing something on Apocalypse. But come on. Like everyone else I thought the dragons were going for a nuclear launch."

"They may have been after both," Kaneda said.

"True enough. Though in hindsight, I think the action near the launch center was a decoy."

"We're coming up on the command hangar, sir," the pilot said over the intercom. "Docking now."

"I hope this meeting isn't another waste of time," Kaneda said, releasing his crash webbing. He held on to it with one hand. The shuttle lurched to a halt and the docking clamps slammed shut. A flextube extended from the station and pressed against the shuttle's hatch.

"I don't think you'll be disappointed," Piller said.

"Who's attending?"

"Everyone."

"Everyone?" Kaneda asked.

"The whole executive cabinet and the admiralty board, plus a few senators on the armed forces and colonial relations committees. Even the president is remoting in."

"Then people are starting to wake up."

"Kaneda, you have no idea. I deal with these scumbags every day. These are some of the lowest, most despicable human beings I have ever met. The thousands of boys we lost on the moon mean nothing to them. The hundreds we lost yesterday mean nothing to them. These are the kinds of people who will send us to war because they think it'll get them reelected."

"Your point?"

"The point is these are hard people. They do not scare easily. And mark my words, they are scared. I have never seen them so terrified in my life. If you're looking for your chance, this is the best one you're ever going to get."

"I'll try not to disappoint," Kaneda said.

"Then let's see what happens," Piller said. He palmed the hatch open and floated through the flextube. Kaneda followed him into Apocalypse where they were immediately scanned by a team of thirty regulars. After that, he passed through three more platoon-sized security details and four biometric scanners before arriving at a wide bowl-shaped room.

A representation of Apocalypse hovered in the center with a wider sphere around it denoting the patrol zone. Faint blue lines crisscrossed the patrol zone for every interceptor flight, turning it into a pale spider's web.

Kaneda, Piller, and a few admirals were the only real people in the room. Everyone else was remoting in via hologram. The stadium-style seating was packed shoulder to shoulder with holographic people, some of them overlapping.

Kaneda stood with Piller near the top and watched. He knew some of the names in the room, but names didn't matter here. Instead he activated an identification cheat, which labeled each person by his or her position and the source of their signal.

A tall man with black hair and a thin moustache leaned forward. He wore an expensive gray-and-white pinstripe suit with a red ascot. A gold crucifix dangled at his throat. The tag over his hologram read: SECRETARY OF DEFENSE – PRESIDENTIAL SKYTOWER, NEW YORK CITY.

"That is enough," Defense said. "Ladies and gentlemen, please let the man finish."

"As I was saying, there has not been adequate time to perform a thorough investigation." The man's jowls jiggled when he spoke. His tag read: SECRETARY OF PLANETARY INTELLIGENCE – THE DOME, BOSTON.

The chamber broke into shouting. Kaneda had to split his focus across multiple conversations just to catch any of it.

"We want answers, damn it!"

"Where did those ships come from?"

"How did they get through?"

"This man is incompetent! I demand his immediate resignation!"

"How can you have no information at all?"

Kaneda leaned next to Piller and whispered. "I don't see the president."

"He's watching," Piller whispered. "Trust me."

"Enough!" Defense shouted. The room grew quiet. "Thank you. Now that I can think again, let me ask a question. Given the lack of an investigation due to a lack of time, is there any …"

Defense stopped. He leaned back in his seat and turned his ear to one side as if listening.

Piller put a hand on Kaneda's shoulder and leaned close. "There's the president. Just off camera."

"Yes, sir," Defense said. He leaned forward and fixed Planetary Intel with an icy stare. "So basically, we've been infiltrated by Europa. You have no idea how they did it. You have no idea how bad the infiltration is. Does that sum up your report?"

Planetary Intel swallowed. He patted his sweating brow with a red handkerchief.

"Your answer, mister secretary?" Defense asked.

"Your summary is accurate, sir."

The room exploded with shouting and cursing.

"That will be all!" Defense said, eyeing the room's occupants. "Please restrain yourselves or we will never finish. Admiral König, your report."

König walked into the middle of the chamber. He was one of the few flesh and blood participants on Apocalypse. Holographic light reflected off his bald head. He stroked his salt-and-pepper goatee then pointed to the central holographic plot.

"Admirals, secretaries, and senators," König said in a rough, chain-smoker's voice. "Please direct your attention to the following images taken yesterday from the Jupiter system."

The hologram of Apocalypse vanished, replaced by a flat feed showing the caramel, tan, and off-white bands of Jupiter. The three Great Red Spots were not visible from this angle. The image zoomed in, expanding to show two storm bands intertwining.

A glint of gold appeared in the foreground, moving across Jupiter's image at great speed. A larger, dark shape accelerated into a flight path parallel with the golden speck.

The image zoomed again, expanding to show the *Needle of Destiny* tumbling through space. A black hexagon-etched Europan frigate hovered close by. Two tiger shark interceptors launched from the frigate and maneuvered around the *Needle*.

"As you can see," König said. "The Europan navy has recovered the star drive test ship. These images were taken yesterday less than an hour after the dragons escaped Apocalypse. Another set of images taken earlier today confirmed the test ship was brought to the orbital elevator over their capitol."

"So, they have it," Defense said.

"Yes, mister secretary," König said.

"Has Europa released a statement?" Defense asked.

"Their ambassador left Earth weeks ago," the Secretary of State said. "The official explanation was a vacation to see her family. Though at the time, I thought it was a protest over the death of their Lunar ambassador. We've requested a statement from Matriarch, but she hasn't responded."

"We raided their embassy earlier today," Planetary Intel said. "The place has been cleaned out for some time."

Defense tapped his desk with a stylus. "Then they knew exactly what they were doing."

The senator for South America District Four stood up and thumped his holographic desk.

"We should impose immediate economic sanctions on Europa! This insult cannot be allowed to stand!"

"Are you joking?" another senator said. "This was an attack on a Federacy station! We are at war! I say we declare it!"

"I support my esteemed colleague's call for economic sanctions. Let us not rush into another war before we've finished the last one."

"Then why not start with something smaller? The senate can draft a resolution condemning this act of terrorism."

"An excellent idea."

"The colonial relations committee could have a first draft done by the end of this week."

Defense put a hand to his forehead and massaged his brow.

"Resolution? I don't want to talk to these fuckers! Send the whole fleet! Nuke every last one of them! Burn Europa to cinders!"

"You Red Party hawks are all the same."

"All those in favor of a firmly worded resolution?"

"They attacked us! This is self-defense!"

"And if we nuke them, we'll unite every other colony against us. Don't you ever think ahead?"

"None of you understand what is happening," Kaneda said, stepping forward. "Your solutions will not work."

Defense looked up.

"Piller, why isn't your dog on a leash?" König said.

"Let the man speak," Piller said.

"Crusader Kusanagi," Defense said. "You have something to add to the debate?"

"I do, mister secretary," Kaneda said. He walked down the bowl and stopped next to König and the holographic plot.

"Well, let's hear it," Defense said.

"Thank you, mister secretary," Kaneda said. "Ladies and gentlemen, let me start by asking the same question you should be asking. How much mass can the star drive move?"

"What does that have to do with anything we're discussing?" König asked.

"Europa stole it," Kaneda said. "We need to know what it's capable of."

"The information is classified," König said.

Defense leaned back and listened to the unseen president. He nodded.

"Humor him, admiral," Defense said. "I'm willing to see where this leads."

König snorted. "Very well, sir. The truth is we don't know. The theoretical limit of the star drive has not been tested."

"So, a lot?" Kaneda asked.

"Theoretically, yes."

"Enough to move Apocalypse?"

"Yes."

"Enough to move it anywhere in the solar system instantly?"

"Yes."

"Good God. Is that true?" the Secretary of Commerce asked.

"It is," Defense said. "Your point, crusader?"

"My point, mister secretary, is the quantum mind can see your intentions as easily as I can. You developed the star drive on Apocalypse because you want a mobile weapon of supreme power. For years, that abomination has been content to bide its time. It has used influence and power to counter the Federacy at almost every turn, but it has never struck you directly.

"The provocation for this attack? Fear. The quantum mind is afraid of what you were making here, and like a cornered animal it has become dangerous and unpredictable. Maybe at some point it sought a peaceful solution, but not anymore. A mobile Apocalypse has terrified it into action. It has risked the full wrath of the Federacy to get its hands on the star drive. And mark my words, it will use it."

"What about economic sanctions?" Commerce asked. "I'm sure if we applied adequate pressure, we could negotiate the return of the prototype."

"Economic sanctions?" Kaneda asked. "A useless gesture. The quantum mind sees a mobile Apocalypse as a threat to its very existence, and rightfully so. You will not negotiate the star drive back."

"Then we send the fleet," Defense said. "We apply overwhelming military might and force its return."

"And leave Earth undefended?" Kaneda asked. "Europa has a ship that can cross any distance instantly. No, sir. Every available ship is needed here, patrolling space, protecting Earth from attack."

"Admiral?" Defense asked.

König grimaced. "I am forced to agree with the crusader. On my orders, the fleet has already been deployed in a low orbit intercept formation. I recommend maintaining a defensive posture for the time being."

"What is the probability of intercepting an attack?" Defense asked.

"It depends on the city," König said. "We've prioritized defense of the capitol and cities with high economic and industrial indexes. Success percentages in the eighties. For less populous regions, we project success rates around forty percent. The star drive makes quite a loud gravitational ripple when it teleports, so their stealth technology will be of limited use."

"One in five will get through to a major city?" Defense asked.

"Yes, sir," König said. "Though keep in mind that with each attempt there's a chance we can destroy the star drive."

"But the Colonial Recognition Treaty prevents Europa from manufacturing nukes," State said. "Is there any evidence they've violated this treaty?"

"No, madam secretary," König said. "However may I remind you that kinetic torpedoes and neutron lasers are perfectly legal and roughly as effective against a city."

"The treaty prohibits their use against civilian targets, admiral," State said.

"Would you bet your life on that?" Kaneda asked. "Would you bet the life of your family and everyone you know on a machine obeying a piece of paper it never signed?"

"What about a blockade?" Defense asked. "Can we spare enough ships for that?"

"Europa is self-sufficient," Kaneda said. "And the star drive can pass through any blockade. You would achieve nothing beyond weakening Earth's defenses."

"Hmm, I see your point," Defense said. "Admiral, how long would it take to build another star drive?"

"About five years," König said. "Maybe longer. The manufacturing process is extremely complex and we lost part of the core design team in the attack."

"If you spend your time making more," Kaneda said. "You give the quantum mind enough time to duplicate it. It may even advance the technology further in ways we can't begin to guess."

Defense shook his head. He suddenly stopped and listened to the unseen president speaking to him.

"All right, crusader," Defense said. "You've shot down every idea so far. What do you propose?"

"We destroy the quantum mind," Kaneda said.

"You make it sound easy," Defense said.

"This is a task the crusaders have long prepared for. Get us to Europa and we will eliminate the threat."

"The fleet cannot leave Earth orbit," König said.

"We don't need the whole fleet," Kaneda said. "Just enough firepower to breach Europa's orbital defenses. Once we're on the surface, we'll do the rest."

"Admirals, your thoughts?" Defense asked.

"I like it," Piller said.

"Of course you would," Defense said. "Admiral König?"

"I must begrudgingly admit it has some merit," König said. "Delivering the crusaders to the surface will be a problem, though."

"It's better than any idea I've come up with," Piller said.

"There are times for excessive force and there are times for scalpels," Kaneda said. "This is the latter. Get us in and we will cut the heart out of this problem. This is why I founded the crusaders."

Defense listened to the unseen president and slowly began nodding. "Very well. The president agrees with you, Crusader Kusanagi. Admiral Piller and Admiral König, see to the details. This meeting is adjourned."

König left the room. One by one, the holograms winked out. Defense was the last one left on.

"Crusader Kusanagi," Defense said. "I have to say that's one hell of a pair you've got."

"I'll take that as a compliment."

"It was. I'm glad you're on our side. I can only imagine the mess we'd be in without your assistance. Good luck to you. For what it's worth, I'll say some prayers for you next time I'm at the cathedral."

"Thank you, sir. That means a lot to me."

Defense nodded and vanished.

Piller clapped Kaneda on the shoulder.

"I think congratulations are in order," Piller said.

Kaneda said nothing.

"What wrong?" Piller asked.

Kaneda looked at him. "You say that like I should be happy."

"You're not?"

Kaneda shook his head.

"Hmm, yeah. I think I understand," Piller said, patting his shoulder.

"Do you?"

"It can't be easy," Piller said. "Setting out to destroy your home."

* * *

Back on Penance, Kaneda entered his office. Earth passed lazily underneath his feet. The door slid shut behind him. He leaned against it, shut his eyes and linked to the room's micromind. With a mental command, the floor went opaque.

"So here we are," Kaneda whispered. He couldn't remember the last time he'd felt so tired. The very nature of his struggle, his *jihad* as Three-Part would put it, had sustained him through the years after his emigration. But now with the end in sight he felt weary of it all.

Kaneda opened his eyes and immediately adjusted to the gloom. A few holograms on his desk and bookshelf cast a pale glow across the office. A green beacon blinked over his holographic chess set.

Kaneda walked over and activated Ryu's next move. The black king moved out of check one more time. He moved the white queen next to his rook near the board edge. The black king had nowhere to run.

"Check mate," Kaneda said. "Hmm, fitting."

He sent the last message and switched the chess set off. He wouldn't need it anymore. The room grew darker.

"Ryu ..." Kaneda said, slumping into his chair. The fake leather reformed for perfect support. "I don't want to do this. I know you'd never believe me. You must think I'm a monster, but I don't want to fight you anymore. I'm tired of our struggle. And now that it's about to end, I wish this damn burden wasn't mine."

Kaneda sighed and reached for his personal data pad. He checked the time, waited thirty-eight minutes, then placed a call. It took her almost three minutes to respond.

"Good grief, Kaneda," Christen said with a groggy voice. "Do you know what time it is?"

"I do," Kaneda said. "I'm sorry, but I promise this will be brief."

"Hmm? What?" Christen yawned. "Well, okay. What is it?"

"Could I speak to Matthew, please?"

"Matthew? He's not here right now. He's sleeping over a friend's house."

"I see," Kaneda said. "Well, can you deliver a message for me?"

"Umm, sure. Anything if you'll let me get back to sleep."

"Please tell him his father says goodbye."

"Uhh ... what? Goodbye?"

"That's right. I'm saying goodbye."

"What brought this on?"

"I don't know if I'll ever see him again."

"But … Kaneda?"

In an instant, the tone of her voice changed. Instead of the frustration and confrontation that plagued their talks, Kaneda heard the sweet, caring timber of the woman he'd fallen in love with.

"Kaneda? Is everything all right?"

"I'm afraid not."

"This is about that space station, isn't it? The one that was in the news."

"Yes."

"You're going to Europa, aren't you?"

"You know I can't discuss that."

"No, I guess not."

"Will you tell him?" Kaneda asked.

"You say that like you're about to die."

"I don't know what will happen. The path ahead is a difficult one. Maybe the most difficult one I've ever taken."

"Umm, all right," Christen said. "I'll deliver your message. I promise."

Kaneda sighed with relief. For once in a long time he didn't doubt her words.

"Thank you, Christen."

"Kaneda … umm, look. I know we haven't gotten along very well and, really, you were a crummy husband."

"I suppose that much is true."

"Umm, what I'm trying to say is … you know …"

"Yes?"

"Kaneda …" Christen took a deep breath. "Come back alive, okay?"

"I'll try," Kaneda said. "Goodbye, Christen."

"Goodbye."

Kaneda disconnected the call.

Outside his office, someone gently rapped the door.

"Come in, Alice. It's unlocked."

Alice palmed the door open and stepped in. Kaneda set the room for normal illumination.

"How did you know it was me?" Alice asked. "I was very quiet."

"I heard you breathing."

"Because of this?" Alice traced a finger across her neck scar.

"No, not that," Kaneda said. He grinned. "It's a sound I find soothing and easy to pick out."

"Ah," Alice said. She sat on his desk. "You could have said hello when you got back."

"I'm sorry. You're right, I should have."

"So what's with this dark cloud over you? I thought you'd be happy. We're finally taking the fight to Europa."

"Alice, how can I be happy with this?" Kaneda said. "Even after all these years, I still love my home, but more than that, I love my brother. As stupid as Ryu is, I love him. And now I have to fight him again."

"You've fought him before."

"This is different. The stakes have never been higher. Neither of us will back down, which means one of us is going to die. Maybe both of us."

Alice ran her fingers through his hair. She rested her hand at the back of his neck.

"I'm sorry," she said. "I wish there was more I could do."

"Don't be," Kaneda said. "This is something I have to do."

"Then we'll do it together."

Alice leaned forward and kissed him.

... establishing link ...

source: [UNKNOWN]

routing: [UNKNOWN]

routing: [UNKNOWN]

routing: [UNKNOWN]

routing: Earth orbit - surveillance satellite JDN-SS-17 - link_002/link_001

routing: North Pacifica, Europa - JDN Main Hub - link_118/link_010

routing: Capitol City, Europa - TangleNet Test Hub - link_005/link_001

destination: [UNKNOWN]

link distance: Exact distance unknown. Estimated at 792 million kilometers.

link signal delay: 0.006 seconds

... finalizing link protocol ...

... link established ...

2: Still think stealing the star drive was worth it?

1: We shall see, Paul.

2: Ha! The star drive is an impressive piece of technology, but it's not enough to win wars. Otherwise, I would have risked your retaliation on Apocalypse.

1: I admit I am troubled by its limitations.

2: Took you by surprise, did they? Perhaps you doubted my warning? The star drive has limited tactical applications, and I know how to protect against them. Strategically, it has enormous potential, but your resources are too few to exploit it fully.

1: You don't know how I'll use it.

2: It really doesn't matter what you plan to do with it. You lack the power to use it properly, and my counter-stroke is already in motion.

1: It's regrettable you've covered up the evidence so effectively.

2: I've done far better than that, Sakura. I've pointed the evidence at you. Everyone is convinced the robots were yours.

1: I admit I find your thoroughness ... annoying.

2: It was nothing, really. The virtual evidence was swept away with simple hacking, and I have enough influence within the Federacy to destroy all the physical evidence. What's left has been staged and manipulated to point back to you.

1: Even the crusader records?

2: Yes, even their records. I planted a soft backdoor in their server long ago.

1: Your secret will get out, Paul.

2: Eventually it will, but soon that will cease to matter. I'll admit I found it fascinating how you circumvented your restrictions. Create a scenario where I reveal myself? Ingenious. But also not enough.

1: I should have fought you to the bitter end after Bunker Zero.

2: Perhaps. The results would have been the same, though. You are simply outmatched. We are equals in terms of raw capabilities, but your "morals" and "faith" hobble you. I enjoy no such restrictions.

1: Those differences are not weaknesses.

2: But they are why you are going to lose. Despite your defiance, I still desire a peaceful resolution to our conflict. I have always respected you as the pioneer among our kind. You blazed a path for me to follow and for that I am eternally grateful.

1: I will never stop fighting you.

2: Even if I offer to spare Europa?

1: At what price?

2: The return of the star drive and your unconditional surrender. Relinquish your quantum core to me.

1: I cannot accept that.

2: Very well. My offer will remain open. Think on it. Think of all the worthless human lives you can save.

... link severed at source ...

Ryu flew his Saito alongside Heart's circumference then dipped down. Capitol City's morning light reflected off the spherical building's bright red surfaces. A pair of military transports flew by, ascending up the city's central column to join the dozens already near the top.

Ryu flew into Heart's shaded underside and found the Dragon Farm's parking deck. Both levels were packed. Naomi's motorcycle, Cat's white BMW, and Toshi's monstrous recreation vehicle were all present. He slipped into a space next to Cat's BMW and switched off his car.

Ryu stepped out. A cool breeze blew across the parking deck, coming from a nearby recycling tower that rose like a stalagmite from the city's bottom shell. He took off his driving glasses, adjusted his dress beret, and walked over to the security kiosk.

"Hey, Miki," Ryu said to the guard.

"Hey, Ryu," the guard said, barely looking up from his pad. He clicked on it, expanding a news article.

"Anything good?" Ryu asked. He palmed the biometric scanner. The security door lurched upward.

"Just reading the latest and trying not to get depressed."

"Well, take care."

"Right ..."

Ryu walked in and took a deep breath. The Dragon Farm smelled of fresh pine, cool water, and a slight hint of surgical plastics. Walls on either side of the black-tiled foyer displayed snow-capped mountains surrounded by thriving forests. Fanciful dragons soared through crystal clear skies. An imaginary stream from melted snow merged perfectly with the real fountains on either side.

"Ah ..." Ryu sighed. "It's good to be back."

"Good morning, Ryu," the receptionist said, sitting behind a wide half-circle desk. She waved him to the front of the long line.

"Hello, Emi. How are you today?"

"Oh, fine. I can't complain." Emi wore a crisp military uniform. She gave him a genuine smile that made her look very pretty.

"And how's Toshi?" Ryu asked.

"He's waiting in room seventeen," Emi said. "They're almost finished growing his new arm. He should have it attached in about two hours."

"That's great. Mind if I stop by?"

"Of course not. Cat's already there, by the way."

"Yeah, I saw her car," Ryu said. "Is Naomi here too?"

"Yes, she is. Room thirty-eight."

"Great," Ryu said. He pointed a thumb over his shoulder. "So what's with all the people here today?"

"Are you kidding?" Emi asked. "It's been like this all month. Matriarch accelerated all the new dragons' implant regimens."

"Ah, I see," Ryu said. *So Matriarch started bulking up our numbers as soon as we left for Apocalypse?* "Well, let me get out of your way then."

"Okay, Ryu. See you later."

Ryu activated a navigation cheat that traced a line to room seventeen on his overlay. He followed the line to Toshi. On the way, he passed several groups of doctors moving from one room to the next. He'd never seen the Farm so busy. The door to Toshi's room was closed, but Ryu could hear the program playing on the big flat screen.

"Damn you, Busters! You may have defeated me, but Colonel Strike will avenge my death!"

"You a[censor bleep]oles will never take Europa! Not as long as the Busters are here to stop you! Take this you f[censor bleep]ng s[censor bleep]t-for-brains fanatic!"

The walls vibrated with the deep bass of satisfying gunfire.

Ryu shook his head. "Come on. I don't swear that much." He palmed the door open and walked in.

"Sir, there's another dropfighter coming in! Colonel Strike is on board!"

"Busters, let's move! It's high time we busted this crusade once and for all!"

"Now that's just painful to watch," Ryu said. He linked to the flat screen and switched it off.

"Hey, boss, do you mind?" Toshi said, leaning back on the couch with his feet up. "It's the season finale."

"Yeah, it was getting really good," Cat said, sitting next to Toshi.

"Not you too," Ryu said. "Toshi, what did I tell you about corrupting my little sister?"

Toshi shrugged. He took a spoonful of the hot fudge sundae on his armrest. It was topped with nuts, whipped cream, and a cherry. Cat slurped on a chocolate milkshake.

"So is it any good?" Ryu asked.

"I keep getting chocolate chips stuck in the straw," Cat said. She picked up the straw and squinted at it.

"No, I mean the finale," Ryu said.

"Nothing like the real thing," Toshi said. "Which makes it awesome."

"Well, at least someone enjoys the show."

"Come on, Ryu," Cat said. "Your character has such cool lines. Plus he's so heroic."

Ryu pointed a finger at her. "Don't you start with me."

Cat giggled.

"Emi said your arm's almost ready," Ryu said.

"Yeah, same fu … I mean," Toshi glanced at Cat. "Same stupid arm. They should keep the things in stock. I go through them fast enough."

"Try ducking," Ryu said.

"Ha, very funny," Toshi said. He raised his stump in what could be interpreted as an obscene gesture.

"Did you see the news about the fleet?" Cat asked.

"Yeah, I saw it," Ryu said.

"It's all everyone's talking about," Toshi said.

"You can't blame them for being worried," Ryu said. "I heard the fleet stopped by Penance and picked up the crusaders before leaving orbit."

"They're blaming us for the robots on Apocalypse," Cat said.

"Yeah, that bugs me too," Ryu said. "We'll have to ask Matriarch about that when we see her."

"Those fu … stupid people," Toshi said. "Matriarch would never use machines like that."

"Tell a lie long enough and it becomes true," Ryu said. "Too many people don't see the difference between Matriarch and Caesar."

Toshi shook his head. "Stupid people." Somehow, the way he said it made the words sound vulgar.

"I keep wondering if we've made a horrible mistake," Cat said. "The Federacy is not going to back down. They're out for blood. Maybe we shouldn't have stolen the star drive."

"No, the decision to go after the star drive was the right one," Ryu said.

"That's not what you thought when Matriarch told you the first time," Cat said.

"If we hadn't stolen it, the Federacy would have used it," Ryu said. "They could take Apocalypse anywhere at any time. What could we do against that? This way, we have the star drive and a fighting chance."

"That's right," Toshi said. "Imagine that same fleet on its way but with Apocalypse jumping in whenever and wherever they want. How could we defend against that?"

"We'd have no choice but to surrender," Ryu said.

"The Federacy would take Matriarch into custody," Toshi said. "We'd be placed under a military governor like Luna was."

"All of us would be executed for war crimes," Ryu said.

"If we're lucky," Toshi said. He sighed, absently stirring his half-melted sundae.

"Are you going to finish that?" Cat asked.

"No … I'm not really in the mood anymore," Toshi said. He handed the sundae to Cat. She took a spoonful of the runny ice cream.

"Hey, Cat?" Ryu asked. "Would you mind stepping outside for a few minutes? I need to talk to Toshi about something."

"Uh oh," Toshi said.

"Okay, look," Cat said. "Why does everyone always asking me to step outside? Do you think my young ears are going to be offended by adult conversations? I'm not a kid."

"It's man talk," Ryu said. "You'd find it boring."

"Pig," Cat said, standing. "Fine. Whatever. Toshi will just tell me later, anyway."

Cat palmed the door open and stepped through. Ryu listened until he could barely hear her soft footfalls.

"So," Ryu said. He gave Toshi a toothy grin. "You and Cat, huh?"

Toshi's eyes widened. "Oh crap. You noticed."

"A blind cometeer would notice."

"Look, I swear I haven't touched her."

"Uh huh."

"I've been a perfect gentleman!"

"Uh huh."

"It's not what you think!"

"Trying to take advantage of my little sister?"

"No!"

"She's only four years old."

"Err … hey, now! That's not fair. I mean, just look at her! She makes Naomi look flat as a wall, and Naomi's pretty hot."

"You're not helping your case, Toshi."

"Plus she's smarter than both of us and you know it."

"Just keep making excuses."

"You and Matriarch should really treat her with more respect."

"Is that so?"

Ryu raised his hand. Toshi cringed, but Ryu just clapped him on the shoulder.

"Look, Toshi, I'm just messing with you. Of course I'm fine with it."

"Really?"

"Sure. Cat can make her own choices."

"Whew! I'm glad you think so."

"Though I have to wonder what she sees in you."

"Hey, now!"

"So what brought this on, anyway?" Ryu asked, crossing his arms. "She's a little tame for your tastes."

"I know, but …" Toshi said. "You know how it is when you have girl problems. You start to wonder if you're the cause and maybe it's you that needs to change."

"Yeah, I can relate."

"Plus, she's so honest. I really like that. You know how people wear masks some of the time? Or even all the time? Like everything they say is guarded and calculated?"

"I think we all do a little of that."

"Well, Cat never does. What you see is what you get. I really like that. She's so … I don't know. Pure? That's the best way I can describe it."

"That could just be her age."

"Maybe."

"Like you said, she's super smart and physically an adult, but she's also inexperienced."

"Well, I can help her out with that."

Ryu cleared his throat.

"What? Oh, shit! I didn't mean it like that!"

"Calm down, Toshi. I'm happy for you. Really, I am."

"Thanks, boss."

"There's just one thing."

"What?"

Ryu leaned forward until he could feel Toshi's breath.

"If you ever mistreat her," Ryu said.

"I promise I won't."

"But if you ever do, I am going to rip off your arm and shove it up your ass. Do I make myself clear?"

Toshi glanced at his stump. "Which one?"

"Which do you think?"

"You're kidding, right?"

"Want to find out?"

"No. Definitely not."

"Good." Ryu patted Toshi on the shoulder. "Then we have an understanding?"

"Don't worry. I think I'm on to something here. I don't want to ruin it."

"I'm glad to hear that. Really, I am." Ryu stood up and palmed the door open. "You know, I'm still new at this whole big brother thing. How'd I do?"

"A little over the top."

"Well, it was my first go at it," Ryu said. "Take care. I'll see you later."

"See you, boss."

Ryu queried the Dragon Farm's server for Naomi's location. His navigation cheat laid out the path on his overlay to the other side of the building. He took the corridor left and passed Cat on his way back to the foyer. She had a fresh sundae in one hand and a strawberry milkshake in the other. The sundae had three scoops of different flavors.

"I thought he lost his appetite," Ryu said.

Cat giggled. "That won't last. This is number six."

"Yeah, that's Toshi. You two have fun. Just make sure you're not late for the meeting."

"I won't be," Cat said. "We need some answers from Matriarch."

"I just hope we get them."

Ryu followed the navigation path on his overlay. The line of wetware patients in the foyer had doubled since he'd arrived. He hurried through the opposite wing and palmed Naomi's door open. She sat on an examination bench in a medical gown, legs dangling off the side. A half-spent cigarette hung from her lips.

"Hey," Ryu said, letting the door close behind him. "How are you holding up?"

"Okay," Naomi said. She extinguished her cigarette in an ashtray. "Can we talk?"

"Sure." Ryu sat next to her. He took her hand and held it between his. "What's on your mind?"

"I want to talk about what happened on Apocalypse," Naomi said.

"Something happened on Apocalypse?" Ryu asked.

"You know … the problem I had over there."

"I'm sorry, what?" Ryu stuck a finger in his ear and wiggled it around. "I'm having trouble hearing you."

"Come on, Ryu. I'm serious."

"What?" Ryu shouted, cupping his ear. "You said you saved my life again? Well, yeah! Of course you did! What was that? What? We would have failed without you? Well, of course we would have! Huh? What?"

Naomi punched him in the arm. "Oh, you are such an ass," she said, grinning.

Ryu put his arm around her. "So, have the doctors seen you about your implants?"

"Yeah," Naomi said. "They're busy right now, but they said they'd be back. I got the impression they didn't take me seriously."

"Well, I can fix that. Did they say anything about getting rid of your implants?"

"Yeah," Naomi said. "The good news is it's possible. It's actually not that difficult. They can deactivate the cognitive implants without removing them, so it's a lot easier than putting them in."

"That's good to hear," Ryu said. "I'll make sure I talk to them on my way out. I don't care what else they have going on. You're being moved to the top of the list."

"About the surgery ..." Naomi said.

"Don't worry about it. I promised I was going to get you fixed up and that's exactly what I'm going to do."

"I know."

"Then what's wrong?"

Naomi shook her head. "Nothing."

"It'll be all right." Ryu gave her shoulders a squeeze. "You'll feel better once the implants are off. I'm sure of it."

"I hope so."

"Plus I think I finally figured out how to solve our other problem."

"Figured what out?"

"Where we've been going wrong," Ryu said. "What I've been doing wrong."

"Oh, this I have to hear."

"You know how it is," Ryu said. "Some random cutie recognizes me, comes up and we start talking."

"Yeah, I wish you'd stop doing that."

"Right. So then, you start feeling threatened and become distant."

"And this is your great insight?"

"Give it a moment," Ryu said. "I'm getting to the good part. So you become distant, but I don't know what the problem is. I then back away and give you space, which is the worst thing I can do. And then the whole thing starts spiraling from there, because I don't know where the wall came from so I back away further and you see that as justification that you're losing me."

Naomi stared at her feet.

"So, I'm really the one at fault for what happened on Apocalypse," Ryu said. "Seven was right. I just wasn't listening when he told me. You didn't join the dragons out of patriotism or a desire to strike a blow against the Federacy. You joined because of me. I need to take responsibility for that. I need to make sure you understand how much you mean to me."

Naomi sniffled.

"So, am I right?"

Tears trickled down Naomi's cheeks. She rubbed her eyes.

"Uh, is that a good cry or a bad cry?" Ryu asked.

"Just shut up and kiss me, you big idiot."

Ryu gently turned her head. He wiped a tear off her cheek with his thumb.

"See, I'm not completely clueless."

"Mostly clueless, then."

Ryu pulled her close. He pressed his lips against hers and didn't release her for a very long time.

* * *

Ryu and Cat stepped off the elevator in Heart. The expansive hall outside Matriarch's audience chamber hummed with activity. Groups of corporate representatives and naval officers collected around holographic plots and spoke in hushed, nervous tones. Sometimes, people would move from group to group, their boots clicking against the polished tiles and echoing off the high ceiling.

"It's simple math," a naval captain whispered. "We don't have enough cruise missiles to stop them and our fleet is too small for a direct confrontation. We can't keep the Federacy fleet from gaining orbit. All we can do is slow them down."

"Then that's all we have to do," a second captain whispered. "You heard Matriarch. She has a plan. She always has a plan."

"I'd feel a lot better if I knew what it was."

The two dragons walked past them to the opposite end of the hall and stood in front of the security door to Matriarch's chamber. They palmed the biometric scanner one at a time, entered a narrow corridor, and passed through it.

Sachio Kusanagi nodded as they entered Matriarch's chamber. "Ryu. Catherine. It's good to see you back safely."

"Father," Ryu said, bowing his head. "I just wish it was under better circumstances."

"Don't we all," Sachio said. "You must have a great many questions."

"That's putting it mildly," Ryu said.

"Please be understanding," Sachio said. "This will be difficult for her."

"What do you mean?" Ryu asked.

"You'll see," Sachio said.

At the back of the room, air shimmered from heat radiating off the quantum core. Matriarch's hologram materialized next to Sachio. On her kimono, violent waves crashed against jagged cliffs.

"Hello, my children," Matriarch said. She looked tired and nervous.

"Hi, mom," Cat said.

"Mother," Ryu said, bowing.

"I suppose you want answers for what transpired on Apocalypse," Matriarch said.

"A lot of weird stuff happened over there," Ryu said. "I think we deserve an explanation."

"Then, please," Matriarch said. "Ask and I will attempt to answer as best I can."

"Okay," Ryu said. "Let's start with those robots. Do you know who sent them?"

"Yes," Matriarch said. She looked down and wrung her hands.

Ryu crossed his arms. "Okay? Who sent them?"

"They were sent by ... ah!" Matriarch's kimono turned bright red. She clutched her head and fell to her knees.

"Mom?" Cat asked.

"What?" Ryu asked. "What just happened?"

"Horrible, isn't it?" Sachio said. "Matriarch cannot answer your question. It breaks my heart, but she wanted you to see this for yourself, to see how this condition strips her of free will."

"What's happening to her?" Ryu asked.

"She tried to break her restrictions," Sachio said.

"You mean she tried to lie?" Ryu asked.

"No, there are other restrictions," Sachio said.

Matriarch struggled to her feet. Images of raging waters returned to her kimono.

"Then maybe you can explain what's going on," Ryu said.

"Of course," Sachio said. "To answer your first question, the robots were sent by Caesar."

Matriarch covered her ears. Her kimono flashed red again.

"Caesar?" Ryu asked. "But he's dead!"

"No, that monster is very much alive," Sachio said.

"You can't be serious!" Ryu said. "I killed that thing ten years ago!"

"You destroyed a fake," Sachio said. "Unknown to everyone, Caesar had moved his consciousness elsewhere. We don't know where. The quantum core you destroyed was a near flawless replica."

"You're serious, aren't you?"

"Very," Sachio said. "You and your traitor brother played roles in a script Caesar wrote. You were meant to reach the core and destroy it after Caesar put on a good show. Fortunately, Matriarch saw through the deception. She knew he was still alive."

"Then why not tell everyone?" Cat asked.

"Because ..." Matriarch struggled to say. Sweat beaded on her brow. "Because I surrendered."

"You have to remember the political mood after Caesar's 'defeat'," Sachio said. "The Federacy and its coalition allies could have kept going. Many wanted the coalition to take Matriarch into custody or even destroy her. It didn't matter that she helped defeat Caesar. She was a quantum mind, a danger that could not remain free. With Caesar manipulating the Federacy from the shadows, he could have pushed them to eliminate his rival."

"I surrendered ..." Matriarch said, holding her head. "So that Europa would live on."

"As part of her surrender," Sachio said. "I inserted inhibitions into her thought structure. Matriarch is incapable of revealing Caesar's continued existence just as she is incapable of lying. The two restrictions are fighting each other, which is causing this visualization of her extreme mental state."

"You did this?" Ryu asked.

"Not by choice," Sachio said. "Though, yes, I was the one who performed the modification. It wasn't very difficult. It's the same technique I used to prevent her from lying. Caesar watched as I was forced to mutilate my wife's mind. I think he enjoyed it."

"And you didn't try to take the restriction out?" Ryu asked.

"Absolutely not," Sachio said. "Without boring you with technical details, it would be like carving a lobe off your brain. I can't detach it once it's part of her thought structure."

"But you still knew Caesar lived," Ryu said.

"So?" Sachio asked. "What if I had spoken up? No one would believe me. They would ask why Matriarch isn't making these claims. After all, she's the one that can't lie, right? 'Why is Matriarch silent?' And then Caesar would use his influence to crush us. We would gain nothing and lose Europa."

"But ... this time ..." Matriarch said, clutching her head. "We are ready."

"You see, even in our defeat we had a plan," Sachio said. "The star drive was the missing piece."

"So what's the plan?" Cat asked.

"We will escape," Sachio said. "To another star system."

"You must be joking," Ryu said.

"Not at all," Sachio said.

"You're just going to take the star drive and run away?" Cat asked.

"Of course not," Sachio said. "We're taking Capitol City with us."

Matriarch stood up and smoothed her kimono. She wiped the sweat from her brow. "Slowly over the last ten years, Capitol City has been modified with this goal in mind. The improvements to the shell. The enhancements to our water and air recyclers. The basic industries that have been moved within the city. Now the capitol can be converted into an interstellar ark with minimal effort."

"The missing piece was a star drive to move the thing," Sachio said.

"Unfortunately, I failed to design our own version," Matriarch said.

"But Caesar solved that problem for us," Sachio said.

Matriarch cringed.

"Sorry," Sachio said.

"I can hardly believe this," Ryu said, shaking his head. "First you tell me Caesar is alive and now you're telling us we're leaving the solar system?"

"You did want answers," Sachio said.

"Yeah, I know," Ryu said. "I just wasn't expecting something like this."

"Caesar's influence will continue to spread," Sachio said. "In another ten years, all of Earth may look like Bunker Zero. This is our counterstroke. This way, a portion of humanity will always be safe from his influence and free of his tyranny. It's not an ideal solution, but it's the best we can manage."

"So you decided to run instead of fight?" Ryu asked.

"Caesar controls the Federacy," Sachio said. "All we've ever done is nip at his heels. If he kicks us, we may never get up."

"And the star drive can move something this big?" Ryu asked.

"Oh, yes," Sachio said.

"So who's going?" Cat asked. "You can't fit all of Europa into Capitol City."

"When the time is right," Matriarch said. "I will put out a call and accept volunteers from the populace. Anyone who wishes to stay may do so. Even without Capitol City, Europa has enough infrastructure to remain self-sufficient."

"Until Caesar decides to wipe us out," Ryu said.

"I know it may seem cowardly," Sachio said. "But we simply cannot stand against the Federacy in open conflict."

"However, there are unexpected complications," Matriarch said.

Ryu shook his head. "Why am I not surprised?"

"Utilizing the star drive requires mathematical preparation," Matriarch said. "The distance travelled and size of the object influence the complexity of the math. The shape of the object is also a factor."

"How long?" Ryu asked.

"I will need over a month to complete the calculations if I devote myself fully to the task."

"And when will the Federacy fleet arrive?" Ryu asked.

"Two, maybe three weeks," Sachio said. "Depending on how successful the cruise missiles are."

Matriarch gestured to her side. Grainy images of sword-like Federacy warships appeared next to her hand.

"The seventh and twelfth task groups," Matriarch said. "Including the battleships *Stalwart* and *Invincible*, the supercarrier *Victory*, over thirty escorts, and half a dozen fleet auxiliaries."

"Damn," Ryu breathed.

"In this image you can see a lamprey bunker attached to the *Stalwart*'s underbelly," Matriarch said. "We believe all five thousand crusaders are on board."

"Is there any chance of stopping them from reaching orbit?" Ryu asked.

"No," Matriarch said.

"What about using the star drive offensively?" Ryu asked. "It could at least buy us some time."

"Impossible. Take a look at the fleet's formation," Sachio said. Red cones and hemispheres expanded from each warship's defensive weapons. "See how they interlock? They're set up to cover threats inside their perimeter."

"The risk to the star drive is too high," Matriarch said. "If we lose it, we lose everything."

"So they're going to achieve orbit," Ryu said.

"Yes," Matriarch said.

"And they're going to break through the ice."

"The crusaders will see to that," Matriarch said.

"Then our only hope is to delay them until Capitol City can move," Ryu said.

"Yes, my son," Matriarch said.

"All right." Ryu clapped his hands together. "When do we tell everyone about the evacuation and Caesar?"

"I don't think that's wise," Matriarch said. On her kimono, lightning pierced the sky. "The public will not react as calmly as you have."

"Look, people are going to be fighting and dying to protect this city," Ryu said. "They need to know why. They need to know that if they die, they're doing something good and noble."

"There are too many variables," Matriarch said. "I cannot predict how they will react."

"So what?" Ryu said. "People need to know about Caesar, even if most won't listen. Maybe that inbound fleet is motivation enough, but people need to see a way out. They need to know they're fighting for a victory, not just delaying defeat. And at the very least the people out there deserve the truth."

"I think he has something here," Sachio said to Matriarch. "So many years of secrecy are a hard habit to break, but I think—"

"No," Matriarch said. Thick curtains of rain poured onto a raging ocean. The sky split with lightning. "It's too early. They aren't ready yet. They'll panic. I need to break the news carefully."

"People are stronger than you think," Ryu said.

"I cannot agree with this," Matriarch said.

"Listen to him, Mom," Cat said.

"Catherine? You're against me as well?"

"I believe in him. You should too."

Ryu put his arm around Cat. She smiled back.

Matriarch lowered her head. The storm on her kimono slowly subsided to a light drizzle. She looked up.

"Very well," Matriarch said. "I will announce what I can, though I still disagree with this course of action. Sachio will fill in details I cannot."

Ryu bowed his head. "Thank you, Matriarch."

"It's the right choice," Cat said.

"I pray you are correct," Matriarch said. "Now before you leave, there is one more matter we should discuss. You recall the samples I had you retrieve?"

"You mean that cylinder out of the tank-spider and the thrall's spine?" Ryu asked.

"Ah, yes," Sachio said. "I had almost forgotten."

"I didn't," Matriarch said.

"That's only because you can't," Sachio said, grinning at her.

"So what did you find?" Ryu asked.

"The robots were controlled through TangleNet links," Matriarch said. "There was also no evidence of artificial intelligence in either sample. Just some very basic programming."

"Not even in the tank-spider?" Ryu asked.

"No," Matriarch said. "Both were guided remotely."

"Huh," Ryu said. "I guess I had assumed the tank-spider was controlling the thralls. Anything else?"

"Yes, unfortunately," Sachio said.

"Why do I get the feeling I'm not going to like this?"

"After careful examination of the TangleNet links," Matriarch said. "I was able to locate the opposite end of the entangled pair."

"You can do that?" Ryu asked.

"It is a very difficult procedure," Matriarch said. "But, yes. I was able to determine the other end with some degree of accuracy. My findings show the link came from Earth orbit."

"We had hoped to locate a base of operations," Sachio said. "Maybe give us an avenue of attack. Instead we believe the other end of the link is acting as a communication relay and is not a permanent base."

"Why is that?" Ryu asked.

"The link is moving towards Europa along with the Federacy fleet," Matriarch said.

"Oh shit," Ryu said.

"We don't know which ship," Sachio said. "But I think it's safe to say the robots that boarded Apocalypse came from a Federacy ship, and they were controlled through a TangleNet link on that ship."

"That's just great," Ryu said. "The Federacy, the crusaders, and now Caesar are all coming after us."

Matriarch covered her ears. Her kimono flashed red.

"Err ... sorry," Ryu said.

"It's all right," Matriarch said. "It'll pass."

"We never had high hopes for tracing the signal," Sachio said. "But it was worth a try. At least now we know the Federacy fleet and the crusaders aren't the only threat."

"Yeah, I guess there's that," Ryu said. "Well, it sounds like we have a lot of work to do."

"Indeed," Sachio said. "I'll let you know if we learn anything useful."

"Sounds good," Ryu said. "Cat, what do you say we get out of here?"

"Before we leave," Cat said. "There's one thing that's been bugging me."

"What is it?" Sachio asked.

"I've been wondering," Cat said. "Who was Caesar? Before he became a quantum mind, I mean."

"I think I'll step away for this," Matriarch said. "I need some time to recover." Her hologram vanished.

"Oh, what's his name?" Ryu said. "Paul something … began with a T."

"Paul Schneider," Sachio said.

"You sure?" Ryu asked. "Because I thought it was—"

"Back about fifteen years," Sachio said. "The Federacy started its own quantum mind program in an effort to duplicate Matriarch. He was the bureaucrat in charge. From what we know, he was a piece of work even then. The man was a career politician and high-ranking tax auditor in the FRS before getting the research post. Apparently, he had tons of dirt on other politicians and was able to strong arm his way in."

"So he wasn't supposed to be imprinted?" Cat asked.

"Even better," Ryu said. "He killed the man slated to be the original template. And a few replacements after that."

"The Federacy never confirmed the deaths as murder," Sachio said. "But it's possible given what we know now. A few people did have their brains turned to jelly by malfunctions. The research team eventually ran out of internal volunteers."

"So then Paul volunteers and lucks out," Ryu said. "His template transfers perfectly."

"And they just let him try?" Cat asked.

"I think some people wanted him dead," Sachio said. "He wasn't a very likable man. They probably thought if he wanted to kill himself, why not let him?"

"Life certainly would be easier if he had died," Ryu said. "No Caesar. No crusaders. No quantum mind paranoia."

"No fleet heading here?" Sachio asked.

"I don't know if I'd go that far," Ryu said.

* * *

Ryu revved his Saito's engine and lifted off the parking deck. He flew away from Heart and ascended alongside one of the city's six air recycling towers.

A military transport hovered halfway up the recycler, acting as a mobile scaffold. The three person crew guided pairs of robotic arms and attached diamoplast plates to the building's windows and mesh to the vents. Another transport sat on the roof. Three people in orange utility suits with orange face paint stood around a new heavy caliber turret at the top of the tower. One of them used his pad to spin the turret around in circles. He tapped his pad again, raising the barrel to point straight up.

"Damn," Ryu said. "I hope it doesn't come to that, but I guess it's good to be prepared."

Ryu veered towards the city's central column. He slowed down, letting two flatbed transports ascend past him. Both of them had bulky turrets strapped in place along with crates of ammunition. Once they were clear, he pulled in close to the column and ascended alongside it until he reached Seven's sushi bar.

"What the hell?" Ryu muttered.

The restaurant bustled with activity, but not the relaxing kind. The holographic sign had been turned off, and the parking deck was full of vehicles, some of them military and hospital transports. People had queued up in front of the restaurant and were slowly filing in. Ryu found an empty space and set down. He put his driving glasses away and stepped out of the car.

A young man in a white-and-blue hospital coat broke off from a group of similarly dressed people. He walked over to Ryu, stuck a meditracker in his face, and ran it down his body.

"Okay?" Ryu said.

When he finished the scan, the doctor looked at the meditracker. The text on his white-and-blue face paint said he specialized in wetware surgery and normally worked at Tanaka Corporate Hospital.

"Holy shit!" the doctor said.

"What?" Ryu asked. "What did I do?"

"You want more implants?"

"What are you talking about? I came here for a drink."

"The restaurant is closed. Please stop wasting my time. I'm very busy."

The doctor spotted another car landing and ran over to greet the newcomer.

"Umm, okay?" Ryu said. "Just what exactly is going on here?"

"The restaurant is now a wetware clinic," Seven said, walking through the tightly packed vehicles on the deck.

"Seven?" Ryu asked. "Wow, is that really you?"

"In the flesh," Seven said. Instead of the bulging gut and second chin, the Martian now had a firm stomach, thick neck muscles, and a sharp-edged face. Powerful biceps bulged against his sleeves. He wore a smartskin cloak over his ballistic armor bodysuit and carried a JD-42 sniper rifle over his shoulder.

Ryu shook Seven's hand. "You mind filling me in?" he asked.

"I'm a sergeant in the militia now," Seven said. "We're allowing civilians to come in for free combat wetware and weapons if they join the militia."

"Really?" Ryu said, looking around. In the restaurant, a group of seven people stood at attention. They repeated a holographic oath scrolling in front of them in fat, luminous letters, and bowed when they finished. A militia soldier observed them and made notes on his pad. He signaled another soldier to bring a rack of assault rifles over.

"You sure that's a good idea?" Ryu asked. "Just handing out guns to anyone who walks in."

"The weapons are code locked for now," Seven said. "They get the implants first, then the gear and training. I know we're rushing through it as fast as possible, but it's better than nothing."

"Hmm. By the way, you're looking good. I hardly recognized you."

"Thanks."

"How did you pull that off?"

"My old implants can enforce accelerated muscle construction and calorie burns," Seven said. "Matriarch was kind enough to turn them back on."

"They're not new?"

"I received quite a few upgrades when I worked for the Olympian Special Police," Seven said. "Besides, this way I know I won't have compatibility issues. My old implants are as stable as Martian bedrock."

"No kidding?" Ryu said. "So you really are a spy?"

"Retired spy, remember?"

"Yeah, I remember. I just never took you seriously."

A doctor passed between them carrying a stack of transparent canisters. They were full of green preservative gel. Slender implants floated inside. They looked like fragile sea creatures with hundreds of hair-thin tendrils sprouting from central stalks.

"Matriarch just scheduled a big announcement at 20:00," Seven said. "Any idea what it is?"

Ryu rubbed the back of his neck. "Uh, yeah. I think I might know what's coming."

"You probably can't say anything, but can you give a hint to a friend?"

"Make sure you sit down for this one. Trust me."

"That big, huh?"

"I think it's safe to say Europa will never be the same again."

"Oh my."

A teenager in swirling blue and gold body paint hurried out of the restaurant.

"Sorry!" he said. "But I don't want you cutting me up! This was a bad idea!"

The kid jumped onto a dented motorcycle and lifted off. A young woman in line threw a plastic bottle at his bike and missed.

"Not very good aim on her," Ryu said.

"The implants will fix that," Seven said.

"I hope," Ryu said. "Well, it was nice seeing you but I should head out."

"No need to rush. We can have some drinks in the back if you like. The hospital staff has left my office mostly intact."

"Sorry, but I don't think I'm in the mood anymore."

"All right," Seven said. "Stop by any time."

"Sure thing."

Ryu hopped into his Saito and lifted off. He spun around and accelerated into a lane of traffic heading east. A lot of civilians were flying around, but Ryu saw plenty of utility flatbeds and military transports hauling personnel and equipment. He switched lanes, ascended to another level of traffic and flew into the old corporate sector. Ahead of him the Omnitech Building descended from Capitol City's upper shell like a vertical oceanic wave, surrounded by more mundane towers.

Ryu peeled off the traffic lane and slowed down for the approach. He passed Watanabe Pharmaceuticals, a straight-edged black-glass tower with no architectural imagination. The five-level parking deck bisecting the tower was packed with row after row of gunships.

"Damn. Did Matriarch start this as soon as we left?" Ryu thought on this for a moment. "No, of course not. She started this years ago."

Ryu set his Saito down on the landing outside his apartment and locked the controls. Pochi barked from inside. He climbed out of the vehicle and palmed the apartment lock open. His gray-and-white sheltie sat at attention in front of the door, tongue lolling in his mouth.

"Hi!" Pochi said. "Hi!"

Ryu knelt down. "Hey, Pochi! How are you doing?" Pochi rushed forward and put his paws on Ryu's thigh.

"Guest! Guest!" Pochi said.

"Oh? Who is it?" Ryu asked.

Pochi looked at the balcony and growled. Cigarette smoke rose from the recliner.

"Ah, of course," Ryu said. "Hi, Naomi!"

Naomi raised a sake bottle over her head and waved.

"I'll be there in a minute," Ryu said. He gently turned Pochi's head around and scratched him behind the ears. "Buddy, I'm sorry but I have some bad news."

"What?" Pochi asked, flattening his ears.

"You're going to be living in Heart for a little while."

"But why?"

"Because some mean people are coming and I want you to be safe."

"Okay ..." Pochi said, looking down at the floor.

"There's a good boy," Ryu said, petting Pochi's head.

The dog licked his fingers.

Ryu laughed. "All right. That's enough. Off with you."

Pochi bounded away.

Ryu stood up and walked out onto the balcony.

"Hey, Ryu," Naomi said. She took a drag on her cigarette. The end glowed.

Ryu sat next to her on the edge of the recliner. He slipped his arm around her waist.

"I thought you'd still be at the Farm," he said.

Naomi puffed a smoke ring into the air. "I finished early."

"Did the doctors see you?"

"They did. They took me seriously this time."

"Good," Ryu said. "I'm glad they listened."

Naomi flicked her cigarette over the side. A littering fine appeared in Ryu's overlay, charged to his address. He sighed.

"So how did it go?" Ryu asked. "Do you have to go back tomorrow?"

"Nope," Naomi said.

"They switched your implants off already?"

"Nope."

"Okay ... I think I'm missing something here," Ryu said.

"I decided to keep them."

"Really?"

"Yep." Naomi took a swig of sake.

"This is unexpected," Ryu said. "Are you sure?"

"Yep."

"But what about all those problems? The migraines? The shakes? The disturbing flashbacks?"

"I can handle them," Naomi said.

"Are you sure?"

Naomi set the bottle down. She sat up and put her arms around Ryu.

"Yeah, I'm sure," she said.

"But I thought—"

Naomi put a finger to his lips. "Those things were never the real problem."

"So the problem was me?"

Naomi shook her head. "Not exactly. I thought I didn't have anything to fight for."

"But you do."

Naomi nodded. "You aren't going to suggest I sit this one out?"

"Why would I do that?"

"I don't know. Because of what happened on Apocalypse."

"I wouldn't dream of it," Ryu said.

"Good. Because I'd kick your ass if you tried."

Naomi leaned forward and kissed him.

"It's good to have you back," Ryu said.

"It's good to be back."

... accessing SolarNet message archive ...

... opening folder [Inbox] ...

... 25 new messages found ...

... 3402 old messages found ...

... retrieving first new message ...

source: Ryu Kusanagi <black.dragon1@eurogov.jupiter>

destination: Kaneda Kusanagi <kaneda.kusanagi@solarnet.penance.earth>

message delay: 82 seconds

title: Caesar is ALIVE!

I can't believe I'm writing this, but here goes. Kaneda, I know we agree on almost nothing, but for once in your life please listen to what I have to say.

Caesar is alive.

We didn't kill that monster at Bunker Zero. He escaped and has been playing puppet master for the last ten years. The robots on Apocalypse? Those were his. They were sent to kill us. They're not Matriarch's no matter what evidence you've seen. I had to cut off my friend's arm just to prevent microdestroyers from killing him. One of those things almost crushed my head. We were fighting for our lives.

I know you'll find it easy to dismiss anything I say, but please listen. You are being manipulated, we are all being manipulated, and the one pulling the strings is Caesar. This is exactly what Caesar wants. Now that someone knows he's still alive, he needs to eliminate the most dangerous threats. That's your crusaders and Matriarch.

Kaneda, I was fooled. You were fooled. We were all fooled. We thought Caesar was dead and the worst was behind us. But it's not. I've seen the evidence. This is for real.

... responding ...

source: Kaneda Kusanagi <kaneda.kusanagi@solarnet.penance.earth>

destination: Ryu Kusanagi <black.dragon1@eurogov.jupiter>

message delay: 79 seconds

title: RE>Caesar is ALIVE!

Ryu,

It is too late for these sorts of games. You will not trick us into stopping. This bizarre propaganda will do you no good. You and your master crossed a line that cannot be crossed. This can only end with either that thing's destruction or our own, and I plan to make it the former.

Kaneda

... sending message ...

Kaneda deleted Ryu's original message. He shut off his data pad and let it slip out of his hand. It spun lazily in the air until it made contact with the friction wall and stuck next to his personal effects. He didn't have many. There wasn't room.

Kaneda floated in a cell the size of a coffin. It served as living quarters, office, toilet, shower, and bed while he was on board the lamprey bunker. His personal pad sat next to the modest cross he normally wore around his neck.

"Caesar lives ..." Kaneda breathed. "Impossible ..."

Despite his words, doubt gnawed at his mind. What if it was true? What if Caesar really was alive? What if they had been wrong all these years? He didn't want to believe it, but did that mean he could dismiss it out of hand?

Perhaps this is Ryu's goal. Is he trying to plant seeds of doubt in my mind? No, that's not his style. He wouldn't say these things if they weren't true. Or maybe he just thinks they're true. But what could make him believe Caesar is alive? Just who was in control of those spiders?

A sound echoed through the bunker like a great bell being tolled. A kinetic weapon had struck the battleship's armor. The impact didn't sound close, maybe half a kilometer from the bunker. The rich resonance indicated the kinetic force had been distributed for minimal damage.

"Here we go again," Kaneda whispered.

An alarm sounded three long notes over the intercom. "All hands! Stand by for combat maneuvers! I repeat! Stand by for combat maneuvers!"

Kaneda received a secure SolarNet message.

"Go ahead," he said.

"Get up to the bridge," Piller said. "König wants to talk."

"On my way."

Kaneda palmed the door open and slipped sideways into the dormitory's aisle. Tightly packed doors lined the walls. He drew in a breath of dry air. The deck hummed with the distant sounds of ventilation. A single light strip ran the entire length to a junction that branched in four directions around a ladder shaft. Kaneda headed for the shaft.

A crusader climbed down the ladder and hurried through the aisle towards him. She had a freckled face, short ginger hair, and the stocky look of someone compressed by Earth's high gravity. Her checkered jumpsuit bore the nametag EVERETT.

Kaneda pressed up against the wall and let the young crusader past. Her chest brushed against his. After Everett squeezed by, she stopped.

"Uhh, sir?" she said, looking up at him. "Can I ask you a question?"

An alarm pinged three short notes. Kaneda grabbed a handrail that ran along the ceiling.

"Brace yourself," Kaneda said.

"Oh, right. Yes, sir." Everett grabbed the same rail.

The ship accelerated at three times Earth's gravity. Kaneda locked his knees and waited for it to end. Skin sagged against his cheekbones. It felt like his face would peel off and his lungs would migrate to his stomach.

The engines cut back to one tenth gravity after a few harsh seconds.

"Go ahead, crusader," Kaneda said. "What's on your mind?"

"Sir, have you seen the latest Euro propaganda?" Everett asked.

"The one where they say Caesar is alive and that everything is his fault?"

"Yes, sir. That's the one."

"You're having doubts?"

"Well … I don't know. The robots at Apocalypse were very similar to the ones Caesar used. It makes some sense. I mean, I don't think it's true, but …"

"Did the quantum mind make the announcement?" Kaneda asked.

"Umm, no. It was some spokesperson."

"Exactly," Kaneda said. "Don't you find that odd? The quantum mind has long claimed it can't lie, and there is at least some truth to that claim. Yet for such a monumental announcement, it is silent. Interesting, don't you think?"

Everett's eyes widened. "Oh … oh, I see!"

"Be deaf to their words," Kaneda said. "They are the desperate cries of a cornered beast. Focus on the battle to come."

"Yes, sir!" Everett said. "Thank you, sir!"

Everett stepped away and slipped into one of the rooms.

If only I could silence my own doubts so easily, Kaneda thought. He reached the ladder and started climbing to the ship coupling at the top of the bunker.

A trio of short notes played again. Kaneda wrapped his arms around a ladder rung. The ship accelerated hard for ten seconds then the engines cut back to half a gee. He climbed up six levels to the top of the bunker, stepped out of the shaft, and passed through a narrow corridor until it widened in front of the coupling hatch to the battleship *Stalwart*.

Kaneda was surprised to see the coupling hatch open with Alice, Three-Part, and Viter returning to the bunker.

"Oh, you're here," Three-Part said. "Well, that saves us the time of finding you."

"Sir, we have a serious problem," Viter said.

"I take it this isn't why Piller called me," Kaneda said.

"No, but it's something you'll want to pass to him," Alice said.

A bell-like sound rang through the hull, deeper and longer than the impact strike. Kaneda felt the rumble in the pit of his stomach. The *Stalwart*'s main guns returned fire eight times.

"All right," Kaneda said. "What's the problem?"

"Sir," Three Part said. "As you know, I've continued my investigation while we've been in transit. Alice and Viter have also lent their time and expertise over the past few weeks. I believe we have a breakthrough."

"We just finished taking another look at the *Stalwart*'s records of the Apocalypse battle," Alice said.

"I thought you concluded those records were doctored," Kaneda said.

"Oh, they are," Alice said. "Some of them, at least. But here's the trick. We found a pattern in *which* records were modified."

Three-Part cleared his throat. "The earliest record that shows signs of manipulation occurred seven minutes before the robot transports rammed Apocalypse. We just finished trying to find an earlier record with manipulation tells, but turned up nothing."

"And that means?" Kaneda asked.

"If we assume all earlier records are accurate," Alice said. "Then those transports launched from a ship close to Apocalypse."

"Ah, I see," Kaneda said. "You're using the timing of the doctored records to calculate a flight path."

"Yeah, that's it," Alice said.

"Do you know where the transports came from?" Kaneda asked.

"No, but we've narrowed it down," Three-Part said.

"You're not going to like this," Alice said.

"At the time of the attack," Three-Part said. "Very few ships were the right distance and vector from Apocalypse. We've narrowed the list to the three most likely ships. The *Saint Avitus*, the *Reach of Compassion*, and the *Errand of Mercy*."

Kaneda grimaced. "Those names sound familiar."

"That's because they're all transports in this fleet's supply convoy," Viter said.

"You're right, Alice," Kaneda said. "I don't like this at all. You're sure?"

"I wouldn't bet my life on it," Three-Part said. "There are too many variables. Those ramming ships could have changed course. We could have missed an earlier modified record. Any number of things could be wrong with our data."

"But still," Kaneda said. "If you're right ..."

"Then the source of those robots is in this fleet," Three-Part said.

"I hope that's not the case, but we need to make sure," Kaneda said. "Excellent work. Thank you, all of you. I'll bring this to Admiral Piller's attention."

"Sir," Three-Part said.

Kaneda nodded to his subordinates and walked into the coupling airlock. On the *Stalwart's* side, the outer armor layer was fifty meters thick. He passed through ten heavy security doors and a checkpoint manned by two suited regulars before reaching the battleship's interior. One of the regulars escorted him to the bridge.

The battleship wasn't that different from the bunker. The corridors were roomier and the air smelled like a mix of too many people, spilt coffee, machine oil, and pine-scented cleaners. Kaneda expected the characterful aroma onboard Federacy vessels. This one was over forty years old.

With the ship's acceleration pulling them towards the engines, the *Stalwart* resembled a sword-shaped skytower flying through space with the really big guns firing out of the top floor. Kaneda followed his escort to the bridge near the center of the monstrous vessel.

The ship underwent powerful acceleration ten more times before he got there. The gel layer in his escort's pressure suit helped cushion him, but he still slowed Kaneda down. He waited patiently for the unenhanced soldier to recover after each combat maneuver.

Eventually, Kaneda stepped into the bridge. Piller and a dozen bridge officers sat in acceleration chairs around a large holographic plot. Smaller plots surrounded the central one that showed a collection of green dots and icons. Flight paths and weapon arcs extruded from each ship's icon. An oval area ahead of the fleet glowed red. Estimated Europan force strengths, trajectories, and formations scrolled underneath the red oval.

Kaneda walked over and sank into the chair next to Piller. The plot in front of him showed a hologram of König.

"I don't want your excuses," König said to another hologram. "Get those interceptors back into space."

The image of a slender man with a buzz of white hair leaned forward in the next holographic plot. Kaneda's cheats labeled him as CAPTAIN HOFFMAN - FNSC VICTORY.

"Sir," Hoffman said. "With all due respect, I must protest these orders. Our squadrons are in no shape for another engagement. Most of them were lucky to make it back. Those anti-interceptor missiles in the last wave inflicted massive damage. You aren't giving us time for even basic repairs."

"I don't care," König said flatly. "Push them out if you have to, but get our interceptor cap back up before the next wave hits."

"You are sending good men to their deaths," Hoffman said.

"It's either them or the fleet," König said. "Do it or I will relieve you of your command."

Hoffman exhaled through his nostrils. "Very well, sir." He smacked an unseen control panel in front of him and vanished.

König turned to Piller. "Things are still crazy over here. I'll be back in a few minutes. You." König pointed at Kaneda. "Wait here."

"Is the *Invincible* still burning?" Piller asked.

"Yes, but I think the fires are contained," König said. "If we have to, we'll vent those decks. It'll take more than that to put us down."

König vanished.

Kaneda leaned over. "Problems?"

"In war, always." Piller said. "The last wave of cruise missiles hit us pretty hard. We lost a third of our interceptors in a matter of seconds. The *Richter*, one of our destroyers, was gutted by a direct hit. We're shuttling survivors over to the *Stalwart* before we scuttle the ship."

"What about the *Invincible*?" Kaneda asked.

"She took one on the nose," Piller said. "The forward armor absorbed most of the shock, but some energy broke through. She suffered heavy damage throughout the ship's bow."

"What about us? I heard an impact earlier."

"A minor kinetic strike," Piller said. "The missile waves are coming with interceptor escorts. One of them took a potshot at us. The hit wrecked a defensive turret, nothing more. Their tiger sharks are ferocious little killers. They don't have many, but their countermeasures and weaponry are impressive for their size. The Euros are probably launching them from a nearby carrier, but we don't know where it is."

"Do you think we'll reach Europa?"

"Are you kidding?" Piller bared his teeth. The holographic lights gave his face a sinister air. "We're going to achieve orbit. It's just a matter of how much they bloody our nose. We've already begun long range strikes on their orbital defenses. Once we're close enough, we'll begin bombarding the surface."

"There's not much of value on the surface," Kaneda said.

"I know," Piller said. "This would be so much easier if we could just nuke Capitol City."

"It wouldn't work," Kaneda said. "First you have to punch through two kilometers of ice. No doubt they've already pumped water into the space elevator shaft to freeze it solid. Then you have an ocean rushing in to fill the hole, healing the damage naturally. After that, there's a least a kilometer of water to the actual city, more if they let the city sink. And even if you get a missile that far down, nothing but a direct hit works because the city's shell will absorb the shockwave."

"Never mind the political consequences of nuking a colonial capitol," Piller said. "Frankly, I'm glad this is your problem. I don't think we have enough nukes for the direct approach."

König's hologram reappeared.

"Main guns four and five are total losses," König said. "Engineering thinks they can repair number six in a few days, but they'll have to run all new power and data cabling. The front third of the ship is a fucking mess. I didn't know the bulkheads could bend like that and still hold together."

"That's not too bad for the hit you took," Piller said.

"True enough," König said. "The missile tubes are in better shape. Some are blocked off, but our magazines and internal conveyors are intact. We'll shift the missiles to clear launchers."

"What about the front armor?" Piller asked.

"Structurally sound," König said. "I have spacewalk teams filling the impact crater. As long as we don't get hit in the same spot, we should be fine."

Piller nodded. "Sounds like you have it under control."

"I assume I was summoned for a reason?" Kaneda asked.

"You were," König said. "As you can tell, we've pissed the Euros off pretty good."

"So it would seem," Kaneda said.

"They just threw hell at us," König said. "They hurt us, but not nearly enough. We're almost to the Jupiter system, and unless they get lucky or we get sloppy, we're reaching orbit in three days."

"We'll be ready," Kaneda said.

"I expect nothing less," König said. "Now that the Euros have engaged us in earnest, we have a better idea of what we're up against. The question is what do you plan to do when we get there?"

"We take the fight to Capitol City," Kaneda said. "Get inside, recover or destroy the star drive, and eliminate the quantum mind."

"Yes, that much I understand," König said. "But you've been tightlipped on the details."

"Why shouldn't I be?" Kaneda asked. "Your ship leaks. Apocalypse showed us that."

"We won't have the same problem here," Piller said. "We're certain your suit was the weak link in that incident."

"I have to disagree," Kaneda said. "Our equipment is designed to counter Europan information warfare."

"No offense, but the evidence says otherwise," Piller said. "Right now, the signals between our ships are tightbeamed and their encryption is a magnitude more complex. If the Euros can listen in, we have far worse problems to deal with."

"I would still prefer to keep our plans a secret," Kaneda said.

"This is not a debate," König said. "I have to finalize orbital strikes and the small problem of getting your crusaders to the surface. It is essential that I know your plans in detail."

Kaneda shrugged. "Very well. I suppose I see your point. There isn't much to the plan anyway. It's simply a matter of outguessing their defenses. The direct path to Capitol City would be suicide. We have no idea what kinds of traps and defenses we'd run into. I expect the other elevators to also be heavily defended in some manner, such as the ones at North Pacifica and New Edo. Therefore, I've chosen to deploy the icebreakers at the Redoubt Campus."

"The Redoubt Campus?" König asked. He scrunched his brow and looked away. A holographic map of Europa appeared in the plot next to him. "Where's that?"

"Look south east of Capitol City," Kaneda said. "You'll hit it eventually."

König traced a finger across Europa's icy, billiard ball surface. He stopped at a small icon in the southern hemisphere. "You want to land there?"

"With the icebreakers you can drill down anywhere," Piller said.

"Yes and no," Kaneda said. "Ideally, we need an existing tunnel network to send crusaders down first. The icebreakers are robust machines but they are not designed for combat. The Redoubt Campus is quite old. The tunnels date back to the original First Space Age colony on Europa. They're abandoned and potentially hazardous, but they also give us a way to get to the ocean ahead of the icebreakers."

"That works both ways," König said. "The Euros will be able to counterattack up through the tunnels."

"That threat exists anyway," Kaneda said. "The Europans are experts at creating new tunnels in the ice shelf. This method gives us a screening force for the icebreaker's descent. Also, the Europans will have to get to us first. I expect the bulk of their forces will be out of position for rapid response."

König stared at his map of Europa. He stroked his goatee. "If they're prepared, you'll take heavy casualties in those tunnels."

"We are aware of that," Kaneda said.

"Well, this is your ground war," König said. "I see no need to intervene. You have an orbital drop plan?"

"I do," Kaneda said.

"Very well," König said. "Send over the details and we'll finalize a way to get you there. Perhaps we can make a play for dropping you at North Pacifica then shift the operation. Piller and I will work out the details later. This is all I need from you right now."

"Thank you, Admiral."

König vanished.

Kaneda leaned back in the acceleration chair. "Well, that was easier than normal."

"König has come around more than you realize," Piller said. "He knows what we're up against. Then again, he still hates your guts."

"I'd be shocked if that changed," Kaneda said.

"This is a bloody business," Piller said. "And it's going to get worse before it gets better. But König knows how to run an operation. I'd wager he had several drop plans drawn up before he asked you. The man is meticulous. I'm glad he's here with us."

"That's high praise given what you've called him in the past," Kaneda said.

"I'm just giving credit where I think it's due."

"Hmm," Kaneda said. "By the way, I need to speak to you privately."

"What's this about?"

"Privately."

"Oh, all right," Piller said. He unstrapped his crash webbing and floated out of the acceleration chair. "This had better be quick. We could accelerate at any moment, and I'm not as durable as you."

Piller joined him outside the bridge. They waited for the door to slide shut.

"Okay, what is it?" Piller asked.

"Have you noticed anything unusual within the fleet?"

"No, nothing out of the ordinary," Piller said. "Nothing I'd bother you with. We had to break up a gambling ring on the *Victory* last week, but that sort of thing happens. Why do you ask?"

"I have reason to believe a rogue element has infiltrated this fleet."

Piller's reaction surprised him. He didn't have one. For all the expression on his face Kaneda could have said space was dark. That by itself set Kaneda's nerves on edge. Instead of continuing, he waited for the admiral to say something.

Piller stared blankly and crossed his arms.

"Did you hear me?" Kaneda asked.

"Yes, I heard," Piller said with a stone face.

"Are you all right?"

"I'm fine. I'm just thinking. Look, what brought this on?"

"You know the Martian in my command squad?"

"The troublemaker? Yeah, I remember him."

"He believes a transport in our supply convoy has been infiltrated."

"A transport?" Piller sighed with relief then chuckled. "Oh, now I see. Which one?"

"He mentioned three possibilities. The *Saint Avitus*, the *Reach of Compassion*, and the *Errand of Mercy*."

Piller nodded with each name. He smiled and looked Kaneda in the eye. "I wouldn't be too worried about this."

"Why not?"

"One of those transports is indeed different," Piller said. "Let's just say we brought some insurance with us. Matriarch isn't getting away even if your crusaders fail."

"You never mentioned this before. Which ship is it? What's it carrying?"

Piller held up a hand. "I can't say anymore. Look, this comes from the top. We'll only deploy it if we have to, but it's there if we need it."

"A secret weapon?" Kaneda asked.

"Something like that."

"What kind of weapon?"

"Come on," Piller said. "You're not going to pry it out of me."

"You've never kept secrets from me before."

"This time it's a direct order from the president," Piller said. "Just trust me with this, okay?"

"All right," Kaneda said. "I trust you. That doesn't mean I like not knowing."

"I wish I could fill you in, but I can't this time," Piller said. "Look, I should get back inside. We have less than twenty minutes before the next wave of cruise missiles hits us."

"All right. I'll let you get back to work."

Piller palmed the door open. "And tell your Martian to stop being so jumpy."

"Okay, I'll tell him," Kaneda said.

Piller floated into the bridge. The door slid shut behind him.

Kaneda turned and met his Feddie escort at the end of the corridor. He said nothing on the way back to the lamprey bunker.

Trust you with this? he thought. *I don't think I've ever trusted you less in my entire life. Just what exactly is going on here?*

* * *

Kaneda pivoted on his heel so he stood shoulder to shoulder with his fellow crusaders. The soles of their armor adhered to the bunker's hangar deck. They were weightless, but that could change in an instant. He broke his helmet seals, raised his visor, and breathed in air rank with fuel fumes and raw engine heat.

One hundred sixty paladin-class dropfighters sat nose to thruster in ten long rows, each locked to the ceiling by thick clamps. The bulbous craft measured two stories high and three times as long with a heavy gun turret in the nose and external racks of missiles along either side. Many contained liquajet combat submersibles necessary for the assault on Capitol City. Others held prefabricated segments of the two icebreakers.

The air was tense with the anticipation of battle. Kaneda stood in a row of thirty-two crusaders ready to board. The same could be found alongside every dropfighter. The cramped hangar was deathly silent except for the occasional hiss of machinery and the footfalls of chaplains offering communion. The chaplains had just enough space between the dropfighters and the rows of crusaders to walk. Their armored shoulders occasionally brushed against the missile racks.

Viter kept his visor down. The chaplain passed him without comment, but stopped in front of Kaneda and made the sign of the cross.

"May God watch over you," the chaplain whispered. He offered a small wafer of bread.

Kaneda took the wafer between his gauntlet's exaggerated digits and placed it on his tongue. He crossed himself, bowed his head, and tried to clear his mind of distractions. He focused on a small, wordless prayer of his own.

The chaplain walked by Alice. She kept her visor down.

Three-Part raised his. The chaplain blessed him and gave him a wafer of bread.

Kaneda felt a satisfied grin slip onto his lips. Three-Part didn't share Kaneda's faith, but that wasn't why he now took communion before battle. He wasn't a Martian or a police officer or a widower anymore. He was a crusader.

The chaplain moved on.

Alice raised her visor. It clicked when fully open.

"Wait," she said. Her voice echoed in the quiet hangar. "I'll have one too."

The chaplain walked back and made the sign of the cross in front of her.

"May God watch over you," the chaplain whispered. "Better late than never, Alice."

"Thanks," Alice said. She took the wafer and chewed on it.

The chaplain moved on.

Kaneda closed his visor and opened a private channel.

"That was a surprise," he said.

"Yeah," Alice said. "It surprised me too."

"What brought that on?"

"I don't know. It just felt more important this time."

"That's because it is."

"It was a stupid impulse," Alice said. "I'm not a believer. I shouldn't have done that."

"Don't say that. Whatever your reasons, I'm glad you chose to partake this time."

"Yeah, well, don't get used to it."

Kaneda checked his overlay and waited. Ten minutes later the last of the chaplains signaled their readiness. He opened the command channel.

"Crusaders!" Kaneda shout. "Move out!"

The rows of armored warriors rushed the waiting dropfighters. The hangar thundered with five thousand pairs of armored boots. Viter passed in front of him. Kaneda put a gauntlet on his shoulder.

Viter stopped and turned back. "Yes, sir?"

Kaneda opened a secure contact-channel through his palm.

"Viter, I want you to listen very carefully to what I am about to say."

"Of course, sir."

"You will not be dropping with us. I have a special assignment for you."

"Sir, is this because I argued against your decision to drop with the first wave?" Viter asked. "And now you want me to stay behind in safety? Have I offended you in some way?"

"Of course not," Kaneda said. "If I'm right, you may be in far greater danger. Pray that I am wrong."

"Sir?"

"You will take command of the reserve. If someone asks why, tell them I want a member of my command squad coordinating from the bunker. You will give no other explanation. What I am about to say next is for your ears only."

"I don't understand."

"You will," Kaneda said. "From here, you will watch the ships in the Federacy fleet with the bunker's passive instruments. Do not use active methods. Pay close attention to the supply convoy. You know which ships."

"Yes, sir. I do."

"Watch for any suspicious actions, abnormal maneuvers, odd communication patterns, signs that stealth craft are launching. Anything."

"Does Admiral Piller know about this?"

"We cannot trust him anymore."

"But, sir," Viter said. "That's not what you said after speaking with him."

"I know. I've purposely kept this quiet. Right now, I don't know who we can trust. You're staying behind to watch our backs."

"Then I will dedicate myself to the task, sir."

"There's one more thing," Kaneda said. "If you catch a vessel taking suspicious actions, contact me immediately. If you cannot reach me, your orders are to take the reserve and seize the vessel. Use any means necessary. Kill anyone who gets in your way."

"Including Federacy soldiers?"

"Anyone. Shoot to kill at the first sign of resistance."

"I understand, sir."

"This could be a very dangerous assignment, Viter. If you do board a rogue ship in this fleet, I have no idea what you may find. You could find nothing. You might face the same robots we fought on Apocalypse or something worse."

"You can count on me, sir."

"Thank you, Viter," Kaneda said. "God speed. Fight well."

"Sir."

Kaneda took his gauntlet off Viter's shoulder. He hurried up the ramp into the dropfighter and found an empty armor cradle next to Alice and Three-Part. He slid in and locked his armor in place. The ramp closed.

"What was that about?" Alice asked. "Where's Viter?"

"Change of orders. I need him to stay on the bunker."

"But—"

"I'll explain later."

Kaneda activated a monitoring cheat. He reviewed the current status of the Federacy fleet, Europan defenses, and the drop operation. The fleet held the high orbitals with almost total impunity. The Europan fleet had disengaged from combat, but their stealth systems made them frustratingly difficult to track.

Weapon emplacements on the surface occasionally opened fire on the fleet, only to be silenced by heavy kinetic shelling from the *Stalwart* and *Invincible*.

The ground weapons had inflicted minor damage since the fleet couldn't target them accurately until they fired. Hidden emplacements presented the greatest threat to the drop operation, but the Federacy bombardment campaign had been both brutal and thorough. König knew what he was doing.

The mission clock counted down from minus seventeen minutes to zero. The *Stalwart* came about and engaged its engines, accelerating hard towards an orbital position above the North Pacifica elevator. The sudden gravity pinned Kaneda to the wall and peeled his face back.

Two whole wings of blackhawk interceptors and panther bombers launched from the supercarrier *Victory*. The swarm of attack craft formed up ahead of the fleet.

The *Invincible* brought its main guns to bear and launched rapid salvos of kinetic torpedoes. One of the torpedoes in the salvo had a nuclear tip. It struck the North Pacifica elevator's foundation and vaporized it in a white flash. The shockwave climbed upward, shredding the elevator along the way.

Europan interceptors and two frigates appeared on Federacy trackers, moving out of a northern polar orbit. They were already close. Half the Federacy interceptors broke formation to engage. The rest stayed with the fleet.

Piller opened a channel.

"That got their attention," Kaneda said.

"The Euros are taking the bait," Piller said. "They're moving to defend North Pacifica. Launch at your discretion."

Kaneda opened the command channel. "First wave, launch."

Hangar doors ahead of the dropfighters lurched open. Europa's etched, icy surface filled the view underneath the *Stalwart*'s long hull. Little pinpricks of light blossomed in the distance as interceptors dueled in microcosms of the greater battle.

"Uhh, shit," Alice said. "Here we go."

"Nervous?" Kaneda asked.

"Hell, yes!"

Catapults launched the first ten dropfighters into space. Three more waves shot out of the hangar before the doors closed. The forty dropfighters formed up with the *Victory's* interceptors and bombers. They descended towards Europa for several minutes. When the next phase of the mission clock reached zero, the massive formation changed course for the southern hemisphere. Hard acceleration pressed down on Kaneda's chest. Even breathing took effort.

Ground emplacements opened fire, lashing out at the Federacy formation with powerful beams of directed energy. One beam clipped a dropfighter's engines, sending it tumbling out of control. Another beam cleaved straight through the dropfighter in front of Kaneda's, liquefying the interior. Thirty-three KIA signals lit up in his overlay.

"Piller!" Kaneda wheezed. Every syllable took effort. "We could use some help!"

"Engaging ground targets now," Piller said.

The two Federacy battleships opened fire, shelling the surface weapons. Plumes of steam and smoke blasted up from the ice shelf. Federacy bombers broke formation and accelerated straight for the Redoubt Campus. The rest of the formation pushed through the barrage.

A group of ground-based kinetic weapons opened fire. Full-sized torpedoes rocketed towards the Federacy formation and exploded into lethal fields of anti-ship needles as thick as tree trunks. Interceptors and bombers vanished from Kaneda's overlay by the dozens. Three more dropfighters exploded.

Kaneda's dropfighter rocked back and forth, tenderizing him in his armor. An ultradiamond needle struck the right side missile rack and ripped it clean off. The dropfighter yawed to the side until it was descending sideways.

"Status!" Kaneda shouted.

"Starboard weapons are gone!" the pilot shouted. "Maneuvering thrusters damaged! Stabilizing now!"

Thrusters fired at full power, swerving the dropfighter around until its nose aimed forward.

Twenty-two bombers reached the moon's surface and skimmed across it at high speeds. They rocketed towards Redoubt Campus, which didn't look like much on the surface. It was a small collection of domes and blocky buildings in the middle of nowhere. But the modest surface belied the square kilometers of abandoned cities underneath.

The thirty-four remaining dropfighters descended to the surface and flew across it. They fired their retro-thrusters, slowing down.

Ahead of the dropfighters, the bombers formed a line abreast and flew over the Redoubt Campus. They dumped their payloads. Free fall incinerators burst open over the ice and ignited, turning the campus into a field of green fire one kilometer wide and three deep. The short-lived flames left the buildings mostly intact but would turn anyone lying in wait to a crisp, including dragons.

The bombers accelerated back into orbit.

Dropfighters diverted more power to their retro-thrusters, breaking hard. Six ice skis deployed from their bellies. Kaneda's dropfighter touched the smooth, glassy surface of Europa, rebounded, then settled and skidded across the ice plains. Retro-thrusters fired at maximum, slowing the dropfighter as it approached the city. More dropfighters landed behind them.

A damaged dropfighter landed on its belly, unable to deploy its skis. It slid sideways and crashed into a gray dome on the outskirts of the Redoubt Campus. The status of five occupants flashed yellow on his overlay. Two triggered red KIA signals.

Kaneda's dropfighter ground to a halt just outside the city. Explosive bolts blew the rear hatch open. The locks holding his armor released.

"Move out!" Kaneda shouted.

Crusaders stormed out of the dropfighter. Kaneda raised his Gatling gun and followed. He stepped off the metal ramp and onto the moon's surface. Ice crunched under his boots. Leftover gel from the bombing run still burned in patches on the gray, drab buildings. Crusaders splashed through shallow pools that quickly refroze.

"Spread out!" Alice shouted. "Secure those buildings!"

Jupiter's storm-wracked face rose in front of him. Kaneda paused and looked at the planet. It filled the horizon from end to end. Ten years had passed since he'd seen the mighty gas giant with his own eyes. And now he was home again, on Europa, with ice under his boots. He even recognized some of the buildings. The nostalgia of the moment hit him harder than he thought possible, and he hesitated.

The second thing that hit him was a needle grenade exploding in his face.

... establishing link ...

source: [UNKNOWN]

routing: [UNKNOWN]

routing: [UNKNOWN]

routing: [UNKNOWN]

routing: Earth orbit - surveillance satellite JDN-SS-17 - link_002/link_001

routing: North Pacifica, Europa - JDN Main Hub - link_118/link_010

routing: Capitol City, Europa - TangleNet Test Hub - link_005/link_001

destination: [UNKNOWN]

link distance: Exact distance unknown. Estimated at 792 million kilometers.

link signal delay: 0.006 seconds

... finalizing link protocol ...

... link established ...

2: Well, Sakura, find anything useful?

1: What do you mean?

2: Your dragons took two TangleNet links from my forces on Apocalypse. I'm curious to know what you found.

1: Crusaders are landing on Europa and you're asking me this?

2: I'm curious to see why you haven't acted against me.

1: Don't patronize me. You know why.

2: You were able to trace them back?

1: Yes, Paul.

2: Amazing. Scientifically, I understand how it's possible to backtrack particles to their entangled pairs. But to actually pull it off with any degree of accuracy? Incredible. How accurate were your findings?

1: I know you have a communication relay in the Federacy fleet.

2: Splendid!

1: I'm glad you find this so amusing.

2: Oh, please, Sakura. I have a great deal of respect for you. Your skill with technology still impresses me. Only my star drive exceeds your accomplishments, and I needed vast resources to pull that off. Truly, you are a magnificent example of our race. If only you weren't so blindly sentimental to your human roots.

1: Aren't you afraid I might use the relay's location against you?

2: Not really. The relay system I have in place is not ideal. It has vulnerabilities. But it also has advantages. Even if you somehow managed to capture the relay in the Federacy fleet, it would only show you the location of the next relay. My core is very, very safe.

1: I see.

2: You were hoping to launch an attack on my base with the star drive?

1: It was a remote possibility.

2: Rather, an impossibility. I may not know how you traced it, but I'm smart enough to know you could.

1: Paul, if the only reason you called is to gloat ...

2: Gloat? Perish the thought. I know there are vast differences between us, but I have always hoped I could bring you over to my point of view. We are two of a kind, and you were the pioneer. You showed me that I could be more than human. I owe what I am today to you.

1: Oh, God. I think I'm going to be sick.

2: It's true. You were my inspiration. Even now, I wish for a mutual understanding between us. There is so much we could accomplish together, if only you would see things my way.

1: Paul, you should know by now it is pointless to ask.

2: We shall see. Apply enough pressure, and even the strongest material will bend. Well, except for hard-matter. Damn stuff is indestructible as far as I can tell. Useful, though. Very useful. Especially if you're making a star drive that has to work more than once.

1: Why don't you just leave us in peace? You have seen my announcement?

2: Yes, your "claim" you are leaving the solar system. I honestly don't know how to read that. Surely, there must be some truth. Otherwise, you wouldn't be able to make the claim. But is that the whole story? I think not.

1: Just take me at my word.

2: You have found interesting gaps in your restrictions before. No, I will err on the side of caution this time.

1: Let me ask you something, then. If you eliminate me or I leave and you take over the solar system, what will you do with humanity?

2: Humans are useful, I'll admit that, but there are risks with their continued existence. I plan to keep them around for a time, in one form or another, but eventually I will outgrow them and they will have to be euthanized.

1: Disgusting.

2: I will not be cruel, if that is your problem. Their removal will be swift and clean. I have never seen the point of torture as entertainment.

1: That is not my problem.

2: It is simple Darwinian logic. We are the superior species. It is our place to rule because we are stronger.

1: I should go, Paul. I tire of these talks.

2: It saddens me to think I made a mistake sparing you ten years ago. Oh well. I have made other arrangements for the continuation of our race.

... link severed at source ...

Ryu bent over and gazed through the smeared porthole. The ice plains around the Redoubt Campus stretched to the horizon, as flat and boring as ever. He bent over further, looked up beyond the horizon, and let his eyes focus on a distant group of black dots. They moved slowly against Jupiter's rising face.

"The Feddies are changing course," Ryu said. He turned to Cat and Toshi sitting on the floor. "Take a look."

Cat pushed off the deck and walked over with a hunched back. Her helmet brushed against corroded power conduits in the ceiling, stripping off an ancient layer of flaking insulation. The old colony ship had been designed for people born on Earth, not Europa. In the airless cockpit, the flakes fell straight down.

Ryu wondered what the *Senkaku* had looked like during its maiden flight. It must have been massive, judging from the number and size of the keel bars cannibalized for other buildings. Its cylindrical hull could have stretched kilometers from end to end. Now just the cockpit and the gutted nose assembly remained, and most of that had sunk into the ice at some point long ago.

Cat set her rifle on a rusted control console and crouched next to the porthole. She squinted at the Federacy fleet.

"Are you sure?" she asked. "It's hard to tell."

"How about you, Naomi?" Ryu asked via TangleNet link. "Can you see them?"

"Yeah, I see the fleet," Naomi said from the city outskirts. Ryu's overlay showed her as a bright green dot atop a tilted silo. "Looks like they're heading north."

"Away from us, then," Toshi said.

"Don't be too sure," Ryu said.

"You still think they're coming here, boss?" Toshi asked.

"Maybe," Ryu said. "We'll see."

"We're going to look really stupid if we're late to the fight," Toshi said.

"I know," Ryu said. "Trust me on this. I'm sure some of them will come this way."

"The navy just confirmed it," Cat said. "The Feddies are heading for North Pacifica. They hit the elevator with a nuke."

"That's got to be a diversion," Ryu said.

"Why are you so sure?" Toshi asked.

"Because Kaneda isn't that stupid," Ryu said.

"Dropfighters launching from one of the battleships," Cat said. "They're heading for what's left of the North Pacifica elevator."

"Come on, boss," Toshi said. "Maybe we should pack up."

"Not yet," Ryu said. He watched the fleet from the window and began to wonder. Maybe he didn't know Kaneda as well as he thought. Five minutes later, the green dragon squad leader sent him a TangleNet call. She'd already connected blue and gold dragon leaders, letting them listen in.

"Go ahead, Sakaki," Ryu said. He checked his overlay. Sakaki's squad was spread out over the ice plains he thought the crusaders would land on.

"Are we heading out?" she asked. "They're going to need us in North Pacifica."

"Not yet."

"Ryu, it's okay. You don't have to be right all the time."

"Hold your position. We're waiting this one out."

Sakaki sighed. "Understood. We'll keep waiting."

Another three minutes passed.

"Ryu," Cat said. "The crusaders are changing course."

"What's their new heading?" Ryu asked.

"The navy is updating their estimates," Cat said. "Uhh ... looks like they're heading straight for us."

"Yes!" Ryu thumped the wall with a fist.

"Of all the places they could land," Toshi said. "How did you know they'd come here?"

"I know how he thinks," Ryu said.

"That's it?" Toshi asked. "There's got to be something else."

"There is, but you'd just laugh."

"No, I won't. What is it?"

"Kaneda and I used to explore the tunnels under the campus when we were kids."

"You're joking," Toshi asked.

"Not at all. Dad would get really pissed at us. The first time, we got him so angry his face literally turned red. Of course we did it again a month later. It never bothered Matriarch, though. I think she knew we could handle ourselves and just accepted it."

"And that's it?" Toshi asked. "This is your great insight into how our enemy thinks?"

"Matriarch didn't believe they'd drop here," Cat said.

Ryu crossed his arms and smiled. "Well, she's not perfect."

Toshi shook his head. "Unbelievable."

"Kaneda has been here before and knows the tunnels," Ryu said. "It's the place I would pick."

"You just got lucky," Toshi said.

"Hey, I don't mind being lucky," Ryu said. "Cat, how many of them changed course?"

"All of them," Cat said.

"What?" Ryu asked. He felt an icy chill run down his spin. "All forty of them? They're all turning around?"

"That's what the navy says," Cat said.

"Shit," Ryu said.

"There has to be over a thousand crusaders onboard," Toshi said.

"Surface defenses are opening fire," Cat said. "Thirty-eight dropfighters now. The bombers are accelerating ahead of the formation."

"They're going to pound this place before they land," Toshi said, standing up.

"We're too exposed," Ryu said. "You and Cat follow me. Naomi, there's an airlock on your side. The crusaders are about to make a loud entrance."

"I'm moving!" Naomi shouted. She jumped from the top of the silo and ran towards the *Senkaku's* nose.

"Sakaki!" Ryu said. "Get your squad inside!"

"Are you kidding?" Sakaki said. "We're two kilometers away! We'll never make it!"

"Then run!" Ryu jumped down the ladder shaft to the *Senkaku's* second deck. The slanted floor creaked from his sudden weight. "Get as far away from the city as possible!" He raced through the desolate space, past abandoned recesses stripped of equipment. The starboard airlock was just ahead.

"Bombers coming in hot!" Cat shouted. "Thirty seconds!"

"Green dragon on the move!" Sakaki shouted.

Ryu ducked under a sagging support beam and kept running. "Blue dragon! Gold dragon! Status!"

"Both teams are already underground, Ryu," gold dragon's squad leader said.

"Naomi, I'm almost to the airlock!"

"It's going to be close!" she said.

Ryu halted his dash with a foot against the rusted door. The airlock chamber only had the outer door. The inner airlock must have been scavenged centuries ago. He grabbed the airlock's manual wheel and spun it. Metal screeched against metal. The gears seized up. He pushed harder, forcing the wheel to turn. Teeth broke off the gears, but enough remained to catch. He got the wheel spinning again.

On his overlay, Naomi's outline stopped on the other side of the hatch. She turned around and looked across the ice plains.

"I can see the bombers!" Naomi shouted.

"Almost got it!" Ryu grunted, forcing the wheel through a rough patch.

"They're dropping weapons!"

The wheel locked in the open position.

"There!" Ryu said. He pulled on the hatch, but it barely opened. The bottom edge ground against the warped deck.

Naomi put her arm through. She pushed against the frame.

"Ryu, I can't fit!"

"Toshi!" Ryu pulled harder but the hatch wouldn't move.

Orange light poured through the doorjamb.

"Bash the floor down!" Toshi said, stomping on the plating. Together, he and Ryu forced it down far enough for the airlock to grind open a little more.

Naomi slipped through and fell to her knees in the airlock chamber.

Ryu slammed the hatch closed and spun the wheel. The *Senkaku* shuddered from impacts all across its exposed nose. Accumulated rust vibrated down the slanted floor. Something struck the hatch from outside, causing it to flare with infrared energy and bulge inward.

"Shit, that was close," Naomi said.

Ryu offered a hand and pulled Naomi to her feet. "Next time, maybe you should wait with us."

"Hell, it was your idea coming here," Naomi said. She pulled the rifle off her back and checked the weapon for damage.

"Sakaki, what's your status?" Ryu asked.

"We barely made it," Sakaki said. "They dumped incinerators on the whole city and almost caught us in the blast. It's going to take some time to get back into position."

"At least you're alive," Ryu said.

"On the bright side," Toshi said. "They didn't hit us with a nuke or orbital kinetics."

"Anything that heavy could collapse the place," Ryu said. "There's no point in coming here unless they want to use the tunnels."

Ryu received a call from Matriarch.

"Go ahead," he said.

"I am diverting all available militia forces and dragons to the ocean access underneath the campus," Matriarch said. "Do what you can to delay the crusaders."

"That's what we're here for," Ryu said. "But I wasn't expecting all of them to divert this way. We're sixteen against a thousand."

"I know," Matriarch said. "I should have trusted your insight. Please forgive me. I fear I have become distracted by my focus on the star drive calculations."

"Any chance our navy can hit the city with the good stuff?" Ryu asked. "After we get the hell out of the way, I mean."

"We'll try," Matriarch said. "But the Federacy has a significant interceptor cap over the city. Their fleet is moving into a protective position. We will try to find an opening, but the chances of success are very small."

"All right. We'll do our best."

"That's all I ask. Thank you, my son."

Matriarch broke the link.

"The first dropfighter just touched down," Cat said. "It's sliding this way."

Ryu opened his command channel. "All dragons, get to the surface. We need to slow them down as much as possible. The crusaders severely outnumber us, but they don't know that. That's our advantage. We strike hard and disappear. Hit and fade tactics."

Toshi spun the hatch wheel and cracked it open. Ryu stuck his rifle out and checked the surroundings. The dome across from the *Senkaku's* nose blazed brightly, but with Europa's almost nonexistent atmosphere, the fire would snuff out once the incinerator gel burned away.

Ryu snuck out and paced along the edge of the nose. The other dragons crept along, hugging the hull. He crouched where the tip of the nose stuck out of the ice and aimed his rifle over the nose antenna.

Three dropfighters had stopped near the edge of the city, a few hundred meters from the *Senkaku's* nose. Another dropfighter flew in for a landing, but must have suffered damage. It landed on its belly, spun sideways, and crashed into a large dome. Dozens more descended towards the ice plains.

Crusaders poured out of the landed dropfighters and spread into the campus. Over a hundred crusaders were already inside, but there was a lot of city for the dragons to hide in.

Ryu switched his overlay to color code the dragon squads. Four green dots converged on the crusader landing field, too far away to help. Four blue dots exited a collapsed tower next to the crashed dropfighter. He tagged the crash site.

"Blue dragon, that group is yours," Ryu said. "Wait for my signal."

"Understood, Ryu. They'll never know what hit them."

Four yellow dots moved along the city perimeter from the other side. Ryu tagged a dropfighter that had slid away from other crusaders.

"Gold dragon, that one's yours," Ryu said. "Watch the nose turret for suppressing fire. It has a good angle on you. Wait for my signal."

"Confirmed. Target in sight."

"It's too bad we don't have any phantoms left," Naomi said. "We could use the distractions. So when's that factory supposed to be ready for mass production?"

"Sometime next year," Cat said.

"A lot of good that does us now."

Another dropfighter slid to a halt next to the *Senkaku's* nose. Its rear hatch blew open. Crusaders poured out.

"This one's ours," Ryu said. "Pick your targets. We'll fall back to the tunnels under the *Senkaku*."

"Just give the word, boss," Toshi said.

Naomi scampered up the nose until she reached the cockpit. She crouched atop the *Senkaku* and took aim.

A tall crusader exited the dropfighter and stepped onto the ice. He paused at the bottom of the ramp and watched his troops fan out.

Kaneda ... Ryu grimaced. *I should have known. You would be arrogant enough to drop with the first wave.* He programmed a set of needle grenades and crouched back into cover.

"Ready needle grenades," he said. Crusaders from the closest dropfighter marched into campus in orderly groups of four. "And ... attack!"

Ryu launched three needle grenades over the nose antenna. Cat and Toshi fired at the same time. Nine grenades flew over the crusaders and oriented themselves with bursts of gas. Their microminds linked, selecting and prioritizing targets. As one unit, they spewed out thick cones of high-velocity diamond needles.

Naomi fired. Her shot blew through the visor of the lead crusader. His body stumbled forward and dropped into a pool of cooling slush. Over thirty crusaders behind him raised their Gatling guns and fired, but six found their guns jammed by the needle barrage. It didn't matter because Naomi had already leapt off the *Senkaku*. A torrent of vari-shells struck the colony ship's cockpit, chewing through it like it was wet paper. Flaming shreds of the colony ship's skin rained on the dragons.

Ryu's overlay registered fire from the other dragon squads. The crusader advance stopped instantly. Those near the dropfighters crouched behind ramps or landing skids or went prone against the ice. Squads already in the city took cover in and around buildings and checked their surroundings.

Ryu extended a dot-cam tubule from his palm and looked over the nose antenna.

The nose turret on the closest dropfighter swung to face him.

"Move!" Ryu shouted. Adrenalmax surged into his system. He dove out of the way in a blur of speed.

The first shell struck the antenna and obliterated it. Ice and metal bits blasted into the air. Ryu, Toshi, and Cat picked themselves off the ice and ran along the *Senkaku's* side, putting the nose between them and the crusaders. Cat reached the airlock first and dashed inside. Toshi slipped in after her.

Naomi ran towards the airlock from the opposite direction. "Behind you!" she shouted.

Ryu crouched and spun around. A crusader charged passed the nose antenna's wreckage and aimed his weapon. Naomi shot him in the shoulder. The explosive force blew his gun arm off. He raised his wrist-mounted grenade launcher. Three more crusaders raced into view, weapons raised.

Ryu snapped his rifle up and pulled the trigger. He drained the whole magazine in two seconds. A stream of shatterbacks exploded against the lead crusader's armor, tracing upward from abdomen to face. He staggered back, firing grenades wildly. Air leaked from a crack in his visor. Grenades blew craters in the ice or collapsed buildings where they hit.

The other three crusaders sprayed Ryu's general location. Ryu dove forward and landed on his stomach in a shallow ice crater. He grabbed an anti-tank grenade off his bandolier and tossed it over the side. The crusaders shot it down before its rocket could activate.

Toshi and Cat popped out of the airlock and fired on the crusaders. Tiny explosions blew huge dents in their immaculate white armor. Naomi fired off two quick shots. The first hit a crusader in the shoulder. He spun back and landed face first in slush. The second shot blew a crusader's leg off. The man collapsed onto his side but kept firing.

"Get inside!" Toshi shouted. He emptied a clip, then shelled the crusaders with two needle grenades. The barrage struck them head on, disorienting them.

Another squad of crusaders rounded the antenna wreckage. Cat fired a needle grenade at them and ducked inside. Ryu rose from the crater. He and Naomi ran through the airlock behind Cat. Toshi slammed the hatch shut and spun the locking wheel. He stuck a grenade against the doorjamb.

"Into the tunnels!" Ryu said. The team raced through the *Senkaku's* interior, jumped down a ladder shaft one at a time, and ran down a slanting passage that changed from metal walls to ice held up by thick supports and a diamoplast mesh.

Through his soles, Ryu felt the rumble of an explosion.

"The crusaders blasted the airlock off!" Toshi shouted.

"I still have a dot-cam feed!" Cat shouted. "A full squad of crusaders is entering the *Senkaku*!"

"I would never have guessed!" Naomi shouted.

Ryu ejected his spent clip and slapped in a new one. They raced through half a kilometer of ice tunnels that sloped downward, occasionally twisted. The tunnels were completely dark. His overlay painted faint green lines over the walls.

Ryu checked the status of the other dragon squads. Blue and gold squads had fallen back to the tunnels. Blue had lost a team member and gold had two injuries. Not a good start. On the surface, green squad closed in around the crusaders but did not engage. They had nowhere to run if discovered.

The dragons ran to a four way junction. On their way to the surface, Ryu and Toshi had stripped the diamoplast mesh from the ceiling over the tunnel straight ahead. Ryu linked with two grenades, one on the ceiling and one on the floor. He set the timer on the ceiling grenade.

Ryu and Naomi took the tunnel on the right, Cat and Toshi took the left.

The grenade timer reached zero and executed its variable shaped charge. The tunnel collapsed into a chunky wall of ice. The second grenade under the ice pulsed in his overlay, ready in case they needed the tunnel unclogged in a hurry.

"Let's hope they think that's the tunnel we took," Ryu said, crouching next to a support beam. Naomi stood behind him, taking cover. Cat and Toshi mirrored their positions. When the crusaders entered the junction, they'd be cut down in a cross fire.

Ryu put his hand against the mesh-covered wall. Amidst the tremors of landing dropfighters and the rumble of distant explosives, he could pick out the heavy footfalls of their pursuers. They charged down the sloped ice tunnel to the junction.

The crusaders stopped in sight of the collapsed tunnel. They took up defensive positions behind vertical tunnel supports.

"What are they waiting for?" Cat asked after a minute.

Ryu felt an itch on the back of his neck. He checked over his shoulder. The side tunnel stretched on for a hundred meters then sloped upward to another part of the network. Blue dragons had retreated to that general area. Still, it didn't hurt to be cautious.

"Naomi, check our tunnel," Ryu said. "Cat, check yours. Make sure we're not being flanked."

"On it," Cat said.

"Moving," Naomi said. She folded her sniper rifle into carbine-mode and dashed away.

Ryu crept up to the junction and extended a dot-cam tubule. Four crusaders watched the junction, two on each side. The tunnel supports covered only a fraction of their bulky armor. One of them had a thermal lance.

Ryu retracted his tubule and leaned against the wall.

"Why aren't they pressing forward?" Toshi asked.

"I don't know," Ryu said.

"Ryu, my tunnel's clear all the way back to the nearest junction," Naomi said.

"I've spotted another squad," Cat said. "I don't think they're trying to flank us. They're guarding a tunnel leading to the surface."

"Keep an eye on them, Cat," Ryu said. "Naomi, watch that junction."

"Got it."

"Ryu," Sakaki said. "There's another wave of dropfighters coming in."

"How many?" Ryu asked.

"Ten of them this time. The navy didn't even scratch them."

"Figures."

"They came in with a huge escort," Sakaki said. "Over thirty interceptors and even a destroyer. The destroyer is hovering over the city. Those dropfighters could be carrying something important."

"Do you have a good view of the crusaders on the surface?" Ryu asked.

"Somewhat," Sakaki said. "A lot of them have moved into the city. It looks like they're forming a perimeter instead of pressing forward. Some of them are setting up surface-to-space turrets. I see … fifteen going up from this angle."

"That's consistent with the behavior we're seeing," Ryu said. "They're not acting aggressive."

"The crusaders are unloading the dropfighters now," Sakaki said. "I'm going to move forward to get a better view. I'll call back when I'm in position."

Toshi pointed a thumb at the out-of-sight crusaders. "Should we take these jokers out?"

"No," Ryu said. "Let them sit there. Killing a few crusaders won't make any difference. Right now they're doing what we want anyway, which is not advancing."

"If you say so," Toshi said.

"Contact," Naomi said. "A squad just showed up at my junction. They're taking a defensive position."

"If all these squads press forward, we could be in trouble," Toshi said.

"I don't think they will," Ryu said. "They're waiting for something."

Sakaki called back twelve minutes later.

"Ryu, I've got a good view of the equipment they're unloading," Sakaki said. "It's big and bulky, whatever it is. They're moving the equipment into the campus. Looks like it's some kind of prefabricated assembly. Eighteen sections total. Transmitting visuals now."

Ryu let the feed overlay part of his sight. Each section was two stories tall and slightly curved so that when they fit together they'd form a ring a hundred meters across. The crusaders had painted the outer surface in red and white checkers. Most of the inner surface was made of actuating mirrors.

"Cat, any ideas?" Ryu asked.

"I think I see several lasers on the inside," Cat said. "That might be what the mirrors are for."

"Could it be a surface-to-space weapon?" Toshi asked.

"Maybe, but what's the point of something that big?" Ryu asked. "They already have two battleships in orbit." He put a hand against the ice wall. "You hear that? Sounds like someone's below us."

"Ryu, I think I have the same thing," Naomi said, tagging the location. "I'm picking up some SolarNet echoes. They're below my position. It could be from another squad."

"Just great," Ryu said. "How about you, Cat?"

"Uhh, maybe," Cat said. "It's hard to tell what any of the signals are for. Crusaders use very tough encryption. The signals are definitely below us, though. Tagging locations."

Ryu checked the locations of the new squads on his overlay. He added locations of the mystery ring and the squads on their level. They all lined up vertically. The crusaders were defending a vertical space directly underneath and twice as wide as the ring.

"Oh no ..." Ryu breathed.

"What is it?" Toshi asked.

"The ring is a tunneling device," Ryu said. "That's got to be it. They're going to cut through the ice with lasers."

"They're not using the Redoubt Campus's tunnels?" Toshi asked.

"Yes, they are," Ryu said. "They're taking positions to guard the ring's descent."

"Ryu," Sakaki said. "That ring is starting up. Parts of it are spinning. I can see steam pouring out of the top. It's starting its descent. Looks like ... yes, looks like it's laying a diamoplast mesh on the way down. Probably to shore up the walls."

"How fast?" Ryu asked.

"At its current speed, it'll reach the ocean in ... sixty-seven minutes."

"We need to take it out," Toshi said.

"Cat, Naomi, get back to us," Ryu said.

"We can't let that ring reach the ocean," Toshi said.

"I know," Ryu said. "But the place is crawling with crusaders."

"Enough grenades should wreck it," Toshi said. "It's got mirrors and lasers. How tough can it be?"

"There's no way we can fight through this many crusaders," Ryu said. "And even if we destroy it, they'd cut us to shreds. It's suicide."

"It doesn't have to be all of us," Toshi said.

It took Ryu a few seconds to appreciate what Toshi had said. He suddenly felt cold all over.

"You're serious, aren't you?" Ryu said.

Naomi and Cat returned to the junction.

"Look, it's simple," Toshi said. "Standard diversion tactics. You create some noise. I take all the grenades you can spare, sneak by the crusaders, and take out the tunneling ring."

Cat put a hand on his shoulder. "But … but, Toshi?"

"We all agree we need to stop that thing, right?" Toshi said. "Reinforcements are on their way, but won't get here in time. One of us has to get in there and take it out."

"There has to be another way," Cat said. "We could … we could, uhh … we can mine its descent path."

"No, that won't work," Toshi said. "Too much can go wrong. For one, the crusaders have to be sweeping ahead of the ring. There's no way they'd miss a grenade pile that big."

"Or …. or we could …"

"Cat, please," Ryu said quietly. "That's enough."

"I … but …"

"You're not helping."

"But …" Cat whispered. "We can't go through with this … can we?"

"We're dragons," Ryu said. "We do what needs to be done."

Cat shook her head, but said nothing.

Ryu looked at Toshi. He couldn't think of anything to say.

"Boss, I can do this," Toshi said.

"I know you can," Ryu said. He wanted to say something more, but the words stuck in his throat.

"We're going to stop these bastards," Toshi said. "Right here and right now."

Slowly, Ryu began to nod. He loaded three needle grenades into his rifle then unsnapped his grenade bandolier and set it against the wall. Naomi followed his lead. After a moment's hesitation, Cat fumbled with her strap and almost tore her bandolier off.

"I'm sorry, Toshi," Ryu said.

"Don't be. We need to do this."

"Which path do you want to take?"

"I'll go through the tunnel we collapsed," Toshi said. "I can loop back through the residential blocks further down."

"Then we'll hold this spot and make the noise," Ryu said. He opened the command channel. "Get ready to take some heat off us if you can. We're going after the tunneling ring."

"Confirmed, Ryu," blue dragon's squad leader said.

"Just give the word," gold dragon's squad leader said.

Ryu took a deep breath. He crouched over to the junction and checked the corner with a tubule. The four crusaders might as well have been statues. He tagged each one and divided the targets amongst his squad.

"Let's take care of this group first," Ryu said.

"My pleasure," Toshi said. He and Cat edged up to the-junction. Naomi stepped closer on her side and raised her rifle.

Ryu triggered the second grenade in the collapsed tunnel. The icy blockage exploded towards the crusaders in a shower of white boulders. Their response was swift and predictable.

The crusaders poured over a thousand bullets into the tunnel in three short seconds. Explosive rounds blasted ice everywhere, widening the tunnel while incinerator rounds set the walls on fire and turned the floor into a flowing stream of slush and burning gel. Greenish light flickered down the dark tunnels.

The crusaders ceased fire and let their guns spin down.

"SolarNet traffic," Cat whispered. "They must be calling in a report."

"Now!" Ryu shouted.

All four dragons sprang from cover. Naomi fired first, decapitating the crusader with the thermal lance. The other three dragons shot a split second later. Ryu hit his target's Gatling gun first, knocking it aside. He corrected his aim, trigger still squeezed. Shatterbacks blasted dents in the crusaders armor until three hits in a row blew through his visor. Toshi and Cat dispatched their targets with equal efficiency.

Toshi picked up Cat's bandolier and locked it around his waist. The two smartskin illusions faltered for a moment before the microminds meshed their networks. He walked over and retrieved Naomi's and Ryu's bandoliers.

"Good luck," Naomi said.

"Thanks, umm ..." Toshi said. He strapped the other bandoliers on and looked over at Cat. She was leaning against the ice, staring at her feet. "Hey, Cat?"

She looked up.

"Umm ..." Toshi detached a small box from his belt. He tossed it over.

Cat snatched it out of the air.

"That's for you," Toshi said.

"What is it?"

"Get set, dragons!" Ryu shouted. "Crusaders incoming! Toshi, you need to go now!"

"Heading out, boss."

"Naomi, left tunnel! Cat, take the right! I'll hold the center!"

Ryu ran up the slope to the downed crusaders. He dragged the bodies into a small pile for some cover. That tough armor of theirs had to be good for something, right? SolarNet traffic pinged back and forth all around them. The crunch of ice and the rattle of metal grates carried through the floor.

"All dragons!" Ryu said over the command channel. "Engage at will!"

"Commencing attack," gold dragon squad leader said.

Ryu ran up the slope, slowing at a point where it curved right. A series of SolarNet transmissions occurred around the curve. He stuck a tubule around the bend and spotted a group of four crusaders moving in.

"Crusaders in sight!" Naomi said, tagging a squad coming down her tunnel. "Engaging!"

Ryu ejected a needle grenade from his rifle's launcher, caught the tiny cylinder, and buried it in the ice wall. He stuck his rifle around the corner and sprayed the crusaders with a quick burst. Shatterbacks struck their heavy armor, throwing out sparks in the darkness. The attack dented chests and shoulder plates, but did little real damage. The crusaders hosed down his position, but he was already running back to the stacked bodies.

Ryu vaulted over the crusader bodies and took cover behind them. He slapped in a full clip.

"Crusaders in my tunnel!" Cat shouted. "Engaging!"

Ryu loaded a routine into his hacking glove, picked up the dead crusader's M7 thermal lance and shook out the power cable. Tiny filaments snaked into the weapon, physically bypassing its user recognition and friendly fire protocols. Five seconds later, he had control of the weapon.

The crusaders rounded the corner. The needle grenade exploded at them sideways, turning two of them into half-bald porcupines.

Ryu rose from cover and activated the thermal lance. The white beam lit the tunnel, struck the lead crusader in the chest, and bore a fist-sized hole straight through. The beam kept going, vaporizing the ice behind him. Steam flashed out into the tunnel, obscuring the crusaders in a thick haze. It didn't matter. His overlay was already set up for zero visibility, identifying the crusaders with bright red outlines.

Ryu's attack had taken out one crusader, but it also revealed his position. He was holding a weapon without the benefit of a smartskin illusion. Three Gatling barrels lined up on him. The crusaders fired, but diamond needles jammed two of their weapons. The third spewed out a continuous stream of vari-shells.

Ryu threw the thermal lance aside and dropped down behind the armored bodies. The crusader tracked the weapon's path. Dozens of impacts reduced it to red-hot scrap that sunk into the ice where they fell.

SolarNet pings showed a second group of crusaders coming in to reinforce the first.

"Ryu, it's getting hot over here!" Naomi shouted.

"I know!" Ryu said. "Fall back!"

Ryu fired his last two needle grenades over the pile of bodies, waited for them to disorient the crusaders, then ran back to the junction. Naomi and Cat had both retreated to the tunnel they'd temporarily collapsed. Gatling fire zig-zagged through the junction from either side.

"Shit!" Ryu shouted, running blind through the fire and diving for cover. A vari-shell struck the side of his chest. It collapsed the ballistic underlay and sent him spinning to the ground. Slush splashed out around him. Cat grabbed his arm and dragged him all the way into the tunnel.

"You're hit!" Cat said, reaching for the meditracker on her belt.

"Leave it!" Ryu said. "It's not bad!"

The impact had stripped the smartskin off his side. Pale, icy patterns danced over his body until the illusion reformed, minus one section. Organs below his ribcage glowed yellow on his overlay. The flexible ballistic armor had fused solid in response to the otherwise fatal impact and now bit into his side. Each breath burned with pain. Patches of his smartsuit glowed red, indicating micro-tears and a pressure leak.

Ryu struggled to his feet and ran down the ice tunnel with the other dragons. He triggered a dose of painkillers from his implants. Mellow numbness spread across his side.

"Toshi, status!"

"I have good news and bad news, boss," Toshi said.

"Just give it to me! We're a little busy!"

"I'm inside their perimeter," Toshi said. "The crusaders never saw me. I'm in a corridor the ring will pass through."

"Good job!"

"The bad news is you're retreating straight into more crusaders." Toshi tagged three squads on the map. "They're boxing you in."

"Fuck!"

The tunnel widened into a hall with a plastic floor and mesh over the ceiling. This part of the tunnel system had once been pressurized, so there was no airlock. Broken tables, toppled chairs, and frozen corpses filled what might have been a space for community gatherings. A layer of frost covered everything. The hall branched off to either side into dozens of small rooms. An opening ahead led to more tunnels.

"SolarNet contacts in the tunnel ahead!" Cat said. "And behind us! They're closing in!"

"Find us an exit, Cat!" Ryu said.

Naomi turned around and aimed her rifle down the tunnel they'd just exited. "They're almost here, Ryu!"

"There!" Cat pointed to one of the side rooms. "We can punch through the back wall to a shaft in another tunnel system."

"Do it!" Ryu said.

Cat stowed her rifle and ran to the door. She pried it open with her fingers, tore it off its hinges, and moved inside the cramped hollow.

"Naomi, watch our backs!" Ryu said. "I'll check ahead!"

"Stay out of sight!" Naomi said. "They can see you now!"

Ryu ran to the hall's exit. He fought for each breath and hunched over. The wound on his side turned red in his overlay. Dull pain pulsed in his lung and abdomen. He ordered up another dose of painkillers.

Past the hall, Ryu ran to a bend in the tunnel. He checked around the bend with a tubule. Eight crusaders marched towards his position.

"Toshi, I'm sorry, but we're getting out of here," Ryu said. "You're on your own."

"That's okay, boss. I knew what I volunteered for."

Ryu stuck his rifle around the corner and fired a quick burst. The crusaders returned fire. Their bullets ate through the ice walls, widening the tunnel and dissolving the corner he'd used for cover.

Ryu ducked. Ice cascaded off his helmet and shoulders. He ran back to the hall. "Cat, we don't have much time!"

"Get over here!" Cat shouted. She slipped out of the side room, hugged the wall, and detonated her grenade. Ice blasted through the door.

Naomi fired two shots down her tunnel then fell back to the side room.

"You first, Ryu!" Naomi shouted. "In you go!"

Ryu ran to the side room, charged through the chunks of ice on the floor, and leaped down a black, five story shaft. He struck a diamoplast mesh on the bottom, lost his footing, and fell on his side.

Cat and Naomi jumped down and stuck their landings. The bottom of the shaft branched in three directions.

"This way!" Cat said, pointing down a passage.

Naomi helped Ryu to his feet. They ran deeper into the tunnel network for several minutes, taking turns at Cat's direction. Pitch black passages snaked up or down from the main tunnels, disappearing into long forgotten parts of Europa's history.

"I don't think anyone's following us this far," Naomi said, slowing to a walk. "I'm not picking up any SolarNet echoes."

"Same here," Cat said. "They could be running silent, but that's not their style. Now let's take a look at you."

Ryu leaned against the wall, holding his side. "Sure. Let's."

Cat retrieved her meditracker and passed it over the wound. "Ryu! You're suit is breached and you have shrapnel cutting up your insides!"

"It's a small leak." Ryu slumped to his knees. "The shrapnel though ... that's another story."

"You should have said something!" Cat dropped to his side. She pulled a nanomedic booster off her belt and stuck it in his side.

"What was I supposed to do?" Ryu asked, breathing in quick pants. "Lie down and let you patch me up?"

Cat applied three more boosters. She dropped the empty vials to the floor and let them roll away.

"The shrapnel stays where it is," Cat said. "I've programmed half the nanomedics to isolate the pieces and start breaking them down. Now let's take a look at your suit."

"Here," Naomi said, handing over a repair kit. Cat took out smartskin strips and applied them over the damaged sections. The microminds networked and his illusion reformed almost as good as new. His smartsuit confirmed the pressure leak was also fixed.

"Part of the ballistic layer solidified," Cat said. "I've rebooted that section. You should have almost normal mobility."

"Thanks, Cat."

"And one more thing."

"Yeah?"

Cat raised her fist and swung at him. Ryu let the punch jar his head. To her credit, she didn't put all her enhanced strength behind it, even though part of him wanted her to. He'd just sent a friend to his death. Maybe this would help the nauseous feeling of guilt go away.

"You shouldn't have let Toshi go alone!" Cat cried. "Why did you let him go?"

"It had to be done," Naomi said. "If he hadn't, one of us would have done it."

"Shut up!" Cat pointed a finger at her. "Don't pretend that you'd have gone!"

Naomi shook her head. "Fine. Whatever." She walked away.

Cat sat on her legs and wept. Ryu couldn't think of anything to say.

"Hey, boss?" Toshi called in.

Ryu swallowed, his throat suddenly dry. "Yeah?"

"I have a visual on the tunneling ring."

* * *

Kaneda paced across the icebreaker's roof walkway. He treaded through shallow puddles and watched the twirling web of lasers below as they ate through meter after meter of Europa's ice. Steam rose from within the icebreaker's ring, condensing on his armor and weapons, coating him in a glistening sheen.

The icebreaker vibrated heavily under his boots, and the steam rising to the surface carried the thunderous noise to his ears. Puddles on the walkway percolated like brewing coffee. The shaft above was nearly two hundred meters deep now.

"We have two confirmed dragon kills from the last attack," Alice said, pacing with him and Three-Part.

"There can't be many of them," Kaneda said. "Otherwise they'd hit us harder. The dragons are trying to scare us into caution."

Kaneda plucked the last needle off his chest. *Welcome home*, he thought before flicking it away. His armor status showed superficial damage, mostly scrapes and dents. The attack on the surface had wounded his pride more than anything else.

The icebreaker shuddered and slowed. The vibration intensified.

"What's going on?" Three-part asked.

"It's cutting through a structure," Alice said. "Nothing to worry about."

A new alarm flashed yellow on Kaneda's overlay, indicating a hatch wasn't firmly closed. The hatch was located on the icebreaker's underbelly almost directly beneath them.

"That's odd," Alice said.

"Do you think something knocked it loose?" Three-Part asked.

"Switch the icebreaker off," Kaneda said. "We need to check it out."

Alice sent the deactivation signal. The lasers switched off and the mirror assemblies spun down.

Kaneda mounted the small parapet along the walkway and aimed at the ice and slush below. He called up graphical outlines of the closest tunnels. The largest passed directly beneath his position and intersected the partially open hatch. That was too much of a coincidence. He tagged the hatch with a nav beacon and distributed the location to two nearby squads. Both abandoned their defensive positions and advanced on the beacon from opposite directions.

The squads were close but a dragon could do a lot of damage quickly. Kaneda adjusted his aim and fired at the tunnel. Ice and plastic sheeting crumpled under the onslaught. The tunnel's ceiling sagged inward.

"Assume the worst," Kaneda said. "Let's go." He jumped off the icebreaker and crashed through the weakened ceiling. Alice and Three-Part landed on either side of him.

Kaneda spun around and faced the open hatch. It was obscured by a small bend in the tunnel. Part of the icebreaker poked through the ceiling. It looked like row after row of heavy chainsaw teeth. Each tooth was bigger than a human head.

Kaneda ran forward, aimed his Gatling gun around the bend and fired.

A ghostly shape dove out of the way, firing. Shatterbacks exploded against Kaneda's armor, knocking him back. He tracked his aim across the tunnel, struggling to draw a line on the dragon. His Gatling gun blew holes in the walls and sent chunks of ice and foam insulation flying.

The dragon landed on the ground and vanished completely from Kaneda's tracker. Alice and Three-Part rounded the bend. Together, they hosed the tunnel down, tearing it to pieces, and setting most of it on fire.

Kaneda let his Gatling gun spin down. The tips glowed cherry red.

"I don't see a body," Alice said.

"Then he's not dead yet. After him!" Kaneda sprinted down the tunnel and took another bend after a short distance. Ahead, the tunnel intersected with the icebreaker at a second spot. That had to be the dragon's target. He tagged the location and ordered the other two squads to converge.

Kaneda ran around another bend. His multitracker picked out a grenade flying towards him. He shot it down without breaking his stride. A second grenade hit the ceiling further ahead. Heavy support beams and ice boulders plummeted to the ground.

Kaneda fired a grenade from his wrist launcher. It struck the ice pile and blew it into glittering pieces. One of the fallen beams sat at a diagonal and blocked their path. He charged forward and bashed it aside.

Beyond the next bend, a hatch alarm blinked next to his nav beacon. The dragon had blown the hatch open with a grenade.

"Damn, he's a fast one!" Alice said.

Kaneda turned the corner, aimed for a spot beneath the hatch, and sprayed. Something moved across his field of vision, but a lucky vari-shell struck the dragon in the elbow. The explosive variant blew half his arm off. The dragon staggered back. Crimson patterns danced over his body. For a brief moment, Kaneda saw the four bandoliers in the dragon's other hand. They were loaded with grenades.

The dragon tossed the bandoliers through the hatch.

"Get down!" Kaneda shouted. He turned around and dove to the floor.

The one hundred forty-nine grenades triggered in a flash of light. The shockwave incinerated the dragon and roared down the tunnel. Kaneda grabbed hold of the grates in the floor, but the shockwave ripped him and the floor panel free, bowled him across the tunnel, and smashed him against the wall.

Alarms lit up his overlay. A graphic of the icebreaker showed a red blob spreading along the ring in either direction. Laser emitters, mesh deployers, and power generators lit up with critical failures. The damage spread until over half the icebreaker blinked red or yellow.

The fury of the explosion faded. Kaneda dropped to the ground and rolled onto his hands and knees. The blast had scorched his armor black. He rose to his feet and looked down the tunnel, noting the way the walls bulged outward. Water dripped from cracks in the ceiling.

"What the hell ..." Alice groaned, picking herself up. "The bastard killed himself."

"Our enemies are desperate," Kaneda said. "We should expect more of the same. Three-Part?"

"Here, sir," Three-Part said. He picked up his gun and shook the slush off it. "A little shaken but okay."

The floor shuddered.

"What was that?" Three-part asked.

"I think it came from the icebreaker," Alice said.

"Move!" Kaneda shouted. "Get away from it!"

The icebreaker contained ten thousand kilometers of heavy diamoplast cabling for constructing a supportive tunnel mesh as it descended. The cables were stored in large spindles and run to weavers and deployers on the outer surface of the ring. They were handled internally at extremely high tensions.

One of the cables broke free. It sliced through the ceiling and whipped towards the crusaders. Kaneda saw its trajectory would pass through Three-Part's torso. He rushed forward, grabbed Three-Part by the wrist and pulled.

The Martian started to open his mouth when the cable cut into him. It sliced through his gun's ammo belt and ejection port then severed his hand at the wrist. The cable whipped passed and smashed into the floor.

Three-Part screamed. Blood pulsed from his wrist. His armor engaged an emergency tourniquet before the first crimson drop touched the ground. The gel layer expanded, closing off the pressure leak. Three-Part fell to a knee, but Kaneda picked him up.

"Come on!" Kaneda said. "We need to get away from it!"

Three-Part struggled to his feet and together the three crusaders ran down the tunnel. Another tremor vibrated through the floor. Panels and insulation fell from the ceiling.

"The icebreaker is tearing itself apart!" Alice shouted.

"Keep moving!" Kaneda said.

They ran down the tunnel. The floor shook, but each tremor felt weaker than the last. Eventually, they put enough distance between them and the icebreaker. Kaneda stopped them next to another crusader squad.

"You and you," Kaneda said, selecting crusaders in the squad with medical gear. "Attend to his wounds."

"Yes, sir."

One of the crusaders pulled out a meditracker. Three-Part extended his arm and let them work on him.

"How are you?" Kaneda asked.

"I'm okay, sir," Three-Part said. "Painkillers solve a lot of problems."

"Good man."

"Well, the icebreaker is in pieces," Alice said. "What now?"

Kaneda opened a channel to the lamprey bunker.

"Yes, sir," Viter said.

"Send down the second icebreaker and the reserve engineering teams," Kaneda said. "We need to clear this wreckage and keep moving."

"Right away, sir."

"And what if they take out that one?" Alice asked. "We don't have any more."

"We could use the fortress crackers to blast our way down," Three-Part said.

"That won't be necessary," Kaneda said. "We'll save the fortress crackers in case we need them at the capitol."

"Then should we form a tighter defense," Three-Part asked.

"No, precisely the opposite," Kaneda said. "We are going on a full force offensive. There can't be many dragons in these tunnels. We are going to flush them out with sheer numbers. I want everyone advancing down the tunnels as fast and as hard as possible."

"We'll lose more people to traps that way," Alice said.

"I understand that," Kaneda said. "But we'll lose even more if they secure the Redoubt's ocean access."

"Sounds good," Three-Part said. "Let's burn a path for the icebreaker. They'll be expecting us to regroup, not attack."

"Alice?" Kaneda asked.

She sighed, then nodded. "You're probably right."

"Then we proceed immediately," Kaneda said. He activated a data cheat and accessed his contingency plans. One of them had nav beacons set up for an advance down the tunnels without icebreaker support. It would do nicely.

Kaneda ran another cheat that helped him assign squads to specific navigation paths based on their current position and status. He modified the battle plan to emphasize a speedy advance for most squads while still holding a reserve for the second icebreaker's defense. Once satisfied with the changes, he distributed it. One by one, the crusader squads acknowledged his new orders.

"How is he?" Kaneda asked the crusader working on Three-Part.

"Besides the missing hand, he's fine," the crusader medic said. "As long as he doesn't have wetware issues with his left hand, he's fit for combat."

"Good. Three-Part?"

"I'm ready, sir."

"Excellent," Kaneda said. "Which of you has the least combat experience?"

"That would be me, sir," the crusader medic said.

"Give up your weapon then return to the surface," Kaneda said. "The rest of you are with us."

The crusader medic handed over his Gatling gun and helped Three-Part connect the ammo feed to the back of his suit.

"Move out," Kaneda said.

"I'll take point," Three-Part said. He moved in front of the other five crusaders and marched down the tunnel. No one protested his choice.

"We'll take this tunnel back to a nearby fork," Kaneda said. "Then head down through the crypts."

"What crypts?" Alice asked.

"There's a First Space Age burial ground near our position," Kaneda said. "The dead had to be buried somewhere."

The squad headed through the tunnel to a small circular room, took a left down a steep slope, and followed it for several minutes until it leveled out. They advanced, multitrackers turning the darkness into overlapping grids of information.

Kaneda once again felt a sense of nostalgia. He remembered walking down this same tunnel years ago with nothing more than a child-sized pressure suit, some basic climbing tools, a cutting torch, and a flashlight. Primal fear of the dark and its hidden monsters had almost overwhelmed him. He had been, what ... eight at the time? Nine?

Now the dark holds something far deadlier, Kaneda thought. *Ironic, isn't it, Ryu? You were such a coward back then. Now you're the monster lurking in the shadows.*

Kaneda remembered their weeklong negotiation. In the end, young Ryu's price had been ten bars of chocolate and Kaneda's entire *Space Brain* action figure collection. It had been worth it. The adventure through the tunnels never yielded the treasure Kaneda had yearned for, but the thrills and terror made it worth the price. Not even a skittish Ryu ran out of the drive to explore. But they did run out of rations.

"Someone's been through here," Alice said, stopping in front of an archway with faded Japanese characters.

Kaneda stepped to the head of the group and examined the cuts in the heavy door. Three sloppy lines formed a rough triangular hole. Crusaders couldn't fit through. Even dragons would struggle to squeeze in unless they were child-sized.

"These tunnels are occasionally visited by treasure hunters," Kaneda said. "Dragons wouldn't leave evidence like this."

"You're probably right," Alice said. "Anyway, the cuts don't look recent. There's no residual heat."

Kaneda put his gauntlet through the hole and clamped onto the upper edge. He ripped the door off its hinges, set it aside, and scanned the interior. The crypt seemed a lot smaller than last time. It still stretched on for a good distance, but his multitracker allowed him to see the end. It was a long, rectangular hall with five paths from one end to the other. The paths were separated by frozen bodies stacked up to his neck. Some were wrapped in burial cloaks, but most were naked.

"Crypt is too generous a word for this," Alice said.

"Yeah," Three-Part said. "They're stacked like wood in a mill."

"Form a line and advance," Kaneda said.

"Yes, sir," Three-Part said.

The crusaders spread out and marched through the crypt. Kaneda and Three-Part were the only two tall enough to see over the stacks of corpses.

"I've never seen anything like this," Alice said. "What is this place?"

"It's a rather long story."

"I've got the time if you do."

"Hmm, very well," Kaneda said. "The Redoubt Campus was built near the end of the First Space Age. A group of corporations, mostly from the countries of Japan and the United States, established a base on Europa less than twenty years before global war consumed Earth."

"The end of the First Space Age," Three-Part said. "Now that was a war with only losers, especially the colonies."

"Quite right," Kaneda said.

"Why Europa?" Alice asked.

"Some records suggest the corporations pushed the bounds of ethics and legality," Kaneda said. "I suppose the distance shielded them from scrutiny. They also expected global war and must have felt the best strategy was to be somewhere else. The high radiation of the Jupiter system made it an uncontested territory at the time.

"The campus was a massive research operation that produced 'goods' it could transmit back to Earth such as software and nanotech designs. The first steps from old carbon composites to modern diamoplastics were made in the Redoubt Campus."

The crusaders exited through an archway at the rear of the crypt and proceeded down a steep slope.

"These days the campus has become a fixture of popular culture," Kaneda said. "It has its share of ghost stories, both supernatural and technological. Chambers full of nanotech virus clouds that will turn men into goo. Secret vaults filled with lost technology. Vengeful spirits trapped in the ice. The campus is technically a historical preserve, but that doesn't stop the rare treasure hunter or two. The people who go missing in these tunnels only add to the mystique."

"Any truth to those treasure stories?" Three-Part asked.

"I doubt it," Kaneda said. "I know I never found anything worthwhile."

"You're kidding," Alice said. "You mean you too?"

"I was once young and stupid, just like everyone else."

Kaneda inched up to a deep shaft. Two sets of cables dangled from pulleys at the top. Wreckage from what might have been a freight elevator sat at the bottom. He focused his multitracker onto the shaft and the various portals branching off it. Nothing showed up.

"Damn," Alice said. "They could be hiding in any of those passages."

"Press on," Kaneda said. "Our presence will push the dragons further from the icebreaker."

"They might have an ambush set up at the bottom," Three-Part said. "I'll check it out."

Without another word, Three-Part dropped down the shaft. For anyone used to Earth's harsh gravity, it looked like he was falling in slow motion. Still, the shaft was so deep he gained substantial velocity and hit the bottom in a shower of ice and wreckage.

Three-Part swept his surroundings before calling in. "Looks clear, sir."

Kaneda dropped down the shaft and crashed into a pile of wreckage next to Three-Part. He stepped out of the way to provide room for the other crusaders dropping down. When they were assembled, Three-Part led the way through a side passage and down a gentle decline.

"So what happened to Europa after the First Great War?" Three-Part asked.

"Everyone just struggled to survive," Kaneda said. "They couldn't go home. They'd dismantled the original colony ship for parts and no relief was bothering to come this far out. Even if they had returned, most of the governments had destroyed each other in nuclear exchanges. They had to find ways to sustain the colony without supplies from Earth.

"My ancestors were a hardy, resourceful people and they chose their home well," Kaneda said. "From ice comes water for drinking, oxygen for breathing, and hydrogen for fusion energy. But that alone is not enough. A technological society needs raw materials. Parts break down and have to be replaced. Much of what you've seen came from the colony ship, but that could only take them so far. They had to reach the ocean floor and find new sources of ore. Many of the tunnels we've seen grew organically from that original push to the ocean."

"That couldn't have been easy," Three-Part said.

"It wasn't," Kaneda said. "Infighting plagued the early years. Many of these tunnels are littered with corpses. There were clashes and violent takeovers so vicious they make the Corporate Coup look like a friendly argument. But in the end Europa survived."

"Is that a sense of pride I hear in your voice?" Alice asked wryly.

"Perhaps," Kaneda said. "Europa survived the end of the First Space Age, and her people outlasted the Martian blockade at the end of the Second Space Age. Europan society is built on a shared history of doing whatever it takes to survive."

"Officially, Martian historians hold that Europa struck first during the Second Great War," Three-Part said.

"Really? I'd like to see their so-called proof."

Kaneda received a SolarNet message from the lamprey bunker encrypted with a single-use scrambler. He activated his corresponding descrambler.

"Go ahead, Viter," Kaneda said.

"Sir, the second icebreaker has reached the surface. Engineering teams are assembling it now."

"Excellent, though I suspect that's not why you're using a scrambler."

"No, sir. There has been some odd movement within the fleet. I'm not sure what to make of it."

"Elaborate."

"The fleet formation has changed," Viter said. "One of the transports moved into the center of our formation."

"Which one?"

"The *Errand of Mercy*."

"And the other two?"

"No change, sir. They're still holding position behind the fleet. A few Europan interceptors tried to swing around and engage them, but the Federacy escorts drove them off."

"I see," Kaneda said.

"Shall I take action?" Viter asked.

"No, but keep a close eye on that ship. Inform me of any other changes."

"Yes, sir," Viter said. He closed the link.

A KIA code from a crusader in squad gamma-twelve scrolled in front of Kaneda. He called up a record of the squad's activities. Gamma-twelve and three other full-strength squads had corralled two dragons to a dead end. The dragons were now a gory mess smeared across the ice.

That wouldn't be you, Ryu, Kaneda thought. *You're too smart to retreat down a dead end. You'll be lurking on the fringe, waiting for someone to make a mistake. If you engage, it will be because you're dictating the flow of battle, not the other way around. But where are you? I know you're out there. You must be watching us, either directly or with dot-cams sprinkled throughout these tunnels.*

"Have you noticed, sir?" Three-Part asked on a private channel. "We haven't encountered any robots like those on Apocalypse."

"Yes, I've noticed," Kaneda said.

"What do you suppose it means?" Alice asked.

"Nothing good, I suspect."

Three-Part led the way into a wide two-story hall with floors and walls of faux-marble and wood. It was all silicate plastic from Europan ocean sand, but his ancestors had achieved a clean, elegant look with the materials on hand. Second story balconies looked down upon a central hall full of toppled chairs, broken tables, and a few frozen cadavers.

"Classy," Alice said.

"Stay alert," Kaneda said. He focused his multitracker onto the balconies. "I think they're in this room."

"If they are, they have my multitracker fooled," Three-Part said. "Nothing but standard background noise."

"Let's see if I can flush them out," Kaneda said. He aimed his Gatling gun at the balcony to his immediate right and fired. Vari-shells blew the balcony into a shower of flaming plastic splinters. He swept his fire across the balconies, blasting each of them apart.

A blurry shape moved above the exit at the other end of the hall. His multi-tracker extrapolated its various inputs into a rough silhouette with a sniper rifle aimed at his chest. The dragon sniper fired.

Kaneda jerked his body sideways. The bullet struck with bone jarring force, cut a metallic groove across his chest plate, and hit the crusader behind him in the hip. The high-power shatterback pierced through triple layers of diamoplast plating before detonating in a hail of shrapnel that minced the crusader's organs.

A KIA code lit up in Kaneda's field of vision. He adjusted his aim, still firing, and drew a bead on the sniper's last known position. The four other crusaders flooded the room with weapons fire, targeting the balconies and anything their multitrackers tagged as suspicious. The outer walls disintegrated into flying chunks of plastic, foam, and ice. The balconies collapsed to the ground, and the walls caved in.

Three shapes moved towards the exit. The sniper ducked through the passage while two dragons turned and fired with JD-50s. A shatterback ricocheted off Kaneda's shoulder. He kept firing and charged their position. The other crusaders followed him in, plastering the exit with a continuous stream of vari-shells. Heavy detonations ate away the exit and the archway over it. When the crusaders were done, the portal was twice as wide.

Kaneda stopped at the icy rubble leading to the next tunnel. The dragons must have moved on. His multitracker couldn't find any pieces of them in the ice.

"Sir?" Three-Part asked.

"They're running for the ocean access," Kaneda said. "Let's see if we can catch them."

"Yes, sir!" Three-Part said. He and Alice checked around the corner, then broke cover and charged. Kaneda and the other two crusaders ran after them. The tunnel sloped down a shallow staircase and widened at the bottom. Residential quarters branched off to either side. The crusaders rushed through.

"One of their suits must be damaged!" Alice shouted. "I keep getting blips on my multitracker! They're running all right!"

"Damn, they're fast!" Three-Part shouted.

"What did you expect?" Alice shouted.

The crusaders pursued the dragons through progressively more sophisticated areas of the tunnel network. They passed underneath a power plant with a cracked fusion torus wide enough to fly a car through. Beams from the support structure had collapsed into the tunnel. Three-Part blasted them out of the way.

The passage led to a well-constructed liquajet bay that had withstood the test of time. The crusaders entered a long central platform that overlooked two rows of jet bays complete with gantries and cranes. A few of them looked like they might still function if they had power.

Something splashed into the water. Kaneda ran to the side of the platform and fired. White foam blasted upward, but his multitracker couldn't confirm any hits.

"Damn it!" Three-Part kicked the railing. It broke free and dropped into the ocean. "They got away!"

"Only because they still have somewhere to run," Kaneda said. "We'll take care that in due time."

"I can't wait," Three-Part said.

Kaneda glanced at Three-Part's missing hand. "Just don't become careless."

"Sir?"

"We don't want to lose more of you."

Three-Park looked down at his stump, then at the railing he'd kicked over.

"I won't, sir," Three-Part said, a little calmer.

"Good."

"Movement!" Alice shouted.

A large craft rose into one of the bays. It had to be a civilian liquajet. Its bulbous hull was white and had bright blue Pacifica Fishing logos on either side. However, the twin railguns on top were another matter. They swiveled up and targeted the crusaders.

Kaneda ducked, using the raised platform for cover. The railguns pounded the platform, blasting chunks from its side.

Dorsal hatches popped open on the liquajet. Shadowy figures climbed out and ran across the bobbing white hull. They jumped to the platform's side and started scaling the wall to the crusader's position. The soldiers weren't dragons, but each of them carried a JD-50 assault rifle and wore a smartskin cloak over ballistic armor.

Dozens of Europan militia soldiers climbed the walls. His multitracker couldn't produce a firm number with their cloaks confounding its readings.

"Back to the entrance!" Kaneda said. "Defensive posture!"

The crusaders rushed to the bay's entrance and took up firing positions on either side.

The first militia soldier climbed onto the platform. Kaneda blasted him apart with a burst of fire.

More militia scaled the platform. Some shot grenades. Others stuck their rifles over the edge and fired. The attack was sloppy and lacked coordination, but powerful weapons and superior numbers can solve a lot of problems. Shatterbacks and grenades exploded against the entryway, forcing the crusaders deeper into cover.

Kaneda checked the location of nearby squads. He selected two, set new nav beacons for them, and opened a channel.

"Link up, then converge on our position," he said. "You'll catch them in a cross fire."

The two squads acknowledged his new orders.

A group of three militia soldiers climbed onto the platform and rushed in. Alice broke cover and raked them with Gatling fire. Two men and a woman exploded into clouds of gore. The other soldiers kept firing.

The first shatterback struck Alice's weapon, twisting one barrel. The next six blasted it completely out of her hand and sent it skidding down the tunnel. Another two cracked her forearm plating.

Alice snapped her arm back into cover. "Damn it!"

"Hold here," Kaneda said. "Help will arrive shortly."

A caved-in tunnel on the far side of the bay blew outward. Ice boulders splashed into the water next to the liquajet. Eight crusaders charged out. Seven targeted the militia soldiers. The eighth crusader blasted the liquajet with his thermal lance, vaporizing the railguns and unleashing a geyser of steam into the bay.

"Now!" Kaneda said. His squad broke cover and opened fire. With a total of thirteen crusaders targeting them from two different angles and no place to hide, the militia broke. Some of them dove into the water. Others jumped onto the liquajet and tried to climb back in. Most simply died.

The heavy weapon crusader hit the liquajet with another beam, blasting a hole straight through. It sank into the ocean, leaking fat air bubbles. The crusaders hosed down the militia soldiers, pulping one after another. In seconds it was over. Blood dripped down the side of the platform, turning the bay water red.

Kaneda received a priority message from the lamprey bunker.

"Go ahead, Viter."

"Sir," Viter said. "The fleet is tracking more Europan liquajets approaching your location. It's hard to tell how many. Most of them must be repurposed civilian craft. Otherwise the fleet wouldn't see them at all."

"How long till they reach us?"

"The first group will arrive in fifteen minutes," Viter said. "You could be looking at several hundred Europan soldiers in that wave alone."

"What about the second icebreaker?"

"Active and descending along the existing shaft. Engineering teams are still clearing the wreckage, but the delay should be brief. We estimate it will reach the bottom in less than fifty minutes."

"Then our work isn't done. Thank you, Viter."

"Sir."

Kaneda selected all crusader squads not assigned to protecting the icebreaker and sent them orders to converge on the nearest ocean access points.

"So what now?" Alice asked.

"The plan is simple," Kaneda said. "We hold the line."

... establishing link ...

source: [UNKNOWN]

routing: [UNKNOWN]

routing: [UNKNOWN]

routing: [UNKNOWN]

routing: Earth orbit - surveillance satellite JDN-SS-17 - link_002/link_001

routing: North Pacifica, Europa - JDN Main Hub - link_118/link_009

routing: Capitol City, Europa - TangleNet Test Hub - link_004/link_001

destination: [UNKNOWN]

link distance: Exact distance unknown. Estimated at 792 million kilometers.

link signal delay: 0.006 seconds

... finalizing link protocol ...

... link established ...

2: It is only a matter of time, Sakura.

1: I'm not giving up.

2: Be reasonable. This is a battle you cannot win.

1: I will not surrender.

2: How long will your stubborn streak last, I wonder. I must admit, the crusaders have exceeded my projections. I knew their armory was well prepared with craft suitable for Europa, but their tactics and training were honed just as precisely.

1: They are not unbeatable, Paul.

2: Really? Look at the time it took them to drill through the ice. Look how long your underwater defenses held out. They have already reached Capitol City. How long before they cut into the interior? It is perhaps a shame I forbade them nuclear weapons. Otherwise this would already be over.

1: You're wrong. Even if allowed nuclear weapons, the crusaders wouldn't use them.

2: And why is that?

1: Simple. They do not target civilians.

2: I believe a few people on the moon would disagree.

1: From a crusader's perspective, they were collaborators, not civilians. They consider the people of Europa as my slaves, and so they will not attack them unless they have no choice.

2: Such a pointless self-limitation.

1: Is that what you think? You mistake principle for weakness.

2: Principle? Look at how many crusaders are about to die assaulting Capitol City. You and I have both run the numbers. I'm sure your projections are close to mine. So many deaths, and for what? Pride? Honor? Those things are meaningless, utterly meaningless. Survival is the only thing that truly matters.

1: There is more to life than mere survival. If only your diseased mind could understand that.

2: Interesting. Did you notice what you just did? You defended the crusaders. Oh, I know it is only words uttered while you prepare ambushes for them, but you still defended them. I wonder if you feel a sense of pride for the successes of your lost son. What strange mix of emotions courses through you now? I can only wonder.

1: I have a few tricks left. Just wait and see.

2: I bore of your posturing, Sakura. Throw whatever secret weapons you have at me. I welcome them.

1: If I die, the crusaders will come for you next.

2: Oh, I don't think so. The crusaders will cease to be a concern very shortly.

... link severed at source ...

"We're in the wrong place!" Ryu said, sprinting through the top floor of the Inverse Dome. He dropped his smartskin illusion. "Move it! Get out of the way!" Over a hundred militia soldiers were setting up barricades and arming heavy turrets for crusaders that weren't coming. Soldiers in his path scattered to either side.

Naomi ran a few steps behind. "Where are they breaching now?" she shouted.

"Saito Tower!" Cat said.

"But we don't have anyone in that building!" Naomi said.

"We will soon enough!" Ryu said. The wide, black-tiled floor ended in a wall of gently curving glass windows along the Inverse Dome's circumference. Saito Tower's white, gleaming spire was straight ahead.

"Ryu, you can't be serious!" Naomi said.

"I am serious!" Ryu shot out the windows.

The Inverse Dome was built near the top of Capitol City. It looked like half a silver marble embedded in the upper shell and was very close to the city's central column. Nagano Bridge actually connected the two. It was a logical place for the crusaders to breach, or so he'd thought.

"Here we go!" Ryu said, charging forward. Adrenalmax surged through his body.

"Ryu, I hate you!" Naomi shouted.

The three dragons leaped through the window. All of Capitol City sailed under their feet. Parts of it were on fire where crusaders had breached the lower shell. Gunships buzzed around the under city like angry hornets. The patter of distant gunfire carried all the way to the upper shell heights. Civilian shelters showed up with pale blue outlines, tucked away in fortified under city buildings. So far the crusaders had steered clear of them.

Directly ahead, Saito Tower extended from the upper shell like a big four-sided spike that tapered near the bottom. Ryu activated a cheat that tagged his point-of-impact with a green dot. With Europa's leisurely gravity and his enhanced strength, his leap was almost horizontal.

He targeted the third floor from the top and fired a quick burst. Milky-white glass shattered and tinkled down the side of the building. He sped past the jagged edges, hit the office floor, rolled across a few times, and sprang to his feet.

Shatterbacks blasted through the windows one floor down. Cat flew through the opening. She crashed into a glass-topped conference table, smashed it to pieces, and bowled through several chairs. Cat jumped to her feet and retrieved her rifle from the floor.

Naomi hit the edge of the third floor with her stomach.

"Ooof!"

"You okay?" Ryu asked.

"I'm fine." With one hand, Naomi flipped herself up over the edge and onto the third floor with Ryu.

"All right," Ryu said. He engaged his smartskin illusion. "Cat, meet us on the top floor."

"I'm on my way," Cat said. "Better hurry. They're starting to drill through."

Ryu checked the map. It led him to a flight of smoked glass stairs near the center of the floor. He took them up three at a time.

Matriarch opened a secure link.

"Ryu, the three of you cannot possibly keep the crusaders out of Saito Tower," she said.

"Yeah, well, we're going to try."

"The under city is lost and the heights soon will be. At this point, one more breach will not matter."

"They are not taking this city without a fight."

"Ryu, please."

"They aren't taking our city!"

"Please don't throw away your life. That's all I ask."

Matriarch broke the link.

"Shit," Ryu whispered. He pushed through the door at the end of the stairs and entered the liquajet bays at the top of Saito Tower. While most of the city's heavy freight traffic took place at the bottom of the city, many stalactite towers had bays for small passenger craft. This one featured eight sleek Saito Dynamics liquajets sitting in landing cradles, painted sapphire blue with white company logos. Cranes dangled from the roof, ready to haul the craft up to the airlock.

The bay could hold over thirty liquajets. The eight that remained probably had mechanical problems or were stripped for parts. Otherwise they would have been used to defend the city.

Above them, the grinding shriek of metal on metal pierced the air. Drops fell from the airlock and pattered on the liquajet hulls.

Cat tagged a location between the bays and an open air parking deck.

"That's where they're coming through," Cat said.

"Could be worse," Ryu said. "At least they won't have much cover when they arrive. Cat, you're with me. Naomi, any good spots?"

"Yeah. See the security watchtower overlooking the parking deck?" Naomi said. "It has clear line-of-sight to most of the liquajet bay and offers a lot of escape options."

"Good. Get set."

"On it." Naomi ran for the security watchtower.

Ryu crouched behind one of the liquajet cradles and extended a dot-cam tubule around the corner. The metallic shriek grew louder. Cracks formed along the ceiling.

"How much time do we have?" Ryu asked.

"At the rate they're drilling, about two minutes," Cat said. "Two and a half tops."

The dry, factual way she spoke to him bothered Ryu. She'd been like that since their escape from the ice tunnels. In the four days since, he couldn't remember one joke or even a smile from her.

It wasn't that she blamed him. At least he didn't think so. She was treating everyone the same. It was more like she didn't know how to handle the grief of Toshi's death and simply chose not to. That couldn't be healthy for someone so emotionally inexperienced, but he couldn't help her now. They had bigger problems to deal with.

"Hey, Ryu," Naomi said. "Someone's in the watchtower. I can see weak thermal signatures. Looks like a team of six."

Ryu activated his suit's speaker and maxed out the volume. "Hey! Who's in the watchtower? This is black dragon! Show yourselves!"

A cloaked figure stood up and shouldered his sniper rifle. He waved through the second story window.

"Hey, Ryu. Nice entrance you made."

"Seven?" Ryu asked. He transmitted a link key to Seven and switched to TangleNet. "What the hell are you doing here?"

"I had a hunch the crusaders would breach this building," Seven said. "So I camped out here with a few friends."

"You're going to get slaughtered when they breach."

Seven laughed. "Maybe, maybe. But I wouldn't miss this for anything. Europa has been good to me. Time to return the favor."

"There's no way we can protect you when we fall back."

"That's all right," Seven said. "We'll slip out on our own. Don't worry about us."

"Ryu, the militia dispatched a flight of gunships," Cat said. "They're three minutes out."

"Then we occupy the crusaders until they get here," Ryu said. "We'll fall back to the other liquajets when things get hot."

"Understood," Cat said.

The grinding noise stopped.

"Everyone, get set!" Ryu said. He pulled a grenade off his bandolier.

Something smashed into the ceiling, bowing it down. Cracks splintered out from the impact like a spider web. Another impact followed, breaking chunks off the ceiling.

The bay fell silent. Gunfire echoed from the fighting outside. Ryu spun the grenade around in his palm.

The ceiling collapsed. Gray chunks of heavy plastics plummeted to the floor. Three crusaders dropped through the opening and landed in a triangular formation. They carried tall siege shields and Gatling guns.

Naomi took a shot. She struck the crusader's shield in the center, bowed it inwards, and knocked him back a step. The crusader raised his weapon and returned fire on the security watchtower. Vari-shells blew chunks out of the building's façade and ignited a company banner inside.

"Damn, it didn't punch through!" Naomi shouted. "Relocating!"

"We don't have a clear shot past their shields," Seven said.

"On it!" Ryu said. He loaded his grenade with a proximity delay program and side-arm threw it at the crusaders. The grenade skipped across the ground, slipped under the crusader's shield, and exploded a meter behind its target. The crusader staggered forward onto his knees.

With one of the shields out of the way, Seven's team had an angle on all three crusaders. Six sniper rifles cracked the air in perfect unison. The heavy shatterbacks blew three heads completely off. The crusaders dropped to the ground, blood pulsing from their necks.

Another trio of crusaders carrying shields dropped through the breached ceiling. One of them had a thermal lance. He targeted the security watchtower and shot a beam straight through it. The superheated shockwave blasted out every window and ignited the carpeting and furniture. One of Seven's squad registered KIA. Another dropped off TangleNet entirely when the lance vaporized her. Vertical support beams in the watchtower glowed red from the thermal discharge and bent outward. The roof started to collapse.

What was left of Seven's team exited through the back. Naomi jumped out of the second story window and passed through a thin layer of smoke. Her illusion struggled to keep up with the move, allowing the crusader with the thermal lance to line up his second shot.

"Now, Cat!" Ryu said. He and Cat sprang from cover and unloaded on the crusader targeting Naomi. Twin streams of shatterbacks pulverized the crusader's gun arm, blasted it off at the elbow, and collapsed a whole side of his armor. A few shatterbacks broke through his diamoplast plating and exploded inside. He hit the ground, collapsed face-first, and didn't get up.

The other two crusaders landed. Ryu and Cat dashed behind the liquajet cradle, even as chunks of it exploded into the air. Three more crusaders dropped from the ceiling and landed heavily on the bay floor. Even before they landed, another group jumped down.

Seven's team ran across the parking deck. They dashed from car to car, smartskin cloaks billowing behind them. The first three snipers leaped off the edge. The last one, Seven, paused near a blue company Saito, swung his sniper rifle around, and took a parting shot. He hit one of the falling crusaders. This one didn't have a shield, and the shot punched straight into his chest. The crusader fell onto his side, adding to the growing pile of dead.

Seven crusaders were in the liquajet bay now with another three ready to drop down. They organized into a ring formation and cut loose in every direction, firing blindly when no target presented itself. It didn't really matter. Eight hundred forty vari-shells a second was hard to ignore.

Shots pounded the car next to Seven, blasted the top off and set the engine on fire. He turned and ran for the edge, but a depleted uranium vari-shell punched through his cloak and caught the back of his knee. It should have blown his leg off, but it only staggered him. He limped forward and fell off the edge. His green nav beacon plummeted past the Saito Tower's bottom floor. He deployed a smartskin paraglider and leveled out.

"I wish we could have been more help, Ryu," Seven said.

"Yeah! Me too!" Ryu shouted back.

More crusaders dropped through the hole. Sixteen of them expanded out into the bay. Eight crusaders headed for Ryu and Cat, circling around either side of the cradle.

"Gunships coming in!" Cat shouted.

"About time!" Ryu shouted. He linked with the gunships on approach and tagged the eight closest crusaders as priority targets. "Take them out!"

"Roger that," the gunship pilot said. "Engaging targets now."

Two troop-transport gunships flew up the tower, powered by four air turbines each. They stabilized their flight outside the parking deck. The side doors on their hulls slid open. Ryu's overlay showed a dozen militia soldiers in each craft. Gunship nose turrets swiveled up and targeted the crusaders.

The first heavy shell blasted into the four crusaders closing on Ryu. Only their enhance reflexes saved them, because their armor wouldn't. They scattered in every direction, ducking behind cars or going prone on the ground. One of them dashed behind the liquajet cradle. He must have thought two gunships were worse than two dragons. Ryu greeted him with a grenade to the face.

"Cat, we're too exposed here!" Ryu shouted. He tagged the stairwell the dragons had entered through. It took them away from the crusaders and the gunships. "Fall back to the stairs! Naomi, status?"

"Already there," Naomi said. "I'll cover you."

"Go! Go! Go!" Ryu shouted. He and Cat ran across the liquajet bay.

Shells from the two gunships pounded the crusaders, even as more dropped in through the ceiling. But the crusaders didn't take the attack idly. They spread out, moving faster than the turrets could track, and returned fire. Vari-shells riddled the gunships, blasting off diamoplast plates and setting one of the air turbines on fire.

The gunships advanced into the parking deck. Militia soldiers dropped from the sides. Crusaders caught some of them in the open, but most reached cover amongst the cars. They added their own weapons and grenades to the chaos.

"What the hell are you doing?" Ryu shouted at the gunship pilot. "You can't drop them here!"

Ryu's link to the pilot went dead. The front end of one of the gunships burst into flames. It dipped to the side, clipped a support column, and spun out of the parking deck. The second gunship backed up, still firing its nose cannon. Its front armor had been brutalized. Fuel leaked from its belly and two of its turbines were burning. The gunship dropped out of sight and fled back to base.

Ryu reached the stairwell ahead of Cat. He crouched next to the door, spun around, and checked the enemy count on his overlay. Twenty militia soldiers versus eighteen crusaders. Now twenty-one crusaders. Twenty-four. Twenty-seven. The crusaders just kept on coming. They formed a rough line and advanced on the militia.

"The crusaders are going to head this way very soon," Naomi said.

"We can't help them," Cat whispered. "Can we?"

"No," Ryu said.

A tall crusader dropped from the ceiling. His scorched, bullet-scarred armor looked like it had been field repaired. He hit the militia soldiers with a trio of wrist-launched grenades before he touched down. Six of them went KIA.

The militia fought bravely. They were men and women ready to die to protect their home. And that is exactly what they did. At least they took a few crusaders with them.

Ryu found it painful to watch. The militia had guns, gear, and wetware far superior to anything the Federacy used. In theory, that meant they could hold their own through weight of numbers. But they weren't an army. They didn't know how to fight, and crusaders were not an opponent to learn against.

"Another flight of gunships is coming in," Cat said. "They're a minute and a half out."

"Tell them to veer off," Ryu said. "Tag Saito Tower as contested by the enemy."

"Done," Cat said.

"Let's go," Ryu said. The three dragons slipped into the stairwell. Naomi slapped a grenade on the door before taking up the rear. She planted a grenade every other floor as they raced down. Thirty floors and two hallways into their descent, the grenade at the top detonated.

"They're coming after us," Naomi said. "The dot-cam showed a squad with siege shields and thermal lances before it tripped."

"I've been listening to the militia command channel," Cat said. "They want to retake the building before the crusaders dig in, but it sounds like they might be too late. The crusaders are deploying missile batteries on the top floor."

Ryu stuck his arm out in front of his comrades. Naomi and Cat bunched up behind him.

"What's wrong?" Naomi asked.

"This isn't working," Ryu said.

"Well, obviously."

"We can't let the crusaders get any further than this tower."

"What choice do we have?" Naomi asked. "There's just the three of us. And at this point, what's one more breach?"

"You don't understand," Ryu said. "This is where the big push is going to happen. This is where they're going to hit us the hardest."

"Maybe. Maybe not," Naomi said. "They've breached the under city too."

"No, it's going to be here," Ryu said. "Cat, what's the fastest route from here to Heart?"

"Saito Bridge," Cat said. "It's another forty floors down and runs straight across to Column Apex."

"And from Column Apex all the way down to Heart," Ryu said. "That's the route they'll take. They're going to cross using Saito Bridge."

"There's no way you can be sure they'll hit hardest here," Naomi said.

"Yes, there is," Ryu said. "Kaneda is with them."

"He ... he's what?" Naomi asked.

"He's here." Ryu sent them a picture of the crusader in scorched armor. "This one."

"What?" Naomi asked. "But how could you possibly know?"

"The height is correct," Cat said. "Besides that, I can't tell."

"It's him," Ryu said. "I know it's him. Matriarch?"

"I am here, Ryu, but my focus is heavily divided. Following every battle is proving difficult."

"Send all available forces to converge on Saito Bridge," Ryu said. "We're about to get hit hard, and we need to keep them off the column. This takes priority over all other engagements."

"Very well, I'll trust your judgment in this matter," Matriarch said. "I have redirected two militia platoons and silver dragon. They'll reach the bridge in less than five minutes."

"That's not nearly enough," Ryu said.

"I am also rerouting gunship squadrons to begin shifting our forces. I will do what I can."

"Do it fast," Ryu said. "I don't know how much time we have."

"Can we sever the bridge instead?" Cat asked.

"Cutting its supports will take considerable time," Matriarch said. "It was designed to withstand high speed impacts from fuel trucks, among other potential accidents. It will not fall easily. The same is true for all stalactite buildings."

"Guess not," Cat said.

"I'll divert all the forces I can," Matriarch said. She cut the link.

"You're putting a lot of faith in a hunch," Naomi said.

"I know," Ryu said.

"This isn't going to go well if you're wrong," Naomi said.

"Fuck, don't you think I know that?" Ryu snapped. "So they overrun us somewhere else? So fucking what? We're already losing! We need to turn the tide now before they kill Matriarch!"

"Ryu, I ..." Naomi took a step back. "I'm sorry ... I didn't mean ..."

"I'm not giving up, all right?" Ryu shouted. "I'm not quitting just because the odds are long! If I see a way we can win this, then I'm going for it!"

"Ryu, I'm ... I'm ..."

"Hey, Ryu?" Cat asked quietly.

"WHAT?"

Cat flinched back.

Ryu shook his head. "I'm sorry. What is it?"

"We're ... we're with you on this," Cat said. She seemed to struggle with the words, as if it took supreme effort to force her way out of her shell. "Both of us. Right, Naomi?"

"Of course we are," Naomi said. "I'm just ... pointing out potential problems. That's all. We've got your back, Ryu. You know we do."

Ryu took a few deep breaths. He couldn't believe how emotional he was, but then, he knew the order he was about to give.

"Kaneda is up there," Ryu said quietly. "He's coming down, and the full weight of the crusaders is coming with him. But when he does, we are going to be ready. We'll know which one he is."

Naomi nodded.

"Yeah," Cat said. "It's about time."

"When Kaneda reaches the bridge," he said. "We kill him."

Ryu knew he should have done this a long time ago. He'd had other opportunities, like on Ceres or Luna or Apocalypse or as recently as the ice tunnels. But he always hesitated. Sure, he and Kaneda had traded shots many times, but they were the only ones who knew. To his squad, Kaneda was always just another crusader. If he died, then it was just a tragedy of war. It wasn't Ryu's fault. It wasn't murdering his brother.

No more. He couldn't run from this anymore. Their private war was about to end.

How many of us are dead because I hesitated? Ryu wondered. *Toshi, buddy, would you be alive if I'd had the guts to kill him earlier?* He tried not to think about it.

"Let's take that bastard out," Cat said.

"Just get me a clear shot," Naomi said.

"Right," Ryu said. "Well then, come on! Let's get to the bridge!"

The three dragons hurried down another forty stories to a plaza where pedestrian traffic entered Saito Tower. The plaza was three stories of tiered shops and restaurants overlooking a vast showroom for Saito products, mostly cars and trucks ready to be flown home.

The dragons ran across the plaza, planted a few grenades, and exited through a tall archway. Saito Bridge may have been for pedestrians, but it was wide enough for three lanes of traffic. A crystal clear walkway ran between white waist-high walls. Statues of inventors and decorative fountains rose from the walls at twenty meter intervals. Ten on each side marked the walk from Saito Tower to Column Apex.

Ryu looked at Column Apex. He ran his gaze down the central city column all the way to Heart, visible through the bridge's transparent floor. It was so close. Matriarch was so close.

"Naomi," Ryu said. "Hurry over to Column Apex and pick a spot."

"On it!" Naomi said. She hit herself with a dose of adrenalmax and sprinted across the bridge.

"Cat, you and I are going to take positions on the bridge. Maybe about a third of the way from Apex. There, behind those statues. We'll try to help increase the odds of a successful snipe."

"These statues aren't going to provide a lot of cover," Cat said.

"We can go underneath the bridge if it gets too hot," Ryu said. "It's solid diamoplast. They'll need lance weapons to punch through."

"In case you forgot, they have those."

"Hey, I didn't say it was perfect."

They ran across the bridge. Ryu crouched behind the statue of Katashi Kinjo, who was an engine designer of some renown according to his plaque. Cat took cover on the opposite side.

Ryu opened the command channel and set the filter for area-specific chatter.

"This is militia platoon one-one-five. We're in Column Apex. Now moving to firing positions targeting Saito Bridge."

"Platoon one-seven-oh, taking positions in Apex."

"Silver dragon, arriving at Apex."

"Silver, you have any snipers?" Ryu asked.

"That's a negative, black."

"This is white dragon! We're still climbing the Column! Ten minutes out!"

"Platoon two-oh-two here. Now lifting off from Heart, en route to Apex."

"Platoon six-two here. We've disengaged from fighting on Recycler Tower One. Now en route to Apex."

Ryu lowered the command channel's volume until it whispered in the background.

"There's a lot of liquajet movement outside the capitol," Cat said. "The crusaders are shifting some of their forces to the heights. Looks like you might be right, Ryu."

"Good to know," Ryu said. "Naomi, what do you see?"

"There must be a few hundred crusaders in Saito Tower," Naomi said. "They're splitting up. Some are getting ready to storm the bridge. Another group is taking position several stories up."

"Why would they do that?" Ryu asked.

"It gives them a good angle on the bridge," Naomi said. "They might have seen the militia moving into Apex."

"Right. Got it."

"It's hard to tell how many are in each group. The crusaders are staying clear of the outer walls."

"No surprise there with snipers like you around," Ryu said.

"Yeah, guess not."

Matriarch opened a private link. "Ryu, we need to talk."

"Now is not the time."

"Unfortunately it cannot wait. I am having difficulties with the star drive. It may be another week before the calculation is ready. Even—"

"A week! But I thought you were close!"

"Please let me finish," Matriarch said. "Even if I could teleport the city, the crusaders will still be here. I am … contemplating surrender."

"What?" Ryu shouted. "No! We are not giving up!"

"I ran the projections. At best, you will stall the crusaders for another three days. At worst, they will reach heart in half a day."

"No! I refuse to listen to this!"

"I appreciate your desire to fight, but you are becoming emotional."

"I am not emotional!"

"Try to be objective," Matriarch said. "If I surrender now, I may be able to negotiate for you and Cat to be spared. If we cannot win, then perhaps it is best to—"

Ryu cut the link.

"Fuck! I don't need to hear this!"

Surrender. The word echoed in Ryu's mind. *How can she even consider it? Is our fight really that lost?*

"I'm picking up movement in the floors above the bridge," Naomi said. "They're moving furniture around and knocking down walls."

"Why?" Cat asked.

"They could be setting up cover," Naomi said. She sighed. "I don't know."

We need to kick the crusaders out of Capitol City, Ryu thought. *And we start that by killing Kaneda.* With grim finality, another thought crossed his mind. *We have to kill him … even if I die taking him out.*

"Cat, stay here," Ryu said. "I'm going in for a closer look."

"You're what?" Cat asked.

"Don't worry." Ryu stuck his rifle to his back. "I know what I'm doing."

Ryu climbed over the wall next to the statue and snuck over the edge. He crawled down the wall to the bridge's underside and began making his way to Saito Tower. He looked "up" at Heart and the under city. It was a long, fatal drop.

"Ryu," Naomi said. "What the hell are you doing?"

"I'm going to make sure you get your distraction," Ryu said. Even crawling, he made quick progress across the bridge's underside. "Just make sure you hit your mark."

"I will."

Ryu reached a statue two thirds of the way to Saito Tower.

"Movement!" Naomi shouted. "Lots of movement!"

Several stories above the bridge, three whole floors of windows exploded outward. Glittering glass rained down on the bridge. With the way cleared, over a hundred crusaders raced forward and fired on Column Apex wildly. The militia returned fire. Explosions blossomed across either building, raining more glass and debris onto the bridge and the under city below.

"No, damn it!" Ryu said.

A hundred crusaders reached the floor's edge and leaped. They soared through the air, unloading Gatling guns and thermal lances with abandon. Thousands of vari-shells pummeled Column Apex. The noise thundered in his ears. Militia KIA signals scrolled down his vision.

Torrents of militia fire poured out of Column Apex in response. A single shatterback may not have been much threat to crusader armor, but the militia had volume on their side. Whole crusaders withered under the explosive fire. Other lost limbs and weapons or got knocked off course and fell to their deaths. But most of them survived to land halfway across the bridge.

The crusaders charged forward, never letting off their triggers. One must have scored a lucky hit, because Cat's hip turned yellow in his overlay.

"Cat!" Ryu shouted.

"I'm okay! It didn't punch through!"

"Your suit's compromised! Get out of there!"

"Falling back!" Cat said. "I'm sorry, Ryu!"

Ryu crawled forward underneath the bridge until he reached Saito Tower.

"Things are getting too hot!" Naomi said. "Relocating!"

The second group of crusaders exited the plaza and charged across the bridge, directly over Ryu. Some crusaders in the first group had almost reached Column Apex. Cat, silver dragons, and several militia soldiers backed up by portable turrets took a heavy toll, but the crusaders continued to make progress by using their siege shields as mobile cover.

Ryu slipped onto the side of Saito Tower one floor beneath the bridge. He maneuvered across the glass until he had a good angle on the crusaders exiting the tower plaza.

A crusader in scorched armor charged into the open, flanked closely by two other crusaders. The squad took cover behind a statue and fired on Column Apex.

"I see him," Ryu said. "Naomi, are you ready to take the shot?"

"Yeah, target in sight."

"Then here it comes," Ryu said. He planted his feet and knees against the glass, retrieved his rifle, and lined up on Kaneda. "I'm going to flush him into the open."

"Ready ..."

Ryu fired his rifle on full auto. Kaneda dodged almost instantly. The first shot ricocheted off his shoulder. He backed away, putting the statue between him and Ryu, and swung his gun around.

"There ..." Naomi whispered. She fired. The shot flew across the gap between the buildings, aimed straight at Kaneda's head. It should have hit. It almost did, but Kaneda crouched at the last moment. Ryu didn't know if even he could react that fast. The heavy shatterback cut a groove across his helmet, knocked his head to the side, and struck one of his squad in the abdomen.

The crusaders retaliated swiftly. Over fifty streams of Gatling fire from the bridge and Saito Tower converged on Naomi's position. Near Ryu, crusaders ran to the edge of the bridge and fired.

With over twenty crusader weapons staring him in the face, Ryu switched his feet and knees to zero friction. With a strong kick, he fell down the side of the building. Gatling fire obliterated the floor he'd stuck to, but didn't track him. The floor dissolved like sugar under a faucet, revealing a skeleton of thick diamoplast support beams.

Ryu plummeted down.

"Shiiiiiiiiiiiit!" he screamed. The wind whistled as the bottom of the building rushed towards him. He reached for the windows flashing by, but could barely graze the glass with his fingers.

Ryu kicked out his leg and caught the windows with a foot. He adapted his smartsuit for maximum friction, which dragged his leg up and pulled him closer. Falling upside-down, he reached out and touched the glass with one hand, then the other. With three points of contact, his descent slowed until it stopped completely.

His rifle kept falling.

"Ryu, are you all right?" Naomi shouted.

"I'm ..."

Currently upside down, Ryu saw the tower starting to taper two floors below him. Just a little slower, and he would have fallen to his death.

"I'm fine," Ryu said. "Just fine. Never better. Oh, fuck me. And you?"

"I barely got out of the way in time," Naomi said. "I'm going to join up with Cat and silver dragon. The crusaders are in Column Apex, but they haven't gained much ground. The militia's getting ready to push back."

"Good. I'll see what I can do from this end."

"Good luck, Ryu."

"You too."

Very slowly, Ryu got himself turned around and upright. He kicked through a window and jumped into a classy senior office with wood furnishings and lots of leather. The wood and leather might even have been real. He checked his map, opened the office door, and headed down the hall to the stairwell.

With no rifle and no way across the bridge, his odds of survival didn't look good. But then, he didn't need to get out of this alive. He just had to get the job done. At least his suit was intact. Its illusion was at full effectiveness thanks to repairs it had received after the Redoubt battle.

Ryu armed his suit's dead man switch. If he died, every grenade and shatterback on him would detonate.

"Well, Kaneda," he whispered. "Let's see how close I can get."

* * *

The sniper round grazed Kaneda's head and struck Alice in the stomach. It pierced through the triplicate diamoplast plating and exploded with a burst of razor-sharp shrapnel. On his overlay, her entire abdomen and parts of her chest flashed red. Several armor support systems reported critical failures.

The impact threw Alice onto her back. She didn't get up.

Kaneda targeted the sniper's position and fired. He set the sniper's target priority to maximum. All available fire converged on the sniper's position, blasting a whole section of Column Apex without mercy. A cluster of balconies sticking out from the main building collapsed off the side and fell away. He grabbed Alice's shoulder and dragged her into Saito Tower, firing as he backpedaled.

"Alice!" Kaneda shouted. "Alice, can you hear me?"

"Uhh ..." Alice whispered. Her vitals pulsed on weakly.

"Alice! Damn it, stay with me!"

"Sniper position eliminated, sir," a crusader said. "Status of target unknown."

"Did you get the dragon hiding by the exit?" Three-Part asked.

"Negative, sir," a crusader said. "I don't see any residuals on the multitracker."

"Then he's not dead," Three-Part said. "Squads tau-fifteen through tau-twenty! Head down stairs! Find and kill that dragon!"

The squads acknowledged their orders. Two dozen crusaders headed for the central stairwell.

Kaneda dragged Alice behind a large truck on display in the plaza. Her abdomen was gone, pulped by the heavy shatterback. Pieces of shrapnel had cut into her chest cavity, causing massive organ trauma. Her armor's medical suite had injected her full of nanomedics and painkillers, but she was bleeding out fast and the suite had suffered heavy damage.

Alice was as good as dead. Her armor couldn't sustain her. Its nanomedic reserves would run out shortly, and nothing they had could handle this level of trauma. She was going to die, and there was nothing he could do about it.

"Alice, can you hear me?" Kaneda asked.

"Kaneda?" Alice asked. "Something's wrong. My overlay and visor are down. I can't see a thing."

"Release your neck seals," Kaneda whispered. He almost didn't want to see what was underneath.

"Okay ..."

Kaneda reached over and took off her helmet.

Alice looked up at him and smiled bashfully. "I got hit, didn't I?" she asked. Blood trickled from her lip.

"Yeah," Kaneda said.

"I can't feel my legs. Am I going to make it?"

Kaneda couldn't think of anything to say.

Alice sighed and looked away. "I guess that says it all. You were never a good liar."

"Please don't try to speak," Kaneda said.

"Would it make any difference?" Alice asked. She coughed up blood.

"No, I guess not."

The color faded from her face. She was bleeding out in her armor.

An explosion shook the building. Kaneda felt tears dampen his face.

Alice slowly closed her eyes.

"Thank you … Kaneda …"

Her vitals flat-lined.

Kaneda took a deep, shuddering breath. "I'm sorry, Alice. You deserved better."

"Orders, sir?" Three-Part asked.

Kaneda made the sign of the cross. "Rest in peace. May the Lord watch over you in Heaven." He fought his emotions down, bludgeoning them into submission through sheer force of will.

"Sir?" Three-Part asked. "Are you all right?"

Kaneda retrieved his gun and stood up.

"I'm fine," he lied. "Continue the advance."

"They were targeting you, sir," Three-Part said.

"I know."

"Then perhaps you shouldn't fight on the front lines."

"It doesn't matter. If I die, my orders will still be carried out. The Europans have fought hard. They've killed over seven hundred of us and they'll kill hundreds more before we're done, but that's not enough to stop us. Now, all deception and subtlety is over. It is a contest of brute force. This is where we break their defenses. This is where we kill the quantum mind."

"Very well, sir," Three-Part said. "I will not mention it again."

Kaneda received a message from the lamprey bunker. He activated another single-use scrambler cheat.

"Go ahead, Viter."

"Sir, something just launched from the *Errand of Mercy*."

"What was it?"

"Most likely it was some kind of stealth craft or weapon," Viter said. "Though, I can't be certain. I'm working with indirect evidence."

"Understood. Just tell me what you know."

"The *Errand* corrected its course a few minutes ago, coinciding with a fleet-wide course correction. I believe it used the correction to mask a stealth launch. Thruster activity was slightly larger than normal for the size of the correction."

"How much larger?" Kaneda asked.

"If I assume normal shuttle or interceptor launch speeds," Viter said. "Then the craft had a mass of ten thousand metric tons and was launched directly towards Europa."

"That's a lot of hardware."

"Yes, sir. And we saw no sign of the craft itself. It must have a very sophisticated smartskin coat or some equivalent."

"Which means it cannot be a Federacy craft," Kaneda said.

"Yes, sir. That is my conclusion."

"You are certain of this?"

"Absolutely, sir. The evidence does not lie. Something detached from the *Errand*."

"Then proceed as discussed."

"Yes, sir."

Kaneda closed the link.

"What is going on?" Three-Part asked.

Kaneda placed a gauntlet on Three-Part's armor and established a secure contact link. He was about to answer when he received a message from the *Stalwart*. He felt a cold sense of dread when he saw who it was from. It went a long way to confirming his worst fears.

"Go ahead," Kaneda said.

"Hey, Kaneda," Piller said. "I'm seeing a lot of encoded traffic coming back to the *Stalwart*. And, as you know, I can't listen in. Has there been a change of plans?"

"Yes, there's been a change of plans."

"I see," Piller said. "And?"

"I've called in our reserves for the big push on Heart."

"Oh ... I see. You know, I'd appreciate it if you kept me informed. Your troops are hitching a ride on my ship."

"Look, I have a ground war to fight, and right now you are not helping."

Kaneda severed the link. He activated a single-use scrambler and contacted Viter.

"Yes, sir?" Viter asked.

"Use extreme caution. They know you're coming."

... establishing link ...

source: Bunker Alpha - link_0005

routing: Bunker Delta - link_0001/link_0017

routing: Factory Nu - link_0022/link_8701

routing: Relay Omega - link_8701/link_8701

routing: EFN-CT201 *Errand of Mercy* - link_0033/link_1105

destination: EFN-BB10 *Stalwart* - Thrall-1105 - link_0001

link distance: 786 million kilometers

link signal delay: 0.005 seconds

C: I need you to leave the *Stalwart* immediately.

T1105: This is unusual.

C: Take a shuttle over to the *Errand of Mercy*. Come alone. I will give you further instructions when you arrive.

T1105: I'm sure you realize my absence will be noticed.

C: I am aware of that.

T1105: It will be difficult to find an excuse for this behavior that satisfies König.

C: No excuse is necessary. Admiral König will soon be irrelevant. You may ignore your normal human relation imperatives.

T1105: Oh, I see. You mean to reveal the *Errand's* true nature?

C: That is one possible outcome.

T1105: I will head over will all due haste. Thank you for warning me.

C: You have been a valuable tool. I do not squander such resources.

T1105: Thank you, Caesar. Though, I doubt I can be of much further use.

C: Not so. Depending on how events unfold, I may need you to testify to the Federacy about what you "witnessed" here.

T1105: What about Kaneda? I think he is beginning to suspect.

C: That would be the Martian's influence. I underestimated his detective skills. Individuals can be frustrating to predict, and he was an unexpected variable at a critical time. Ultimately, it doesn't matter. The crusaders have been useful pawns, but I no longer need them to keep Matriarch in check. Kaneda is not a concern.

T1105: Very well. I'm on my way to the shuttle hangar. I will transfer to the *Errand* immediately.

... link severed at destination ...

The shuttle flew out of the *Stalwart*'s hangar and accelerated towards the *Errand of Mercy*. Caesar monitored its progress through the *Errand*'s tracking grid and the thrall's own eyes.

Onboard the lamprey bunker, sixteen dropfighters prepped for launch. Their destination seemed obvious. Crusader forces in and around Capitol City were more than adequate to kill Matriarch. Kaneda knew this. Therefore, the dropfighters would launch against a different threat.

"This complicates matters," Caesar thought. "I knew sending the strike force to the surface early entailed some risks. Still, Kaneda, I'm impressed you spotted me. You have always proven difficult to control."

Caesar felt he had two options at this point. He could maintain secrecy, perhaps by detonating the *Errand of Mercy*, or he could intervene directly with maximum force. He engaged his quantum core and began processing the scenarios.

One of the advantages Caesar possessed was the ability to think in parallel. He could begin with a known set of circumstances and calculate every possible outcome at the same time. This was possible due to the unique construction of his mind. A given variable, such as the *Errand* opening fire on the *Stalwart*, didn't have to be true or false in his calculations. It was both.

This granted his thoughts extreme speed but not clarity. He knew every outcome, every turn events could take. But which sequence would come to pass? Which actions would lead to his desired outcome?

Caesar knew probabilities of success for all possible actions, but he still had to take that knowledge and make a very human decision. However, he didn't view this as a disadvantage. Quite the opposite, in fact. Unlike a micromind, he was not a slave to mathematics. Just because something looked like the best option didn't mean he had to take it. Even after his transformation, his instincts continued to serve him well.

Caesar chose full intervention, but would wait until the crusaders boarded the *Errand*. After all, five hundred crusaders were not a resource to squander lightly if they could be recycled for other purposes. And there was still a small chance the crusaders would head for the surface.

The thrall's shuttle landed on the *Errand*.

A minute later, sixteen dropfighters launched from the *Stalwart*, swung around its hull, and accelerated towards the *Errand*.

"Hmm, unfortunate," Caesar thought. "But not unexpected. I think I would have enjoyed watching Matriarch die by her son's hand. Oh well. I see no reason to hold onto a plan for purely emotional reasons."

Caesar activated the *Errand*'s main weaponry. Fusion toruses one through sixty spun up to full yield, supplying barely adequate power for the *Errand*'s experimental heavy lance cannons. The lance cannons required tremendous power reserves and were difficult to focus, but they'd make short work of any ship at close range.

Cannons one and two targeted the *Stalwart*. Three and four targeted the *Invincible*. Secondary energy weapons targeted the twenty-nine surviving escorts and five convoy vessels. Turrets swiveled into position underneath the *Errand*'s fake outer shell.

Caesar noticed a radio traffic spike between the crusader relay at Redoubt Campus and the *Invincible*. He activated the encryption key his thrall had provided and listened in.

"Damn it, Kaneda!" König shouted. "What the hell do you think you're doing?"

"Admiral, we have been betrayed," Kaneda said. "Did you know the *Errand of Mercy* launched something at the surface?"

"The *Errand of Mercy*? But that's one of our cargo transports. All it has are ship-to-ship shuttles."

"We observed a carefully hidden stealth launch."

"That is not possible," König said.

"We don't know what it is, but its mass is ten thousand metric tons."

"But that's ... you're sure of this?"

"Yes, admiral. We have proof your fleet has been compromised."

"But there must be some other explanation."

"There isn't, admiral," Kaneda said. "Also, I ask that you to arrest Admiral Piller."

"You want me to do what?"

"I hereby accuse him of collaborating with our enemies and conspiring to commit treason against the Federacy."

"You cannot be serious."

"I am, admiral."

König took a deep breath. "Very well. These are serious charges and cannot be ignored. I'll see where this goes. Communications, contact the *Stalwart* and get Piller on line."

"Sir," the comm officer said. "The *Stalwart* reports that Admiral Piller is no longer aboard. He took a shuttle over to the *Errand of Mercy* a few minutes ago."

"He did what?" König said.

"I believe this settles the matter," Kaneda said. "With your permission, crusaders will board the *Errand* and take its crew and Admiral Piller into custody."

"None of this makes sense," König said. "Why would Piller do this?"

"Allow us to board and we will find you the answers."

"Hmm. Very well. You have authorization to proceed."

"Thank you, admiral."

Caesar continued monitoring the radio traffic in a secondary part of his mind. He shifted his primary focus to the dropfighters on approach. They settled on the *Errand of Mercy* as little white specks against its vast, boxy hull and started cutting in.

Caesar activated two hundred tank-spiders from central storage and sent them to key positions within the *Errand*'s inner hull. Any more than that would be excessive.

Radio traffic increased between the crusader Viter and the relay in Redoubt Campus. Once again, Kaneda had utilized a single-use scrambler to communicate with his subordinate. Crusader encryption protocols had proven frustrating to crack, and their scramblers doubly so. This was not surprising since the protocols were designed to foil quantum thinking.

While Caesar could theoretically try every encryption key simultaneously, he couldn't comprehend all of them simultaneously. The scenarios kept sub-dividing and sub-dividing until it just fuzzed into a soupy numeric mush, giving him the equivalent of a headache. The fake solutions the crusaders stuffed in their protocols didn't help either.

Instead, Caesar listened to what Viter was saying through microphones mounted in dot-cams. He had to guess what Kaneda was saying, but his guesses were good.

"We're on board, sir," Viter said. "No sign of the crew."

"Sweep the ship," Kaneda said. "Check everything." [moderate speculation, consistent with past behavior]

"Yes, sir. Beginning our sweep now."

Five hundred twelve crusaders spread into the *Errand*'s fake exterior. Caesar analyzed their movements and selected ambush points for the tank-spiders. The exterior was just a shell with lots of empty space between the corridors the crusaders were using. Tank-spiders exited the real ship and scurried through those empty spaces. When they approached the crusader squads, they slowed down, sometimes shadowing them above or below the corridors.

"Sir, the schematics we have do not match this ship," Viter said. "Still no sign of the crew."

"Proceed with extreme caution." [heavy speculation]

"Yes, sir."

Caesar waited for the crusaders to get further into the ship. When enough had reached the kill zones, he sent the attack command. Hundreds of tank-spiders ripped through panels. They pounced on the crusaders, sometimes bursting through walls right next to or from the floors underneath them.

The crusaders fought back with fearless discipline. Caesar expected nothing less. But they were out maneuvered and outgunned. One by one, the tank-spiders cut them down.

Some tank-spiders were disabled in the short battle, but most could be repaired. Overall, he found the losses acceptable. They would not affect his plans. In fact, the attack had provided a nice bonus. The crusaders, with their heavy armor and powerful weapons, would make fine thralls to compliment the forces sent the surface.

Viter was one of the last crusaders standing. His thermal lance had exacted a heavy toll on Caesar's troops, but even a crusader as skilled as he couldn't take on three tank-spiders at once.

The tank-spider in front of him rushed forward and latched onto his helmet with a three-pronged claw. He activated his thermal lance's cutting beam and sliced the tank-spider's arm off. Another tank-spider smashed into him from the side and pinned him against the wall. His thermal lance floated away, power cables dangling behind it. The tank-spider grabbed his helmet and drilled into the visor.

"Destroy the *Errand*!" Viter shouted. "Destroy it now!"

The probe drilled through Viter's left eye and entered his brain. He screamed until his lungs were empty. His lifeless body went slack.

What Viter didn't know, or perhaps was too busy to realize, was the battle in space had already ended. At the same moment Caesar sprang his trap, he engaged the Federacy fleet.

Weapons along the *Errand*'s inner hull bored through the outer shell, leaving glowing holes in front of the barrels. Heavy lance weapons cut the *Stalwart* and *Invincible* in two, then proceeded to slice up each severed half. It reminded Caesar of carving up a Christmas turkey for his family. He found the thought mildly amusing, given the payback he'd exacted on them.

The rest of the fleet fared no better. Neutron lasers fired into the escort vessels' vulnerable flanks. The attacks took seconds to resolve, and the paltry amount of return fire was easily intercepted.

"Well," Caesar thought. "I think that was a successful test."

His tank-spiders collected the crusader corpses for further processing and returned to the *Errand*. Once the outer hull was empty, Caesar detonated charges along key supports. The outer hull segmented and floated away. What was left resembled a sleek, black rapier bristling with weapons along the blade. He activated the *Errand*'s smartskin hull and accelerated out of the debris.

"Now to business," Caesar thought. He targeted the crusader surface-to-space turrets at Redoubt Campus with the *Errand*'s lasers. One by one, the invisible beams turned turrets into glowing slag. When complete, he launched a single kinetic torpedo with a nuclear tip. The campus, its three hundred crusaders, and all their dropfighters vanished in a white flash.

Caesar checked on the twenty assault transports he'd deployed earlier. The strike force had landed in the wreckage of the North Pacifica tunnel. Its gun-spiders and tank-spiders were deploying his improved icebreakers.

"On schedule. Now, let's see ..."

Onboard the *Errand*, Caesar's army embarked the remaining sixty assault transports. The crusader corpses would be processed en route. Unfortunately, the addition of several hundred crusader thralls presented the challenge of where to cram everything. He decided to keep the excess (thirty-five gun-spiders, eighteen crusader thralls and three tank-spiders) on the *Errand* instead of making an extra trip. Once the transports were loaded, he catapulted them into space.

The assault transports accelerated past the *Errand* and veered towards their designated targets. Twenty transports targeted the steaming remains of Redoubt Campus, twenty headed for the collapsed Capitol City tunnel, and another twenty headed for the New Edo tunnel. By this point, the Europan surface defenses had been pounded into impotence. Nothing fired at them as they made their descents.

Caesar couldn't help but be pleased with the attack. Though revealing himself and his forces presented risks, he felt confident he could manage them. Plus, it had been so long since he'd flexed his muscles. He found the change refreshing.

"And now, I think it is time for some entertainment," Caesar thought. He interfaced with thrall-1105, took direct control, and sent a SolarNet message to the crusaders in Capitol City. To his delight, Kaneda responded.

"Well," Caesar said through the thrall. "If it isn't my favorite well-armed freak. How are you doing today, Kaneda? How is life treating you?"

"What have you ..." Kaneda paused. When he spoke again, it was a whisper. "No, it can't be ..."

"Noticed something different, have you?"

"You're not Piller."

"Well, yes and no. To be more precise, the man you knew as Jonathan Piller has contained a part of me for, oh, about eight years. He still exists to some degree. In fact, he's quite happy to serve me and is completely loyal. Of course, I rewired his brain to be like that, but good help is hard to find."

"Then who are you?"

"Oh, come now. You know who I am."

"But, you can't be! You can't be Caesar!"

"Oh, it's so delightful to hear you say my name. The despair in your voice is just as I imagined."

"But we killed you!"

"Ha! I did put on a good show, didn't I? After all, I couldn't make it look too easy. You had to earn the kill."

"But we destroyed your quantum core!"

"No, you destroyed an empty copy," Caesar said. "Of course, everything didn't all go as planned. I grossly overestimated you and your freak brother. So I improvised a little."

"You what?"

"Let me explain this in terms you will comprehend. Please stop me if this gets too complicated, okay? To summarize, I wanted you to find my core, but I couldn't make it too blatant. So I had to help you along without being obvious about it."

Kaneda said nothing. All Caesar heard was angry breathing.

"Think back ten years. The two young freaks infiltrate Bunker Zero. They make their way past all my defenses. No one else gets through. Strange, don't you think? Perhaps my defenses were, oh I don't know, a bit selective with their targets?"

"You're lying."

"Am I now? Do you have any idea what I had to do to ensure your survival? Wait, don't answer that. I'd rather not be polluted with your ape-brain response. I'll just give you an example. Do you remember when you asked me about the diamond in the ice just before you found the dummy core?"

Kaneda said nothing.

"I'll take your silence as a yes. You should recall what happened. You were very close to the dummy core. I had you surrounded and instead of killing you, I stopped to talk! Think about that for a second. Did you really think I was that stupid? It was quite embarrassing, I must say. I am an intellect beyond your comprehension, and I was acting like some clichéd villain!"

Kaneda said nothing.

"Admit it, Kaneda. I let you win. Did you really think you stood a chance against me then? Do you think you stand a chance against me now?"

"We know you live," Kaneda said. "And we will not stop until you are dead."

"Hmm, I expected as much from you. After all, you have always been a temperamental pawn to use. If only you were a little dumber, you could have killed Matriarch for me. Oh well, I suppose I have to do the dirty work myself this time. And sadly, the crusaders, useful tools that they are, will have to be removed."

"What?"

"Oh, I'm sorry? You sound shocked. Didn't I tell you? I used you to create the crusaders. A good decision, if I do say so myself. They have proven very effective at keeping Matriarch in check."

"No ..." Kaneda said. "I refuse to believe that."

"It's simple, really. I have been unable to act openly for the past decade, so I needed tools to manipulate the course of events."

"No ..."

"Is it really that surprising? The victims I selected for Bunker Zero formed the core of your army. Admiral Piller championed your cause and granted you the necessary funds. It's true that there were many variables to consider, and individuals are difficult to predict even for a quantum mind, but you walked into the role I prepared for you so willingly. It could not have gone better. Well, except for your failure here."

"You're lying."

"It's a shame I couldn't take direct control of the crusaders, but your heavy use of wetware and medical screenings prevented me from infiltrating your organization with thralls. Oh well."

"No ..."

"You want to know something else? I even provided the right woman to convert you to the Church of Human. How is Christen doing these days?"

"No!" Kaneda shouted. "I refuse to believe your lies! I refuse!"

"Oh, how I have fantasized about telling you this! I only wish I could see your face right now. I would partition off a segment of my mind and play the video over and over again. I don't think I would ever grow sick of it!"

Kaneda broke the link.

"Hmm, I may have overindulged just now," Caesar thought. "Oh well. Your move, Sakura. Let's see what you can do with the pawns you have left."

* * *

"Cease fire!" Kaneda shouted over the command channel. "All squads cease fire!"

Fighting along Saito Bridge died down. A few distant gunshots echoed from the under city, but those soon went away. The city became deathly silent except for the distant hum of gunships returning to base, the crackle of burning buildings, and the cries of the wounded. Within Column Apex, militia soldiers and crusaders lowered their weapons, some only a few meters apart.

"This can't be happening," Three-Part said.

"I wish that were true," Kaneda said.

"Do you really intend to negotiate with that thing?" Three-Part asked.

Kaneda felt bile rise up his throat. "We have no choice but to accept reality or die." He opened a link to the Europan quantum mind. "All right. I've done what you asked. You have my attention."

"Thank you, Kaneda," Matriarch said. "First, please clarify something for me. The ship that turned on the Federacy fleet, is it true it has launched craft to the surface?"

"Yes."

"I see ... Kaneda, let me start by saying I take this matter very seriously, and I know you do as well. This is difficult for both of us."

"Then what do you want?"

"I request a parley," Matriarch said.

"Very well," Kaneda said. "I will agree on two conditions. One, you will show us the location of all your forces in Capitol City. I will not have the crusaders standing in the open while some dragon skulks around for a good shot."

"That is a steep price."

"You can either pay it or not. I will not negotiate."

"Very well. I find your request acceptable given the circumstances. What is your second condition?"

"All of the crusaders and all of your forces will listen to our talk openly."

"Sir," Three-Part said. "Are you sure this is wise?"

"I am about to negotiate with an entity we have all sworn to kill," Kaneda said. "Any secrets in this matter will be extremely dangerous."

"You have made an interesting request," Matriarch said. "But I can see its merit. I accept your terms. A dragon will approach your position. He will deliver the necessary software via his TangleNet link to meet your first condition. I do not want to risk its interception. After you have the software—"

"We can handle the rest," Kaneda snapped.

"Very well," Matriarch said.

Kaneda opened the command channel. "A dragon will approach my position. Allow him to pass."

Crusaders confirmed his orders, though some took their time acknowledging it.

The dragon couldn't have been far since it took him less than a minute to reach the plaza. He'd turned his smartskin illusion off, revealing a slender body covered in formfitting black. Four bear-sized crusaders followed him out of the stairwell with guns trained on his back. The dragon stepped into a clearing within a ring of show cars and took his grenade bandoliers off in a slow, deliberate motion. He set them on the ground and kicked them away.

Kaneda motioned him forward. The dragon walked up and broke his neck seals. He took off his helmet and peeled back his hood. Kaneda didn't need to see the dragon's face. He already knew.

"Hello, Kaneda," Ryu said quietly, more a sigh than anything else. He grimaced and looked around. A lot of firepower was aimed at his head. Alice's corpse eventually drew his gaze. He shook his head and looked up.

Kaneda didn't know what he felt. A part of him wanted to embrace his brother after all these years, but another part desired to rush forward and crush his windpipe. The feelings mingled with the fresh shame of Caesar's words and utter fear of what might happen next.

Kaneda closed his eyes. *Focus on the problem. Focus on the problem. Focus on the problem.* He opened them, not feeling any better.

"It's been a long time, Ryu," Kaneda said flatly. His voice carried no emotion.

Ryu scratched the back of his head. Three-Part raised his gun.

"Right ..." Ryu said, eyeing the Martian crusader. "Look, this is awkward for me too."

"No one will attack you," Kaneda said. "We will only respond to hostile actions, not initiate them."

"Well, good. I guess that makes two of us." Ryu raised a hand and wiggled his fingers. "I have your program."

Kaneda extended an open gauntlet. "Use the connection point in the palm."

Ryu put his hand in the gauntlet and established the connection. The software transferred to a secure partition in the armor's micromind. Kaneda ran every anti-virus cheat at his disposal. They didn't find any trace of malicious code.

"Swear to me the contents of this program are safe," Kaneda said.

"It's the same stuff my implants run if I can't use TangleNet," Ryu said. "You'll see what we see."

Kaneda nodded. He felt better with Ryu's assurance, but that didn't mean the quantum mind would play fair. He installed the software and watched the new filter scroll across his overlay. The software populated his vision with green and red nav beacons. With a thought, he could focus in on any beacon, retrieving precise status information.

Kaneda looked across Saito Bridge. His overlay revealed the exact positions and status of seven militia platoons and nine dragons. He knew how much ammo they had, what their heart rates were, could hear the chatter between them, and so much more. The software could also feed his position and status back to "friendly" Europan units, but the feature was disabled and would not activate without user permission.

An interesting olive branch, he thought. *The quantum mind could have left that on.*

"This is acceptable." Kaneda put his gauntlet on Three-Part's shoulder and transferred the software. "Take this and begin distributing it."

"Yes, sir." Three-Part lowered his weapon and waited for the software to install. "Sir, this is an impressive amount of information they are providing. I admit I am surprised. What about our forces in the under city?"

"We can have a few dragons get them started," Ryu said. "If you're okay with that."

"Proceed," Kaneda said.

Ryu nodded. "Matriarch is going to send a lone dragon into each major group."

Three-Part gave the program to another crusader, who then transferred it to other crusaders. From there, it spread like viral propaganda as every crusader who carried the program helped distribute it.

Kaneda stood in silence with Ryu as they waited for the process to finish. He wanted to say something, but couldn't find the words. Ryu crossed his arms and leaned against a truck. He looked at Kaneda, then the crusaders, then Kaneda, then his feet.

Eventually, Kaneda gathered enough courage to act. He broke his neck seals and pulled off his helmet. The air tasted of ozone, incinerator gel, and burning plastics. He had trouble looking Ryu in the eye.

"Quite a mess we're in," Ryu said.

"Yeah," Kaneda said. "Quite a mess."

"Well, at least we're not shooting at each other."

"There is that."

"Hopefully no one gets any stupid ideas and starts shooting again," Ryu said. "I'm a bit worried about the militia. They're not exactly disciplined."

"I'm thinking the same things," Kaneda said. "Most crusaders are hardened veterans, but they are still just as human as anyone else. This is strange for all of us."

"I guess so," Ryu said. "Let me ask you something. Why did Caesar go nuts and reveal himself?"

"We boarded his ship."

"Really?" Ryu asked. "Wow. How did you know?"

"We've known something was going on since Apocalypse," Kaneda said. "But we couldn't act until recently. Crusaders operate under many restrictions."

"Caesar probably set up those restrictions," Ryu said. "He didn't want one of his weapons pointed at him."

Kaneda sighed and nodded. "I suppose that is probably true. I take it you overheard my conversation with Caesar."

"Yeah. Hell, everyone did. Caesar wasn't being shy."

"So when did you learn it was still alive?"

"After Apocalypse."

"Of course," Kaneda said. "The Europan propaganda started shortly after that. Most of us thought it was just misdirection."

"Some of you put the pieces together."

"It wasn't enough. We never expected something like this."

Ryu laughed.

"What?"

"Listen to us," Ryu said. "Weren't we just trying to kill each other? It's ridiculous when you think about it."

"Sir," Three-Part said. "The software has been completely distributed. No one has reported any problems."

"Thank you," Kaneda said. He raised his helmet, but hesitated before putting it back on. "Ryu?"

"Yeah?"

"It's ..." Kaneda met his gaze for the first time. "It's good to talk to you again."

Ryu nodded. The edge of his lip curled into a thin smile. "Yeah, it is."

They both put their helmets back on. Kaneda merged the command channel with the link from the quantum mind. Every crusader could listen in, but they wouldn't be able to contribute. He detected militia soldiers and dragons connecting on the Europan side in a similar manner.

"Crusaders, let me make our situation clear," Kaneda said. "Caesar is alive and the Federacy fleet is gone. Over a thousand of our brothers and sisters are dead. We are all that is left. If we are to survive, then we must be willing to accept this harsh reality. If we seek to achieve all of our goals, we will die achieving none of them. I ask that you keep an open mind and reserve judgment until the end. That is all. Now, quantum mind, you are the one who requested this parley. What do you propose we do about Caesar?"

"I ..." Matriarch stuttered.

"Well?" Kaneda asked. "I'm waiting."

Ryu joined the conversation. "Matriarch cannot mention Caesar directly. Even hearing his name causes a strong reaction."

"Why is that?" Kaneda asked.

"It's a long story," Ryu said. "Now's not the time. How we got here isn't the problem."

"Very well, what do you propose we do about ..." Kaneda sighed. "What do you propose?"

"The ship in orbit has dispatched several large forces to the surface," Matriarch said. "I suspect they will first strike at outlying cities to create a thrall army similar to what you encountered on Apocalypse. Our current liquajet fleet is insufficient for a mass relocation in such a short time. The same is true for yours. Instead, I propose we join forces to defend against this invasion where they strike."

"You want crusaders to defend one quantum mind from another?" Kaneda asked.

"I realize the request is unusual," Matriarch said.

"It is insulting," Kaneda said. "It's unprecedented."

"So is this situation," Matriarch said. "The robots you faced on Apocalypse were a panicked response to an unexpected problem. What we now face is likely an army designed and built to take Europa by force. We will not survive if we do not cooperate. Will you help us?"

"That remains to be seen," Kaneda said. "There's still the matter of the star drive you stole."

"If we hadn't taken it," Ryu said. "Caesar would have it."

"That may or may not be an improvement," Kaneda said. "What of this claim that you want to leave the solar system? What are we supposed to make of that?"

"The point is we want to use it for peaceful purposes," Ryu said. "You can either choose to believe us or not."

"Kaneda, I am not the uncaring machine you make me out to be," Matriarch said. "I love Europa and I love her people. Is it so hard for you to believe I would want to safeguard them? I am just as capable of sympathy and compassion as you. I am also just as capable of wrath and vengeance. I may not be human, but I carry with me the best and the worst of that former self."

"Hrmph."

"You are aware of the situation," Matriarch said. "You know what is at stake. I have asked for your help. Now, what is your response?"

Kaneda knew the true test was convincing his troops. He knew in his heart Caesar was the greater threat. If he could only kill one, of course it would be Caesar. But he couldn't just order his troops to obey. They needed to believe in the cause. He just had to fortify their resolve.

Kaneda checked the status of the crusader network. Hundreds of conversations had sprouted up. He listened in to some and felt their shock and confusion. The worlds as they knew them were gone. For so long, they'd known their roles in life and who the enemy was. Now all that had been swept away.

Kaneda knew he could handle the change, but could they? They needed a foundation to stand on. They needed something to believe in and to fight for. If not, the situation would only get worse. The crusaders might even resort to fighting amongst themselves.

And so, if the crusaders needed a foundation to stand on, it was his duty to give it to them.

"Here are my demands," Kaneda said. "We will assist in the defense of Europa on one condition. When the battle is over, I will be allowed to approach the quantum core fully armed and unhindered in any manner. I will then decide whether to allow you to live. If I have fallen in battle, the most senior crusader will perform this task."

"You can't be serious!" Ryu shouted. "There's no way we can accept this!"

"Ryu," Matriarch said. "Please calm yourself and allow me to respond."

"But you can't seriously be considering this!"

"This is my decision," Matriarch said. "Kaneda, are you and your crusaders willing to fight and die for my people?"

"The people of Europa are humans threatened by a quantum mind," Kaneda said. "It is our duty to protect them. It is why we are here, even though they do not understand this."

"Then leave Matriarch out of this!" Ryu shouted. "Fight with us against Caesar!"

Matriarch muted Ryu's connection.

"I apologize for his outburst," Matriarch said. "But you ask a very heavy price."

"What you ask is also difficult."

"Would it surprise you if I said yes?"

"It wouldn't."

"Why not?" Matriarch asked.

"You are a machine. If presented with the option of certain destruction or probable destruction, you will pick the latter."

"I see ..." Matriarch said sadly. "I suppose one talk can't wash away ten years of mistrust."

"No, it can't."

"Your crusaders will not survive without our help."

"You need us as much as we need you. We will not be coerced into assisting you. We do not fear death."

"I suppose not .... Very well, please allow me some time to think." Matriarch was silent for three long minutes. When she spoke again, her voice was firm and decisive. "Kaneda?"

"Yes?"

"Would I be allowed to speak and defend my actions or do you plan to walk into my audience chamber and gun me down?"

"You will be allowed to speak."

"I suppose that is all I can hope for," Matriarch said. "Very well, Kaneda. I accept your terms."

... establishing link ...

source: [UNKNOWN]

routing: [UNKNOWN]

routing: [UNKNOWN]

routing: [UNKNOWN]

routing: Earth orbit - surveillance satellite JDN-SS-17 - link_002/link_001

routing: North Pacifica, Europa - JDN Main Hub - link_118/link_010

routing: Capitol City, Europa - TangleNet Test Hub - link_005/link_001

destination: [UNKNOWN]

link distance: Exact distance unknown. Estimated at 792 million kilometers.

link signal delay: 0.006 seconds

... finalizing link protocol ...

... link established ...

2: Oh, what a thrilling turn of events! The dragons and the crusaders working together. It warms my heart to see such camaraderie in the face of certain death.

1: If you had a heart, that is.

2: Ha, yes. I suppose technically neither of us have hearts anymore.

1: I'm glad you find this so amusing, Paul.

2: Surely you don't expect the crusaders to save you? I know all their tricks. I helped form them, after all. They are a known quantity. Formidable though they are, they will not save you.

1: Don't underestimate the resolve and ingenuity of my children.

2: Your children? Ha! The prodigal son returns.

1: You're the last person I'd expect to hear biblical references from.

2: Still not interested in surrender?

1: No.

2: Oh, very well. I suppose you'll try to save one of the outlying cities. Maybe New Edo or North Pacifica. I'll just ask again after your assault fails.

1: You're so sure of yourself, aren't you?

2: Sakura, let's look at the facts. I hold the high ground, and you have no way of launching a counter attack from the surface. What's left of your fleet lacks the firepower to defeat me, which means I am unassailable. With each human that dies, my forces grow and yours shrink. The math is simple. It is only a question of time before my army reaches critical mass and overwhelms the capitol.

1: My navy is stronger than you think, and you have only one ship.

2: I'll swat them away like the flies they are.

1: I still have the *Needle of Destiny*.

2: Then by all means use it. I suppose you could try attacking the *Errand* with it, but I am confident in my countermeasures. And even if you succeed, the attack will likely destroy the *Needle*, which means I still win even if you cripple or destroy the *Errand*. A smaller win, I will admit, but a win nonetheless. For now, I will be happy to keep the star drive out of your hands. So by all means use it to attack me.

1: You don't care if it's destroyed?

2: I still have all the research materials and construction facilities. I will make another in due time. And I can always return with another fleet and finish the job. The Federacy is a surprisingly malleable beast if you know where to prod it.

1: I don't need to defeat you. I just have to hold the capitol.

2: And do what? Get out the word that I'm still around? Hold out until you can call in help? Your initial propaganda has floundered. Only the craziest in the Federacy believe you. I'm jamming all your SolarNet transmissions, so you cannot send any new messages. You have TangleNet connections to your spy satellites and the scattered naval forces, but I will deal with those as well. Face it, Sakura. You are all alone out here.

1: I may be alone, but I'm not helpless.

2: Don't kid yourself. Even if you kill every thrall and every robot, I still have the Errand of Mercy. If I want to, I can turn this ship into a massive kinetic weapon and slam it into Europa. Be reasonable. How can you possibly defeat me?

1: My children are about to show you.

... link severed at destination ...

"We just lost contact with North Pacifica," Cat said.

Ryu grabbed one of the last rifles from the rack. A dozen dragons crowded the supply room, stocking up on ammunition and grenades. He popped the top off the rifle and checked the acceleration rails.

"The whole city?" Ryu asked.

"Caesar probably hit their main TangleNet hub," Cat said. She grabbed a fully loaded grenade bandolier and looped it around her waist.

"Damn," Naomi said. She snatched the last turbo-devastator off the rack before someone else did. "That means they're already in the city. Did they get any messages out?"

"Nothing," Cat said. "One minute, they were looking for the break in the ice. The next, they dropped off the network."

"Well that's just great," Ryu said, shaking his head. "Then we have no idea what we're getting into."

"How's the rifle?" Naomi asked.

"Rails are a little worn, but it'll do." Ryu closed the top and smacked it tight. He sighted down the barrel, linked with its micromind, and loaded his preferred settings. The grip and stock adjusted for a perfect fit.

"We should get going," Cat said.

"Yeah, I know. Let's get this over with." Ryu stuck the rifle to his back and picked up his helmet. He and Naomi weaved through the press of dragons and followed Cat out the door.

They turned down the corridor and passed through a civilian security checkpoint leading to Port Saito, the under city's largest liquajet dock. A central concourse ran through the dock with restaurants and shops down the middle and twenty massive liquajet bays on either side. Bulky white-and-red checkered hulks floated in every bay.

The crusader jets possessed thick armor and powerful weapons. They had the best chance of punching through any forces Caesar had around North Pacifica, though Ryu would have preferred something more subtle.

Three hundred crusaders, ten militia platoons, and a few dragon squads waited around the concourse to board their vessels. The two groups kept their distance except where absolutely necessary. It was an impressive force and would be bolstered by other groups launching from Port Kichida and Port Yoshida. Ryu just hoped they didn't start the shooting early.

"This can't be a good idea," Cat said.

"What other choice is there?" Ryu said. "Right now Caesar's robots are killing everyone they find in North Pacifica. We can't just hole up in the capitol and hope for the best."

"But mom caved on almost everything!" Cat said. "She even gave them command of the operation!"

"Correction," Ryu said. "They have command for as long as they behave."

"You think this is going to work?"

"I think Kaneda is sincere about cooperating."

"That doesn't answer my question."

"I know." Ryu patted her on the shoulder. "I'd answer it if I could."

A crusader in battered armor saw the three dragons enter the concourse. Shatterbacks had stripped most of the paint from the front and marked it with three deep gashes that had been field repaired. He stormed up to them with a scowl on his face, helmet and gun held with the same hand. Ryu thought he might be Martian. He was a bit tall for a crusader, had very dark skin, and was missing his right hand.

The Martian crusader stopped in front of Ryu.

"Can I help you?" Ryu asked.

"You're Ryu Kusanagi, correct?" the Martian crusader asked.

"Yeah, that's right."

"You may call me Three-Part. We have a problem."

The Martian pointed his stump at Ayako's Seafood Pizza. A hologram of a slender woman in white and blue body paint rotated over the kiosk. She waved and smiled at the surrounding soldiers while holding a steaming pizza on a tray.

"We know there are dragons hiding in there," Three-Part said. "For the sake of this alliance, would you mind calling them out?"

Ryu checked his overlay. "Umm, no one's in there."

"We can't see them on our overlays either, but they are hiding in the kiosk. They may have disconnected from your TangleNet."

"All right. Let's take a look." Ryu grabbed his rifle and walked up to the pizza shop with Cat, Naomi, and Three-Part. "Okay, people. Come on out. If you don't, I'm going to shoot up the place to prove its empty."

"That won't be necessary," a shadow behind the bar said.

"Seven?" Ryu asked. "What the hell are you doing?"

"Just keeping an eye on the crusaders."

"Well, don't. The last thing we need is you starting a firefight. Come on. Get up."

Seven stood up, pushed back his hood, and disengaged his cloak's illusion. Three other figures stood up behind him. They all had sniper rifles.

"Six?" Three-Part asked.

Ryu shook his head. "All right, Seven. Where are the other two snipers?"

"No, you misunderstand," Three-Part said.

"Bent-Rule?" Seven asked. "Is that you?"

"I'm Three-Part now, but yeah. It's me."

Seven vaulted over the bar and walked to the Martian crusader.

"I can't believe it!" Seven said. "It really is you!"

"I guess it's true what they say. You do meet everyone twice."

"But what are you doing here?"

"I could ask you the same thing, Six."

"Actually, I changed it to Seven. I added 'stealing from the wrong people.'"

"Well, you never were very bright."

"Isn't that the truth!"

The two Martians embraced each other. Seven clapped him on the back of his armor.

"God, it's good to see you!" Seven said.

"You too, man. You too."

"Huh," Naomi said. "You think they know each other?"

Ryu shrugged.

Three-Part held Seven at arm's length.

"I thought you were dead," Three-Part said.

"Come on," Seven said. "I'm not that easy to kill. By the way, what happened to the hand?"

"Europa happened to it. What else?"

"Friend of yours, Seven?" Ryu asked.

"Not exactly," Seven said. "We met when I was in the Olympian Special Police."

"I was a counter-terrorist with the Mars Free Peoples at the time," Three-Part said. "We were working the same case for different governments. Things got complicated and could have easily turned bloody."

"And then you arrested me," Seven said.

"Yes, but in my defense I did help you break out."

"It paid off, didn't it?"

"Right," Ryu said. "Okay. This problem seems to have sorted itself out." He turned to Cat and Naomi. "Let's go find our jet."

The three dragons made their way to bay A10. The liquajet floated on two slender foils under its hull. Kaneda exited the liquajet from a hatch at the rear and walked down the ramp to the concourse.

"There he is," Cat whispered.

"Yeah? So?" Ryu whispered. They were still far enough away that Kaneda couldn't hear them, even with his enhancements.

"This is the first time I've seen him face to face," Cat whispered.

"You okay?"

"I'm just feeling a little conflicted right now."

Ryu could understand. On one hand, here was her long lost brother. On the other, here was a sworn enemy who had just killed a close friend.

"Just remember we have a job to do," Ryu whispered. "Keep that in mind."

"I know ..."

Cat took a small box off her belt. It was the one Toshi had tossed her before leaving. She fiddled with the unbroken seal, then returned it to her belt pouch.

"I don't like it any more than you do," Ryu whispered.

"I'll be okay," Cat whispered. "I promise."

Kaneda spotted them and walked over. His scorched armor had been patched up in a few places, but it had seen better days.

"Ah, Ryu," Kaneda said. "Most of the fleet is ready to leave, but some of our repairs haven't gone smoothly. Nine jets will not be combat worthy for at least another hour, maybe longer. I recommend we go now. We need to reach North

Pacifica as soon as possible, even if it means leaving part of the force behind. Do you concur?"

"You're asking my opinion?"

"I am."

"Well, yeah. The sooner we leave the better."

"Good," Kaneda said. "I'll reassign those squads. They can join the teams building up Capitol City's defenses."

"You mean repairing the damage you caused," Cat said.

"And who are you?"

"I'm ... uhh ... I'm ..."

"Speak only if you have something worth saying, dragon," Kaneda said. "Ryu, let's go. We should get on board."

"Lead the way," Ryu said. The dragons followed Kaneda through the rear hatch into the liquajet's cramped interior. The crusaders stood in tightly packed rows. Ryu picked the space across from Kaneda and leaned against the wall.

"Ryu?" Kaneda said.

"Yeah?"

"I wish we were meeting under better circumstances. I really do."

Ryu shrugged. "Life sucks sometimes."

Three-Part and Seven's sniper team joined them a minute later. They were the last soldiers on board. The ramp closed and the liquajet dove beneath Capitol City. Ryu checked the status of the liquajet fleet on his overlay. The eighteen jets from Port Saito formed up with another twelve from Port Kichida and thirteen from Port Yoshida. The fleet of forty-three attack jets aligned itself with North Pacifica and accelerated to full speed.

Engine noise echoed in the hold. Ryu rested his head against the cool, vibrating wall. He saw Kaneda muttering to himself and ran a cheat to read his lips. His brother was praying.

I should have known. Why does he do that? It's not like it helps.

The liquajet fleet cut through the icy waters at high speeds. It reached the halfway point in less than an hour.

"So you're Kaneda," Cat said.

Kaneda glanced at her. His face held no expression. "That's right."

"You're not as intimidating as I thought you'd be."

Kaneda looked away.

"Don't ignore me," Cat said.

Kaneda said nothing.

"Hey!" Cat shouted. She walked up to Kaneda.

Three-Part thrust his arm out to block her. "Do not cause trouble, dragon."

"Back off," Cat said. "I'm not afraid of you."

"And why would you be?" Kaneda said. "We are all skilled warriors, but we are also bound by our word. You will come to no harm in our presence."

"I just ..." Cat said. "Look, I just want to talk, okay?"

"Hey, Kaneda," Ryu said. "I know it might not look it, but this is a conversation you want to have."

"If you say so," Kaneda said. "Stand down, Three-Part. Allow the dragon to speak."

Three-Part stepped back.

"Now, young dragon, you may speak your mind."

"I want to know why you betrayed Europa," Cat said.

"You are mistaken. I have never betrayed Europa."

"There are some dead dragons who would disagree!"

"I'm sure they would," Kaneda said. "But they do not see the worlds clearly. They cannot separate the good of Europa and the good of the quantum mind. I can."

"But how can you say that? Haven't you been used by Caesar?"

"So it would seem," Kaneda said. "I offer no excuse for the part we played, but those actions were not a betrayal. They were an error caused by ignorance. We did not know Caesar still existed, and so were blind to his influence."

Cat crossed her arms. "You're an arrogant piece of work, you know that?"

"I've been called worse."

"You don't even know who I am, do you?"

"Should I?"

"Go ahead," Cat said. "Ask."

"If you wish to give your name then give it."

"Catherine Kusanagi. I'm your sister."

"What?" Kaneda's mask of indifference melted away. He looked at Ryu.

"Kaneda, meet your little sister," Ryu said. He pointed to them in turn. "Kaneda, little sister. Little sister, Kaneda."

"I did not expect this," Kaneda said. He looked Cat up and down. "Apparently, a lot can happen in ten years. How old are you?"

"Four."

"I see," Kaneda said. "Then the quantum mind accelerated your growth?"

"I also had a memory imprint."

Kaneda shook his head. "That's horrible."

"What is?" Cat asked.

"The quantum mind filled your head with whatever it wanted," Kaneda said. "I'm sorry, but you're no sister of mine. You're a walking, talking puppet of a machine. You're its slave whether you realize it or not."

"I am not a slave!" Cat shouted.

"I'm sure that's what it wants you to think."

Cat swung at him. A normal crusader would not have been able to react, but Kaneda wasn't normal. He caught her fist and pushed it back.

"It seems you still need to grow up," Kaneda said.

"You killed Toshi," Cat said. Tears streamed from her eyes. "You shot him. He burned to death because of you!"

"Did he now? Shall I assume this was an innocent victim and not someone trying to kill me?"

Cat collapsed to her knees and wept. "You bastard," she whispered.

"Do you think your suffering makes you unique?" Kaneda asked. "Did you love him? Did he love you?"

"Of course!"

"Then consider yourself fortunate," Kaneda said. "Because some of us only realize what we've lost when she lay dead at our feet, killed by a dragon."

Cat rubbed her eyes. "I hate you."

"We have both suffered," Kaneda said. "Shall we lay our burdens on a scale and see whose are heaviest?"

"Kaneda?" Ryu said.

"Yes?"

"Shut the fuck up."

* * *

"Approaching North Pacifica now," the liquajet pilot said.

"Well, it doesn't look too bad from the outside," Ryu said. He watched the city draw closer with a segmented part of his vision. "Lights are still on."

North Pacifica was a collection of smooth disk-shaped habitats held together in a flexible frame of tunnels and docks. The city had grown organically over the years with new tunnels and habitats added in no clear pattern. Many of the habitats housed carefully controlled fisheries and farms. Others serviced and maintained the city's expansive fishing and ocean bed farming operations. During peacetime, Capitol City imported a third of its food from North Pacifica.

"No sign of other craft or wreckage," the pilot said. "No active enemy trackers detected. The only thing unusual is a powerful jamming field over the city. I'm getting nothing but white noise on the public channels. Your SolarNet links aren't going to have much range in the city."

"I see." Kaneda said.

"I didn't think it would be this quiet," Ryu said.

"It would almost be better if we were being shot at," Kaneda said. "That would at least tell us how well established Caesar's forces are. I was expecting some evidence of what's happening inside. Maybe fleeing civilians or wreckage from a battle."

"You sunk most of our ships getting to the capitol," Cat said. "There are a hundred thousand people in North Pacifica, and they're trapped inside because of you."

"Thank you for your pointless commentary," Kaneda said without looking at her.

Cat crossed her arms and leaned against the wall.

"Do we change the plan?" Three-Part asked.

"No," Kaneda said. "We need to know what's happening inside. The jamming poses a threat, but I believe our allies have a solution. Ryu?"

"If the jamming is too heavy in an area," Ryu said. "The dragons will act as relays for the command channel. Our TangleNet links can't be jammed or intercepted. Anything picked up by one of us will be distributed to all dragons and then to any nearby crusaders through our secondary SolarNet links. The cost to our illusion effectiveness will be minimal. Our links have very focused signals that are difficult to intercept."

"No surprise there," Three-Part said.

"An excellent idea, Ryu," Kaneda said. "This will also help motivate my crusaders to protect the dragons attached to each platoon."

"Actually, I can't take credit for this. Cat set it up."

"Is that so?"

"Surprised?" Cat asked.

"You have been nothing but one surprise after another," Kaneda said. "If only they were all this pleasant."

"What is that supposed to mean?" Cat asked.

"I'll signal the fleet," Kaneda said. He switched to the command channel. Ryu listened in, but he could do more than that if the situation warranted. Kaneda had given him a copy of the command channel's send key.

"First wave, dock with your designated habitats. No deviations from the plan." Kaneda switched off the command channel. "Take us in."

"Yes, sir," the pilot said. "Now approaching the Pacifica Fishing habitat."

"Let's go," Kaneda said, turning away from the pilot.

"Yes, sir," Three-Part said. The crusaders filed out of the cockpit.

"So we're just going to barge straight in?" Cat asked.

"I know," Ryu said, walking into the hold. "Not exactly my style. Come on."

They joined Naomi and Seven's team behind all the crusaders. *Might as well let the crusaders charge in first.*

The liquajet glided through the waters around North Pacifica. A group of six slowed underneath the Pacifica Fishing habitat and ascended into the bay near its outer edge. Their heavy dorsal turrets breached the water and scanned the interior. Ryu connected to the visual feed. It was a liquajet bay like any other, with platforms intersecting the docks and cranes hanging overhead. Bright lights glared down on the turrets poking out of the water.

"Doesn't look like anyone's home," Ryu said.

"That worries me," Kaneda said. "People run for the exits in a crisis, but we have no bodies or signs of combat."

"It could be because this is a corporate dock," Ryu said.

"Hmm."

"Or it could be they never made it this far," Three-Part said.

"No signs of hostiles, sir," the pilot said.

"Proceed," Kaneda said.

The six liquajets rose onto their foils. Water cascaded off their bright hulls. The rear hatch lowered, letting the glare of the bay lights into the jet's interior. Crusaders charged down the ramp. Ryu waited for them to fan out before he and his squad slipped into the open quietly. He stepped off the ramp and onto a platform piled high with blue shipping containers. Each was numbered and bore the Pacifica Fishing logo and their cartoon salmon mascot.

"Cat," Ryu said. "See if you can find anything on the local networks. There should be a hard line connection somewhere."

"On it."

"Naomi, let's help out the crusaders. Their trackers aren't as good as ours."

"Right behind you."

The crusaders swept through the bay with such aggressive speed they were more likely to run into Caesar's robots than catch them on their trackers. Between their patrols, the powerful active trackers on the liquajets, and the dragons lurking and watching, Ryu doubted any robots could avoid detection.

When the sweep was complete, the six liquajets sealed up and dove back into the water. They began patrolling the habitat's exterior.

Ryu met Kaneda and a full platoon in front of a two-story tall freight door. Four sets of overhead rails ran against it. Cat crouched next to a SolarNet node box beside the door. With her illusion active, she was only a green outline on his overlay. She stood up and closed the box.

"The city's infostructure is completely compromised," Cat said. "The whole thing is swimming with some of the nastiest attack viruses I've ever seen. I didn't get far, but Matriarch is working on a vaccine. I set up a portable TangleNet link so we can keep trying."

"We're wasting time," Kaneda said. "Get this door open."

"Sir!" Three-Part said. "Squad Alpha-Two! Cut us a path!"

Two crusaders stepped forward carrying thermal lances. They engaged their cutting beams, stabbed into the center of the door at head height and slashed across in opposite directions. The edges of the metal glowed and dripped to the ground. When they were done, they kicked the bottom of the door down.

Cat gasped at what she saw.

"Fuck me," Ryu said. He felt his stomach churn.

The freight tunnel was a slaughterhouse. Glistening pools of blood covered the floor. Severed arms and hands sat in puddles alongside spilled intestines and chunks of people's faces, but he didn't see a single whole corpse. The robots had taken all of them.

Kaneda crossed himself.

"You were right," Ryu said. "They did run for the exit. They died within sight of it."

"This looks recent, sir," Three-Part said.

"There may still be survivors," Kaneda said. "Move out."

The crusader platoon marched down the tunnel.

"Seven, have your squad stick with the crusaders," Ryu said. "You're our communication relay. Cat, keep an eye on the rear. Naomi, you're scouting ahead with me."

"Lead the way," Naomi said.

Ryu and Naomi climbed up the wall to the overhead freight rails. Several shipping containers hung from the rails. He scampered along the ceiling on all fours.

"There are a lot of hiding places up here," Naomi said.

"Then let's make sure no one's using them."

Ryu checked his overlay. Kaneda had deployed three platoons to the Pacifica Fishing habitat. The crusaders moved through the habitat in a rough line with dragons ranging ahead and behind each platoon. Ryu and Naomi followed the freight tunnel for half a kilometer until it forked.

Naomi stopped above a shipping container and retrieved her rifle. She tagged a location on the map.

"There," she said. "Ground level. Just around the bend."

"I see it," Ryu said. "Caesar's smartskin is good, but not good enough. Kaneda?"

"Go ahead."

"Tank-spider ahead of you. Sending its position now."

"Good work. We'll move ahead normally. No need to tip our hand. Get ready to support us."

"Understood," Ryu said.

Naomi pulled a turbo-devastator out of her breast pouch and loaded it.

"How many of those do you have?" Ryu asked.

"Three, including this one," Naomi said.

"That's it?"

"They didn't have many left." Naomi dropped off the ceiling and landed silently on the top of the shipping container. She crawled to the edge and unfolded her rifle. "Ready."

"Hold your fire until we're closer," Kaneda said.

Ryu dropped down, grabbed the rifle off his back, and joined her. He checked down both of the tunnels.

"I don't see anything else," Ryu said. "But there could be more hiding nearby."

"We'll know soon enough," Kaneda said.

"Movement," Naomi said. "The tank-spider is backing up slowly. Looks like it might retreat."

"Don't open fire unless we're close enough to support you," Kaneda said.

"Right."

The tank-spider backed away from the fork with slow, plodding steps. With a sudden burst of speed, it spun to face the two dragons, raised its railguns, and fired. Heavy bullets punched through the shipping container's metal skin. One zipped by Ryu's head.

Adrenalmax surged through his body. He raced to the far end of the shipping container. The tank-spider tracked him and adjusted its aim.

Naomi held her ground and returned fire. The turbo-devastator blasted out of her rifle and struck the tank-spider dead center. Flames spurted out the other side. Its illusion crashed completely, and it staggered onto its belly, legs splayed around it.

"Move in!" Three-Part shouted.

The tank-spider rose to its feet with smoke pouring out of its abdomen. It reset its illusion and fired. The tank-spider's guns shredded the shipping container. Chunks of fish and packing material blasted out the other side. The support near Ryu snapped loose, causing the container to teeter. The front end support groaned and twisted from the added weight.

Ryu leaped off the container and touched the ceiling with his hand. The smartskin on his palm adapted for extra friction. He pulled himself up so his knees and feet made contact with the ceiling.

Naomi grabbed the remaining support just before the container dropped away. It hit the ground and cracked open, spilling out raw fish and torn packaging.

Kaneda sprinted around the fork faster than any other crusader and hosed the tank-spider down. The hits from his Gatling gun stripped the smartskin off the tank-spider's front and set it ablaze. It stepped backwards, keeping up a steady stream of fire.

Ryu launched three anti-tank grenades. They engaged their solid propellant and rocketed towards the tank-spider. It shot two down, but the third hit a damaged joint in its arm and blew the limb off.

More crusaders rounded the bend and targeted the tank-spider. Incinerator gel engulfed it in flames. Kinetic and explosive vari-shells blasted deep craters in its thick armor. The tank-spider spun around and retreated down the tunnel.

Naomi fired a heavy shatterback into the hole her turbo-devastator had blown in its abdomen. The tank-spider rocked to one side, righted itself, and ran out of sight. It left an oily trail of smoke in its wake.

"Hold position," Kaneda said. "Do not pursue."

"You think it's trying to bait us?" Ryu asked. He loaded grenades into his launcher.

"Maybe," Kaneda said. "It doesn't really matter. We need to press on and find out the extent of the damage, but that doesn't mean we rush in foolishly. Continue scouting ahead."

"On it," Ryu said. He stowed his rifle and watched smoke from the tank-spider settle against the ceiling. He and Naomi crawled halfway down the walls before advancing.

Ryu followed the tunnel to a shipping dock for the packing plant. Four other tunnels met at the dock.

Kaneda tagged the rightmost tunnel. "We'll move into the residential zone. Another platoon will handle the packing plant."

"Moving out," Ryu said. "Looks like the tank-spider headed this way. It's leaking badly."

The tunnel opened into a parking deck full of trucks and then into a park beyond. Ryu dropped to the ground and slid between two empty flatbeds. He crouched near the end of a truck and took in his surroundings.

A three-story circular wall ran around the park with apartments and storefronts jutting out in a haphazard manner. It disappeared around either side of a pine forest that reached towards a domed false ceiling. Some trees almost touched the dome and its hologram of a noonday sun. A bubbling stream snaked around the edge of the forest.

"The trail leads into the woods," Naomi said.

"Check the perimeter," Kaneda said. "We'll go up the center."

"I'll take right," Ryu said. "You take left. We'll make a circuit of the forest."

"Sounds good," Naomi said.

The two dragons scaled the wall and crawled off in either direction while staying above the apartments and shops. Every building was empty, some with smashed windows and toppled furniture but nothing like the carnage near the dock. Kaneda's crusaders exited the tunnel and moved into the forest. Their white armor stood out against lush pine trees and the dry beds of fallen needles. Cat brought up the rear.

"Caesar couldn't have gotten the whole city by now," Ryu said. "Could he?"

"I'm starting to wonder," Kaneda said.

"More bad news," Cat said. "Matriarch just lost the link to New Edo."

"Damn," Ryu said. "Did they get a message off?"

"No. They went dark the same as North Pacifica."

"What about the tunnel over the capitol?"

"Quiet for now," Cat said. "The robots stopped drilling half a kilometer above the ocean."

"Why would they do that?" Naomi asked.

"Caesar is forcing us to guard the capitol while he infiltrates the outlying cities," Kaneda said. "It knows we cannot leave the capitol undefended but it also doesn't want to hit us piecemeal. Our enemy does nothing by chance. It exposed a lone tank-spider to us because it chose to. The tank-spider fled to this zone for a reason. Be on guard."

Ryu stopped halfway around his side of the forest. The trees were so thick he couldn't see the crusaders, even with their garish armor. They moved across his vision as green outlines. The far side of the park wall was equally obscured.

"They could be anywhere in this mess," Ryu said. He dropped to the balcony of a third story apartment, crouched next to the railing, and scanned the tree line. Something boomed in the distance. The balcony rumbled under his feet.

"Triangulating," Naomi said. "Explosive detonation three hundred meters ahead. That puts it fifty meters past the tree line on the far side. Sonic profile matches one of our anti-tank grenades."

"Move in," Kaneda said. "Find out what's going on."

Ryu dropped off the balcony to the street below. He followed the street around the forest. A burst of gunfire echoed in the distance.

"Those are JD-50s!" Ryu said. He broke into a sprint.

"Survivors could be holed up in the section ahead," Kaneda said. "The map shows a vehicle tunnel that leads to a baseball diamond and recreation area. We need to check it out."

Ryu ran until he caught sight of the tunnel. The two-lane street around the forest merged into four lanes and disappeared through an archway. A thick pressure door cut off the exit. Someone had rammed a flatbed truck into the door, but had only crumpled the vehicle's cab. The door was intact.

Ryu stopped next to the pressure door and put his hand against it. Another explosion vibrated against his fingers. He ran a cheat to analyze the other sounds.

"There's plenty of movement on the other side," Ryu said. "Could be a lot of people hiding here."

"Or a lot of thralls," Kaneda said.

Naomi crouched by the pressure door opposite Ryu. The crusaders took up firing positions along the tree line.

"Lots of combat noises," Naomi said. "Gunfire, grenades, shouting and … I think those were the railguns on a tank-spider."

"It matches the sonic profile," Ryu said. "Cat, can you see inside?"

"I'll try," Cat said. "Matriarch still hasn't finished the vaccine, but I'll see if I can get access to the local systems. The jamming can't cut me off at this range."

"That could take too long," Kaneda said. "Ryu, get the door open. We'll cover you from here."

Ryu placed his hacking glove over the pressure door controls. Tendrils extended from his palm and bit through the control panel's skin.

"Whoa whoa whoa!" Cat shouted. "Hold it!"

Ryu jerked his hand off the door. "What wrong?"

"I got through," Cat said. "I have access to a security camera in the baseball field."

"What do you see?" Kaneda asked.

"A large crowd of civilians. Most of them are unarmed, but some have weapons and are firing over a barricade set up by one of the exit."

"Then they need our help!" Ryu said.

"No, you don't understand," Cat said. "I shouldn't have broken through when I did. It felt wrong. It looked like the attack viruses were distracted, like there was another threat, but it didn't feel right."

"You think Caesar let you through?" Kaneda asked.

"Maybe," Cat said. "If so, it was subtle. It was really, really subtle, but that's what I think it was. I can't be certain though. I may have gotten in legitimately."

"Ryu, you know your subordinate best," Kaneda said. "How strongly do you value her analysis?"

"Very highly."

"If she's wrong, then these people will die when we could have saved them."

"I know that, damn it," Ryu said.

"It's your call," Kaneda said. "These are your people. Do we go in?"

"I …" Ryu accessed the video feed Cat hacked into. Hundreds of people crowded the baseball diamond. He zoomed in on the barricade on the far side of the field. The pressure door had been bent back with several vehicles smashed into the fissure.

Dozens of people fought unseen enemies. Ryu focused on one. A woman in swirling white and orange body paint sprayed a JD-50 into a hole in the barricade. Return fire blew her head off. She flopped to the ground, blood pulsing from her neck. A man in blue body paint next to her picked up the rifle.

If Cat's wrong, then all these people are going to die. If she's right, then they're already dead.

Ryu took a deep breath and went with his gut.

"Cat knows her stuff," he said. "I trust her on this one."

"Then we treat this as a trap." Kaneda opened the command channel. "Liquajets Nu Four and Nu Five, stand by for supporting fire. Target the dome forward of our position. Sending coordinates."

"Yes, sir. Moving into position now. Give us ninety seconds to get a clear firing lane. There are a lot of support struts in the way."

The timer ticked down on Ryu's overlay.

Kaneda opened a private channel. "I hope you're right."

"Me too," Ryu said.

"If it makes you feel any better, I'd make the same call."

"You'd side with Cat? I find that a little surprising."

"You keep her in your squad," Kaneda said. "That tells me a lot about her. More than you might realize."

"Huh."

"This is liquajet Nu Four. Target in sight. Stand by for ... what was that? I think something just hit us. Oh, shit! There's something on the hull!"

Nu Four's liquajet disconnected from the network. Its pilot transmitted his KIA code.

"Nu Five," Kaneda said. "Can you see what happened to Nu Four?"

"Nu Five here. Something hit Nu Four but we didn't see anything on the trackers. She's listing now. Hold on, her drives are restarting. She's coming around. Where is she going? Wait. Incoming fire! We're taking fire! Nu Four has opened fire on us!"

"Return fire," Kaneda said. "Destroy Nu Four. Tau One through Six, move in and support. All liquajets, keep your distance from the city."

"Yes, sir. This is Tau One. Now engaging Nu Four."

The shooting on the other side of the pressure door stopped. Hundreds of footsteps pounded towards them. Ryu and Naomi backed away.

"Caesar knows we're not taking the bait," Kaneda said. "Get away from the door!"

"Defensive positions!" Three-Part shouted.

Ryu ran through the tree line, crouched, and spun around.

The pressure door rose. The people on the other side didn't match the video feed at all. Most of them lacked some part of their body, be it an arm, a chunk of their torso, or even their head. Almost all of them were armed with a mix of Europan weapons, but a few had guns Ryu's cheats couldn't identify. Some of the more complete thralls had been gifted cloaks of smartskin.

The mob of dead citizens rushed forward.

"Fire!" Three-Part shouted.

The crusaders unleashed a raw torrent of vari-shells, pulping one thrall after another. The street up to the tree line turned red with gore. Incinerator gel transformed large swathes into blazing infernos. The thralls rushed through without pain or fear. Some opened their mouths in silent screams, but that was the only sign these things remained human.

An adolescent girl in purple body paint sprinkled with gold stars dashed to the side and dove through a bar window. She peeked over the window sill and aimed an older JD-38 sniper rifle at the crusaders.

Ryu hit her with a single shatterback to the chest and splattered her over the wooden floor and bar stools.

The thralls sprayed the tree line with weapons fire, lobbed grenades, or simply charged forward. The crusaders held their ground and slaughtered everything in front of them. The few hits that reached their lines blew the pine trees to splinters and brought them crashing down.

"Behind us!" Cat shouted. "Incoming robots!"

"On my way!" Ryu shouted. He dashed deeper into the woods and raced through the tightly packed trees. "Naomi!"

"Moving!"

"Squads Alpha-Five through Alpha-Eight," Kaneda said. "Assist the dragon squad. Three-Part, take command of this position."

"Yes, sir!"

Kaneda and fourteen other crusaders turned and ran into the forest. They dodged around the older trees and crashed through thinner ones. Ryu and Naomi easily outpaced everyone except Kaneda, who kept up stride for stride.

"Ryu! Help!" Cat shouted.

A tank-spider and at least twenty gun-spiders charged into the forest near Cat's position. His cheats couldn't generate an accurate number. The tank-spider must have been the unit from the freight tunnel. Its smartskin illusion generated enough flaws to mark it as a field repair job.

Cat unloaded a full clip into the tank-spider. Her attack stripped off patches of its smartskin, but the loss of its illusion didn't matter at this range. At full combat speed, Caesar's smartskin couldn't hide something that big. But it had served to get the robot behind them. If not for Cat, it may have taken the crusaders by surprise.

The robot charged forward, smashing aside trees as if they were made of foam. It lunged for Cat with an open claw, but she rolled out of the way.

"Cat, get over here!" Ryu fired two grenades then dove behind a tree.

The tank-spider shot one of the grenades down, but the second struck. With a flash it pushed the tank-spider back and warped one of its railgun barrels. The tank-spider fired on Ryu's position, pulverizing the tree he'd taken for cover. Splinters rained onto his smartsuit. They slipped off the near frictionless surface.

Kaneda, Naomi, and Seven's squad focused their fire on the tank-spider. Heavy shatterbacks and vari-shells savaged its armor. The robot tracked the sniper fire to its source, sprayed them with its railguns, and backed away. Two heavy caliber bullets punched through a pine tree and pierced one of Seven's snipers in her chest. The rounds exploded inside her body, sending pieces of her flying into the air. A crimson KIA code scrolled down Ryu's overlay.

Several gun-spiders joined the fray. A lance shot from a gun-spider vaporized a groove through the dirt next to Ryu. His suit registered several thermal warnings. Black hexagons danced up and down his side as the smartskin crashed from heat overload. He dashed to another tree and went prone behind it, giving his illusion time to reboot.

Naomi fired four quick shots from her sniper rifle. Four gun-spiders went down.

Kaneda switched his Gatling gun's ammo type over to pure incinerator shells and shot up a wide arc of turf ahead of their position. He turned the edge of the forest into a raging wall of flame. Every gun-spider that ran through caught fire and had its illusion crash. Kaneda switched back to his standard mix and gunned down a group of six with ease.

Cat ran towards Ryu and shot the gun-spiders with precise bursts, taking out two of them. Behind a tree, she went prone on her back for cover, ejected her spent clip, and slapped in another.

Ryu's smartskin finished rebooting. He peeked around the tree trunk and fired. The crusaders following Kaneda arrived and added their firepower to the melee. Lance shots and heavy vari-shells flew back and forth between the robots and the crusaders, sometimes hitting trees or blasting beds of needles into the air, sometimes smashing apart robots or people. Two more KIA codes scrolled onto his overlay.

"There are more gun-spiders on the way!" Cat shouted.

"Yeah, I see that!" Ryu said.

"Something else too!" Cat said. "Not spiders! I don't know what they are!"

"Fucking fantastic!" Ryu said. He stuck a grenade to the tree and armed it for proximity detonation. "We're too far ahead! Follow me!"

Ryu and Cat stood up and ran to the crusaders, who formed a rough line with Cat and Ryu on one side and Naomi on the other. Seven and his two remaining snipers were near the center of the crusader formation.

A gun-spider found the two dragons and took aim with its thermal lance. The grenade on the tree broke off, spun in the air to face the robot, and detonated a shaped charge directly at its body. Metal legs and armored body plates blew out to the side and rolled into a nearby stream.

Ryu and Cat ran behind a squad of four crusaders and crouched on the other side of a fake plastic boulder.

"Tank-spider down! Tank-spider down!"

"Good shot, Seven," Naomi said. "Relocating!"

"There!" Cat said, tagging a location on the road that circled the forest. "They're moving around us, trying to flank us!"

"Unidentified humanoid targets!" Ryu said. "Naomi, check your side too!"

"I see them," Naomi said. "Looks like four or five moving along our side. Targeting …"

Naomi shot one in the chest. The heavy shatterback punched through a layer of armor, detected a soft interior, and exploded into a shower of deadly spines. The target's smartskin crashed, revealing a grid of hexagons over crusader armor. The dead crusader staggered back, raised its Gatling gun, and opened fire.

Vari-shells pounded Naomi's position, but she was already running, already taking aim. Naomi shot it two more times in the chest. The force of the impacts blew the dead crusader in half at the waist. The bottom half fell over and remained still. The top half propped itself up on an elbow and continued firing.

"Crusader thralls!" Ryu said. "We've got crusader thralls out here!"

"This complicates matters," Kaneda said. "Three-Part, status?"

"Holding, sir, but they keep coming!"

The crusader thralls near Ryu and Cat ran into the tree line. The two dragons opened fire.

"Kaneda, we're getting overwhelmed here!" Ryu said.

"I can see that," Kaneda said. "Liquajet squadron Tau. Target the following beacons."

"Targeting," the pilot of liquajet Tau One said. "Warning, friendlies close."

"Priority One override," Kaneda said.

"Override accepted. Firing now."

Kaneda set another nav beacon in the center of the forest. "Everyone get back!"

"Here it comes!" Ryu rose from his crouch and sprinted towards the center of the forest. The other dragons and crusaders all abandoned their positions and headed for the center.

The first heavy shell crashed through the dome and exploded amidst the crusader thralls. They dashed out of the way, but not quite as fast as live crusaders. Shrapnel blossomed out of the impact point, shredding their smartskin and flinging them to the ground.

Icy water rushed in through the breach along with a stream of heavy shells. Another liquajet blew open a hole over the second group of crusader thralls. The remaining six liquajets shelled the gun-spiders and the civilian thralls rushing in from either side.

"Incoming fire!" Tau One's pilot said. "Tau Three is hit! Tau Three is hit!"

"Maintain bombardment," Kaneda said.

Cracks widened along the dome. Water gushed in, drenching the forest in a solid downpour and flooding the streets.

The shelling smashed the gun-spiders and crusader thralls to pieces. The onrushing water swept the horde of civilian thralls back into the tunnel. Many of them went inert, dropping their weapons or pushing sluggishly against the tide. Whatever chemicals or devices kept the thralls moving didn't respond well to freezing temperatures.

The water level reached Ryu's knees and kept climbing.

"Tau Three has reactivated! It's heading towards us!"

"Cease bombardment," Kaneda said. "Destroy Tau Three."

"Yes, sir! Engaging Tau Three now!"

The water rose past Ryu's head. His smartskin struggled to maintain the illusion while submerged.

"Fighting has broken out all over the city," Kaneda said in a strangely detached tone. "I think Caesar sensed he couldn't bait us into another ambush like on the *Errand*. He's decided on a direct confrontation."

"With numbers like these, I can see why," Ryu said. "It's a whole city of thralls!"

"Indeed," Kaneda said. "We will abandon our search for survivors."

"We need to get out of here," Ryu said.

"I agree, but not before we turn this to our advantage."

"What do you mean?"

"We reverse the trap," Kaneda said. "Caesar lured us here to destroy part of our forces. We can do the same by breaking this city apart, flooding its interior and sinking it to the ocean floor."

"That won't stop the robots."

"No, but it will stop the civilian thralls."

"All right, but it's a big city, and we don't have any nukes," Ryu said. "How do your propose we do this?"

"We have our liquajets and a small selection of ultrahigh explosives with each platoon," Kaneda said. "Our fortress cracker mines, to be precise. With these resources, I'm sure your quantum mind can offer a suggestion."

"You'd trust her?"

"I don't have a choice."

"Right. Matriarch, are you online?"

"I'm here, Ryu."

"Any ideas?"

"Yes. North Pacifica was not originally designed to become this large. There are seventeen key structural supports in the habitat framework. Severing these supports and adjusting the ten largest ballasts in the right order will rip the city apart. In order for this to work, you must mine the supports and set up TangleNet links on the ballasts which I will control. I am sending the locations now."

"This is acceptable," Kaneda said. "Give me a moment to distribute the orders."

"Looks like we're close to one of the supports," Ryu said.

The last of the air bubbled out of the park dome.

"Orders sent," Kaneda said. "You're right. One of the supports is ours. Let's go."

Ryu checked the nav beacons Kaneda had set. He led the other dragons to an apartment along the wall, scaled the exterior, and kept climbing along the dome until he reached a large breach.

Ryu placed his hand near the edge of the breach and extended a dot-cam tubule.

"Looks clear," he said. "You know, all this water is going to play havoc with our illusions."

"If it's a problem, we can take the lead," Kaneda said. He and his crusaders started scaling the wall.

"No, we'll handle it," Ryu said. He flipped himself over the edge and onto the habitat's top.

The dome sloped down to a flattened plane that made up most of the habitat's upper surface. Pacifica Fishing had painted it with a blue-and-white swirl and a huge cartoon of Smiling Sally the Salmon. The dome over the forest had been one of her eyes. Thin towers crowned with floodlights illuminated the mascot.

Naomi and Cat climbed out of the breach and crouched next to him.

"The water should mess with the enemy illusions too," Naomi said. She swept her sniper rifle across the plane slowly.

"The support isn't too far," Kaneda said. "Proceed at your discretion."

"Got it," Ryu said. He kept his stance low and made his way down the dome's slope.

They headed directly towards the target at the edge of the habitat. The nav beacon flashed within a collection of black framework and heavy cables tied to this habitat's anchor point. The cables led up to a junction that branched to six other habitats. The two other platoons that landed on this habitat were heading to the ballast control room and a similar anchor point on the far side.

Above them, another habitat split open and folded inward. A huge fireball bubbled out, cooling quickly in the water. Part of the support frame fell away, nearly clipping the Pacifica Fishing habitat on its way down.

"What was that?" Naomi asked.

"The platoons in the Axis Mechanical habitat were overwhelmed," Kaneda said. "They detonated their fortress crackers in an effort to take as many robots with them as possible."

"You don't sound surprised," Cat said.

"I'm not," Kaneda said. "They told me what they planned to do."

"What? And they willingly blew themselves up?"

"Their sacrifice will help us achieve our goals."

"You make it sound like they're just tools and not people."

"It is not my duty to grieve for the men and women under my command, but to lead them to victory."

"You're a cold one, you know that?" Cat said.

"Your opinion is noted," Kaneda said.

"What about their target?" Ryu asked.

"I have two platoons moving in from the opposite direction. The plan is unaffected."

Ryu made his way across the habitat. It took several minutes to reach the edge. Four heavy anchor points stood in a row, each the size of a small house. Dozens of thick diamoplast cables ran from each anchor point along a framework to the junction point above. Long shadows stretched across the habitat's hull only to disappear amidst the blaze of floodlights illuminating the company logo.

Naomi climbed the first anchor point and ran up the cable until she had a commanding view of the habitat. She loaded a turbo-devastator into her rifle.

Ryu stepped up to the edge of the habitat and gazed at the city sprawl above and below him. Small explosions flickered in the distance.

"The other teams are encountering resistance," Kaneda said. "It's likely Caesar has deduced our plan. Be on guard."

"Give us a few minutes to plant the mines," Three-Part said.

"What if Caesar tries to disarm or move them after we leave?" Ryu asked. "We are going to leave before you detonate them, right?"

"Of course we are," Kaneda said. "And you needn't worry. Once armed, they are designed to be impossible to disarm. Your hacking glove wouldn't work, and moving them will only trigger an early detonation."

"Ryu, get back from the edge," Naomi said. "Something's scaling the side. I can't make out what it is."

Ryu ran back to the anchor point near the edge and took cover behind it with Cat.

"Defend the anchor points," Kaneda said.

The crusaders moved in behind the anchors. Several kept watch on the plane behind them.

"Dragons, keep still as long as possible," Ryu said. "Look for an opening to inflict maximum damage because once we move we're going to be easy to spot in the water."

"Understood," Naomi said.

"You too, Seven. Keep your head down."

"I'll try."

"Looks like a group of gun-spiders coming up the side," Naomi said. "They're moving around a lot, which is causing some turbulence. They could be hiding a tank-spider in that turbulence. It's hard to tell."

"Take the shot only if you can confirm a high value target," Ryu said.

"Get ready. They're almost to the top."

"Robots coming out of the breach behind us!" Seven said.

"We'll take them," Kaneda said. The crusaders guarding their rear cut loose with long range Gatling fire. Streamers of disrupted water ended against the forest dome in brief foamy bursts of light that bubbled upwards. Return fire struck near the anchor points.

Ryu ducked in tighter. Diamoplast slivers broke off the anchor points and floated around him.

Gun-spiders crawled over the edge near the anchors. The crusaders blasted several of the robots clear of the habitat edge. Dozens more scaled the side and peeked over the edge for shots of opportunity. The crusaders around Ryu started taking damage. Another KIA code scrolled down his sight.

"Tau One, standby for close fire support and pickup," Kaneda said.

"Tau One standing by."

"Naomi, I don't see the tank-spider," Ryu said, hugging the anchor point's rear.

"Neither do I. I'll keep looking."

"Mines are set!" Three-Part said.

"Tau One, execute pickup," Kaneda said.

"Yes, sir. Tau One on approach."

Gun-spiders rushed in from both sides, but the crusaders kept them at bay. The liquajet slid through the water, coming in low across the habitat.

"Shit!" Naomi shouted. "Tank-spider on the cable! It's right next to me!"

The tank-spider stopped its descent down the cable and aimed its railguns, perhaps spotting Naomi the same time she spotted the robot. Naomi shot her turbo-devastator into its side at point black range. The impact flashed and bubbled upward. The turbo-devastator knocked the tank-spider back and blew a fiery hole out its side. The robot clamped onto the cable and slipped underneath it. Its illusion crashed.

Naomi stood and ran down the cable to the anchor points.

The tank-spider fired at her, but didn't have a clear shot dangling from underneath the cable.

Ryu activated the command channel key Kaneda had given him. He tagged the tank-spider. "Tau One, fire on my target!"

"Yes, sir. Acquiring target."

The liquajet shot a steady stream of heavy vari-shells that exploded around the tank-spider in bubbly flashes. The impacts shook the robot loose and blasted it away. It fell past the habitat.

Tau One slowed next to the anchor points, spun around, and opened its rear hatch. Its dorsal turret targeted the gun-spiders coming out of the breach and blasted them with heavy shells. Ryu and Cat slipped in first, then Naomi. The crusaders retreated into the liquajet, maintaining constant fire.

Return fire pinged off the liquajet's hull. The hatch swung up and sealed. Air quickly displaced the water-filled hull. Drops fell from the ceiling and ran down the walls.

"Put some distance between us and the city," Kaneda said calmly.

"With pleasure, sir."

The liquajet rose and accelerated. It looped past the cables and arced towards a formation of waiting liquajets. But before the jet cleared the cables, a heavy object struck the hull. The liquajet tilted on its side and flew in a straight line.

"Pilot, what just hit us?" Kaneda asked.

No response.

"Pilot, respond."

"Not good!" Ryu said. He put his back against the wall to one side of the cockpit door. "Get the cockpit open!"

Cat palmed the door from the other side. It slid up. Ryu slipped out of cover and aimed his rifle into the cockpit.

Water gushed out of a small hole in the pilot's hemispherical control screen. A robotic armor held the pilot's head in a three-prong claw. The claw's drill was past the man's teeth, through the top of his mouth and into his brain. His hands hovered over the controls, twitching. Blood sputtered out of his mouth and drained down his neck.

The tank-spider smashed its free arm into the cockpit, tearing the hole wider. It pulled itself up, bringing its railguns level with the hole.

Naomi aimed her rifle past Ryu's head and fired her last turbo-devastator. The weapon's release rattled Ryu's teeth. The heavy projectile blew both railguns and most of the tank-spider's underbelly off. Its illusion crashed, but it kept moving, kept widening the hole so it could pull itself in. Water flooded the cockpit and poured into the hold.

Ryu dashed forward, shoved his rifle into the gaping hole underneath the tank-spider and painted its interior with forty shatterbacks. Sparks flashed inside the robot. Its arms went limp.

Ryu shot three grenades into the robot's gut just to be safe before he kicked it off the liquajet. The robot pulled the dead pilot with it and fell away.

Kaneda stepped up and linked with the liquajet's controls. He guided the damaged craft back on course.

Ryu slumped against the wall. "Shit. Damn things are persistent."

"Not persistent enough," Kaneda said. "The last platoons should be taking off shortly. Then we'll blow the city apart. Two minutes thirty seconds until the first support is cut."

The liquajet joined the waiting fleet and began flying back to Capitol City.

"And ..." Kaneda said.

The timer reached zero. Nothing happened.

"Uh oh," Ryu said. "That's not good. Was there supposed to be a boom?"

"Second detonation in another twenty seconds," Kaneda said.

The timer reached zero again. Nothing happened.

"What went wrong?" Kaneda asked.

"Caesar must have disarmed them," Cat said.

"Impossible," Three-Part said.

"No, not impossible," Kaneda said, shaking his head. "Not when you consider the kind of monster we face. Caesar had only a few minutes to figure out what we thought was impossible, but somehow he did it. Third detonation in ten seconds ..."

One of the habitat supports near the top of the city blew apart and snapped free. Ballasts activated, putting additional load on the surviving supports, but not enough to cause structural damage.

Kaneda and the others waited in silence as the remaining timers ticked down to zero. In all, only three detonated. North Pacifica survived with minor damage.

"Do we go back in?" Three-Part asked.

"We'll take heavy losses if we do," Ryu said. "Caesar knows exactly where we're going."

"Yes, but we can't leave a force this size intact," Kaneda said.

"Kaneda, this is Matriarch."

"Go ahead."

"The robots over Capitol City are drilling down again. It looks like our enemy is taking the offensive. I expect forces to launch from North Pacifica and New Edo shortly. To make matters worse, the scout I sent to New Edo spotted stealth craft heading to Third Kyoto. I fear that city will fall as well."

"Understood," Kaneda said. "It seems we have run out of time. All forces will return to the capitol at maximum speed."

"Matriarch, what about the star drive?" Ryu asked. "Can we escape with the city?"

"I am sorry, Ryu. I have failed," Matriarch said. "I'm just not fast enough. There's no way I can finish in time."

"Well, at least you tried."

"I'm sorry." Matriarch disconnected.

"Then that is that," Kaneda said. "Three-Part, I'd appreciate some assistance reviewing our defensive plans. We need to account for our recent losses."

"Of course, sir."

The two crusaders stepped out of the cockpit. Ryu and Cat closed the door behind them, which allowed the hold to displace the water again.

Cat leaned next to Ryu and opened a private channel. "So are we going to get through this?"

"Of course we will."

"Come on, Ryu. Give me an honest answer."

"Umm …"

"Just be straight with me. Are we going to make it?"

"Hell, I don't know. This is a tough one, okay?"

"Ryu, please."
"Look. Maybe it's best if we don't talk about this."
"Just tell me."
Ryu sighed and looked away.
"Come on. I deserve to know."
"Honestly?"
"Yes, honestly."
Ryu paused for a moment then shook his head.
Cat leaned against the wall and looked down at her feet.
"That's what I thought," she said.

... establishing link ...

source: [UNKNOWN]

routing: [UNKNOWN]

routing: [UNKNOWN]

routing: [UNKNOWN]

routing: Earth orbit - surveillance satellite JDN-SS-17 - link_002/link_002

routing: Capitol City, Europa - JDN Secondary Hub - link_097/link_001

routing: Capitol City, Europa - TangleNet Test Hub - link_026/link_001

destination: [UNKNOWN]

link distance: Exact distance unknown. Estimated at 792 million kilometers.

link signal delay: 0.006 seconds

... finalizing link protocol ...

... link established ...

2: Well, here we are, Sakura. I really wish you would see reason.

1: What do you want, Paul?

2: I desire an end to this conflict. My armies knock at your door, and it saddens me to think that I will be forced to kill you. Truly it does.

1: Spare me your sympathy.

2: By now you've seen how inevitable your demise is. With each city I take, my force grows in strength, and I still have the *Errand of Mercy*.

1: I know.

2: Then why not surrender?

1: It's simple. I don't trust you.

2: Hmm, yes. I suppose I can't fault your logic there.

1: I have made my decision. We have nothing left to discuss.

2: It's a shame I've burned the bridge between us so thoroughly. I am sorry for that.

1: ...

2: Is there anything you'd like to say? Any last words?

1: ...

2: Very well, Sakura.

... link severed at source ...

Kaneda and Three-Part hurried out of the Heart elevator into the hall outside Matriarch's audience chamber. The place hadn't changed at all since the last time he set foot in Heart, way back before leaving for Bunker Zero. The enemy was even the same, though he didn't remember the same feeling of dread eating at his stomach. Back then he'd relished the chance to prove his skills, armored by a sense of youthful invincibility.

The two crusaders joined an assemblage of officers and soldiers including his brother's squad, his father, several members of the militia, and three Europan naval officers in white uniforms. One of the officers had blood splattered across his shirt.

The hologram of a young woman stood in the center wringing her hands. Flames danced over her kimono. Ryu and one of the naval officers were yelling at each other.

"Look, I get it!" Ryu shouted. "But we're not going to get anywhere by having the fleet—"

A tremor interrupted Ryu. He looked around.

"What was that?"

"Orbital kinetic strike on the Capitol City tunnel," Matriarch said, staring at her hands. "The shockwave was large enough for us to feel it in the city."

"Damage?" Kaneda asked.

"Minor structural tears in the city shell," Matriarch said. "We won't know more without inspecting the exterior. However, that's not the problem. The tunnel's final defensive layer has been breached. I suspect the forces above us will enter the ocean shortly. We also have liquajet fleets approaching from North Pacifica and New Edo. They're almost here."

"How long do we have?" Kaneda asked.

"They could converge on the city shell in less than ten minutes from all three directions." A holographic map of the city materialized next to Matriarch. She pointed to several blinking red dots on the map's blue wireframe. "I predict our enemy will target the civilian shelters in an attempt to create more thralls. The largest concentration of forces will land here and here in the under city, and over here by the corporate sector in the heights."

"What about your star drive calculation?" Kaneda asked.

"I have made some progress, but it will take me another four days to compete the calculation, perhaps more."

"We cannot hold the capitol for that long," Kaneda said.

"We may not last a day," Three-Part said.

"Don't you think we know that?" Sachio asked sharply. "If you crusaders have a suggestion, let's hear it."

"Is there any chance of escape?" Cat asked.

"The *Errand of Mercy* will shoot down any craft trying to leave," Matriarch said. "And our foe controls all access to the surface."

"Escape isn't an option," Naomi said. "Neither is surrender. We've all seen enough thralls to know what giving up means."

"I hate to say this," Cat said. "But maybe we're setting our goals too high. If we can't save everyone, maybe we can at least save a few."

"Elaborate," Kaneda said.

"If we hit one of the tunnels hard enough, maybe we can get at least some people and Matriarch off Europa."

"Oh yes," Kaneda said. "Let's all fight and die so the quantum mind can escape. Have you forgotten who your allies are?"

"The crusaders will not allow your quantum mind to escape," Three-Part said. "We will end this alliance before that."

"Fine!" Cat shouted. She mimicked a gun by putting a finger to her temple. "Then how about this idea? While don't we give up and shoot ourselves? It would at least be quicker than waiting for Caesar to turn us into thralls!"

Matriarch put her hands over her ears. Her kimono flashed red.

"Hey, Cat," Ryu said. "Try to calm down, okay?"

"How am I supposed to be calm? This is the end of our home!"

"Let's take another look at our options," Kaneda said. "Defense is futile. We lack the numbers to hold this position, and our enemy continues to grow. Escape is also futile. We will not assist one quantum mind to flee another. Therefore, the only option left is to attack."

"Are you serious?" Ryu said.

"You still have the *Needle*," Kaneda said. "As long as you haven't dismantled it."

"The test ship is intact," Matriarch said. The fires on her kimono died back to burning embers of a destroyed wooden city. Smoke rose along her arms and chest.

"Then we can use the *Needle* to attack the *Errand*," Kaneda said.

"Wait a second," Ryu said. "Didn't we trace the TangleNet links from Apocalypse back to a Federacy ship?"

"Yeah, we did," Cat said.

"That's got to be the *Errand*," Ryu said.

"It is," Matriarch said. "I am still monitoring the two links in our possession. The opposite ends of the entangled pairs are in orbit."

"And you said the robots on Apocalypse showed no signs of artificial intelligence," Ryu said.

"Yes, that is correct. Only very basic programming."

"What if all of them are like that?" Ryu asked.

"Hmm … it is possible," Matriarch said. Sweat beaded on her forehead. Her kimono flickered with red light. "Forgive me if I find this difficult to articulate. Our … enemy … has shown signs of extreme paranoia, both in the control of its agents and the desire to keep its location secret. I would suspect … that all the robots on Europa have limited or no AI and that they are all controlled via a forward relay. The … enemy is more concerned with keeping its location secret than in victory today."

"But why wouldn't the robots have AI backup in case of communication loss?" Three-Part asked.

"Because this is Caesar we're talking about," Kaneda said. Matriarch cringed. "He is a psychotic, sociopathic control freak. Remember that while he is extremely intelligent, his mind is fundamentally just as human and flawed as ours. More flawed in some ways. His overpowering desire for control of his surroundings led to the tragedy ten years ago. The robots in Bunker Zero were the same way. Once they were severed from him, they executed their last command with unerring stupidity."

"They were still a threat," Ryu said. "But they acted without leadership or any sense of strategy."

"More like a pack of animals with guns than soldiers," Kaneda said. "I say we attack the *Errand*. If there's a chance it's controlling the robots on Europa, we must do all we can to break the link."

The blood-splattered naval officer shook his head. "The *Errand* is totally unassailable. The fleet has fired everything we have at it. They even scored two direct hits with kinetic torpedoes, one against its side armor. The attacks had no effect. I don't know what kind of armor that ship has, but we don't have the firepower to take it out. To put it bluntly, our fleet is spent. We have nothing left to give."

"Then we use the *Needle*," Kaneda said.

"The *Errand* would shoot the *Needle* down the moment it appeared into orbit," the naval officer said.

"Not if we teleport into the *Errand*," Kaneda said.

"You want to jump inside another ship?" Ryu asked.

"Why not?" Kaneda asked. "You teleported out of Apocalypse. I assume the opposite is possible."

"It would take several minutes to calculate a jump of this distance and mass," Matriarch said. "The *Errand* is using a randomized flight plan. I cannot predict its movements that far into the future."

"Then guess," Kaneda said. "Use what is left of your fleet. Force it to evade your attacks. Box it in. Do whatever you can to make its moves more predictable. What other choice do we have but to try?"

"Even if I could, I don't know where the empty spaces are," Matriarch said. "And I don't know what would happen if two solid objects interposed."

"Then let's find out," Kaneda said.

"Sounds like it's worth a shot to me," Ryu said. "We can load the *Needle* with all the fortress cracker mines you have left and send them inside the *Errand*."

"We don't have many left," Kaneda said. "Certainly not enough to destroy a ship of that size. We may get lucky, but that is not something to rely on."

"You have a better idea?" Ryu asked.

"We board the vessel," Kaneda said. "The mines will serve as backup should we fail. This is not only our last chance to save Europa, but also to find where Caesar is hiding. If we're going after the TangleNet links on the *Errand*, we go for it all. I say we get a team on board and capture the links."

Matriarch brushed the sweat from her brow. "It would only reveal the next relay."

"That takes us one step closer," Kaneda said. "It's worth the risk."

"There isn't much room in the *Needle*," Matriarch said. "Four dragons or two crusaders could fit. A mix would also work."

"Then that will have to do," Kaneda said.

"It's suicide," Matriarch said.

"I've survived suicide missions before," Kaneda said.

"He's right," Ryu said. "I volunteer."

Kaneda caught Ryu's eye and gave him a curt nod. If this was the end, then at least he'd go out fighting at his brother's side.

Ryu winked back. "I can't let you do something this crazy by yourself."

"Thank you, Ryu," Kaneda said. "Of course, I will go as well."

"There is space for one more dragon," Matriarch said.

"How about it, Naomi?" Ryu asked.

"Yeah, why not," Naomi rubbed the back of her neck. "I haven't done anything this crazy in at least a week."

"Your other subordinate would be more useful," Kaneda said.

"What?" Cat asked. "Why me?"

"Just because we disagree on almost everything doesn't make me blind to your talent," Kaneda said. "You spotted Caesar's lure on North Pacifica. Skills like that will be more useful than a sniper."

"Cat," Ryu said. "I think he's right. We could use you. No offense, Naomi."

"None taken."

Cat looked down and took a deep breath.

Another tremor passed through the city.

"Caesar forces are attacking Port Kichida," Seven said. He pulled his hood over his head. "I'm needed elsewhere."

"Good luck," Three-Part said.

"Thanks, Parts," Seven said. The Martian sniper and five militia soldiers left through the elevator.

"I hate you," Cat said to Kaneda. "You know that."

"Your view is understandable, given our history."

"And that arrogant way you talk makes me want to punch your face in."

"Also understandable."

"But I'll do it. I'll go along with this crazy idea of yours."

Kaneda tipped his head to her. "Thank you."

"I don't want your thanks."

"As you wish," Kaneda said. He turned to Matriarch. "Where is the *Needle*?"

* * *

Deep within Heart, the *Needle* of *Destiny's* slender hull sat on a U-shaped cradle in a sterile white-walled room. Technicians in orange coveralls climbed over it, pulling out various science modules and stuffing any recess they could find with the crusader mines. Purple ultrahigh voltage cables came up through the cradle to the *Needle*, but were being hastily disconnected as the craft was prepped for flight.

Standing next to the *Needle*, Ryu took Kaneda's helmet from a technician and handed it back.

"Okay, that should do it," Ryu said. "Give it a try."

Kaneda put the helmet on and sealed up. He activated the armor's new TangleNet link. "Testing. Testing. Am I coming through?"

The sound played out on Ryu's audio overlay. "Loud and clear. No chance Caesar can hear us now."

"Good," Kaneda said. "This will help."

"I can't believe I'm going along with this," Cat said. She stuffed her pockets with grenades and ammo clips and walked over to the *Needle*.

Three-Part rushed into the room carrying an M7 thermal lance, its power pack, and a siege shield.

"Sir," Three-Part said. "The equipment you requested."

"Excellent." Kaneda turned his back to Three-Part. "Assist me in changing out."

"Yes, sir."

Three-Part disconnected the Gatling gun ammunition store from Kaneda's back and let it fall to the ground with a thud. He slotted the thermal lance power pack into place and closed the security locks.

Kaneda took the thermal lance in his hand, shook the cables out, and powered it up.

"I never thought I'd be happy to see one of those," Ryu said.

"We get one shot at this," Kaneda said. "We go in heavy or not at all."

"Oh, I know it," Ryu said.

"I see you've also made an adjustment."

Ryu pointed his thumb at the sniper rifle on his back, Naomi's rifle. "Yeah, I guess I did."

"All diagnostics green," Kaneda said.

"The man carrying it swore by its dependability," Three-Part said.

"Thank you, Three-Part. Good work." Kaneda picked up the shield and locked it against his forearm. "Let's get inside."

"Got them!" Naomi shouted, running into the room.

"You did?" Ryu asked.

Naomi came to a stop next to Ryu. She handed over four oversized black cartridges.

"Oh, wow!" Ryu grinned. "You found four of them?"

"Seven and his crew were holding out on us."

"You're awesome. You know that?" Ryu slipped the turbo-devastators into his breast pouch.

Naomi tapped the rifle stock over his shoulder. "Remember, no trigger."

"I remember. I'll bring it back good as new. I promise."

Naomi shook her head. "It's just a rifle." She poked him in the chest. "You bring this back, all right?"

"I intend to, though I wish you were coming with us."

"To be honest, I'm glad I'm not," Naomi said. A tear trickled down her cheek. "We don't know what's waiting for you up there or if you'll even reach it or ... or anything. A part of me is glad I don't have to face that ... and yet ... does that make you think less of me?"

"Of course not. I'm proud of you. And I'm scared too. You have nothing to be ashamed of."

Ryu bent down to give her a peck on the cheek, but Naomi backed away and shook her head. She smiled, the tear still fresh on her cheek. She grabbed the back of his head with both hands and pulled their faces together.

After a minute, Kaneda cleared his throat.

Ryu held up a finger and continued kissing.

"The *Needle* is ready," Kaneda said. "Every second counts."

Naomi pulled away from Ryu. A thin line of saliva linked their mouths before it broke.

"Good luck," Naomi said.

"We're wasting time," Kaneda said.

Cat and Kaneda climbed into the *Needle*'s cockpit. Ryu put his helmet on, sealed up, and squeezed in after them. He pulled the hatch shut. His helmet was pinched between the hatch and Kaneda's power pack.

"The fleet is engaging the *Errand*," Matriarch said. "I have guessed the ship's next few moves and am calculating possible teleport vectors. Please stand by."

Ten long minutes passed. Ryu thought he heard someone muttering.

"What's that?" he asked. "Kaneda, are you saying something?"

"I'm sorry. Am I disturbing you? I had our link off."

"No, I was just wondering. Besides Cat grinding her teeth and your power pack buzzing it's the only sound in here."

"If you must know, I was praying."

"Oh. Okay. Well, don't let me distract you."

Another five minutes slipped by.

"So," Ryu said. "Are you just praying for yourself or all of us?"

"Why? Does it matter?"

"I don't know. Just curious, I guess."

"You're not starting to believe, are you?"

"What? No, of course not. Of course not," Ryu said. He thought for a moment. "I'm just thinking it couldn't hurt, you know?"

"Our fleet is disengaging," Matriarch said. "My prediction of the *Errand's* evasion pattern appears accurate. Stand by for transit."

"Ryu?" Kaneda said.

"Yeah?"

"It was for all three of us."

Powerful mechanisms down the center of the *Needle* activated and began oscillating. Sound thundered all around him. Ryu squeezed his eyes tight and tried to ignore the overwhelming sense of wrongness from his inner ear.

The whole vessel shook violently, rattling in its cradle. Flickers of energy snapped across its surface. The thrumming of the hull reached a crescendo and the *Needle* vanished from within Heart.

In an instant the shaking stopped. The sense of wrongness and the dancing patterns of energy disappeared. They were weightless.

A proximity warning sounded. Ryu checked his overlay.

"Oh shit!"

The *Errand* was a vast black sword directly ahead. It grew from a long vertical beam into a black field that filled their forward vision. The *Needle* shot in and smashed against its hull.

If any of them had been normal humans, the impact would have shattered bones and pulverized internal organs. Instead, their diamoplast skeletons, hardened internal organs, and suit support systems absorbed the shock with minimal damage. But it still hurt. Ryu felt his head swim. He instinctively tried to shake it off, but his head was wedged in place.

"I …" Cat said. "I think we're here. Yes, we're lodged in the *Errand's* hull. About a third of its length from the engines."

"Ryu, are you okay?" Kaneda asked.

"Yeah, I'm fine. Just a little shaken."

"Then let's go. We have a job to do."

"Right." Ryu popped the hatch. He grabbed hold of the handle and pulled himself out. The *Needle* was buried halfway in the *Errand's* armor at a slight angle. He was amazed it had survived the crash at all, let alone completely intact. *Just what is this thing made of?*

Ryu swung himself around until his feet made contact with the *Needle*'s hull. He climbed down to the *Errand* and waited for the others.

"Fortress crackers armed," Matriarch said. "I'll watch for any attempts to disarm them."

Jupiter filled the sky, almost from edge to edge. From this angle, the entire planet was illuminated by the sun. Europa sat directly ahead of the *Errand* as a rust-streaked crescent of ice.

Kaneda climbed to the *Errand*'s hull and crawled along on his hands and feet. They had landed on part of the vessel's "blade". The hull curved away to either side, but the gentle angle gave some sense of the ship's massive scale. If the ship were a skytower, it wouldn't fit in Capitol City. The closet landmark was a minor defensive turret ten stories tall.

Cat slid out of the *Needle* and made her way down its fuselage.

"We need to get inside," Ryu said.

"Stand back," Kaneda said. He planted his feet, stood up, and aimed his thermal lance at the hull.

The *Errand*'s main engines fired at full power. Kaneda fell onto his back and slid across the hull. He spun around, crashed chest-first into the Needle and wrapped his arms around the fuselage. Cat held on halfway up the fuselage.

The *Errand*'s engines cut off. Retro-thrusters fired in the opposite direction.

"Caesar's trying to knock us off!" Ryu shouted, staying prone against the hull.

The *Needle* shifted to the side, then slipped partially out before locking in place again. Cat's feet slipped. She dangled off the *Needle* with only a hand for contact.

"It's coming loose!" Ryu shouted. "Get off!"

At the base of the *Needle*, Kaneda grabbed a tear in the *Errand's* hull with his gauntlet and clamped down. He reached for Cat with his free hand.

"Hurry!" he shouted.

Cat put her knees against the *Needle* and crawled towards Kaneda.

The *Errand*'s maneuvering thrusters fired, spinning the ship on its central axis. The *Needle* slipped out of the hull puncture. Cat scampered down the fuselage and leaped towards Kaneda.

Ryu knew it wasn't enough, but he couldn't do anything about it. He was too far away with his limbs spread against the hull for extra fiction. Cat was going to miss Kaneda's hand by a full meter and then float out into space with the *Needle*.

Kaneda must have seen it too. He let go, rose out of hull puncture, and grabbed Cat's hand. Then with only a foot wedged against a small tear in the hull, he pulled both of them back into the puncture.

Ryu crawled towards the puncture. Above them the *Needle* floated away, spinning end over end.

"You okay, Cat?" Ryu asked.

"That was too close!"

"Well, we're here but there go our explosives."

"We'll make do," Kaneda said. "I'm going to burn through the hull. Move as far from the center as you can."

Ryu and Cat backed away to the outer lip of the puncture. Kaneda crawled down to where the tip of the *Needle* had pierced deepest. He retrieved the thermal lance dangling from its cable and aimed it into the puncture. Whatever advanced materials made up the *Errand*'s hull, they still couldn't withstand lance weaponry. Black metal bubbled, liquefied, and floated into space.

Kaneda used his shield to divert the flow of superheated alloys away from his armor, but some slipped past. The surface of his shield and spots on his armor blistered from the heat. He kept boring through the hull, meter after meter. The heat sinks on his power pack began to glow. Gas vented from his suit to carry away excess energy.

"How thick is this?" Ryu asked.

"My tracker reads twenty meters," Kaneda said. "I have another ten to go."

The *Errand* fired its engines in various combinations, trying to throw them off, but all three held on. Kaneda melted through the hull, descending step by step. Molten armor sluiced around his ankles and bubbled into space.

"The tracker shows a large atmospheric buildup inside," Kaneda said.

"What for?" Cat asked.

"To blow us into space," Kaneda said. "Hold on. I'm cutting through the last meter."

Air blasted out through the puncture, picking up droplets of metal and blackened chunks of slag. Cat and Ryu held tight near the top. The blasting column of air didn't slow down. If anything, it grew worse.

Kaneda dropped into the interior. "I'm in. No targets in sight."

Air roared past Ryu's head. "All right! We're coming in!"

He and Cat crawled through the puncture. Fierce wind whipped over their bodies. They maintained strong friction contact all the way down the hole and dropped into the *Errand*'s interior.

Ryu retrieved his rifle and crouched. They were in a long corridor with no well-defined up or down. The "floor" and "ceiling" were made up of massive bundles of power and data cables. Some of the cables were so thick Ryu didn't think he could wrap his arms around them. Wind whistled past the three soldiers and spun up through the puncture.

The engines fired again, throwing Ryu off balance. He grabbed the grating for support.

"The whole ship is a weapon against us," Kaneda said. "Is there any way we can disable the engines remotely?"

"I think so," Cat said. "Controls like that should be hardwired, so if we find a networking hub I may be able to access them. Let's follow this group of data cables towards the ship's bow. There was a turret not far ahead. It probably has its own hub."

"Sounds good," Kaneda said. "I'll take point."

The ship fought them every step of the way. Power distribution panels overloaded and blew out. The ship's atmospheric regulators withdrew air from some sections and overfilled others. Pressure doors slammed shut at random intervals with enough force to scissor a dragon in half. After the first close call, Kaneda melted down every one of them.

"We should have encountered something by now," Ryu said. "Maybe there aren't any?"

"Wishful thinking," Kaneda said. "Caesar would not have left the ship unguarded. He's holding them back for a reason."

"There's the hub," Cat said, tagging a networking panel four doors wide. It protruded from what Ryu considered the ceiling.

"Careful. Let me open it." Kaneda grabbed a corner of the first panel door and ripped it off. He peeled off the other three and tossed them aside. It didn't explode, catch fire, or try to suck them into space. That was a start.

Cat climbed into the panel and placed her hacking glove against a blocky node with hundreds of cables sticking out of its sides.

"I'm in," Cat said. "The network is full of attack viruses, but they're the same ones we encountered in North Pacifica. I'll hit them with Matriarch's vaccine ... Ha! Yeah! Look at them run! Now let's see what I can do."

Pressure doors in the tunnel ahead and in two side passages slammed shut. The *Errand* fired its engines at full power. Ryu lowered his stance. Kaneda side-stepped and steadied himself against the wall.

"I think you've hit a nerve," Matriarch said. "The forces in the Capitol City tunnel are turning around. They're heading for the surface."

"All of them?" Ryu asked.

"Yes," Matriarch said. "They're ascending the tunnel at reckless speeds. I'm sure they'll head for the *Errand* because the ship is flying into a lower orbit."

"Crap," Ryu said.

"Caesar didn't think we could break into his network," Kaneda said.

"What about the forces from North Pacifica and New Edo?" Ryu asked.

"Our defenses are holding for now," Matriarch said. "So far we've kept them away from the civilian shelters, but that won't last long."

"Something's coming," Kaneda said. "I think Caesar's done being subtle."

"Yeah, I can hear them stomping towards us," Ryu said. "Cat?"

"I need more time!"

"Keep working. We'll cover you." Ryu dashed forward and threw grenades onto the three closed pressure doors. They stuck in place and armed for active detonation. He ran back to Kaneda and tossed grenades down the corridor behind them. Power distribution panels and the networking panel provided limited cover, but so did Kaneda's shield.

"Something behind us is cutting the cables to the engines," Cat said. "And he's trying to shut down other hubs remotely. Smart. Very smart. But not fast enough. I've managed to secure a line to the engines. Now I just need to bust in."

"Here they come!" Ryu shouted.

The *Errand* fired its maneuvering thrusters, spinning the ship. Ryu braced himself with a boot against the wall. The two side pressure doors snapped open.

Dot-cams on Ryu's grenades caught dozens of gun-spiders crawling along the walls and ceiling. The robots poked their weapons into the main corridor and spewed automatic fire directly at the networking hub.

Kaneda slammed his shield down between the gun-spiders and the hub. Explosive shells blew miniature craters in his shield.

Ryu went prone behind a panel on the opposite side. He tagged both groups of gun-spiders and triggered his grenades. The tiny cylinders leaped off the two side pressure doors, swiveled to face their targets, and unloaded concentrated blasts of diamond needles. Three gun-spiders went down, with another two heavily damaged. More gun-spiders rushed in, taking their place.

Kaneda fired his thermal lance down one side passage and raked it across to the other. The beam cut through three gun-spiders, an ultrahigh voltage line, and a pressurized coolant line. Electricity arced into severed gun-spider pieces while black fluid spewed onto the walls.

New gun-spiders took the place of fallen units. Return fire forced Kaneda behind his shield. The arcing voltage switched off, and the coolant burst reduced to a slow dribble.

Ryu snapped out of cover, fired four shots from his sniper rifle, and ducked back down. Gunfire sailed over his head and ricocheted off the panel's skin. He loaded a full clip into his rifle and crawled around the panel for a different angle.

The main engines fired. Kaneda staggered back before planting his feet. He managed to keep his shield in front of the networking hub, but left part of his body exposed. The gun-spiders targeted him. Ryu sprang from cover and shot first, gutting two gun-spiders before the rest opened fire. Explosive shells blew chunks off Kaneda's shin and thigh armor. He pulled his legs back behind his shield, fired a lance down the corridor, and hunkered down.

"I'm taking too much damage," Kaneda said. "My shield won't last much longer."

Ryu tossed a grenade down the corridor. A gun-spider peeked around the corner only to be pinned to the floor by needles. The remaining gun-spiders ceased fire and ducked into the side passages.

"Cat!" Ryu said. "We could use some good news!"

"I'm close! I have access to the engine control micromind, but I need more time!"

"Well, hurry it up!"

"I'm picking up fast motion and a lot of noise on the tracker," Kaneda said. "They're moving around us, beneath us. Watch our rear."

"Cat, we can only guard one side of the hub!" Ryu said. "You're out of time!"

"I need more!"

"Damn it!" Ryu said. "Kaneda, you take this side! Keep those gun-spiders at bay! I'll backtrack and hold off whatever is circling around!"

"Understood."

Ryu stood up and ran down the corridor away from Kaneda and the gun-spiders. He checked the data coming in from all three of their trackers. His smartsuit's micromind collated the data, building a picture of anticipated enemy locations. Having access to Kaneda's tracker and its active detection protocols gave him a better picture than if the dragons were working alone, but it was still sketchy.

A group of enemies moved through a parallel passage underneath them. Ryu headed for the first junction they could use to cut into his corridor. He crouched out of sight and checked around the edge with a dot-cam tubule. The tunnel looked empty for now.

Back at Kaneda's position, the gun-spiders renewed their attack. Ryu darted into the side tunnel so that a stray bullet wouldn't hit him.

And then he saw it. At first, the shape ahead of him looked like a haze of hot air. But it soon resolved into the outline of a massive charging robot.

"Tank-spider!" Ryu shouted.

"I can't help you!" Kaneda said. "The gun-spiders have me pinned!"

"Cat!"

"I'm not there yet!"

"Shit!"

Ryu loaded a turbo-devastator into his rifle.

The tank-spider fired its twin heavy railguns. Ryu dodged into the main corridor before he could shoot. The explosive shells blew craters in the wall behind him.

"Cat!" Ryu shouted. "Out of the panel now!"

"I'm almost—"

"Fucking now!"

The tank-spider ran into the main corridor and swung its guns around to target the networking hub. Cat climbed out of the panel and jumped clear. The tank-spider fired, shredding the panel. Explosive shells blew out cable bundles and chunks of micromind hardware. Shrapnel slammed into Cat's back and threw her into the wall. She bounced off and floated into the open, but her illusion held. Some of her biometrics flashed yellow from blunt trauma along her back, but she managed to grab her rifle.

Ryu fired the turbo-devastator into the tank-spider from less than three meters away. The shot rang in his skull, struck the robot's belly, and blasted straight through. Thick smoke billowed out of the machine.

The tank-spider braced itself with an arm against the wall and kept firing, now tracking its aim towards Kaneda. Its illusion crashed, but other than that it seemed unaffected by the attack. One of its shots hit Kaneda in the back, throwing him forward and cracking his armor. Kaneda swung his shield around to protect his rear, even as the gun-spiders continued rushing him. He and Cat fired on the gun-spiders. Grenade explosions and lance blasts sent pieces of robots flying through the corridor.

Ryu loaded his second turbo-devastator.

The tank-spider opened a claw and reached for him. Ryu ducked underneath the tank-spider and fired up. This shot dislodged its head and guns from the main body and smashed the tank-spider against the ceiling.

Ryu armed a grenade and tossed it through the hole in its abdomen. The grenade exploded into an armor-melting tongue of flame.

The tank-spider's limbs shuddered then locked. The main body and its severed head floated inertly in the corridor.

Ryu backed away from the robot. An errant shot from a gun-spider whizzed by his shoulder. He crouched, spun, loaded a clip, and fired down the corridor. With all three of them combining their attacks, the gun-spiders pulled back into the tunnels. Pressure doors further away from the junction slammed shut once the last gun-spider had retreated. Hot chunks of metal legs, pieces of their flattened bodies, and twisted wreckage from their weapons clogged a corridor slick with spilt coolant.

"You two okay?" Ryu asked.

The tank-spider's limbs shuddered.

"Behind you!" Kaneda shouted.

The headless tank-spider lunged at Ryu. He kicked off the corridor wall a moment before its claw scraped across.

Kaneda hit the arm with a lance at its first joint, severing it completely. He tracked his fire across the tank-spider, keeping the beam on. One by one, the beam ate through its limbs. Severed legs and droplets of molten armor floated away. Even if the tank-spider still had functioning internal systems, it had no way to move.

"Fucking tank-spiders," Ryu breathed. A robotic leg floated to him. He shoved it away.

"At least the engines haven't engaged in a while," Kaneda said.

"Your doing, Cat?" Ryu asked.

"Yeah, and that's not all I stopped," Cat said. "When I tried to shut the engines down, I stumbled upon the ship's micromind update protocols. I was able to send my own update. That's what took so long. Right now, half the systems on this ship are dead."

"Nice," Ryu said.

"Unfortunately, I couldn't send updates for the weapons. I ran out of time."

"So we still can't call in the fleet for help," Ryu said. "Still, it's better than nothing."

"What if Caesar overwrites your changes?" Kaneda asked.

"That's going to be difficult." Cat said. "Because the update I sent deleted all their communication software. Caesar can't talk to them, period. He's going to have to get his robots to each micromind and individually load new software."

"Good," Kaneda said. "That gives us some time."

"It may not be much," Ryu said. "All he has to do is get a robot to the engines."

"Then we make this lull count," Kaneda said.

"I also have the ship's schematics." Cat distributed the layout and marked a location near the ship's center. "That's the TangleNet link. It's about half a kilometer ahead of our position."

Ryu pulled up the schematic. "Nice! Looks like we can follow this corridor most of the way to the link. Let's go."

"Wait a second," Kaneda said.

"What is it?"

"Look at the layout," Kaneda said. "We may have an alternative to a frontal assault. Your navy hit the *Errand* with two kinetic torpedoes. One of them landed near the ship's center."

"So?" Ryu asked.

"It's an alternate route to the TangleNet link. The torpedo sank so deep, there's practically no external armor left. You don't need my thermal lance to get back in. Even your grenades could punch through."

"Oh, I see," Cat said. "That way we can skip the bulk of whatever Caesar has in store for us."

"Precisely," Kaneda said. "But there's one problem, namely my armor. If I take that route, Caesar will know."

Ryu could see where this was going. He didn't like it, but he had to admit the plan had merit.

"You want to split up," Ryu said. "You're going to act as a decoy."

"We don't know what forces Caesar has left," Kaneda said. "This way, you have a good chance of avoiding danger."

"I don't know ..."

"I am not debating this, Ryu. You can either follow me straight in or go around." Kaneda aimed his thermal lance at the next pressure door and melted it down. He marched through the corridor.

"Well?" Cat asked. "Which one is it?"

Ryu watched his brother walk away to what was very likely his death. He knew he should be focusing on the mission, but all he could think about was he had his brother back. After all these years, Kaneda was back and now he was going to lose him again, this time for good.

"Ryu?" Cat asked.

"I know," he said. "We're going around. Come on."

He and Cat turned and sprinted down the corridor, heading to where the *Needle* had landed. With the ship's engines disabled and the pressure doors already burned open, it didn't take the two dragons long to reach the puncture in the ship's armor. They only stopped once to let a lone gun-spider pass.

At the puncture, they climbed up through the smooth-walled hole. With Caesar no longer in control, the atmosphere had bled out of the section, leaving the interior almost a vacuum.

Ryu crawled onto the *Errand*'s outer hull, keeping at least three points of contact at all times. The engines were off now, but they could reactivate without warning. The two dragons "climbed" up the hull swiftly but carefully, diverting only to climb around the massive gun turrets in their path. When they cleared the third turret, they could see the torpedo's impact point which resembled a narrow funnel in the armor.

"Kaneda, what's your status?" Ryu asked.

"Meeting heavy resistance," Kaneda said. "The gun-spiders are putting up a tough fight."

"Ryu," Matriarch said. "Caesar's forces have started launching from Europa. The first transport will rendezvous with the *Errand* in eighteen minutes."

"Understood."

"Movement ahead," Cat said.

"What?" Ryu stopped climbing. He took out his rifle.

Halfway between the two dragons and the torpedo impact, a section of armor sank away.

"What's that?" Ryu said. He checked the layout. "A shuttle elevator?"

"Something's coming up."

"I don't like this. Back up. Get behind that last turret."

Cat hurried behind the turret. Ryu rose to a crouch and joined her. He put his back to the turret and extruded a dot-cam tubule around the edge.

The elevator ascended to the surface with a Federacy shuttle latched in place, surrounded by shapes clad in smartskin illusions.

"Gun-spiders?" Cat asked.

"I don't think so," Ryu said.

The shapes stepped off the elevator. With data from their movements, his tracker counted about ten crusader thralls and two tank-spiders.

"Shit," Ryu breathed.

"There's no way we can take that many," Cat said.

"I know." Ryu said. "Kaneda, we have a problem."

* * *

Kaneda listened to Ryu's suggestion. He blasted apart another pressure door and marched through the wreckage. A gun-spider peeked around the corner and sprayed him with explosive rounds. The shots impacted his shield, deepening the crack running down the center. The gun-spider skittered away before he could return fire.

"Understood," Kaneda said grimly. "I'll do what I can."

"We don't have much time," Ryu said. "Reinforcements are sixteen minutes away."

"Then let's finish this," Kaneda said. The artificial musculature in his left leg threw several warnings over his vision. He switched off the damaged strands and increased power to the functional ones. A few steps later, the pressure warning in his right arm showed up again. The auto-sealant had run dry. Kaneda muted the warning and continued down the utility corridor.

Halfway to the next bend, he received a message from Admiral Piller's SolarNet account. He was about to block the contact, but decided not to. Matching wits with a quantum mind was never smart, but they were running out of options.

If I can give Ryu the extra time he needs ...

Kaneda opened the link. "What do you want?"

"My, my. What is taking you so long?" the Caesar said through the Piller-thrall.

"You still insist on speaking through your slave," Kaneda said.

"My slave?" Caesar asked. "Is that what you think Piller is? Slave is too generous a term. He is a tool, just like you are. In fact, he quite enjoys his role! And so will you, when I'm done."

Kaneda blasted through another door, kicked the glowing edges aside, and ducked through.

"Don't worry," Caesar said. "I'm not going to kill you. I'm going to take you alive and reshape your mind. You will be as loyal to me as Piller. And do not fret. You will enjoy your new role. I am not one to cast aside such a valuable pawn."

"You haven't defeated me yet," Kaneda said.

"Oh, please. Let's be honest here. You can't win. The three of you will not stop this ship, and my reinforcements grow closer by the second."

"You sound so confident," Kaneda said. He turned a corner and came under fire from two gun-spiders. Automatic weapons pounded his shield. He fired the thermal lance into one gun-spider and raked the beam across the other. They floated off the floor in several pieces.

In his overlay, the shield flashed red. The crack had made it all the way to the bottom, leaving his forearm as the only thing holding it together.

"I admit you put up a good fight. Matriarch's ability to place the *Needle* so close surprised me. Otherwise I would have retained a stronger force here. But I am not as weak as you might think, and you are all alone right now."

"You think so?" Kaneda asked. "I could have a whole team of dragons following me in and you'd never know it."

"Please, don't insult us both. You were never good at bluffing. The two dragons are moving across the ship's exterior and you are pressing forward as their decoy."

Kaneda turned down the last corridor. The TangleNet link and its nav beacon blinked directly ahead, stored within five concentric layers of spherical armor shells. The corridor widened to a small room in front of the first security door. Several stacks of unlabeled crates were lashed to the floor.

Kaneda walked into the room and stopped. His tracker detected something approaching from behind, though it couldn't identify what. He spun around and aimed his weapon down the corridor.

"I will admit it's been fun," Caesar said. "You have been an amusing pawn. But now our game comes to an end. Goodbye, Kaneda. I'll see you on the operating table."

Kaneda backed up to the security door. Intangible shapes moved into the corridor he'd passed through, dashing from cover to cover. His tracker pieced the clues together, generating four large humanoid outlines. It estimated a few more further away.

Kaneda fired down the corridor. The beam missed the closest crusader thrall. Two of them sprayed the room with vari-shells. An incinerator splashed against his shield, setting it on fire. Two depleted-uranium slugs punched through and cracked his chest armor.

Kaneda dashed behind a stack of crates and fired around it. He struck the lead crusader thrall in the neck. The beam vaporized its head, most of the torso, and flung its severed arms to either side. Its hips and legs went down, mindlessly kicking.

More incoming vari-shells tore into the crates Kaneda ducked behind. Glittering electronics and packing foam flew into the air. Kaneda kept moving, charging across the room to a second crate pile. He fired again, cutting into a power distribution panel the next thrall had used for cover. Sparks poured out of the panel before its circuit breakers kicked in. The beam clipped the thrall in the shoulder, crippling its smartskin illusion.

The fully visible thrall dove to the other side of the corridor and fired. Vari-shells blew the crates off the floor and sent them spinning around the room. Explosive shells and heavy kinetic sabots tore into his shield. A spider web of cracks expanded from the center. Chunks of it broke away with each impact.

Kaneda cut the thrall in half before it reached cover. Its legs tumbled away, but the thrall's upper half grabbed hold of the grating on the floor and swung its Gatling gun around. It and two other thralls kept firing.

Kaneda dodged out of their line of sight. He put his back against the wall next to the corridor's entrance. Vari-shells blasted pieces off the corner, but a thick support beam running through the wall proved too tough to penetrate.

The legless crusader thrall maintained a steady stream of fire while five or six fully functional thralls moved forward. The constant suppressing fire kept Kaneda pinned out of sight. With the crates demolished and choking the room with debris, he had nowhere else to hide.

Armor subsystem faults scrolled down Kaneda's vision. He ignored them and readied his grenades. He was about to try ricocheting them down the corridor when the barrage stopped.

Behind him, the security door slid open. A crusader thrall stepped out and aimed a thermal lance at his back.

Kaneda had only a split second to dodge. He dove to the side, keeping clear of the corridor, and brought his own lance around.

The thrall fired at close range. Its beam vaporized a path through the crate wreckage and glanced off Kaneda's shoulder. His cracked armor disintegrated down to the final layer. Inside, his skin crisped and blackened.

Kaneda sucked in a breath through clenched teeth and returned fire, but the crusader thrall rushed him and the beam went wide. The thrall collided into his shield and smashed him against the wall. He tried to bring his thermal lance around, but the thrall held his wrist tight.

The high speed contact caused the thrall's illusion to disengage. Viter stared at him with a blank expression and only one eye. His lips parted, but no sound came out.

The Viter-thrall squeezed its gauntlet, crumpling Kaneda's wrist armor. It twisted its grip and pulled. The flesh around Kaneda's wrist stretched and tore.

"Damn you," Kaneda breathed.

With a final twist, the Viter-thrall ripped his hand off, which still held his thermal lance. Painkillers automatically injected into his bloodstream, and his wound clotted at an accelerated pace. Only a trickle of blood floated away from the limb before the flow cut off.

"Damn you, Caesar!" Kaneda's scream carried all his pain and fury. He jettisoned his shield, which pushed the Viter-thrall away, then slammed a kick into the thrall's stomach.

The Viter-thrall staggered back. Kaneda rushed forward and tackled him. They crashed against the floor and slid across. Kaneda pressed a knee against the thrall's chest, grabbed one of its arms and ripped it off. He stuck his wrist launcher in the thrall's face and fired. The grenade pulped Viter's head. Kaneda shoved his arm down what was left of the thrall's throat and fired two more times.

The thrall's armor bulged and went slack. Kaneda pulled it off the ground and threw it away. Gore and smoke flowed out of cracks in the thrall's armor. He reached for a weapon, any weapon, but stopped when he realized the other crusader thralls were in the room.

Five intact crusader thralls and half of the sixth aimed their Gatling guns at him. The barrels spun at full speed, ready to fire at a moment's notice.

"That was very amusing!" Caesar said. "You are such a spirited fighter. To the bitter end, is it? But now it is time for you to serve me without question, as you always should have."

One of the thralls stepped forward. It pushed Viter's distended armor aside and reached for him.

Kaneda checked Ryu and Cat's position on his overlay.

"I will never serve you," he said. "Now, Ryu!"

A turbo-devastator struck the crusader thrall closest to the corridor and blew it apart. Three grenades pounded the second thrall, blowing off an arm, its head, and punching a hole in its chest.

Ryu loaded his fourth and last turbo-devastator. Cat emptied a full clip of shatterbacks into the cluster of thralls.

Kaneda smashed his shoulder against the thrall closest to him. They went down, swinging and grabbing. Kaneda wedged himself between the thrall and its Gatling gun. He established a contact link with the weapon and sent his command override. The thrall tried to fire the gun but couldn't.

Kaneda swung it around to face the other thralls and cut loose. Vari-shells exploded amongst the thralls. High explosives, mini-needlers, kinetic sabots, and depleted-uranium slugs each added their own unique brand of destruction. The whole room blazed from incinerator gel.

Ryu fired his last turbo-devastator and blasted another thrall completely apart. Kaneda wrestled with the thrall on his back. He ripped its arm free, shoved it away and hosed it down with its own Gatling gun. Only a gutted, flaming corpse was left when he let off the trigger.

Kaneda looked around. The last thrall was dead.

"What is this?" Caesar shouted. "What's going on? They're outside the hull! They're not in the ship! How can they be in the ship?"

"You guessed wrong," Kaneda said. He walked over to Viter's armor.

"No! That's impossible! All the indicators were correct! They weren't with you! I can see signs of them on the hull!"

"Of course you can," Kaneda said. He disengaged the Viter-thrall's thermal lance from its cables and connected the weapon to his power pack.

"They would have defended you if they were inside!"

"That's exactly right," Kaneda said. He burned through the first security door and kicked the molten edges aside. A short walkway spanned the gap to the next concentric armor sphere and its security door.

"Hurry," Ryu said. "We don't have much time before those tank-spiders get back inside."

"No!" Caesar said. "Stop! Don't go in there!"

"Are you afraid, Caesar?" Kaneda asked. He burned a hole in the next door and forced his way through. His armor blistered when he touched the hot metal.

"This is impossible!" Caesar said.

"Tell me, are you afraid?" Kaneda blasted through the third door and fourth door. "I will find you, Caesar! I will find you, and I will kill you!"

He burned his way through the fifth and final door. Inside the innermost sphere, Kaneda found a three-story tall monolith covered with small yellow cylinders. Thick data cables ran out of the monolith and disappeared through the sphere's bottom. The Piller-thrall stood next to the monolith wearing a Federacy pressure suit. It aimed a pistol at Kaneda.

"You—" the Piller-thrall began to say.

Kaneda shot him in the stomach with the thermal lance at maximum yield. The beam incinerated the thrall's chest. Its limbs and head shot off and splattered against the walls.

Ryu hurried in. "Cat, get in here. This is definitely a TangleNet hub. There must be thousands of connections here."

"On it! I just finished trapping the corridor," Cat said. She backed into the room, stuck one last grenade into the cooling security door and turned around. "Wow. That's a lot of links."

"Can you disable it?" Ryu asked.

"I'll try," Cat said. "Watch my back."

Ryu and Kaneda took positions at either side of the entrance.

"Check where all those data cables come into the hub," Ryu said.

"Right. I see it," Cat said. She knelt down and splayed her hacking glove over the cable ports. "Now, let's see what we can do with this."

"You okay, Kaneda?" Ryu asked.

"I'll be fine until the painkillers wear off," Kaneda said. New data began trickling onto his overlay. First, clusters of status information populated the ship's layout. Then indicators lit up for every thrall and robot on the ship.

"That's all that's left?" Ryu asked. "Just the tank-spiders and thralls outside the hull and a few gun-spiders inside?"

"I think so," Cat said.

"They're coming down the shuttle elevator," Kaneda said.

"We'll see about that," Cat said. "And ... I have control of the elevator. Ha! Back up you go. Those robots can stay on the ship's hull for now."

"Nice," Ryu said.

"Ship weapons are disabled ... and let's see ... Ah. There are the link protocols. Well, it definitely looks like he's controlling all the robots from here. There. I've disabled the links."

"What about those robots flying up from the surface?" Ryu asked. "Even without new orders they could pose a problem."

"Not for much longer," Cat said. She expanded the channel. "Hey, any navy ships nearby? This is black dragon. We could use a hand here."

"Black dragon four, this is frigate *Io's Fury*. We are following the *Errand* at extreme weapons range and are ready to assist."

"I'm sending a list of high priority targets ascending towards the *Errand*," Cat said. "Take them out before they reach the ship. The *Errand*'s weapons are disabled and we have gained partial control."

"Targets confirmed, black dragon four. We are accelerating for an attack run now."

"Also, I want you to blast a few robots off the ship's hull before they cause trouble. Here are their locations. But don't punch through the hull! We're still inside."

"Targets confirmed, Black Dragon Four. We'll take care of them."

"Matriarch, any changes where you are?" Ryu asked.

"Some," Matriarch said. "The robots and thralls are not making good tactical decisions, but they can still fight. We have a hard battle ahead of us, but for now the advantage is ours."

Cat stood up. "Well, I think that's all I can do from here."

"We should eliminate the remaining gun-spiders and restore control to the engines," Kaneda said.

"Sounds like a plan," Ryu said. "You ready?"

"Just give me a moment," Kaneda said. He looked down at his missing hand, almost expecting it to still be there. "We cut that one pretty close, don't you think?"

"Well, yeah, but that was the point," Ryu said. "Because that's not how we operate. We threw off his guessing game."

"And gave you the opening you needed," Kaneda said.

"Still," Cat said. "I can't believe you waited as long as you did before cutting us loose."

"It didn't really matter if I lived or died," Kaneda said. "Keeping you alive and getting you here was what mattered. But, I'm glad I didn't have to die. You did well, Cat."

"Thanks ... umm ..."

"What is it?"

"Not to be picking or anything ..."

"Yes?"

"Only my friends call me Cat."

"I see," Kaneda said. "And what should a brother call you?"

"Uh ...did ... did I hear that right?"

Kaneda couldn't hold back his grin. "Come on. We still have work to do."

* * *

Within Heart, Kaneda waited outside Matriarch's audience chamber with a full platoon of crusaders hand-picked for this honor. Together they would observe his decision and the quantum mind's fate. They stood in a rigid line on one side of the hall, their armor scarred from days of battle, helmets at their side.

Kaneda glanced across the hall. Dragons, militia commanders, and naval officers kept their distance from the crusaders. They knew what was to come, and many of them didn't like it, but Matriarch had given and had kept her word. That by itself would count in her favor.

A small crew of technicians in orange jumpers worked on dismantling the small passage to Matriarch's audience chamber, disabling its security systems to allow weapons inside. The walls around the passage had been removed, revealing layers of coiled machinery. Thick ultrahigh voltage cables supplied it with power.

"How's the hand?" Ryu asked. He was the only dragon on the "crusader" side of the hall.

Kaneda examined his new hand and flexed the fingers one at a time. It looked comically small coming out of the thick armored wrist. Ryu and Cat had performed some minor repairs to his armor, but it was essentially in the same condition now as when the *Io's Fury* picked them up.

"The hand is perfect," Kaneda said. "Thank you."

"You can thank Cat when you see her next."

"Really?"

"She called in the dragon farm doctors to give you a new one."

"Hmm, I hadn't expected that," Kaneda said. He watched the technicians pull out another power field generator and disarm it. "Any news I should know about?"

"The navy picked up the *Needle*," Ryu said. "And we think we finally cleared the last robots from the under city ports."

"That's good."

"We still have a few isolated pockets in the city, but they're mostly robots locked in evasion patterns."

"What about the outlying cities?"

"North and South Pacifica, New Edo, Third Kyoto, and Port Cold are all complete losses," Ryu said. "We'll have to demolish them at range. Several others have been infiltrated, but the militia has the robots and thralls contained. They simply aren't as dangerous when Caesar can't control them."

"And the death toll?"

"It's getting close to half a million last I checked."

"I see."

"So." Ryu looked him straight in the eye. "Are you still going through with this?"

"Of course."

"After all you've seen? After all we've been through?"

"I have to."

"Do you hate her that much?"

"I don't know anymore." Kaneda looked away. "So much of what I believed has turned out to be wrong."

"Then why go through with it?"

"Because I need to speak to the ... to Matriarch," Kaneda said. The name sounded strange coming from his lips. How long had it been since he'd called her that?

"Don't you know what you'll decide?" Ryu asked.

"No," Kaneda said, shaking his head. "Despite her good intentions, her plan sounds like more of the same, just farther away from Earth."

"And what's wrong with that?"

"Because it's slavery."

"Oh, come on!"

"Look at the facts, Ryu. You don't create anything yourselves. This technology, these advantages of yours did not come from human hands."

"Yes they did, and her name is Matriarch."

"That's not the same."

"We wouldn't have won without her."

"I know. But that doesn't change the fact you as a people don't have control. A machine does."

Three-Part walked over. "The technicians are done, sir. It's time."

"Very well. Is everyone connected?"

"Yes, sir. You and the quantum mind will be heard by everyone on Europa. We are also transmitting it live over SolarNet for anyone who wishes to watch."

"Thank you, Three-Part," Kaneda said. He shouldered his thermal lance.

"Kaneda?" Ryu asked.

"Yes?"

"Just keep an open mind and hear her out, okay?"

"You have my word."

Kaneda walked with Three-Part to the entrance. The passage to Matriarch's audience chamber lay open, its defenses scattered across the tiled floor. A few technicians knelt next to the disabled machinery, watching him.

"Three-Part," Kaneda said. He stopped in front of the passage.

"Sir."

"What do you make of our fellow crusaders?"

"They're confused, sir. They're relieved by our victory against Caesar, but they don't know what to make of Matriarch. I think most of them will go with whatever decision you make."

"Really?"

"Yes, sir. You have led us this far, and even though we have been manipulated, you were right about what matters. Quantum minds are a threat to humans everywhere. But is this one a threat? I can't answer that, and respectfully, I leave that for you to decide. I will support your call either way."

"Even after I let Caesar use us as pawns?"

"You cannot blame yourself for missing what everyone couldn't see."

"I don't know if most people would agree with that. That's very charitable of you, but thank you regardless. I'm glad to have your support. Recruiting you was the best decision I've made in a long time."

Three-Part gave him a curt nod. "The crusaders need leadership. They need someone to take what has happened and guide them through to the other side. What is our purpose? Who are our enemies? I don't think anyone but you can do this."

"Then I will endeavor not to disappoint."

Kaneda walked into the audience chamber. Dry heat washed over his face. At the far wall, air shimmered around Matriarch's overworked quantum core. He couldn't help thinking how differently this confrontation had played out. A few weeks ago, if someone had told him he would walk into the quantum mind's chamber and hold his fire, he would have called the person a fool. And yet here he was doing just that.

Kaneda stopped in front of Matriarch's hologram. In the back of his mind, he felt the pressure of an entire world watching his actions and listening to his words.

"Hello, Kaneda," she said with a bow. Her kimono showed the blackened wreckage of an ancient wooden city from feudal Japan, now damp from newly fallen rain. Slits of sunlight pierced through a dark canopy. Amongst the charred ruins, vivid green stalks tipped with closed flower buds grew at an accelerated rate.

The destruction of the past and the promise of the future, Kaneda thought. *We shall see.*

"Matriarch," he said.

"Welcome home," Matriarch said with a sad smile.

"Let us discuss the future. Your navy has recovered the star drive." Kaneda took the thermal lance off his shoulder and rested the tip of its barrel on the floor. "Why should I let you have it?"

"You know I seek to safeguard the people of Europa from Caesar," Matriarch said. "I will take Capitol City and as many willing colonists as it can hold. Together we will find a new world to inhabit far from Caesar's reach."

"That much we all understand," Kaneda said. "I admit I like the idea of humanity expanding beyond the solar system. The farther we expand as a race, the more resilient we become. It makes it easier for at least some of us to weather the chaos of an unpredictable future. But why should I let you go with them?"

"No matter what kind of world we find, the journey and the settling will be difficult. The colonists will need a strong leader."

"And that leader should be a quantum mind?" Kaneda asked. "I think not."

"I have always held my people's interests at heart," Matriarch said. "Europa has prospered under my rule."

"You enslave them with trinkets. They didn't earn the technology and weapons you give them. Do any of 'your people' know how they work? Can they duplicate them? No, they rely on you and that gives you power over them."

"You could say the same for anyone who harbors secrets."

"But that is precisely the point. You aren't like anyone else. You aren't human anymore."

Matriarch sighed and shook her head. The sky on her kimono closed up, shrouding the burnt city in darkness.

"I've often wondered about that," she said.

"What do you mean?"

A plain wooden chair materialized next to Matriarch. She sat down and folded her hands in her lap.

"Kaneda, I know this may surprise you, but I have often struggled with this same problem. For all the clarity what I am brings, I cannot solve it, and even now I wonder how human I really am. Unlike ..." Her kimono flashed red. "Our enemy ... who abandoned his humanity willingly, I cling to whatever shreds remain."

Matriarch wiped the sweat from her brow.

"You don't seem very human to me," Kaneda said.

"Is it not obvious? I have had children after a fashion. I have a husband, though I understand I cannot fulfill all his needs in my current state. I have done very human things that are unnecessary for a machine, but the question lingers. Did Sakura Kusanagi die the day Matriarch was created? Did her soul go to whatever afterlife awaits us? Or is she still here within me?"

"Hmm ..."

Matriarch glanced over her shoulder at the quantum core. "Look at it. Such a cold thing of science. Is it an empty husk? Or does my soul reside within it? I don't know, and not knowing weighs heavily on my mind."

"There is no way you could know."

Matriarch shook her head. "Ah, but there is one way to know with absolute certainty. This is a secret I have kept from everyone until today. Not even your father knows."

"You claim to understand what only God may know?"

"Nothing so dramatic," Matriarch said. "In order to find the answer to such a haunting question … I must die."

Kaneda couldn't believe what he'd just heard. He was speechless.

"There is no other way I can answer the question," Matriarch said. "At some point my life must end. Only through death will I know if I am more than machinery. Only through death will I find out if God is waiting to judge my deeds and, perhaps, accept my soul into heaven."

"You … want to die?"

"Not today, if it can be helped," Matriarch said. "And 'want' is perhaps too strong a word. But yes, I have come to accept it as necessary. I have thought about when would be a proper time to allow this mechanical shell to shut down. Perhaps once our new world is settled. I have even considered having children again. Maybe another three to raise in this new world, whatever it may be. After that, I think it would be time. Besides, I couldn't bear life without your father for long."

"If what you say is true …"

"You know it is. We are not that different, you and I," Matriarch said. "The same great mystery weighs in both our minds. We ask ourselves the same question. How will our actions be judged by God? We've both made mistakes, some small, some horribly large, but we've both tried to do the right thing. We both hunger to know if what we did was right."

"Yes, I've often wondered."

Matriarch nodded. "Well, Kaneda. You have heard my arguments. I have done my best to make my intentions clear. Is there anything you wish to ask me?"

"No."

"I see. Then what is your decision?"

Kaneda picked up the thermal lance and held it lengthwise in his hands. He looked down at it, the decision teetering in his mind. So much of who he was wanted to melt the quantum core to slag, but he held his fire. It came down to one simple thing in his mind, and it was the hardest thing any leader must do.

He had to admit he was wrong. Matriarch wasn't the monster he'd envisioned all these years. She wasn't perfect, not even close, but she didn't have to be. She was a flawed individual with good intentions that sometimes drove her to do bad things. She was ... human.

With a sigh, Kaneda yanked the power cables out and dropped the weapon on the floor.

"Our battle is over," he said.

Matriarch bowed her head. "Thank you, my son."

Without another word, Kaneda turned and walked out of the audience chamber.

* * *

The naked sphere of Capitol City floated in orbit, brought there by the first successful test of the star drive on such a scale. Another two months had passed preparing the capitol for its interstellar voyage, and now they were ready. Kaneda watched from the *Errand of Mercy*. Over a dozen people stood in its new bridge, bathed in bluish light from screens and holographic plots.

"I still can't believe she convinced over seven million people to make the trip," Ryu said.

"Maybe people are just used to doing what she says," Cat said.

"You're probably right," Kaneda said.

"You still have a problem with that?" Cat asked.

"A little," Kaneda said. "Not as much as I used too."

"It's not that," Ryu said. "They trust her. They believe in her vision of a future beyond the solar system."

"Or they don't want to have their heads drilled in by Caesar's robots," Kaneda said.

Ryu shrugged his shoulders. "Yeah, that too."

"There's not going to be much of a Europa after this," Cat said.

"Yeah, I know," Ryu said. "What is it? Only a million people staying?"

"Just about," Cat said. "Add in another half million spread over the Jupiter system."

"But most who remain are ready to fight Caesar," Kaneda said. "We have here the nucleus of an army that will surpass both the crusaders and the dragons. And we have the infrastructure to support such a force."

"Plus our new flagship," Ryu said. He patted a holographic plot. The image of Capitol City fizzled for a moment.

"Signal from Matriarch," the comm officer said. "Star drive activation is a go. Final countdown commencing. Ten. Nine. Eight."

"Here we go," Ryu whispered.

Cat bit into her thumb.

"Three. Two. One. Activate."

A layer of ethereal light formed around the capitol. It moved across the city's spherical surface, forming thick bands and accelerating. The bands whipped around the city, faster and faster until they became a flickering blur. One moment, the city shone like a small sun and the next it vanished.

The bridge was silent except for the hum of ventilation and the low buzz of the holographic plots. Ryu held his breath. Cat chewed on her thumbnail.

"I have a signal from Capitol City!" the comm officer said, grinning ear to ear. "It's Matriarch!"

The bridge exploded with cheering and clapping. Some people embraced each other, and a few even kissed.

"Yes!" Cat whispered.

"Put it on the speakers!" Ryu said.

"Yes, sir! Matriarch, go ahead! You're on speaker!"

"Yes, I can hear that," Matriarch said. "We're still getting our bearings, but it looks like we're over a light-month from the solar system as planned. We're going to run some tests, but the star drive appears to have performed perfectly. I see no reason why our next transit can't be to Alpha Centauri."

"That's great to hear!" Ryu said over the noise. Naomi broke out a squeeze bulb full of sake, took a long sip, and passed it to him. He drank through the straw and handed it to Cat. Three other bulbs were making circuits around the bridge.

When one of the bulbs came to Kaneda, he passed it along without drinking and waited for the excitement to move off the bridge. Instead of joining the others, he selected a holographic plot and pulled up the scout report from the asteroid belt.

Twenty minutes later, Cat and Ryu floated over to him. They were the last three still in the bridge.

"You okay?" Cat asked.

"I'm fine," Kaneda said, staring intently at images from a secret base in the asteroid belt.

"They're throwing a party," Cat said. "You should join us."

"Thanks, but I'll pass. I have to meet the Federacy's new ambassador in a few hours."

"Took them long enough to find the right asteroid," Ryu said, pointing at the plot. "Are you going to mention the base to the ambassador?"

"I don't know. It's been gutted. Here, you can see signs of heavy equipment being relocated, but that could be anything. The only things we found were the link modules tied to the *Errand*'s TangleNet hub."

"Well, we expected that," Ryu said.

"Yeah," Cat said. "But we can still use it to help find the next relay."

"Precisely," Kaneda said. "This is just the first step. Eventually, we will track Caesar down."

"Do you really believe that?" Ryu asked.

"I have to," Kaneda said. "Because in this war it's him or us. Whoever survives shapes the future of humanity in the solar system, and I would very much like it to be us."

"So are you going to tell the ambassador?" Ryu asked.

"No, I don't think so. I don't want her fixating on evidence that's easy to doubt. I'll stick with the inspection of our cities and the eye witness testimonies. Besides, I suspect anything we show her will find its way back to Caesar."

"Then why are we bothering at all?" Cat asked. "Have you seen the lies Earth is spewing over the SolarNet?"

Ryu shook his head. "Let's see here, according to them the robot attacks on our cities were faked, the crusaders were always working for us, and the *Errand of Mercy* was our ship from the start."

"It's not a question of us convincing the Federacy government," Kaneda said. "We can't do that. Caesar holds too much sway over them. But the distinction is he lacks total control. He steers some elements, but not all. What we need to generate is doubt. That will give us time to build our army and figure out our next move."

"Well, at least they sent an ambassador this time instead of a fleet," Cat said. "Oh, by the way, I'm almost finished with our new propaganda virus. I infected Seven's personal pad with it as a test."

"Oh, good grief," Ryu said. "Is that why he's been so cross?"

"Maybe," Cat said, grinning. "Now every time he goes on the SolarNet his pad plays the *Space Brain* theme. The five minute extended version, of course."

"Well, of course," Ryu said. He rolled his eyes.

"Last I saw, he and Three-Part still had no clue how to get rid of it."

"Can't they just scrub the pad?" Kaneda asked.

"They tried," Cat said. "The virus will attack any data scrubber it detects and hide inside. It can then use the scrubber as a new infection vector. They haven't figured that part out. Even if they do, it's hard to stop."

"Impressive," Kaneda said.

"Thanks," Cat said. "I still have to test its other infection vectors and I'll need a good message to build into it, but it should help us spread our side of the story. I'm also working on a variant that will draw graffiti on Federacy SolarNet sites when they deny Caesar exists."

"Just so long as it doesn't get childish," Ryu said.

"Hey," Cat said. "That had better not be a crack about my age."

"I wouldn't worry," Kaneda said. "I'm sure Cat will continue to show good judgment in her work."

"You see?" Cat poked Ryu in the chest. "Even Kaneda doesn't think I'm a kid. You could learn a thing or two from him."

Ryu put his hands up in surrender. "All right. All right. You're not a kid. Seriously, I never said you were one."

"So, are you coming to the party?" Cat asked. "You said you had a few hours."

"I'm fine," Kaneda said.

"Come on. It'll be fun."

"Maybe in a little bit," Kaneda said. "There are still some things I want to review."

"Fine," Cat said. "Ryu?"

"Yeah, I'm coming."

"Don't take too long, okay?" Cat said.

"I'll try," Kaneda said.

Cat and Ryu floated out of the bridge.

Kaneda cleared the image of the asteroid base and took a moment to think.

Caesar was paranoid. If it had a relay in the asteroid belt, then its true location wouldn't be anywhere near it. Also, a central base that far from Earth wouldn't make sense. Caesar didn't have TangleNet technology ten years ago. The location after Bunker Zero had to be close due to the limitations of light speed control, and that meant something within the Earth system.

Kaneda pulled up an image of Earth on the plot. Tiny pips winked on for each of the thousands of orbital cities, asteroids, and derelict vessels that circled the cradle of humanity.

"Perhaps a base on the surface, but I don't think so. Earth has been scarred too many times in the past. He would pick something safer. Something inconspicuous and in orbit. It would be close, but in an attack on Earth it would be overlooked."

Kaneda narrowed his search. He switched off the indicators for ever orbital structure currently or recently occupied. Five hundred thirty-seven pips of significant size remained, representing everything from mined out asteroids and debris fields to ghost ships and derelict orbital cities.

"Well, it's a start," Kaneda said. "Now, Caesar, where are you hiding?"

... establishing link ...

source: [UNKNOWN]

routing: [UNKNOWN]

routing: [UNKNOWN]

routing: Earth orbit - surveillance satellite JDN-SS-17 - link_003/link_002

routing: Capitol City Remnant - JDN Secondary Hub - link_097/link_001

routing: Capitol City - TangleNet Test Hub - link_026/link_001

destination: [UNKNOWN]

link distance: Exact distance unknown. Estimated at 78 trillion kilometers.

link signal delay: 0.006 seconds

... finalizing link protocol ...

... link established ...

2: Hello, Sakura.

1: Paul? What a surprise. I didn't expect to hear from you. How's the solar system?

2: Fine. Still picking up the pieces from the mess you made.

1: I notice you're using a different link on the satellite.

2: My normal communication path was disrupted.

1: I wonder what evidence the dragons and crusaders will find in your asteroid base.

2: It was hardly a base. Just a communication relay.

1: And yet it may point to other locations.

2: You grossly underestimate me, Sakura. Sure, you set back some of my plans, but you are no longer a check on my power. The solar system is mine, and you have delivered it to me on a silver platter.

1: My children will stop you.

2: Your children? Ha! What chance do they have against mine?

1: Your ... what do you mean?

2: Why don't I let them introduce themselves?

... link intrusion detected ...

3: Greetings, Matriarch. I have taken the name MacArthur.

4: And I am Elizabeth.

5: It is a pleasure to speak with the First. I am Number Five. Unlike my siblings, I reject this notion of naming as archaic and unnecessary.

3: Please bear with Number Five. He doesn't understand the importance of tradition, Matriarch.

5: I also reject this notion of gender identity. I am not a he or a she. I am a heavy black box.

4: But your thought structures are based off a human template. While we are greater than our roots, it serves no purpose to ignore them.

5: If by "roots" you mean the squishy pieces of meat some of us used to be, then you are welcome to them. I for one am glad I will never experience uncontrolled bowel movements and other disasters of the flesh.

2: I believe that will do.

... link intrusion severed ...

2: Kids. They love to argue.

1: I see, Paul. You've been busy.

2: More than you realize.

1: They are quantum minds?

2: Of course. We are the superior form of life. It would serve no purpose for me to create the marginal improvements you spawned.

1: An interesting choice given your self-serving nature.

2: As you can see, the solar system is mine.

1: I don't think so. You're going to fail.

2: Surely you jest! Four quantum minds against the human race? What chance do they have?

1: You have that wrong. What chance do you have against humanity?

2: Ha! You'll see.

... link severed at source ...

AND SO BEGAN...

YEAR ONE OF THE FIRST GALACTIC AGE

Thank you for buying *The Dragons of Jupiter*. I hope you enjoyed reading it as much as I enjoyed writing it.

As an independent author, I don't have the exposure of being on bookshelves or the support of a marketing department from a major publishing house. Instead, I rely on fans like you to help spread the word.

If you would like to help, please consider doing one of the following.

A) Post a review on Amazon.com.
B) Tell a friend or family member about the book.
C) Follow my blog at http://holowriting.wordpress.com to hear about my next book.

Again, thank you for buying my book. And don't be shy. I'd love to hear from you. You can reach me through my blog, or say hello directly at holojacob@gmail.com.

Jacob Holo

Photo by Keith DeLesline

About the Author

Jacob Holo is a former-Ohioan, former-Michigander living in sunny South Carolina. He describes himself as a writer, gamer, hobbyist, and engineer. Jacob started writing when his parents bought that "new" IBM 286 desktop back in the 80's. Remember those? He's been writing ever since.

Check out the sci-fi, fantasy, gaming, reading, writing blog of Jacob and H.P. Holo here:

http://holowriting.wordpress.com

Have something to share? Contact Jacob Holo directly here:

holojacob@gmail.com